"*Masquerade* captures that ephemeral blossom of youth, of carefree days bumming smokes from crushes and spilling cocktails on strangers, as well as the dreaded anticipation of loneliness and self-doubt on the last train home. From here, it provokes the reader to take part in an irresistible mystery. Mike Fu's writing is vivid and cinematic, unforgettably rendering the vibey-cool of diasporic Shanghai and the restless pulsing of New York's heart."

—Xuan Juliana Wang,
author of *Home Remedies*

"Sensuous, sexy, and at times surreal, Mike Fu's *Masquerade* paints an unforgettable portrait of a young man standing on the cusp of creative agency. *Masquerade* is a mesmeric fever dream of a novel about the powers and boundaries of life, love, and art. Through writing that pulses with animus, danger, and—at all times—beauty, Fu introduces hidden, decadent corners of the singular cities of Shanghai, old Shanghai, and New York. A Nabokovian puzzle with a hint of Hitchcock and an altogether original cast."

—Juli Min,
author of *Shanghailanders*

"Stylistically daring, with jigsaw plotting, lush sensuality, and a tender emotional core, Mike Fu's *Masquerade* is a subtle and self-assured debut. A book that is as much about the brittle threads of reality that bind us as it is about how easily they are shattered." **—Jinwoo Chong**,
author of *Flux*

MASQUERADE

MASQUERADE

a novel

MIKE FU

TIN HOUSE
PORTLAND, OREGON

Epigraph credit: James Baldwin, *Notes of a Native Son* (Beacon Press, ©1955, renewed 1983, by James Baldwin).

Copyright © 2024 by Mike Fu

First US Edition 2024
Printed in the United States of America

Manufacturing by Kingery Printing Company
Interior design by Beth Steidle

Library of Congress Cataloging-in-Publication Data

Names: Fu, Mike, 1985– author.
Title: Masquerade : a novel / Mike Fu.
Description: First US edition. | Portland : Tin House, 2024.
Identifiers: LCCN 2024025339 | ISBN 9781959030843 (paperback) |
ISBN 9781959030911 (ebook)
Subjects: LCGFT: Novels.
Classification: LCC PS3606.U225 M37 2024 | DDC 813/.6—dc23/eng/20240626
LC record available at https://lccn.loc.gov/2024025339

Tin House
2617 NW Thurman Street, Portland, OR 97210
www.tinhouse.com

DISTRIBUTED BY W. W. NORTON & COMPANY

1 2 3 4 5 6 7 8 9 0

To those who continue to seek,
and to those who yearn to be found

We cannot escape our origins, however hard we try, those origins which contain the key—could we but find it—to all that we later become.

—JAMES BALDWIN,
"MANY THOUSANDS GONE"

CONTENTS

Prologue · 1

Part I
THE LOOKING GLASS · 7

Part II
IN BLOOM · 95

Part III
SEASCAPES · 211

Part IV
THE LUNATIC · 251

MASQUERADE

Prologue

HE DISCOVERS THE BOOK ON A PALE JUNE MORNING WHILE scrabbling around Selma's apartment in a hungover haze. He should know better by now, he thinks as he furiously rifles through kitchen drawers and lifts every single fern and philodendron, than to trust himself to be a morning-of packer. Where could that damn passport be? Even though there's no chance that he would have wedged it between her vinyls or stuffed it in the back of the linen closet, Meadow ferrets and fumbles through obscure nooks where he surely hasn't even hazarded a glance, let alone decided to store something important, in the few days that he's been holed up here. He grits his teeth, T-shirt clinging to his chest from a light sheen of sweat. According to the wall clock, it's already nine. His flight is at eleven, which means he's teetering on the precipice of disaster—the minutes whizzing by on this stupid search, while the window of time he has to get through the airport and on the goddamn plane rapidly dwindles.

After looking under Selma's bed, in her writing desk, and near the windowsill again, Meadow cries out in anguish and circles back to the living room. He's half thinking of a contingency plan if he happens to miss his flight, wondering how long the airline will put him on hold, the likelihood of a steep penalty, what outlandish excuse he can invent for his parents, as he kneels at the coffee table, pulling out both of the shallow wooden drawers he neglected to check earlier. One drawer is filled with unopened packs of Seven Stars lined up neatly in a row, along with a matchbook that depicts a stylized red rose on a black background. Typical Selma, he smirks as he slides it shut. The other drawer, at first glance, contains just a single book. He sets it aside on the couch, hoping against hope that maybe he'd decided to stash his passport here in an absentminded daze and simply forgot all about it. But there's nothing else inside except a stray button and a few pieces of lint. He's about to scramble to his feet when his eye lands on the book again, a thin hardcover in faded green that stands out against the burgundy of the couch. He gives the title a cursory glance, and then does a double take when he notices the letters printed at the bottom.

Meadow snatches the book and lowers himself to the couch. The front panel has the title embossed in gold leaf—THE MASQUERADE—but it's the name printed below it that stirs up the muddy adrenaline coursing through his veins. *Liu Tian*, reads the antiquated typeface. It's his name in Chinese. The book can't be more than two hundred pages, the paper lightweight and clean. There's something old-fashioned about the styling of the cover, its worn edges betraying a hint of age. It looks like the kind of hardcover that was commonplace last century, and is nowadays relegated to the bottom of the bin at garage sales and flea markets. When he flips it open and glances at the front matter, he's startled to discover that it appears to be a translated novel from 1940.

Despite his curiosity, a pang of nausea and the throb of his headache pull Meadow back into the present moment. He snaps the book shut, stuffs it into his carry-on backpack without a second thought, and continues searching for his passport. The grim certainty that he'll have to change his flight looms. But a few minutes later, just as he's about to admit defeat, he spots a familiar dark blue edge sandwiched between two piles of Selma's mail on the thin console table in the hallway. He must have put it on top of the mail so he could spot it more easily, then unthinkingly buried it beneath more mail, though he can't quite recall doing either of those things. "Halle-fucking-lujah," Meadow sighs with relief. He pulls out his smartphone to hail a ride to JFK, throws the passport into his backpack, and rummages through his suitcase one more time. Thankfully, he isn't missing anything else.

THE AIRLINE STAFF MEMBER who helps him is a young woman in her early twenties, dutiful and patient, if somewhat unreadable in face of his garbled attempts to explain his predicament. Her eyes widen when Meadow shows her the boarding pass on his phone. With terse but not unfriendly commands, she whisks him to the front of the check-in line, then a special security gate for airport personnel. They pass through the area in a whirl of movements resembling an avant-garde dance. The gate is at the far end of the concourse, so they run the rest of the way, the young woman looking back occasionally to make sure she hasn't lost her charge. Meadow nearly forgets about his hangover as they sprint past duty-free displays, dour sandwich kiosks, and glassy-eyed travelers with paper cups of coffee.

They arrive at the gate just as the final passengers are boarding. "Thank you so much," he pants gratefully, "for your help."

The young woman cracks a smile for the first time. "Have a wonderful flight, sir," she says, straightening her gray vest and matching skirt. Meadow notices she hasn't even broken a sweat.

Only after he boards the plane does the nausea come back to him with a leering warm intimacy, the discomfort magnified by the judgment he imagines in every person who catches his gaze. Should never have stayed out late, he grumbles to himself as he proceeds dolefully down the aisle and tries to take deep breaths. Though come to think of it, he can't quite remember getting home. It was Peter's birthday party, an occasion he simply couldn't miss, early flight be damned, and even though he'd vowed to himself to go home around midnight, he found he was all too eager to be strung along from an East Village dinner to that horrendous gastropub that Annika had chosen for the main event, and then— And then what? He vaguely recalls taking a cab somewhere, maybe eating something. He remembers setting his alarm for seven, which should have given him ample time to leisurely pack and get ready for the journey to Shanghai. But then he woke up at quarter to nine on the couch and spent the rest of the morning flailing about.

He shuffles in penance all the way to the back of the plane, at last settling into his aisle seat next to an elderly couple who are already asleep. Here we go, Meadow braces himself. Every day a new beginning. Within the span of a single week his life has become almost unrecognizable. He's been derailed from the story he thought he was in, the bloom of romance that had restored, for a while, his faith in New York. Luckily for him, moving from his sublet into the even more temporary abode of Selma's was arduous enough a task to distract him for a while and keep him from moping too hard, at least so far. He knows the despair will come eventually, expects it to materialize by his side like a spiteful shadow. There are many long hours of solitude ahead, even among the hundreds of passengers who share the aircraft with him.

As the pilot comes on the intercom in a jaunty Australian accent and tells the flight attendants to please be seated for take-off, Meadow clutches his belly and closes his eyes. The heat of the cabin is oppressive, familiar. He considers how banal an experience this has become: New York to Shanghai, an arc between his present and past. How many hundreds, no, thousands of hours has he lost to unseen trade winds, glazed eyes glued to deep-sea trenches marked on a digital map? It's as if crossing these meridians once or twice a year, rather than the act of living, has caused him to age. This nowhere-space is his home, excruciating and perfect for someone like him, a grown-ass man still clueless about who he is or what he's doing. By the end of the summer, he'll have lived in New York for ten long years, conferring a supposed legitimacy on his claim to the city. Yet he feels more detached than ever, unable to sink roots no matter how hard he tries. And this fate seems perfectly encapsulated by his current age of thirty-one: a prime number, indivisible and impenetrable. No spring chicken, but far from middle age.

He thinks of Diego, now just one more phantom to count among his ex-lovers. Ghosted by my own ghost, the nonsensical phrase comes into his head. It's enough to make him laugh aloud, a wheeze that he barely hears over the roar of the jet engines. Oh fuck, Meadow thinks as his hangover resurfaces, fluttering his eyes open. A surge of nausea overcomes him as the airplane climbs into the chalky gray skies of New York. Breathe, breathe. Meadow tries to concentrate on the sense of routine, this familiar upward plunge into the heavens. It's all he can do to hold it in while the seatbelt sign is mercilessly illuminated. He takes short, shallow breaths, followed by long deep ones, directing air in and out through his nostrils or his mouth. The minutes tick by, one eternity after the next, wisps of cloud streaking past the window in this purgatory of sky. He feels the plane bob up and down, the pressure changing, his stomach distended and compressed over and over again. The second the seatbelt sign turns off with a melodic ding, Meadow unbuckles and rushes for the lavatory, trying to dispel the other thought that just came to him in the agonies of ascent: the notion that he must have lost a piece of himself at some point on these journeys crisscrossing the Pacific, and maybe that's why his life still feels lousy and incomplete. It's so dismal an idea that a pit of existential dread instantly opens in him, as he imagines his ghostly likeness straggling in the sky, floating mournfully from cloud to cloud. A lost soul looking for companionship in no man's country. The dread churns and churns in him as he barges into the bathroom and slides the metal lock on the door, turns around and lifts the lid of the toilet. Before he can think any more about his shadow or his ghost, would-be lovers and lost souls, the dread fountains out of him and into the sterile gray plastic of the airplane toilet. Awful and sour, yellowish gray, the liquid keeps coming, wave after wave, his stomach wrenching all the dread and doubt and sadness from his body until he's quivering from the strain, eyes clouded over with tears and throat raw. Every day a new beginning, he tells himself. Every day, another chance. His story begins again.

PART I

The Looking Glass

1

SHANGHAI IN JUNE IS A SWELTERING CONTINUUM OF NEON and glass, its colors and textures either smudged by gloom or rendered aggressively crisp under the harsh sun. Meadow cocoons himself in his parents' high-rise flat in Xujiahui for several days, gently adapting his circadian rhythms to this side of the world. Time is a circle, he thinks whenever he visits. Even though his adolescent years in the city are long past, and he sleeps in the guest bedroom of an apartment where he has never lived, there is a kind of primal intimacy in the mundane. He has come to associate the floral coverlet and floor-to-ceiling wardrobe of the bedroom with the tedium and ease of family life, these bland furnishings forgivable in the presence of decades-old knickknacks that his parents have kept since their stateside days in Tennessee: a ceramic incense holder shaped like a rabbit, a Great Smoky Mountains mug crammed full of ballpoint pens, a framed Gustav Klimt print on the wall.

He messages a few people, including Selma, to make plans for the coming week, but otherwise he enjoys taking it slow. The sloth feels nearly adolescent—thirty-one going on thirteen—as he whiles away the daylight hours watching inane historical dramas on television, going on long walks with Papaya, his parents' skittish golden retriever, or trailing his mother at the vegetable market.

It's so intense a disconnect from the late nights and breezy banter of his Brooklyn life. His parents, Meadow sometimes considers, are partially to blame for freezing him in time. He's lived more than half his life apart from them, so it only makes sense that they often regard him as a recalcitrant teenager. He has made his peace with it mostly, just as they have also come to accept immutable truths about him. That weekend they celebrate his mother's birthday with a leisurely dinner at a Taiwanese steak house. Meadow presents her with a designer handbag that he bought at a secondhand shop in Nolita, which she effusively receives.

The next day, when his mother is at her dance class, he opens the carry-on backpack to look for the tube of hand cream he brings when flying. The first thing he pulls out at random is a green book with gold lettering. Meadow is still in his underwear, sprawled across the bed, but the sight of *The Masquerade* jolts him awake. He scrambles upright as he examines the cover again, his name printed at the bottom. Amid the turmoil of his last morning in Brooklyn, the discovery of the book completely slipped his mind. Now he looks at it anew, turning it over in his hands. The book is remarkably well-preserved for being nearly eighty years old, though the pages have a stale whiff to them. The binding does feel somewhat fragile, as though it might come apart if not carefully handled.

"The Masquerade," he mutters, opening the book and scrutinizing the title page. "'A tale of deviance and deception.' By Liu Tian, translated by Barnaby Salem." What a weird coincidence, he thinks, that the writer has the same name as him—or at least he presumes so based on its romanization. There's a chance that the surname Liu is a different character than his own, while *tian* too could be written any number of ways. Nonetheless, he likes the strange serendipity of it, imagining that he and the book's author might share this common name by which countless Chinese men, and some women, have been known over the centuries.

His gaze flickers over the roman numerals of the publication year on the copyright page. The era piques his interest, fragments of his past life in academia flickering in the recesses of his mind, a black-and-white montage of marching soldiers, trams and trolleys, waltzing couples, planes jittering over a cityscape. Somehow it doesn't surprise him that Selma has this tome among her possessions; maybe she even meant to gift it to him and simply forgot to mention it. He turns to the first page and begins to read:

Just after nightfall, a man in a black tuxedo jacket alighted before a splendid estate in Shanghai's International Settlement. The house was bone-white beneath the full moon, surrounded by ample gardens on all sides, several fountains along the driveway, and ornate balustrades on the upstairs balconies.

The man's finery was suitable for making an entrance at such a locale. He strode with a self-possessed air in his starched shirt and tuxedo jacket, his patent-leather shoes clopping on the pavement. In addition, he was accoutered in another accessory stipulated by the organizer of the evening's festivities: a mask.

The plain white mask was fitted around his head with an elastic band and had two eyeholes through which he peered. This simple adornment over the man's deep-set eyes and the sensuous ridge of his nose rendered him practically anonymous. An expectant smile formed on his lips as an attendant opened the front door with an obsequious nod, and laughter and music wafted amiably towards him. This would surely be an evening to remember, Mizuno felt, spinning on his heels to survey the revelry. The delight that welled up in his chest was like that of a man claiming triumph in his bets at the horse races.

A veneer of peace had settled over Shanghai in the past months. Gone was the threat of bombardment by sea and by aeroplane, those great metallic birds whose eggs had laid waste to railway tracks, palaces of entertainment, and squalid tenements alike in mere minutes, to say nothing of the countless lives that were consigned to the conflagration. The Pearl of the Orient had held steady through months of chaos, and now she emerged again like a defiant queen, benighted and wounded, but still in reign.

On this night, the events of the previous year's summer could scarcely be imagined, those wretched months evaporated like a dream upon waking. Thank goodness, thought Mizuno as he accepted a glass of champagne from a masked servant. This was the most cosmopolitan city in the world, and it had been dreary to see things grind to a halt as ships and tanks duelled well into the autumn. Just over half a year later and the ease of modernity could be felt once more in the gilded pleasures of Shanghai nightlife, with its vigourous music, beautiful women, and epicurean delights.

It is only human nature to seek pleasure and diversion. Some may even choose to ignore the violence or, worse yet, rationalize it for the greater good, deluding themselves to believe that a measure of cruelty is necessary to wrest control of collective destiny. Whether one considers this frame of mind utopian or maniacal, all forms of desire in this mortal coil are mere illusion: like the mirror's reflection of a flower, as the proverb goes, or the water that contains the likeness of the moon. Dear reader, pay close attention to the story that unfolds. The tale of Mizuno will shock and amaze you . . .

Meadow devours the first twenty pages as the glare of daylight grows brighter beyond the bedroom window. The novel plunges him into the world of a masquerade ball in high society Shanghai in the late 1930s. Mizuno turns out to be a Japanese newspaper editor, a man dispatched to the freewheeling Pearl of the Orient to oversee cultural reportage for the sizable community of his compatriots. He apparently speaks some measure of Chinese and has made himself a fixture in the social scene, hobnobbing with the international elite. After being interrupted by Japanese military incursions a year earlier, the city's nightlife has come roaring back with a vengeance. The first pages of the book offer lengthy descriptions of the lavish interior of the German-style estate where the party is being held, as well as a survey of those in attendance. The impeccably appointed serving staff make their rounds with trays of cocktails and canapés, while Mizuno's fellow party guests don all manner of masks, from Peking opera and South Asian deities to Venetian Carnival and Greek theater. A few times, Meadow turns back to the title page and stares at the name—his name—printed on it. Liu Tian, translated by Barnaby Salem. He shakes his head in disbelief.

Whoever Barnaby Salem was, he certainly managed to translate the novel into flowing English prose, even peppered with the antiquated locutions of a bygone era. Meadow can picture the characters so vividly, his mind conjuring up the lush visual textures of this world by way of filmmakers he has long since internalized. He can't help but think that a Shanghai masquerade ball would be the perfect canvas for the sentimental stylings of Wong Kar-wai or the dreamy opulence of Chen Kaige. He figures this book tells the tale of star-crossed lovers whose romance is thwarted by the tides of history, or something like that. The setting directly recalls the research that once consumed him in grad school, a memory still tinged with regret so many years later.

Papaya's wild yipping at the front door snaps him out of his thoughts. "My darling Tian," his mother singsongs from the foyer, "what do you want to have for lunch?" The book gets relegated to the nightstand as Meadow puts on a shirt and stumbles out of the bedroom.

Over the next days, he manages to get out of the house a few times to jog, to have coffee or dinner with friends, or to perambulate through Hengshan Park. Most of the people he socializes with are former classmates from grad school in New York, or acquaintances he's accumulated by chance. Sandwiched between his early life in Tennessee and adolescence in Indiana, the few years he lived in Shanghai feel like an outlier and oddity, a blip in his existence. Like a pebble tossed into a pond, the ripples still gently purling outward to its edges. For his parents, this city has been home for more than twenty years. Meadow is unable to make any such claim of his own, having been dispatched at age fourteen to Auntie Marilyn's suburban home in what he retrospectively considered his era of midwestern longing, followed swiftly by the northern Californian reverie of his college years, and then the gaping maw of New York. Of all places in the world, he has lived in New York the longest. But Shanghai still has a hold on him in some way, even though it has always been difficult to articulate the reason for it.

Images and sensations flood his brain when he lies awake at odd hours, or descends precipitously into heavy slumber in the middle of the day: the faces of his parents, the smell of summer rain, a stranger's smirk. The tobacco-stained interior of a taxi, a fruit vendor's listless call. China is a topsy-turvy place he could never claim, and yet to which he is inextricably bound. Shanghai's gleaming buildings and traffic-choked arteries feel like a splendid illusion, a façade beneath which lies some primordial substance that remains elusive, unknowable. Even now, as his experience of the city has become nearly blasé with routine, there are times when he detects a whisper of meaning in the mundane, which he strains to decipher. He replays these experiences with his eyes closed, picturing himself wandering through this ghostly metropolis with attentiveness and caution. Always at the brink of epiphany, it seems, he takes one wrong step and slips into a crevice in the sidewalk. The summertime air billows around him, sweet and soporific, as he plunges deeper and deeper into the dark nowhere of the in-between.

HE FINALLY ARRANGES to meet up with Selma for lunch on Monday at her subleased flat. By that time, he is so preoccupied by the slew of recent activities and excursions that he completely forgets to mention the book to her. The address she provides leads him to an old-fashioned residential alley near Changshu Road. When he asks for directions from the security guard sitting in a squat booth, the old man gestures vigorously at the lane behind him. "Just straight back there, young chap," he bellows. "Then left, then another left. You got it?" Meadow thanks him and walks on, feeling the fabric of his shirt cling to his back in the sticky heat.

Selma lives in a building with a tiny yard where clothes have been hung out to dry. He lets himself in through the gate and ascends the open stairwell to the second floor. There's only a single door at the far end of the dim corridor. He strides over and knocks three times.

"Coming!" a voice exclaims from inside.

A flurry of footsteps, then the door flings open. Meadow sees only the silhouette of a woman in the doorway, dramatically haloed by afternoon light on the far wall behind her. A blast of cool air from inside the apartment wafts over him. Selma's features come into view, the familiar intensity of her gaze offset by an affectionate smile. As always she is a vision of timeless composure, her pale blue dress billowing in a languid breeze, the dull shine of a single jade clip in her hair. She leans forward and wraps her arms around him.

"You're a sight for sore eyes," says Selma. "Come in, come in."

"Hey, stranger. Fancy running into you here."

Meadow steps inside and takes off his shoes, closing the door behind him. He finds himself looking out onto a cozy living room with a black marble dining table and a low leather couch. Hazy rays of afternoon sun filter in through a curtainless arched window. A velvety-voiced jazz singer croons from an unseen speaker. The room is suffused in the light fragrance of a rosemary candle, along with something savory on the stove.

"Make yourself at home," Selma calls from the kitchen. "Lunch will be ready in a jiff." The kitchen is rather cramped, with minimal countertop space but modern appliances. Selma presides over a saucepan with a wooden spoon, a rice cooker counting down nearby. When she notices Meadow peeking in, she exhorts him to take a seat and relax.

He acquiesces and flops onto the leather couch. "Nice place." He whistles, eyes still roaming. "I just knew you'd land yourself some stylish digs."

"Oh, I got lucky," Selma says. She tells him she's subletting this apartment from a friend of a friend, a Brazilian designer who is away for a few months. It's been the perfect launchpad for her to explore Shanghai, a city she's visited only once before, while getting settled into the artist residency. As she talks, she glides over holding a tray with a tall glass of soda water and two bowls of snacks, then sets it on the dining table. "Here we have scallion crackers," she says, "and some wasabi peanuts that I paid way too much for at some fancy basement supermarket."

"Amazing." Meadow smiles. "You've really found your groove here. By the way, you'll be happy to know I haven't killed any of your plants yet. I can't tell you how grateful I am—"

"My dear Meadow," Selma interrupts, shaking her head, "say no more. You're the one who's doing *me* a favor. But how have you been? Flight was okay? How are your parents?"

Meadow reaches for the soda water and some crackers. Too much has happened since they last saw each other in May. Getting ghosted by Diego, schlepping his sad suitcases over to Clinton Hill, Peter's birthday party, the past days in Shanghai—all of these events unspooled at a dizzying pace. "I just got dumped," he sighs. "Or ghosted, I should say."

"Oh no!"

"Remember the guy from the Chinatown party? Well, we had a thing going for . . . almost a month? God, I hate how ridiculous it sounds. But it felt so good for that stretch of time. It felt so *real*. Then he disappeared on me."

The rice cooker announces successful completion of its task with a beeping melody. "I'm so sorry to hear that, my dear," Selma says airily as she roots around in a kitchen cabinet. "Is it something you want to talk about?"

"You know what? Not really."

Soon they're seated across from each other at the marble table overlooking a beautiful lunch spread. Apart from the two bowls of rice, there is braised beef with daikon, Chinese broccoli in oyster sauce, and an assortment of vegetables Selma says she pickled herself. "Wow, you've really gone local," Meadow says. "Looks delish."

"When in Rome," Selma replies, picking up her chopsticks. She tells Meadow about her meager attempts to learn conversational Mandarin, the familiarity of Chinese ideograms for someone who'd grown up with Japanese, the utter impenetrability of other aspects of the language. Luckily, most everything related to the residency, sponsored by one Gallery Potemkin, has been carried out in English. Selma's main point of contact has been Anya, a firecracker of a woman who insists on dragging her not just to art openings, but to experimental music venues, far-flung flea markets, and hidden teahouses. The program has also furnished her with a studio in Jing'an district, which has become an oasis amid this endless bustle of activity.

"I've been waking at five in the morning and catching the first train," Selma says, pouring more soda water into their cups. "It's already daylight by then. The sun rises so early in this part of the world, but the streets are still mostly empty at that hour. It's an absolutely magical time to be out in the city."

"Jesus, we're on opposite schedules then," Meadow remarks, stabbing into a piece of broccoli. "Five is when I go to bed after a late shift at the bar."

"You know what I mean, don't you, though? About a certain kind of consciousness that you can tap into only in those early morning hours."

Meadow nods. It's a time of day he knows well, offering a dark serenity that verges on the spiritual. Not just because of the physical relief of returning home, taking a hot shower, and conking out after endless hours on his feet, but for the peace that comes with being almost completely submerged in solitude. Even Atlantic Avenue and Fulton Street, usually a cacophony of brash bus drivers and scrabbling pedestrians, are part of this ethereal, slightly ominous plane of existence whose humming quietness seems to blot out any sound and color that dare remain.

Earlier that year, as she was settling the details of her residency, Selma asked Meadow if he would mind watering her plants while she was away for the summer. He agreed without too much thought. Bartending, after all, allowed him a flexible enough schedule, and they were less than twenty minutes from each other by foot. At the time he had been living in the garden-level apartment of a Bed-Stuy brownstone, renting a tiny room from a white environmentalist couple in their early forties who brewed their own kombucha and tended to a sizable herb garden in the backyard. Their schedules, opposite Meadow's, meant that he barely saw either of them, but their interactions were always superficially pleasant. In the spring, the couple sat Meadow down just as he was getting ready for the early shift at the bar and broke the news: they were expecting. After accepting his congratulations, they gently informed him that they would need to repurpose his bedroom as a nursery. He was given until the beginning of June to find a place to live.

When Selma heard this, she made up her mind immediately that Meadow should stay in her Clinton Hill apartment for the summer. "You don't need to pay rent," she said. "Just look after the plants and keep it tidy."

"But—"

"But nothing. The gallery is covering my housing expenses in Shanghai. You should take it easy and find yourself a new place for September. You can always stay on my couch longer, too, if you need."

Meadow could think of no real reason to reject this offer, so he thanked her profusely and agreed. He'd also racked up enough goodwill at the bar to take a bit of time off. The opening reception for Selma's show at the residency happened to fall close to his mother's birthday. The more he considered it, the more he realized that it might just be the perfect occasion for a summer getaway.

After lunch, they decide to take the train to check out an exhibit at the Power Station of Art, where Selma hasn't been yet. Meadow marvels at the way Selma moves through Shanghai with an almost preternatural sense of direction, barely needing to consult her phone as they navigate the subway or streets. She simply flows through crosswalks and alleys while remaining detached in some way, as though cushioned by her own pocket of air. The museum is a massive industrial building that once purveyed electricity to the urban environs, and now serves as a gathering ground for baby-faced hipsters and ladies of leisure. They wander absentmindedly through the exhibits, eventually making their way out onto an expansive terrace with wooden floors. The sky is a hazy bluish gray that Meadow equates with summertime in China. They walk to the edge of the terrace and take in the gritty view, the few boats drifting lazily down the Huangpu River, lost in their own thoughts under the sun.

That night they land at a tapas restaurant back in the thick of things, in the French Concession. The restaurant is tiny, with only four tables and a row of stools at the bar, the doleful accordions of Astor Piazzolla as a soundtrack. They sit side by side at the counter and consume plate after plate of Spanish omelette, smoked sausage, grilled eggplant, cheese and tomato. Selma regales Meadow with more anecdotes about her residency, the extraordinary people and situations she has been encountering at every turn. At times he gets so engrossed in her stories that he forgets about their surroundings. It could almost be any other night in New York, one more dinner outing to add to all his existing memories of their friendship. They share a conversational ease, an intuitive understanding of each other's rhythms and idiosyncrasies. Meadow feels himself being constituted in her gaze, as though the particles of his existence were being reassembled, his contours made more solid, simply by being in her presence.

An aimless post-dinner stroll leads them to a brutalist bar called Sans Soleil. Meadow initially scoffs at the name, but he discovers that there's a literal meaning to it: there are no windows in the room. More bunker than bar, the washed concrete of the interior is lit up in garish neon pink and sickly green like some retro-romantic vision of the future. By the cash register, the tangerine globules of a lava lamp wobble and warp in their sparkly liquid. Mariah Carey provides an incongruous soundtrack to the whole affair, crooning about fantasy and rapture, dreaming while awake. Meadow becomes aware of a mild ache in his legs from walking all day. Surprisingly stuffed from tapas and beer, and soon two cocktails deep, he starts to space out and stare at his reflection in the mirror that wraps around the length of the bar.

They are the only customers in Sans Soleil. Their silhouettes in the mirror are distant and defamiliarized; at a glance, they could be any other couple in Shanghai, siblings or lovers, classmates or coworkers. Selma has one elbow on the counter, chin against her palm, as she gazes at the lava lamp. Before Meadow even realizes it, the whole story of his romantic misadventure with Diego comes pouring out of him, in spite of his trying not to be a maudlin drunk. Or maybe it's just the effect Selma has on him, coaxing him to name the feelings that burble in his core.

"That's quite the story," she says at length. "I'm so sorry that happened to you."

"Forget it," Meadow grunts, turning to face her. He takes a swig of his gin gimlet, savoring the cold and sour tang. "I should know better. Still fall in love too easily."

"It's not a terrible trait," Selma muses, "so long as you know how to protect yourself."

Meadow hesitates. He wants to say something about these two things being at odds, surrendering to love versus shielding his heart. He knows that to show vulnerability can sometimes be fatal, especially early on in the dating game. But he's never been able to put on the brakes before. Rather than dwell on the matter, he changes the subject and asks what time he should drop by her exhibition tomorrow.

"The reception starts at six," she says, "but that's too early. Come closer to eight and we can go to the afterparty together."

"At your benefactor's place, right?"

Selma laughs. "Sounds downright Dickensian. Douglas is just a collector and patron of the arts." She lifts her glass and takes another sip. "Anyway, I think I should call it a night after this drink. Still have a few loose ends to tie up for tomorrow."

"Of course," Meadow replies. "We had a long day. I should head back, too. The dog always gets too excited and wakes everyone up when I get home."

Moments later, they exit the air-conditioned stasis of Sans Soleil and find themselves back in the real world of Shanghai in June. Compared to the bar, the streetscape of Julu Road is a subdued symphony of orange light and black shadows, clouds dawdling in the bruise-colored sky overhead. The dark swelter of the city still thrums with life. Unseen cicadas screech from treetops while a sonorous ballad wafts out from a residential lane. A howl of laughter erupts in the distance. A breeze swishes through the plane trees and sends an aluminum can rolling down the curb.

Meadow slips a Chunghwa into his mouth and offers the pack to Selma. Even without looking directly at her, he can feel her gaze on him as she extracts a cigarette and holds it gingerly between her fingers. Just as he starts to pat his pockets for a lighter, she beats him to the punch. She strikes a match and holds it to his cigarette, then hers. "Thanks," he murmurs. For a fleeting instant, Selma's face is illuminated by the flame. Her sharp features give her a perpetually pensive expression, but the dark embers of her eyes are filled with empathy and something close to wistfulness. It was this intensity of feeling that brought them together, Meadow thinks, years and years ago. A desire or predilection to grasp at the spongy substance of living, to squeeze the essence out and make some sense of it. Selma takes the cigarette from her mouth to blow gently on the match.

They traipse through the French Concession and puff on their cigarettes in silence. After a few minutes, Selma looks at Meadow. "You fall easily into this kind of story," she says. "I hope you don't mind my telling you that."

"Come again?"

A flash of light illuminates the sky and casts an expressionist glare over the street. Meadow detects a metallic whiff in the rising wind just as a peal of thunder crackles above.

"For as long as I've known you," Selma continues, "you've been so eager for love. And you're good at finding it, again and again. I'm sorry to be so blunt. I think you just . . . you let yourself get carried away. You're searching for that perfect, graceful story." A plume of smoke slips out from between the dark red of her lips as she contemplates how to finish the thought. "Remember that the story is always yours to control. When it veers off track, you can invent a new one and start over."

He takes a long, thoughtful drag of the cigarette and blows smoke into the air. "Easier said than done," he mutters. He knows that Selma's words aren't intended to wound, but he can't help but clam up a little bit at her provocation. Invent a new story, he repeats to himself. If only I had any idea where all this was going. He's long since lost the thread, wallowing in the inertia of his early thirties. But this much, he suspects, Selma already knows.

After a short walk, they bid each other goodbye on Huaihai Road beneath a stretch of gleaming malls and office towers. "Sure you don't want me to walk you home?" Meadow asks.

Selma waves one hand dismissively. "I could find my way back blindfolded by now. Get some rest, Meadow. I'll see you tomorrow."

"Good night, then. Thanks for spending the day with me."

A wan smile flickers across her face. Selma in a pale blue dress, her willowy figure against concrete and glass, awash in the milky fluorescence of city lights—this image will resurface in Meadow's mind weeks later when he's back in Brooklyn. He'll scour his memory for a clue, like groping in the darkness for an object that may or may not be there. He'll strain to remember if there was anything strange in what she said to him, whether she carried herself any differently than usual. It won't be the first time that Selma has occupied his thoughts like so, as though she were a vengeful spirit that can communicate only through obtuse signs and hidden messages. He'll alternate between feeling vexed and fearful, incredulous and skeptical.

But none of this has come to pass. Meadow has no idea yet about the sordid tale that's on the cusp of unfolding. So for the moment, he just leans in, kisses her on the cheek, and turns toward the stairs leading to the metro.

HE MET DIEGO on a Saturday in May, that fleeting season in New York when everything seems aglitter with spring sunlight and possibility. The city had finally and fully thawed out: merry birdsong filled the air, shiny green leaves burst forth from the trees. Even the clouds seemed to move with a swiftness and clarity of intention, their contours crisp white as they transited across the sky and dazzled the eye. Selma had invited him to a house party in Chinatown that night, declaring it would be their last chance to hang out before she went to Shanghai. They had an early dinner at a Southeast Asian joint beforehand, filling their stomachs with Hainanese chicken rice, curry laksa, sautéed snow pea shoots, and an oyster omelette.

The party was being held at the home of an acquaintance of Selma's, a creative director at some magazine Meadow had never heard of. It was a gut-renovated fifth-floor walk-up with a spectacular view of the East River ablaze in dusky color. Lorenzo, the host, kissed Selma's hand when they arrived. "Miss Shimizu," he said, "how lovely to see you." He greeted Meadow with affable indifference, then swanned away to flirt vigorously with a gaggle of models in crop tops and fisherman hats. Meadow was surprised at how many people were crammed into the apartment at such an hour. Later he overheard that there'd been a boat-related excursion earlier in the day.

He drank glass after glass of Johnnie Walker while squeezed against a wall with Selma, who seemed unfazed, an enigmatic smile on her face as she talked with whoever drifted into their path. Someone was going around taking photos with an expensive-looking DSLR, though it was unclear whether it was for business or pleasure. Eventually Meadow got separated from Selma and found himself wedged into a love seat in the living room next to a handsome fellow in a colorful woven shirt. They nursed their drinks while flipping through a gigantic tome of Nobuyoshi Araki photos, all female nudes and cutaway breasts juxtaposed with macro shots of glistening pistils and yearning stamens.

"Well then," the guy in the shirt said, cocking an eyebrow and looking at Meadow. "Sex really *is* everywhere." They laughed and struck up a conversation, turning their attention to the self-serious artists and club kids who hung about in clusters around the apartment. His name was Diego, he said, and he was from East Los Angeles, newly transplanted to the city. With his tortoiseshell glasses and hesitant smile, he exuded a kind of innocence that made him seem slightly out of place, almost vulnerable, among these pouty fashionistas and preening party boys. They managed to have a long conversation in spite of the thumping drum and bass. A goddamn puppy, Meadow thought to himself tipsily. Diego's dark eyes were shimmering as they talked, and Meadow felt a tectonic tremble deep in the core of his being. When he saw Selma gesture at him from across the room to have a cigarette, he nodded and stood up to meet her. He asked for Diego's number before he walked away.

They had dollar oysters and martinis in the Lower East Side on their first date. Meadow was shocked to discover that Diego was only twenty-five. There was a thoughtfulness and maturity in the way he carried himself, deliberating over his words whether they were talking about movies or industrial fishery or apartment hunting in New York. Diego's parents had immigrated from Ecuador and now owned a restaurant in Boyle Heights. He had an older sister who was a real estate attorney. By his telling, none of his family members were too pleased when he decided to move to New York. But there was an opportunity he couldn't refuse.

"Tell me about your name," Diego said suddenly, changing the subject.

Meadow smiled. "What about it?" he asked coyly.

Diego wrinkled his brow. "It's different. I've never met anyone with your name before. It sounds kinda . . ."

"Girly?"

"Well, I wasn't going to say that."

"All good." Meadow leaned back and took a sip of his drink. "My dad was really into English poetry back in the day. Like, Tennyson and Lord Byron. He can still recite them on demand." He cleared his throat. "'Over the thorns and briers, / Over the meadows and stiles'— In that vein. He liked how the word 'meadow' sounded, so I ended up with that as my name."

"Is he a poet?" Diego asked earnestly.

Meadow laughed. "No, he's an engineer."

"It is a nice-sounding name," Diego affirmed, staring at the tray of oyster shells upturned on ice before them. "My last name is Selva, which means 'forest.' We're both creatures of the great outdoors."

"I like that," said Meadow. "Nature boys in the city."

After oysters, Meadow convinced Diego that it would be the perfect time to walk across the Manhattan Bridge since they both needed to get back to Brooklyn anyway. It had been an unseasonably hot day. Now, a cool breeze was whipping through their hair beneath a glorious electric pink sky.

"Look over there," Meadow said when they were halfway across the bridge, pointing at the fantastically iridescent skyline. They stopped walking and drew closer to the chain-link barrier that kept pedestrians from plummeting into the murky waters of the East River. Before them twinkled towers of glass and steel thrusting skyward from the edge of Manhattan. A boat skimmed the surface of the water and sent a white froth billowing in its wake.

Diego gasped. "It's like a dream," he murmured.

Meadow felt a lightness in his body as the wind continued to push on his back, through his fingers. He looked at Diego, whose golden skin was bathed in the glow of twilight, and felt a sudden ache of affection for this young man he hadn't even known existed a week ago. That they could share this sunset walk together now, giddy from martinis and oysters and the ease of a good date, filled him with a long-forgotten tenderness.

"It's beautiful, isn't it?" Meadow said softly. "It damn near always is."

The whole bridge began to shake as a train lumbered its way down the track parallel to the footpath, the rumbling of steel and concrete overtaking the whizzing of traffic on the other side. Diego turned to face him. "What did you say?"

Meadow leaned in and kissed him. He felt Diego's lips tense and then soften into sweet warmth as the world around them melted into this fugitive moment: seagulls circling on high, clouds darkening into dusk, hot and cool air, the Q train screeching past, and the two of them, strangers really, pressing against a chain-link fence, hearts thumping wild. Heart damn near bursting with joy.

DIEGO HAD DINNER PLANS with a girlfriend that night, so they parted under sunset skies in Dumbo with another kiss. Meadow felt like he was practically levitating on the twenty-minute walk back to his sublet. The deepening hues of gold and dark amber that seeped out into the world with nightfall cast a romantic sheen over every street scene, each storefront and bus and traffic light aching with poignancy. He's an unknown quantity, Meadow thought, telling himself to chill the fuck out. Nonetheless, invigorated from the date and still buzzing from martinis, he ended up doing laundry, cleaning his room, and cooking a wholesome meal for the first time that week.

A few days later, he had to work the afternoon shift at Barley with his favorite coworker, Monique, a Haitian American poetess and podcaster, who was extolling the virtues of a community garden she'd recently infiltrated. "I can't garden for shit," she was saying, "but there are always some cuties circling around there. I make sure to ask for their advice. That way I can at least get a date, if not some luscious fucking tomatoes."

"Damn, double duty," Meadow laughed. "You're so efficient."

It was late afternoon and nearing dinnertime. The sky was overcast, gusts of wind occasionally whistling through the open window, riffling the fronds of the bar's greenery and sending a menu or two flying into the air. The rhythmic crooning of Stevie Nicks infused the atmosphere with a teasing energy. A few customers came up to the bar, and Meadow closed out a credit card tab while Monique poured drinks.

"Thanks, guys," Meadow said, accepting a signed receipt on a clipboard. "Enjoy your night." He took the piece of paper and deposited it into a drawer. When he looked up again, his heart skipped a beat.

Diego stood there, a shy smile belying the intensity of his gaze from behind the tortoiseshell glasses. "You said to drop by whenever, so I took your words to heart. Hope it's not an intrusion."

"Not at all," Meadow said, catching his breath and trying to contain his glee. He could feel Monique giving them a sidelong glance from the other end of the bar. "It's great to see you. Care for a beverage?"

"Well," Diego said, taking a seat on a stool across from Meadow, "now that you mention it, I am a bit parched. Could I get a gin and tonic?"

"Coming right up."

Diego had on beige trousers and a dark purple gingham shirt, the sleeves rolled to his forearms. He said he'd just spent the afternoon walking through Prospect Park and poking around the Brooklyn Museum on a whim. "Ah, that's right," Meadow said. "I keep forgetting you're a newbie. How nice to see the city with fresh eyes."

"Untainted as of yet." Diego stuck out his tongue.

"We'll see how long that lasts," Meadow teased. He placed the gin and tonic on a coaster before him. "Cheers. It's on me."

"Are you sure?"

"Absolutely. I'm so glad you stopped in."

Diego thanked him and raised the glass. He asked about what Meadow had been up to in the past few days, when he was moving. They'd talked a bit about his upcoming trip to Shanghai and his summer stay at Selma's during their first date. For his part, Diego shrugged off his week as rather bland. He worked as a coordinator at a nonprofit, a role he described as irredeemably tedious, a means to an end. When an older couple came up to the bar, Meadow excused himself to take care of business.

"Do your thing," Diego said. "Don't mind me."

After he downed the last of the gin and tonic, Diego stood up and waited patiently for Meadow to finish serving the couple. With his hands jammed in his pockets, he affected an earnestness that seemed nearly old-fashioned. "Hey, so I was going to ask when you got off work," he ventured, a hesitant smile flickering over his face again.

"I'm done at eight today," Meadow said coolly.

"Oh, that's pretty soon," Diego said, looking relieved. "Well, I know this is kind of last minute, but . . . If you don't have any plans later, I thought it would be fun to get a drink. Pick up where we left off."

"I think I could fit that into my schedule," Meadow replied. "Just let me know where and when."

For the remainder of Meadow's shift that day, Monique bobbled and danced every time she squeezed past him. "Love is in the air," she trilled, "and I love to see it." Her mood was infectious—or maybe it was Meadow's excitement that was rubbing off on her. Nonetheless he tried to play it cool and admonished Monique not to jinx things. Thunder purred every now and then with all the malice of a sleeping cat. Though it didn't look like rain quite yet, the howling wind forced them to close the windows after the hanging plants by the entrance began to sway a little too precariously over the two-tops.

Once eight o'clock rolled around, Meadow left Barley and took the C train to Hoyt-Schermerhorn, then walked down to Cobble Hill. He found Diego in a dive bar around the corner from the main drag on Smith Street. Framed against brick and glass, he looked contemplative, even a touch moody, in this shadowy nook of a mostly empty bar. "You made it," Diego said, standing up and wrapping his arms around Meadow. His body was hot to the touch, even through the fabric of his clothes. They lingered there for only a second, but when they pulled apart Meadow caught the imploring expression in Diego's eyes, softened by drink, at once an invitation and demand to follow the path that snaked forth from their feet.

"So where were we?" Meadow asked after he bought them a round. "Where did we leave off with our conversation the other day?"

"Family drama," Diego grinned. "Work drama. New York."

"Life," Meadow mused. He took a sip of his vodka soda and grimaced. "Damn, this is strong as shit."

"No complaints here," Diego said.

"Oh, I'm not complaining."

What was there to say about New York? They were at separate points of their journey. Meadow was going on his tenth year, Diego his third month. But they both felt an attachment to the city. "To be honest," Meadow said, "I don't really know what the hell I'm doing anymore. But New York still feels like home, more than any other place I've lived. It's thanks to the people I've met, I guess, who've given me space to figure things out."

"Space," Diego considered, "is so important." He began to recount, via spirited impressions, how his parents had fought tooth and nail against his moving to the East Coast. But they had always been like that, he explained, overprotective and unable to fathom what drove him to do the things he did. They'd been horrified by his poetry phase in high school. Even nowadays they wheedled him constantly to follow his sister's example and get into real estate, where there was surely more upward mobility than in his current work.

"Immigrant parents think alike, don't they," Meadow offered. He told Diego how his parents were none too pleased about his working at a bar. It was yet another disappointment to stomach after the initial shock of Meadow quitting his grad program for a job pushing paper at the university. Even now, years later, his parents relentlessly dogged him to consider business school, or maybe a legal career. They couldn't reconcile with the reality that neither of those futures was even remotely viable for their son.

As they talked, Meadow became aware that the wind had intensified to a high-pitched shriek while white flashes lit up the leafy residential street outside like a stage. It was easy to pay the storm no mind while they yammered on and drank with abandon, intoxicated by the tacit eroticism of the evening. They were sitting so close that their knees occasionally brushed against one another. When he leaned in at certain parts of the conversation to hear better or to punctuate a story, his skin would tingle at the faint heat he could feel emanating from Diego.

They casually retraced their histories, meandering through memories of California beaches, shrooming in Joshua Tree, road trips up to the Pacific Northwest or over to Vegas and Arizona. Reaching further back, they recalled fragments of stories about their younger selves and extended families, the tailwinds that propelled their movements from country to country. The utter serendipity that allowed their forefathers to survive when so many others perished because of catastrophes wrought by man or nature, or simply bad luck, being in the wrong place at the wrong time. How tenuous, all the things that linked them to the present moment, this stormy spring night in Brooklyn, sitting knee to knee: the minor miracle of seeing another person take shape before one's very eyes.

It was close to two in the morning by the time they left the bar. In high spirits, they stumbled out into the sweet-smelling rain that was coming down in curtains and lashing the streets. Diego's umbrella was laughably small for the two of them. Then there was the wind, a brisk nocturnal draft that seemed to funnel precipitation toward them as they made their way to Atlantic Avenue. The world was a bleary mess slick with splotches of neon and chrome, their borders bleeding into one another. Meadow asked if they should get a cab.

"Let's just run for it," Diego said. "It's not that far."

And so they sprinted down the street, laughing and shouting all the while, as rainwater splashed against their faces, soaking their hair and light jackets, their sneakers and jeans. At some point they had to wait for a few cars to pass before crossing at a red light, and suddenly they were pressed up against each other on the metal grate of a storefront, mouths working furiously, playful bites on the lips, hands searching wet hair and sliding under shirts to caress the smooth tension of backs and shoulders.

In Diego's apartment they tore off their clothes as though in a scene from a movie. Thunder crashed as they tumbled into his bed, stripping their sopping shirts and socks and flinging them to the far end of the room. By the time they were down to their underwear, they had found a cozy corner of the bed where they simply lay silent, catching their breaths, peering at each other in the dim glow of a desk lamp with newfound wonder.

Diego got up and walked to the kitchen area of his studio. He filled a glass of water at the sink and promptly gulped it down, then filled it again and brought it over to Meadow. "Gotta hydrate," he said, rubbing Meadow's thigh with one hand.

It was only then that Meadow felt a pang of hunger and realized he hadn't eaten dinner. He drank the water, set the glass on the nightstand, and pulled Diego toward him. "Come here," he growled. Diego's skin was deliriously hot, the weight of his body invoking a feeling close to ecstasy. Meadow stretched out and wrapped his arms around Diego's torso, legs twined around his legs. The kisses were soft now, on his mouth, then down the nape of his neck, tracing the collarbone to his nipple with a playful lash of tongue.

The storm continued to rage outside as they tumbled in unison, gasping in bursts of breath that were redolent of sweat and cologne, May lightning. The thought occurred to Meadow that he'd never been so hungered in his life, overtaken by this primal demand to consume. He could feel the same intractable urge from Diego toward him, the excitement of discovering a lover's body for the first time. Part of it was seeing the full bloom of another's humanness, their fragile, animal compulsions laid bare. But every lover was also a mirror that manifested you anew, their desire an incantation that willed you into existence and gave you substance. He longed to know the entirety of Diego, trace and retrace these paths like a city he'd claimed as his own, every sensual curve and surface scar, tender sward or sturdy citadel. The universe was spinning on an invisible axis, or else they were whirling themselves through fabric and flesh in exhilaration. Diego's hair still wet with rain, this was the sensory snapshot that Meadow would carry with him long past this night. Cold rain and hot sweat, a blur of bodies in which Meadow nearly forgot who and where he was until a vision of Diego appeared prostrate before him, face against pillow, whispering and entreating Meadow to give him what he had been waiting for, what he had wanted so badly and needed for so long.

2

THEY MOVED TO SHANGHAI OVER TWENTY YEARS AGO, THE
summer before Meadow entered fifth grade. He had spent his
whole life in Nashville until then, progressing through grade
school with the same group of kids whose mothers contributed
trayfuls of hot chicken and biscuits for field day and regularly
invited the Liu family to their church gatherings. Shanghai felt
different at the time, more insular and unpredictable, its rough
textures not yet buffed to inoffensive smoothness by the forces of
globalization. The silver and pink spheres of the Oriental Pearl
Tower were still the sole centerpiece of the Lujiazui skyline in
that era. The building looked futuristic yet awkward the first
time Meadow saw it with his parents. He could imagine it either
shooting a laser beam into the sky or folding up into a gigantic
piece of stationery. China itself was like that, both unsentimental and full of brazen yearning.

He'd been born in Tennessee, where his parents had met as
graduate students, a region brimming with the kind of bucolic
Americana that partially inspired his name. Meadow's mother,
Ailing, who went by Eileen in English as a matter of course,
was a database administrator for a healthcare firm, a stable if
unglamorous position that justified her weekend indulgences
at the mall. His father, Stephen (an approximation of Xiwen,

which he'd discovered was indecipherable to Americans), was a professor of engineering who had devoted more than a decade to the American dream. But then a multinational firm came knocking with an offer he couldn't refuse. So they sold their home in the suburbs, shipped an absurd number of boxes by sea, and flew back to Asia on Northwest Airlines, exchanging the oppressive mugginess of the American South for the clammy climes of China's eastern seaboard.

Even as a child, Meadow was perceptive enough to recognize there were at least two sides to Shanghai. On the surface, it was a gleaming metropolis with the fanciest subways he had ever seen. The closest point of reference he could conjure up was New York, where he'd been a few times on family vacations. Shanghai had none of the scurrying rats and mysterious urine stenches of Manhattan, but there were indeed pockets of disarray when you veered away from the tourist areas. Social interactions were either curt or laborious, the unspoken rules ever so confounding. The swarms of people everywhere seemed to cleave and coalesce, over and over, by an endless wild energy. He felt as though he saw more faces in his first week in Shanghai than he had his entire life before that point.

The company that Stephen was working for had enticed him with a suite of attractive benefits, including a housing subsidy, a driver, and annual tuition for his son at an international school. They spent the summer settling into a residential complex in Hongkou district called Giardini di Roma. The two-bedroom felt tiny compared to the house they'd had back in Tennessee. When their boxes of things arrived from the States, they spent the greater part of a week deciding what to throw out. Meadow's parents would make their home in a number of similar communities in the years to come, all of them gated enclaves of thirty-story buildings towering over a patchwork of greenery and lackluster fountains. Aspirational names like Giardini di Roma and Oriental Montmartre announced the worldly desires and upward mobility of the inhabitants; it mattered not that their European namesakes looked nothing like these high-rises jutting out near every major transit hub or within walking distance of several luxury malls.

For the next four years, Meadow attended a British-run school a full hour's commute from home. His entrance into this world shocked his young sensibilities. In Nashville, he'd had the same friends since kindergarten, more or less. Their community was considered diverse, meaning the school boasted more than just a single token minority in each homeroom class. Meadow's three best friends were Vietnamese, Indian, and white; they'd bonded over video games and cartoons and all lived within roller-skating distance of each other's homes. Before Meadow left, his friends bade him goodbye over pizza and sodas at the mall one last time, promising to figure out the time difference so they could instant message him on AOL.

The international school in Shanghai taught primary and secondary school students alike. Though the younger kids had class in a different wing of the building, it was the same bus that picked up all students who lived within a certain neighborhood, so Meadow got used to sharing a ride with gum-smacking girls from Hong Kong and swaggy Korean boys who wore too much cologne. He'd never been around so many Asian kids of such eclectic backgrounds before; the white students were the minority here. With a few exceptions, almost nobody had been born in Shanghai. His classmates were Taiwanese but raised in Kyoto, British Bangladeshi from London, Beijinger by way of Macau, Malaysian Australian transplanted from Melbourne. It was a dazzling environment that made his head spin, almost as much as the posh accents of most of the teaching staff, a far cry from the light and friendly drawl of his grade-school instructors in Tennessee.

When he turned ten, his first birthday in Shanghai, his parents took him to eat at a fancy high-rise hotel where the handsome waiters wore immaculate vests, the gold cutlery was gleaming bright, and they could see the historic buildings of the Bund wreathed in fog below.

"You're growing up fast, son," Stephen said. "Ten years old now, already a little man."

Eileen looked lovingly at him. "How quickly time passes," she sighed. "I still feel like you were just born!"

That day at lunch, his parents poured him a tiny amount of red wine for the first time, enough for two mouthfuls. As he took his first sip from the glass, grimacing at the unexpected sourness, he thought about how much had happened in the span of mere months. Not only had he moved across the world, he'd also started attending a new school and met so many kinds of people. It was amazing how different this life was from the one he'd known, with its church picnics and country music festivals, strip malls and summer block parties. It was hard to imagine these two worlds could exist in parallel.

I'm growing up, thought Meadow, gazing out at the handsome waiters. Still, he could not say with certainty whether this was the world to which he truly belonged.

WHEN MEADOW AWAKENS in the morning, his mother is already out of the house. He stalks out of the guest bedroom in navy shorts and a faded T-shirt to find the apartment empty, hazy sunlight streaking in through the windows. Papaya pads over and licks his knee in greeting. In the kitchen, he discovers three baozi on the counter in a flimsy plastic bag, next to a note from his mother informing him that she is at yoga and will be back around noon. The baozi are fluffy and massive, almost as big as his hand, but he scarfs down all three while Papaya watches with jealous whimpers. The dough is the perfect consistency and lightly sweet. Each baozi has a different filling: vermicelli with chopped chives; braised pork with radish; and chicken, mushroom, and cabbage. He glugs a can of cold soda water in between bites and brews himself a cup of coffee from the fancy industrial-grade machine that sits hulking by the fridge.

It's his second to last full day in Shanghai, and he feels surprisingly unenthused about going back to Brooklyn. Usually he finds himself eager to return to routine, the familiar cycles of work and social life punctuated by the occasional date or excursion out of the city. Later, as his mother whips up lunch and cheerfully shares updates on the romantic entanglements of her yoga friends, all he can think of is the solitude that awaits at Selma's apartment. Eileen produces a delectably balanced meal of fried rice with a side of leftover greens and ground chicken. Meadow scarfs down the bowl, topped off with a generous scoop of chili garlic sauce, in no time flat. Professing sleepiness, he slinks off to the guest bedroom after helping wash the dishes. But he doesn't slip easily into a midday nap, filled with a restless melancholy. He opens his eyes and catches sight of *The Masquerade* on the nightstand. Reaching a hand out for the book, he starts reading where he left off and returns to the scene of a lavish party some eighty years past.

MIZUNO ENJOYS A GLASS of champagne and admires the jazz band playing in the grand foyer at the foot of the stairs. A massive chandelier casts iridescent white light on the entrance and the people congregated there. There are probably a good two dozen guests already, a remarkably cosmopolitan mix of people. Only about half of them appear to be Chinese. Among the rest are a smattering of boisterous English speakers with big bellies and self-satisfied postures, cigars dangling from their mouths, as well as some Europeans, who cluster and chitter awkwardly in their incomprehensible languages. At the far end of the foyer, Mizuno glimpses a woman in a plumed headdress who he overhears is a Mexican heiress. But it's truly impossible to tell who is who, given that everyone, including the musicians and waitstaff, wears a mask on their face.

Once the jazz band wraps up its number, a clinking sound rings out over the din of the guests' applause. "Ladies and gentlemen," cries out a voice in Shanghainese, "please proceed to the inner courtyard for a few words from Master Du Kuo-wen." The same message is repeated in English for the benefit of the foreign guests. And so, following the crowd, Mizuno filters through the foyer, an ornate dining room, and a lounge that has a panoramic view of an enclosed garden with another fountain. He steps through the double doors of the lounge and into the garden, illuminated by torches blazing in each of the four corners. The party guests array themselves along the wall, looking around to see if Master Du is among them. Just as the group begins to grow restless, a cloaked figure emerges from the doorway on the opposite side of the courtyard. Striding into the light, the silhouette reveals itself to be a tall man with a black cape fastened by an obsidian brooch on his neck—and a grotesque rubber mask in the likeness of a pig. Everyone grows silent.

"Good evening, friends," the pig booms authoritatively in English.

"Boss Du!" squeals a woman in Shanghainese. "How sensual you are!"

A few people titter in laughter. From beneath the pig mask, Du lets loose a baritone chuckle of his own. "I am Du Kuo-wen," he announces, "host of tonight's party. I've not had the pleasure of meeting all of you yet, but I look forward to our hours of merriment and intrigue ahead.

"We gather here on the night of the full moon to celebrate the life of common prosperity that awaits us on the horizon. Though we are several more lunar cycles away from the harvest moon celebrated in our Mid-Autumn Festival, I have invited you to my home this evening to remind us all of the bond we share in the brotherhood of man. We have suffered greatly in recent memory, but I trust you will join me in creating together a glorious future for our city, our young republic, and all of the Asian continent."

A few cries of affirmation ring forth from the crowd.

"But let us put politics aside for the moment," continues the man in the pig mask, "and make merry. I promised that there would be special entertainment, and indeed the performances of this evening have just begun. In addition"—he pauses here dramatically as two more figures come through the doorway behind him—"I am most pleased to invite you to a game that will last into the early hours of the morning." Two women take their place on either side of Du Kuo-wen. They wear silver damask dresses and matching facial adornments that taper upward and toward their ears, the identical outfits embroidered with patterns of swirling clouds. Du looks from side to side with apparent pleasure. He clears his throat and recites, "*Spring splendor this garden cannot restrain . . .*"

"*A branch of red blossoms yearns past this domain,*" the two women complete in unison.

Du Kuo-wen laughs heartily, as though enjoying a secret joke. He repeats the couplet again in Chinese, his sonorous voice filling the courtyard, then says in English, "Some of you know that I once harbored aspirations of becoming a poet. Then I came to my senses and found my bearings in the world of international commerce." A few of the gathered guests emit knowing chuckles. "Tonight we have two special guests whom I have enlisted through my recent work in the business of cinema. You may know them by other names, but for the purposes of this party, we shall call them Orchid and Peony." The women each give a bow, palms pressed against stomachs, as Du names them. "When one of them approaches your side and recites the first half of this lyric, you will be obliged to complete the line—and then declare whether it is Peony or Orchid who makes this entreaty. Those who correctly identify their interlocutor will receive a prize. Those who guess the wrong name will be led to one of my upstairs chambers for their punishment: a game of mahjong."

"I want to be punished," cries a guest, eliciting more laughter from the crowd.

An attendant approaches Du with a tray of wide-bottomed glasses. "But enough talk," says Du. "We must have a toast with this special cocktail that my friends at the Cathay Hotel have concocted." He gestures at the bevy of serving staff who have materialized with more trayfuls of drinks. The identical glasses are filled with ice and clear liquor, a single dark fruit leaving a blood-red plume along the edges. Mizuno accepts a cocktail from a nearby server. "Ladies and gentlemen, friends from near and far, let the subtly intoxicating sweetness of the Phantasm usher us into this night of merriment. Together we stand on the cusp of a new world. May our hearts be light, may our hours be filled with pleasure—"

THAT NIGHT MEADOW DINES with his mother at an upscale Hunanese restaurant overlooking the frenetic throngs of People's Square. "A taste of your roots," she declares as they settle into the booth. Stephen is in Tianjin for a business trip, so it's just mother and son on this outing. They peer through leather-bound menus with a dizzying array of options until Eileen proceeds to order a bounty of chopped ham with pickled green beans, shredded potatoes in vinegar, stewed beef, and jellyfish salad. The bright lighting of the restaurant interior contrasts with the blue shadows and pink-streaked clouds outside. Black-garbed waiters move deftly between the tables, conveying steaming plates of noodles and bowls of salted peanuts to customers.

Eileen declares that she's in the mood for some red wine. She orders a glass of Sangiovese, while Meadow opts for a beer instead. When the drinks arrive, Eileen offers a toast, as is her custom. "To your future," she says with lighthearted sincerity.

"Um, to your health," Meadow returns. They clink.

"I'm so glad you could come celebrate my birthday," Eileen says, taking a sip. A tentative smile floats across her face as she regards her son. "So what's next, my darling Tian?"

"What do you mean?"

"Have you given any more thought to your career? Now that you've had time to consider different paths . . ."

Meadow frowns, examining the bottle of Tsingtao before him. "There are always options, I guess. I just haven't figured out which one is right."

"Maybe your environment is holding you back," Eileen offers vaguely. "What if you came back to Shanghai for a while longer? Or even found a job here?"

"I'll think about it," Meadow says blandly, though he has absolutely no intention to do so. He loathes talking about the future, but especially when it comes up with his parents. No matter their good intentions, they never fail to rile up his insecurities and indignation. Though Eileen is a sensitive and nurturing figure who has long been the peacemaker in the family, Meadow still finds himself reluctant to engage. He sips his beer and wonders idly if Stephen put her up to this discussion.

Uproot himself and move to Shanghai? He can scarcely imagine a scenario that would justify tossing aside everything to make such a dramatic change.

"It would be nice," Eileen adds casually, "if you could find someone to settle down with, too." Meadow withers and retracts into himself further at this throwaway statement.

"It would be nice," he echoes glumly.

Soon the dishes arrive in quick succession. The conversation eases into extended family gossip, Meadow's lingering errands in Shanghai, and Selma's show. Eileen recuses herself from attending the opening, citing Papaya's need to be walked. Neither of Meadow's parents are the type to patronize galleries, much less when it comes to contemporary art. They exist in a different stratum of Shanghainese society that is more pragmatic and enclosed, concerned with vintage wines and photogenic vacations over artistic expression. "Tell your friend hi for me," she says. "The Japanese girl, right?"

"Yeah, the one you met at the Brooklyn Botanic Garden last year."

"How nice that she's letting you stay at her apartment. You two seem to have a special friendship." Meadow intuits that she harbors a secret suspicion, or hope, that his relationship with Selma is deeper than he lets on. Though it annoys him that she could even entertain such a fantasy, part of him feels somewhat guilty, as though he were truly deceiving his mother in some way.

After dinner, they ride the metro together part of the way before Meadow transfers to another line. "Don't drink too much," Eileen says gently as they pull into the station. She looks like she's about to say something else, but then changes her mind.

Meadow nods. "I won't," he says half-heartedly, bounding off into the station. "Bye, Ma."

The gallery is nestled deep within the West Bund art district, a former industrial zone on the banks of the Huangpu River transformed into a cultural hub, per capitalist logic. Some of the establishments in this area are spacious standalone buildings of two to three floors that exhibit work by Yayoi Kusama, Wing Shya, or the latest hot-ticket names circulating in the art worlds of New York or Berlin. Other venues occupy a single room in a long corridor of galleries, not unlike the clusters of art spaces found in Chelsea. Selma's exhibition and summer residency are sponsored by Gallery Potemkin, which sits alongside several boxy structures and faces a modest courtyard.

Meadow approaches a slate-colored building with the gallery name over the doorway in both Cyrillic and blocky roman letters. Just inside is a reception area that leads into the gallery proper. An overhead light casts a glaring brightness onto the wall across from the entrance, where the exhibition title, *Selma Shimizu: Terra Incognita*, is painted in crisp black. He picks up two flyers from a table and stuffs them into his tote bag.

About a dozen visitors mill about between the two rooms of the gallery, college students with dramatic haircuts and a few stray tourists. An ambient soundtrack of chimes and woodwinds lends the space an airy quality, in spite of its lack of windows. The first room features an enormous map that depicts a jagged coastline and an archipelago. Faint colors distinguish the land masses and bodies of water on beige parchment, while brushstrokes and symbols depict mountainous terrain, arid regions, and settlements or natural formations along the coast. Meadow remembers seeing a prototype of this work at Selma's studio in Brooklyn. For all its painstaking intricacy, the map is a complete fabrication and unrepresentative of any real place on this planet.

There is a pedestal in the middle of the room with a hexagonal vessel atop. The exterior is a handsome walnut color, while the inside panels are mirrors. The hexagon is filled with soil, in the center of which sprouts a reddish stalk with clusters of white berries growing on all sides. With a single dot of black on each berry, the plant looks like a grotesque flowering of eyeballs, the cascading reflections of the mirrors multiplying their numbers many times over. Nearby, an oversized hourglass filled with sedimented water is attached to a contraption that gradually flips the whole thing upside down so the sparkling liquid pours back and forth between the two vessels at regular intervals.

Meadow finds Selma in the next room, where a series of silver gelatin photos are placed between dazzling watercolors of the sea. The black-and-white photos are extreme close-ups of body parts that resemble natural landscapes: an outcrop of slender fingers with knuckles for ridges, a clavicle with the sturdy elegance of a tree trunk. Each painting depicts a turbid swash of water in dramatically different hues, from the celadon and gray of an overcast day to a sunset's luminescent magenta and orange. A stocky woman in thick-framed glasses is talking animatedly with Selma in the corner. As Meadow approaches, Selma turns and smiles beatifically at him. She wears a dress of black silk, a turquoise and copper scarab hanging on a gold chain below her neck.

Meadow offers his congratulations and embraces her, catching a sweet, faintly metallic whiff of perfume. Selma thanks him for making time to come. "This is Anya," she says, turning to the woman in glasses. "She's the owner of Gallery Potemkin and the person who generously invited me here for the summer."

"Nice to meet you," Anya says with a toothy grin, her voice shockingly loud. She extends her hand. "My name is Anya Wu."

From her first name alone, Meadow had imagined her as a Slavic expat this whole time, a no-nonsense executive with a grim wardrobe and elaborate coiffure. The effusive young woman standing before him is a whole other kind of character.

After they make quick introductions, Anya notices that their hands are empty. "That won't do," she cries. "Let me get you drinks!" She returns with plastic cups and a bottle of prosecco. "So, are you Shanghainese?" Anya says, switching to Mandarin as she gives Meadow a healthy pour.

"Eh, no," Meadow says. "Well, my parents live here. I used to a long time ago, too. But we're from inland. Are you a local?"

Anya chuckles and shakes her head. "No way. You hear my accent, don't you? I'm from the northeast." Anya rushes off and deposits the bottle on a distant table. She comes back with a business card. "A bit old-fashioned, I know," she says, "but my WeChat contact info is also on there."

Meadow studies the card and finds himself surprised a second time. "So Anya is your Chinese name, too."

"That's right. *An* as in 'calm,' *ya* as in 'elegant,' although I'm neither calm nor elegant." She bursts into laughter, then turns to Selma. "Sorry, just making a joke about my name," she says in English, repeating the explanation. "My dad is from Harbin," Anya continues, "a city way up north. He got hooked on Russian literature back in the day, so that's how I ended up with this name." Anya goes off on a tangent about the Russophilia of previous generations, back when communist solidarity was still in vogue, and sketches something of her family circumstances through a few anecdotes. Then her eyebrows arch and she casts a conspiratorial glance at Meadow and Selma as she asks for the story behind their given names.

"My English name comes from an opera singer," Selma says. "My Japanese name was a popular girl's name when I was born, I guess. My parents must have liked the alliteration of 'Selma' and 'Saeko.'"

Anya nods vigorously and turns to Meadow. He briefly recaps the poetic origins of his English name. "They came up with both at the same time, actually," he says. "English and Chinese. Although my Chinese name is just *tian*. Like, 'field.'" He shrugs. "I guess it's pretty plain in comparison."

Anya widens her eyes at his explanation as she finishes her cup of prosecco. "You are a man of dualities!" she shouts, wiping her mouth. "What an interesting story. Liu Tian is a nice name, but I have to agree, it's not quite as lyrical. It gives a different feeling. It's . . . What can I say—"

"Basic?" Meadow interjects with a smile.

Anya titters and then offers to pour them another drink. The gallery fills up a bit more as visitors trickle in from other parts of the West Bund. A gray-haired man in a linen shirt and straw hat descends on them before Meadow has a chance to speak much to Selma. Despite his appearance of a dad on a solo fishing trip, the man turns out to be a curator from Hong Kong by the name of Benedict. Benedict seems to know many of the same people as Anya, who rushes around chattering loudly in Mandarin and English. "The art world is small, too small," he says, leaning in with a coy smile. "You know everyone's secrets, after a time."

Douglas Koh arrives on the scene in short order. Fortysomething Koh, a benefactor of Gallery Potemkin, is the type of man who looks like he was born in a suit. He wears an oxblood blazer and steel-gray trousers, yet somehow also manages to affect a lackadaisical air. Meadow has heard about him from Selma and understands that Koh is responsible, in some vague fashion, for facilitating her residency in Shanghai this summer. With his casually slicked hair, thin mustache, and ornate rings, Koh seems to be the embodiment of a blue-blooded prodigal son embracing a life of dissipation. He greets Selma and Anya with a kiss on the cheek and acknowledges Benedict with a nod. Koh's hand is baby-soft and limp when he introduces himself to Meadow.

A few more cupfuls of prosecco later, there is a mass migration from Potemkin to the afterparty. By then, Douglas Koh has long since disappeared. Meadow manages to pick up on a few tidbits of hearsay as they gather themselves to move to the next location. Hailing from Singapore, Koh has installed himself in Shanghai for the last decade and made himself a fixture in the Chinese art world. Someone mentions that he attended London boarding schools in childhood, a conjecture that makes sense with his antiquated air of deflection. Another person asks if he's gay, to which Anya shrugs. "He's what we call a confirmed bachelor," Benedict offers. Selma whispers to Meadow that Koh's private life has long been a matter of speculation, obfuscated by the vein of gossip and exaggeration that the rich tend to inspire.

More silhouette than man, Meadow thinks. A vessel for all the disdain or admiration a person wants to project. He understands intuitively how someone like Koh can appear dashing to some, repugnant to others. They step outside into the balmy embrace of Shanghai summer. Anya gives hurried instructions to the remaining gallery staff as she heads with the group into the evening. They hail cabs by smartphone, Meadow sharing a ride with Selma, Anya, and Benedict. In the taxi, Meadow presses his face against the glass and watches the cityscape unfurl with its tapestry of parasol trees shuddering in the light breeze, convenience stores and municipal billboards flickering past the windows.

Meadow half expects Koh to live in a high-rise development like his parents', so he's surprised when they pull up in front of a residential lane not unlike Selma's sublet in the French Concession. Anya clambers out to guide the way.

"Is it all right to show up empty-handed?" asks Meadow.

Anya laughs. "There's nothing we can bring that Douglas doesn't already have."

They walk for a few minutes in silence, save for the clop of their shoes on pavement and the muffled sounds of television from the cramped residences on either side. Then they reach a detached house enclosed by a brick perimeter and metal fence, set apart from the rest of the lane. It's not a large home by any means, narrower and shorter than the average Brooklyn brownstone, with only two floors, but its careful maintenance is apparent in the trimmed hedges by the windows and flower beds on either side of the walkway just past the gate.

A white woman greets them at the front door, introducing herself as Adele. With her smokey eye makeup, pearl choker, and layered updo, she looks like a French pop singer from the '60s. They slip off their shoes in the foyer and follow Adele down the corridor, the bright pep of Charlie Parker inviting them inward and softening their intrusion. When they enter the living room, they find Douglas Koh holding court in an elegant, minimalist space. "Ah, here they are," he pronounces from a stately arm-chair, twirling the stem of a cocktail glass in one hand. "Selma Shimizu and the guests of honor!" He flashes a smile and beck-ons them to sit down. "Come, come. Make yourselves at home."

"Champagne, anyone?" Adele calls from the kitchen as she withdraws a bottle from the refrigerator. Without bothering to wait for the replies, she pops the cork and pours into a few flutes that are arrayed on the counter. The minute she finishes distrib-uting the drinks, the doorbell rings again. "Oh, dear," she says.

"Must be the other half of our crew," says Anya, who is already plopped onto a chaise lounge and stroking a Siamese cat that peers aloofly at the guests.

Adele excuses herself and disappears down the hallway. A few moments later, a handful of people from Gallery Potemkin sur-face in a breathless flurry of activity by the door. Over the course of the night, Meadow gets introduced to them by Anya or Selma through halting snippets of conversation. There's a German nightclub promoter who works at a record store in Changning district, a Tunisian professor researching Sino-French cultural flows, and an art history grad student specializing in Manchu fashion. With the air of a seasoned diplomat, Douglas circulates among the guests, assembling threads of viable conversation, ensuring they have drinks in hand and no compunction about casually exploring his home. "I have nothing to hide," he says breezily. "By the way, I think I'm in the mood for something a touch stronger than champagne. Would anyone care to join me?"

Meadow and Anya take him up on his offer. Douglas inspects the liquor cabinet set in the corner of the kitchen, hands on his hips, and picks out several bottles in succession, setting them on the counter. Then, in languid, feline movements, he crosses into the kitchen, retrieves a cocktail shaker, fills it with ice, and begins to measure out portions of chartreuse and gin. While Douglas busies himself, Meadow quietly takes in the full sweep of the house for the first time. The interior is surprisingly modern, with high ceilings, metal casing around the windows, and pendant lights for illumination. A bay window and sliding door look out onto the dark green expanse of the backyard, while the other side of the living room leads into an office with a desk and several bookshelves. The kitchen has ample marble countertops and shiny steel appliances. A few gleaming curios are scattered around the room, including a golden kaleidoscope and a vintage globe on a circular wooden stand. On the far wall hangs an enormous print of a shirtless man with a rack of ribs slung over his chest, Chinese characters in black ink painted all over his face and bare chest.

"Is that Zhang Huan?" Meadow asks Anya in Mandarin.

"You got it." She teeters restlessly on her heels next to him. "Douglas has a nice place, doesn't he? Used to belong to his family back in the day."

"I thought Douglas was from Singapore?" Meadow scratches his head.

"Ah, but his mother's side of the family is Shanghainese. They got the hell out of here in the '40s, you know. A tale as old as time. We Chinese all suffered plenty before that, but they probably would have met worse fates had they stayed."

As the party settles with cocktails and conversation, Meadow ends up talking to a few other colorful characters in the kitchen or on the staircase, marveling at the weird serendipity of sharing a space with all of them. There's a limber, bright-eyed Chinese boy in a denim shirt who introduces himself in English as Cotton, an artist and musician from Sichuan in his early twenties. A child, Meadow thinks, sipping the strong, greenish concoction that Douglas has made. He wonders if he used to have that same dreamy look that Cotton has in his eyes. The bearded South Asian man with a shaved head is Subodh, a native of Mumbai. Currently a visiting scholar at a local design school, he is conducting a transnational research project on the preservation of indigenous crafts. When Subodh asks about what he does, Meadow smiles weakly. "I'm a bartender," he says. He feels a twinge of envy about people who can clearly articulate an identity based on their creative talent or professional interests, as though it were as plain and simple to share as their name.

"You should be the one making drinks then," Subodh says jovially, clapping him on the back.

"Oh, I could do it," Meadow replies. "I just don't want to step on anyone's toes." He glances at Douglas, who is gesticulating wildly in conversation with Selma.

"He won't mind," Cotton says slyly. "He wants us to enjoy ourselves to the fullest here. He always does."

The prosecco-fueled tipsiness of the earlier evening smoothed out on the cab ride over, but now Meadow feels champagne and liquor lifting his spirits again, infusing a sense of possibility and abandon into this night that he expected to end much earlier. They begin to circulate more freely in the house as everyone loosens up and talks to one another, the cat sidling past their legs every so often to inspect the newcomers. Meadow follows a group upstairs and into Douglas's bedroom, where they loll on his bed and against the cushions lining the wall. Besides the king-size bed, there's only a zebra-skin rug and an antique dresser in this room. The austere atmosphere is offset by Douglas himself, who reclines against the dresser with one knee bent while doling out his opinions of various world leaders, ordering the downstairs revelers to bring trays of snacks to them, and occasionally disappearing to make another round of that deliciously strong gin and chartreuse beverage.

In the slickness of inebriation, Meadow almost forgets where he is again. He slips away into the bathroom and sighs with relief when he locks the door behind him. It feels like any other weekend outing in New York, after which he can stumble onto the subway or catch an easy ride back home. As he splashes warm water on his face, he remembers that he has no physical home to call his own. For now he has the purgatory of the guest bedroom at his parents' house. Then he'll return to the transitional space of Selma's apartment, where he is also a mere interloper, even if it's for the rest of the summer. How did things turn out this way? A full-grown man with so few attachments in this world. When he looks up into the bathroom mirror, he has an instinct to reach out his hand. He stands in tense equilibrium for a moment, eyes fixed on his reflection and fingertips slowly closing the distance between them. He takes a breath and presses three fingers against the glass. The mirror is cold and smooth to the touch. The faint print of moisture left by his fingertips dissipates quickly.

A few more guests arrive in the next hours. It turns out to be quite a party, this old Shanghainese house filled with people from the world over: a painter from Oaxaca visiting her boyfriend, an Australian ironsmith. Meadow is pretty sloshed by the time he checks his phone and realizes he'll never make the last train. What the hell, he thinks. It's an evening in celebration of Selma, one of his oldest and dearest friends. But even as he tells himself this, he realizes she's been fading in and out tonight, talking quietly or disappearing into the background for stretches of time. She is usually the most commanding presence anywhere she goes, yet her aura here is strangely smothered by the frenzied dynamic of this diverse crew. Meadow decides it must be due to fatigue, given the incredibly taxing hours she told him she has been keeping.

There are long lulls during which he simply listens to the people around him while staring at a plant or admiring the grain on a piece of furniture. The lighting of the house has dimmed, or the space has shrunk. He feels like he might dissolve into the shadows if he doesn't focus hard enough on what's happening. The next thing he knows, he's in the kitchen scooping ice into the cocktail shaker and whipping up drinks to the delight of several onlookers. He has been dabbling in everything tonight, prosecco and vodka, champagne and gin. He figures it won't hurt to return to whiskey, and besides, Douglas has all the provisions for mint juleps. A few people cheer when he pours the cocktails into tumblers, garnishing each with a sprig of mint from the bundle that lies on the cutting board nearby. "Why, thank you for this, Meadow," Douglas says close to his ear, pressing a hand on his back.

"My pleasure," Meadow says perfunctorily, a tingle of heat rising in his chest.

Douglas declares that they've had enough jazz for the evening, goddamn it, and demands that the music be changed. Meadow is surprised to see Cotton nodding vigorously in acquiescence as he scrolls through his smartphone to find a new playlist. He'd assumed it was under Douglas's control this entire time. After distributing the mint juleps, Meadow takes a hurried sip of his own and decides that it turned out decently. He watches Douglas stand close to Cotton now to supervise the music selection and feels the same prickle, halfway between nausea and arousal, about what exactly is going on.

His eye drifts to the living room, where he sees Selma sitting alone, staring at the garden outside. He crosses over to check on her. "Big night for you," Meadow says, settling in on the chaise lounge.

She gives a weary smile. "It's been a memorable one. I'm so glad you could be part of it, Meadow. Thanks for coming all this way. I was just thinking of going out for a cigarette. Care to join me?"

They step into the back garden, where he is startled to discover a luminous silver disk of moon has risen high in the sky. Selma offers him a cigarette from her pack of Chunghwas. She seems to ease up outdoors, away from the flamboyance and tightly coiled energies of the party. As she smokes, she takes broad, deliberate steps back and forth on the patio, her black silk dress swishing in the thick nocturne. With her features obscured, save for the barest glimmer of an outline under the moonlight, Selma looks like a phantom hovering above the greenery that surrounds this old house, merely a blotch of empty space. Meadow asks if she'll be able to relax now that the show is officially up. Selma shakes her head. "I have a few other projects coming to a head," she says. "And there are more things I want to do while I'm in China."

"I see." Meadow takes a drag of the cigarette, head tilted to the sky. He asks if she has anything concrete in mind, but Selma demurs. She meanders instead into fragmentary impressions she has accumulated over the past five weeks. The sensory overload of the city, how multiple temporalities seem to exist together, a confusing and exciting state of affairs.

"It's so strange," she continues softly, "how people here see me and they don't, at the same time."

"You mean, not being immediately identifiable as a foreigner?"

"No, it's more like . . . I feel transparent. Like what happens here isn't real, because this isn't the same plane of existence as New York."

As she talks, Meadow's mind begins to wander in his state of soft intoxication, floating in the firmament against the milky glow of starlight. Selma's invocation of New York makes him think of how he'll be soaring through the sky to return to his city of solitude in another day and a half. Going back means contending with the reality of being single again for the summer, an all too familiar situation. He'll have to get by without Selma, too, at least until the end of August. Silence accretes in the garden while the music, laughter, and light from inside the house shift and tease. Eventually the two of them make their way back inside.

The party dwindles as the hours drag on. Every so often Meadow wonders idly when he ought to leave. At some point he decides he'll go when Selma makes a move, but everyone is remarkably complacent, or perhaps just too drunk. They find themselves back upstairs in Douglas's bedroom, where Cotton is expertly preparing lines of cocaine on the flat circle of a tray, tidying them into neat parallel formations. Anya chortles and recuses herself, saying she is much too full of energy already to need a chemical boost. Benedict puts forth his age as an excuse. Meadow, for his part, has sworn off drugs since turning thirty, but the alcohol has made him all too suggestible and unable to resist the novelty and allure of indulgence in this kind of atmosphere. When Douglas offers him a rolled-up banknote, he accepts without much consideration.

The night takes on an electrified edge as they do a few lines each. Soon they're marching up and down the stairs, changing the music, and rooting around for water and other refreshments. They search for the most comfortable configuration in which to lounge around any room. A '90s Mandopop playlist infuses a spirit of maudlin whimsy into the house even as the conversation drifts into heavier, more existential topics. Douglas insists that they are living through the end of history, that political leaders around the world have all charted out a course for the demise of mankind. "Surely you feel that in America, don't you?" he asks, narrowing his eyes at Selma and Meadow while fiddling with one of his rings. "That slow but pernicious buildup of rage and despair that finds expression in your politics."

"The last few years have been rough," says Meadow, gritting his jaw. "Honestly, I don't have high hopes for the next election either."

"Rage and despair," Benedict muses. "We've seen plenty of that in Hong Kong these days."

"It's everywhere," Selma adds. Her face is unreadable, save for the slight tremble of her eyes. "It's the animus of our late-capitalist world, manifesting to different degrees of intensity. There won't be a happy end to it."

"Shanghai feels pretty insulated, though," Anya cuts in. "Not to say that it's a good thing, necessarily. Most of China is like that, operating in its own bubble. We like to pretend that things happening in the rest of the world don't matter much to us, so long as people can continue to make money and live the lives they want to live."

"Time is a circle," Douglas says flatly. "It's business as usual until it's too late. I think we're living through the last gasps of stability at this very moment."

"What do you think the inciting incident will be?" asks Subodh. "A civil war in America? The collapse of North Korea?"

"Doubtful," proclaims Douglas. "Something much more unpredictable than that. But whatever it is, it's going to be made worse by the pettiness of the men in power."

Sitting in an armchair, Meadow realizes he has been restlessly playing with the vintage globe on the table next to him, watching the pastel-colored countries of yesteryear spin by. Indochina. Yugoslavia. Belgian Congo. These arbitrary shapes and borders, drawn by militaries and madmen. Folly that tragedy could be so trite, a few events determining the fates of how many hundreds of millions, setting a course for generations of bloodshed or centuries of strife. "I do agree that we are standing at a precipice," Benedict says softly. Meadow looks up and sees him sitting cross-legged by the wall, the straw hat resting on his lap. "This era recalls something of the 1930s, when conflicts of a local scale were gradually building toward global catastrophe. Perhaps hindsight will make this all seem more black-and-white than it does now."

Selma stands abruptly and leaves the room. They all fall silent for a spell, with only the nostalgic warble of Faye Wong to fill in the gaps. Meadow looks behind him and finds that Cotton has the golden kaleidoscope pressed against his eye. "It's a dreary thing," Douglas mutters, "this end of history business. Shall we have another drink?"

They transition back into cocktails, with Anya leading the charge this time. Meadow has the presence of mind to message his mother and let her know he won't be back this evening. He should take Selma home later and probably crash on the couch there. He wonders if she woke up at five today, per usual. That would mean she has been awake for nearly a full day now. It's no surprise then that she has grown reticent. Cotton interrupts his train of thought when he hands over the kaleidoscope. Without a word, Meadow squeezes his left eye shut and presses the viewfinder to his right eye. Like all things in Douglas's home, this curio must be rare, or at least expensive. The multicolored beads in the kaleidoscope are translucent and bright, creating fractals of fuchsia and amber, turquoise and obsidian as Meadow turns the cylinder in his hand. Beyond the mirrored glass, he can vaguely make out shapes or colors in the room itself, flesh and egg white, marble and steel. The colors and patterns cleave and cohere endlessly in mathematical beauty, chaos rendered into logic by repetition and reflection. Only when someone thrusts a drink in his hand does Meadow put the kaleidoscope down.

They drink on and on into the early dawn of June, the moon drawing an arc of descent in the sky outside. Douglas invites Meadow and Cotton upstairs for another few bumps. The sour taste of liquor on Meadow's tongue and the bitter tang of cocaine in his throat are perfectly balanced for a while, so that he feels impervious and self-assured, millions of miles away from the blundering confusion of the everyday and the disappointed gazes around him or within him. He loses track of who is even at this party anymore, what time it is, why he is here. Some people have departed, some have fallen asleep, he notices when tiptoeing back downstairs to fetch a bottle of water from the kitchen. The pale light of dawn is breaking over the garden, and still it does not occur to him to wonder where Selma is or when she left, because he has been sharpened too much by the horrid, heavy conversations of this evening and the unspoken erotic edge of this home, which he feels stirring in him with surprising vigor as he creeps back up to Douglas's bedroom. He finds Douglas with his shirt half-unbuttoned, straddling the smiling form of Cotton, who lies with his arms splayed comfortably over his head. Douglas presses a finger to his lips and gestures at Meadow to close the bedroom door, then beckons him over, taking the bottle of water from him and setting it on the zebra-skin rug. He strokes Meadow's cheek with his cold, soft hand and brings their lips together. Meadow sighs quietly as he releases his body to the bed, his head against the hard edge of Cotton's hip bone, feeling excited breaths quicken in his belly. Their movements are deliberate and unhurried, as though the three of them share in a tacit fatalism: the past irrevocable, the future predetermined. The present moment is nothing more than a pane of glass under pressure from both sides, a story revealed in a spiderweb of cracks.

3

MEADOW STARES AT THE ASHEN SCENERY FLANKING THE
freeway on the way to Shanghai Pudong Airport. As usual, he
feels some measure of uneasiness before the long-haul flight.
This morning he's doing his best to alleviate it by making tepid
conversation with his mother as she muses about planning a
family vacation around Christmas. They haven't been to Europe
in a while, so maybe Spain? Or perhaps somewhere down south,
closer to home, Hainan or Hong Kong. Luckily there's no con-
gestion on the Outer Ring Expressway and they arrive at the
airport with plenty of time to spare. Eileen steps out of the car
to give him a hug and a kiss. He waves at her from the curb, then
wheels his suitcase into the departure lobby.

There was a time when he still marveled at the quintessential
modernity of air travel. That you could hurtle in a metal tube
for hours and end up on the opposite side of the country, let
alone the world, was nothing short of astounding. In his teens,
as he got used to traveling solo to and from Shanghai, he always
found himself agape at the signboards listing all the arrivals
and departures. People were coming from or leaving for places
as far-flung as Rome, Nagoya, Helsinki, Brisbane. He, too,
was part of this miraculous flow, this churn of humanity. The
romance of it has worn off, Meadow thinks now as he waits to

get his passport stamped at immigration. Adulthood has made him more blasé or pragmatic or both. When the plane takes off, he closes his eyes and tries to ignore the pressure at the base of his spine. Departures recall too much of the sediment of his younger years, being torn away from all that he knew and cared about—a world within which he could feel safe, if not entirely happy—to plunge headlong into yet another new beginning. Fresh starts, over and over. Ceaseless becoming. No wonder an instinctive sense of mourning overtakes him with every upward ascent. He feels it tugging on him even as the jetliner continues to gain altitude and put distance between him and Shanghai—this city he still barely knows, but which remains interlocked with his fate.

He arrives in Brooklyn on a stifling Monday afternoon, technically only a few hours after departing Shanghai. Somewhere in transit, he has recouped a half day while crossing meridians. After a mostly sleepless flight listening to old playlists and watching a few inane movies, Meadow is practically hallucinating by the time he reaches Selma's in Clinton Hill. He sighs with relief once he drags his suitcase up the three flights of steps, a stack of her mail tucked under his arm. The inside of the apartment is warm and faintly sweet, a whiff of paper and fabric intermingling in the stale air. The sight of open drawers and scattered objects in disarray gives him a start. Then he remembers his madcap morning, turning the apartment upside down to look for his passport, and chuckles to himself. Once he wheels the suitcase into the bedroom, he cracks open all the windows in the apartment and starts to put things back in order. While in the living room, he stoops to check the soil in one of the potted plants and discovers that it's bone-dry. In a stroke of industriousness, he picks up the metal watering can next to the windowsill, fills it up at the sink, and starts to make his rounds, from the fig tree, overgrown baby jade, and snake plant in the vicinity to the philodendron, parlor palm, and smaller pots in the hallway and bathroom.

Meadow's eyelids grow heavy while he's watering the rubber tree in the hallway. He stands with a yawn and puts the watering can back. Just a short nap, he tells himself as he makes his way to the bedroom. A little rest and then dinner. The enticement of sleep sweeps over him with a soft urgency as he blinks at the silhouettes and flecks of amber that dance on the walls in the early evening light. Within minutes of lying down, he falls into a slumber as dark and featureless as the bottom of a well.

WHEN HE OPENS his eyes again, it takes a minute to recall where he is. Shanghai, his brain immediately intuits, and he half expects to turn onto his side and see the evening view of the courtyard from his parents' twentieth-floor flat. But no—this is Brooklyn, Willoughby Avenue. An early summer evening in Selma's home, the night sky a deep blue. "Shit," he croaks when he checks his phone. He has been passed out for hours, and now it's close to ten.

He doesn't have any shifts at Barley until later in the week, giving him a few days to get reacclimated. While he is grateful for the cushion of time, the solitude of his predicament seems amplified by the stoic silence of the apartment. He's never had so much space to himself before. In another world, another life, he might have been able to share the tender novelty of this situation with someone else. Blinking dumbly in the darkness, Meadow imagines nestling in bed with Diego, maybe watching a movie, ordering takeout, uncorking a bottle of wine. He'd tell Diego about his trip, the things he ate, the conversations left unfinished, the smells and sounds of Shanghai in June.

Groaning at his own maudlin tendencies, Meadow sits up and slides out of bed. He lumbers into the living room and plops down on the burgundy couch, still not entirely awake. On the far wall, near a window overlooking the residential street below, hang two totems, a leering demon mask made of burnished wood and a sleek white fox with its features traced in blood red. The fig tree and overgrown jade plant dominate different corners of the living room, a walnut credenza and shelf between them. Inside the credenza is a pile of sketchbooks, while Selma's modest record collection sits on the shelf. Glass animals, a ceramic bodhisattva, a set of matryoshka dolls, and other figurines nestle among decorative bowls, stacks of coasters, herb planters, and tiny succulents atop the mantelpiece.

Meadow's gaze falls on a Japanese lacquered box with shimmering cranes atop the credenza. A brilliant idea comes to him. Why didn't he think of it before? After all, Selma told him he could help himself; he'd simply forgotten until this very moment that she always keeps a stash. He squats down and opens the box, a pungent whiff of sour diesel tickling his nose. Just what the doctor ordered, he thinks. Something to dispel his ennui and ease him back to bed.

Half a joint later, he's sprawled on the couch and listening to *Lovers Rock* on vinyl, vaguely aware of cars whooshing down the street outside, distant voices floating in on the breeze. Meadow yawns and flops onto his stomach. A fat roach sits on the lip of a glass ashtray, while a pile of orange-speckled marijuana spills out of the lacquered box. Eventually he decides to clean up and starts to sweep the loose leaves into a neat pile with his palm. He deposits these back into the box, then springs to his feet as he realizes that he's ravenous. To his delight, he discovers that there are a few eggs left in the fridge, along with a block of cheese, an unopened package of shiitake mushrooms, and a single wilted scallion, everything he needs for a bowl of instant noodles. He decides to roll another joint while waiting for the water to boil.

After eating, Meadow washes the dishes, takes a quick shower, and starts to unpack his suitcase. In the distance, an ambulance wails down the streets of Brooklyn like a mournful ghost seeking solace. A chorus of crickets offers mild reassurance, cushioning the harsh urbanity with their steady song. It takes him until this moment to notice the Sade record has long been over, the music replaced by a gently pulsing void. The scratchy nothingness emitted by the record player adds a sticky texture to the apartment after midnight. Nocturnal torpor drips over him like a thick, black sludge, slowing his movements. Meadow moves back into the living room to turn the record player off. Time for bed, he tells himself. Nothing good can happen at this ungodly hour.

THE NEXT EVENING, Meadow meets Peter for dinner in Koreatown. They catch up over piping hot stews, each accompanied by an egg and a metal bowl full of white rice, an array of banchan and a bottle of soju between them. For good measure, they also order a plateful of glistening dumplings, a seafood scallion pancake, and rice cakes slathered in gochujang. "You must be so jet-lagged," Peter remarks, cracking open the egg and sliding the golden yolk into his bubbling soup.

"Yeah, I kind of fucked up," Meadow says. "Fell asleep as soon as I got back to Selma's in the afternoon. I thought I could just get high, eat something, and go back to bed, but I ended up tossing and turning until five in the morning."

"Oof. Enjoying your house-sitting gig otherwise?"

"More or less. I dragged most of my shit over before Shanghai. Threw the rest into storage." He takes a spoonful of jjigae into his mouth. "Honestly, it's a pretty luxe setup. I almost feel guilty."

"Med, my man, whatever for?"

"I don't know. It's a relief to not have to pay rent for a few months, and Selma made it very clear that she never planned on subletting her apartment to a stranger or anything like that. But she's doing me a huge favor, obviously. I guess I don't understand what she's getting out of it. Apart from me keeping her plants alive, knock on wood."

Noticing their empty glasses, Peter pours them both some more Chamisul and slides the shot over to Meadow. "There's the ticket," Peter says.

"Huh?"

"Racking up more spiritual debt with your manic pixie artist girlfriend . . ."

"I wouldn't really call her 'manic,' per se. At least not lately."

"Until one day, when the chickens come home to roost," Peter continues, affecting the dramatic tone of a tabloid newscaster, "and mademoiselle enslaves you as a live installation piece, à la Tilda Swinton sleeping in a glass box."

Meadow rolls his eyes but can't help but laugh. He lifts his glass of soju. "Forget I said anything. Why don't you tell me about the rest of your birthday party instead? Do you, um, remember when I left? Because I don't."

"My memory of the evening is a bit sketch, too, if I'm gonna be honest with you. You hung out until pretty late, though. Definitely were there for pizza, and then that Alphabet City dive."

"We had pizza?!"

Peter stabs into a morsel of the savory pancake and dips it in the shallow dish of vinegar nearby. "It was your idea," he says nonchalantly, plopping it into his mouth. "I reminded you about your early flight more than once, but you just showed me the alarm you'd set on your phone . . ."

"Fat lot of good that did me."

". . . and screeched, 'Let me live my life!' I thought you Irish-exited when you disappeared for like an hour, but then you were back with us and shoving bourbon in my face."

Meadow raises an eyebrow as he refills their soju glasses. "Well, I guess I was trying to conjure up the spirit of your twenty-fourth birthday party again."

"You've been doing that every year, man," Peter grins. "You don't know how much I appreciate it."

Peter was his first roommate when he moved to New York. Meadow's college friend, who'd gone to high school with Peter in Texas, had put them in touch when she realized they were relocating to the city at the same time. It was a stroke of fate and good fortune. The two of them got along famously from the get-go. They were both entering grad school, although in very different fields: Peter was an aspiring architect, while Meadow was starting a doctorate in comparative literature.

Peter grew into his handsomeness sometime in his late twenties, Meadow always thinks. Nothing about his physical appearance changed; he had had the same broad, pleasant features and respectable height when Meadow met him for the first time at a coffee shop in Morningside Heights. But something seemed to click into place for him, after living in New York for many years. Maybe he was better groomed now, or had become more attentive or thoughtful in some way. With his dark, well-trimmed mustache and prominent cheekbones, the dapper Peter of today could play the part of a virtuous gentleman on some Korean drama.

Meadow feels a fondness and contentment swell in his chest as they tuck into their meals and Peter rambles on about what he's been doing since they last saw each other at his birthday festivities. They were roommates for seven years, almost the entire arc of their twenties. He was not surprised or resentful when Peter moved in with Annika, a radiant Swede, just months after they'd started dating. Meadow and Peter were on the cusp of twenty-nine then; he knew that Peter was anxious for a long-term relationship, perhaps having also internalized some amount of pressure from his family. Just as well that he met someone like Annika, a devoted humanitarian who worked at the United Nations, a daily practitioner of yoga and excellent cook, to boot. Meadow didn't realize until after the fact how much not having Peter in his daily life would leave a void.

"How often are you at Barley, by the way?" Peter asks as the meal winds down.

"Four nights a week, usually, plus a daytime shift here and there. You should stop in sometime."

"I'd love to. You know, it's kind of sad, but I barely find myself in Brooklyn anymore. Between long work hours and the new apartment . . ."

"I warned you about moving to Queens!" interjects Meadow, only half jokingly.

"Yeah, yeah. And you, sir, still need to come over for dinner since you missed our housewarming. Annika's been in my ear about it."

"Sure," Meadow says perfunctorily. "Let me know when."

Earlier they were able to get seated without much of a wait. A throng of frowning would-be patrons now congregates at the entrance of the restaurant, swiveling their heads to survey the seated diners with a mixture of envy and resentment. Peter and Meadow hasten to finish the bottle of soju as a server comes by to pick up their plates.

"Nightcap?" Peter asks.

"You read my mind. Let's head somewhere else, though. I'm getting death stares from up front."

"Good call." Peter raises his hand and scans the restaurant for a server. "*Chogiyo!*"

Soon they're back out on Thirty-Second Street, weaving through tottering groups of girls in heels, college students wielding bubble tea, ajummas and their grocery carts, and the occasional bewildered tourist gazing dumbly at the density of neon signs overhead. Peter says he knows a dive bar not far from there, a bit off the main drag. They head east and then north beneath puffs of cloud tinted a crisp pink and lavender by the sunset. Turning a corner, they come upon an unmarked wooden door nestled between a flower shop and a curtained storefront advertising psychic services. Peter guides them into a long and narrow bar with sticky floors and the pungent waft of cheap beer. The place is so dark that Meadow would have assumed it was closed if he'd just walked past. A grizzled man in a suit is the lone patron, seated on a stool while tapping out a message on his phone.

Peter buys them a round of bourbon from the bartender, a disgruntled young woman who slaps the change on the counter next to their cups. While this transaction is happening, Meadow delights in the beat-up jukebox with its double piping of neon green and yellow that he finds next to the bathroom. Fishing a few singles from his wallet, he spends a while flipping through its surprisingly robust collection. They slide into a booth in the back just as the strains of "You Give Good Love" by Whitney Houston filter through the speakers. A layer of sentimentality seeps out over the dingy bar as they pick up their conversation from dinner.

Though he saw Peter before traveling to Shanghai, Meadow didn't have a chance to regale him with the full tale of what transpired between him and Diego. Talking about it again feels like probing a wound that hasn't fully healed. But the wincing tenderness of it is reassuring, in a way. The story becomes more and more neutralized with each retelling, no longer as intense a source of anguish or disappointment, transformed instead into another tally on his scorecard of fizzled romances. So Meadow strives to be as detached and dispassionate as possible in presenting the narrative: He met a man; things were great. He thought that the ground they stood on was solid enough. Then he got ghosted. It was more of a shock than heartbreak, at first. He'd never imagined that things could end so abruptly.

Simple as that.

Ghosted. A funny word, Meadow considers later, when he lurches back to Selma's after several bourbons with Peter. Diego may have ghosted him, but it's he who feels like a ghost in this third-floor apartment. It's decidedly weird to be here alone, as though he has passed through the looking glass into a realm where Selma is disembodied and invisible, while her presence in all nooks of the apartment, in every trinket or mundane appliance, is somehow more potent than ever. Absence is its own kind of energy, Meadow thinks. Dark matter, negative space. Selma and Diego, both snipped clean from his life. Of course, the major difference is that she'll return from Shanghai at the end of the summer. But for now, she, too, exists as abstraction and memory. The guilt he mentioned to Peter at dinner is more complex than his inability to reciprocate for the windfall of staying here rent-free. Rather, Meadow can't help but feel as though he's trespassing. All homes are manifestations of the psyche; home is the material expression of one's state of being, the interior made exterior. Even if he is here by Selma's invitation, to sleep in her bed and move through her apartment as if it were his own strikes him as brazenly intimate.

It's close to midnight. Meadow feels nowhere near sleepy, probably owing to the fact that he woke up at one in the afternoon. He flicks on the kitchen light and squats down to examine the contents of Selma's formidable liquor cabinet set against the wall. One more bourbon couldn't hurt, he decides. And a joint to call it a night. He pours himself two fingers from an open bottle of Suntory, then fetches the crane box from the living room. While rolling the joint, a thought skims the surface of his mind. Phantoms and ghosts. They used to joke that her apartment was haunted, he and Selma. He helped her move in around five years ago. In the beginning, he remembers now, she would complain that she was having bouts of insomnia or that her memory was growing fuzzier ever since she'd moved. She began to misplace things or discover objects she didn't recall ever owning. *It's your ghost*, Meadow would tease, though Selma chalked it up to her sense of physical insecurity in a new home. *I'm probably just being absentminded*, she said. *I've hauled too many belongings around the world and forgotten what I've collected.*

The ghost became something of a running gag between them, a casual conversation they might have over cocktails or while walking around Manhattan on the weekend. It was the source of all her technical troubles, naturally, from a laptop battery issue to an inconsistent electrical current that caused her bathroom light to flicker. She would blame the ghost for hiding her keys and making her late for a dinner date or movie. Sometimes they would discover an unfamiliar piece of glassware wedged in the back of a kitchen cupboard, a lighter or earring that Selma swore she'd never seen before in a drawer. They agreed that it was most likely a benevolent ghost who simply wanted her attention, or to give her presents as a sign of goodwill. The joke quietly faded over time as Selma got settled into the apartment, the two of them drifting closer and farther apart and then closer again. Meadow wonders why this is emerging from the depths of his memory now, as he takes a sip of Suntory and sparks the joint at his lips.

For a long spell, he just lies on the sofa with the single living room lamp for illumination, feeling the heat of the June night waft in through the windows. He and Selma share the minor idiosyncrasy of eschewing AC, with a general tolerance for temperatures that others might consider to be disagreeable at best, agonizing at worst. Summertime in New York is nowhere near as muggy as it is in Shanghai, anyway. A breeze is enough to cool down the apartment on a night like this. As he feels the amber liquid swish in his stomach, Meadow closes his eyes, stretches his legs, and wriggles his toes. Against the faint illumination of the lamp, he can make out patterns on the backs of his eyelids, brown and black splotches whose contours undulate and dissolve into one another. Red-purple shapes appear and turn into half-melted triangles and whirling discs, their forms never stable, borders constantly merging or dividing. In the static materializes a dark semicircle, smoother in texture and more cohesive than all else. It moves slowly and steadily into the center of his vision, then extends outward from the bottom until the other symmetrical half of the circle appears. A perfect circle, Meadow thinks dully, just as the edge of the shape takes on a sliver of brightness like the glint of a blade. Or the cold arc of a crescent moon. A moon—

A thud startles him to attention. Meadow opens his eyes, lifts his head from the cushion, and looks around. Nothing seems to be out of place. It sounded like it came from the hallway, a knock from behind a closed door. He rises unsteadily from the couch and looks back and forth between the darkened hallway and the kitchen. There. Not a noise, but some activity in his peripheral vision. His heart begins to beat faster. Could he have imagined it? He swears there was a flutter of movement at the end of the hall, something darting quickly into the bedroom.

Then he hears the sound again, a muffled knock or perhaps a rattle. It's hard to distinguish whether the noise is coming from within the apartment or outside, a backyard or building next door. The neighbors could be doing yardwork or having a party.

It's midnight, a voice reasons in Meadow's head. On a Tuesday. Instinctively, he begins moving toward the bedroom, inebriated adrenaline overpowering any sense of anxiety. Dashing down the hallway in quick steps, he flicks on the overhead light and scans from floor to ceiling. Nothing suspicious. His eyes must be playing tricks on him.

Just when Meadow turns to go back to the living room, he hears it one more time. This time, a series of raps, two in succession, from what sounds like the far wall of the bedroom. Selma's bedroom is sparsely decorated, with just a queen-size bed, a nightstand, a writing desk, and a cheval mirror in the corner by the closet. As he creeps inside, Meadow finds himself drawn to the mirror, a slim antique-looking piece in a rosewood frame. It occurs to him that he is stoned, in addition to having downed considerable amounts of liquor this evening. He moves closer, but what he is looking at is not himself, but rather the bedroom's reflection. The cheval mirror is tilted slightly backward so the expanse of the room is visible from a short distance. Meadow finds himself crouching as he approaches, his attention fixed on the reflected bed, nightstand, and writing desk, all of them oriented exactly opposite to how he is used to. He blinks slowly as he feels the whirring exhilaration of earlier catching up with him.

The closer he gets to the mirror, the more he's convinced that it is indeed the source of whatever sound he heard. But what could it have been? The mirror is but a single pane, no more than a few inches deep, including the frame. Down on his knees, he peers at the back and sees only the same rosewood paneling as the rest of the frame. He crouches and faces the front. It really is a beautiful piece, the joinery seamless and well-proportioned, the glass an unblemished oval several feet in height. Come to think of it, the mirror is remarkably pristine without a speck of dust. The reflection of the bedroom is so sharp that he almost feels like he could step right into that world. The longer he looks without blinking, the more his eyebrows, eyes, nose, and mouth seem to wobble and float independent of one another. The curve of his ears, his stubbly chin. A shimmer of light. Did something move in the mirror? Meadow gasps and scoots even closer. At first he thinks it must have been a trick of the light. But upon closer inspection, he sees that something really has changed. The surface of the mirror looks fluid and unsettled, like the gentle undulation of a pond.

"No way," he hears himself say aloud, his voice hoarse and alien. As he leans his head forward, Meadow notices that it's not the entire reflection, but rather just his face that seems to be shifting in the surface of the glass. Maybe he smoked something else in that joint, he gulps. It must be the quality of light at this angle. But somehow the effect persists even when he stays completely still. Squinting at the mirror, he seems to perceive time and age layering on or sloughing off his face as the seconds tick by. He has a brief, startlingly clear vision of himself as a teenager, then an adult; a child, a man. It is not that his physical attributes are changing in the reflection. His face remains the same size, his hair doesn't get any longer or shorter. But there is a shift in the light of his eyes, the tone of his skin, even the shape of his lips as he stares into the mirror and, for a moment, when he catches sight of what looks like his teenaged self, he feels a wave of tremendous sadness.

A sudden pang of loneliness engulfs him, remembering what it was like to be that age. Living with his aunt in the boonies of Indiana, secretly pining for some boy at his high school, not a soul he could talk to. Long drives into the countryside, staring up at the stars, wondering if he would ever have someone to call his own. Or if anyone could ever know him entirely, find him in this crevice where he was lodged, pull him out of it. Someone who would kiss him on the eyelids and smile warmly, take him into their arms.

Tears pearl at the edges of his eyes. His face mere inches from his reflection, he has a strange compulsion to reach his hand out now, as though to comfort the boy he sees. When his fingers finally touch the glass, it is not a solid surface he feels but something tense and viscous, molten but without heat. His breath catches. He swipes a finger across the mirror, then brings it to his face. A patch of something metallic, shiny and colorful like an oil slick, covers his fingertip. As he blinks, the material evaporates quickly until he sees only the whorl of his fingerprint.

He pushes two fingers against the mirror this time. Instead of encountering a solid viscosity, they push right through the glass. It feels cold, but not unpleasant. He reaches farther and farther until his whole hand is inside and he stands wrist to wrist with his mirror-self. Suddenly there is that knocking sound again, and this time he sees that the cheval mirror indeed moves, jerking in its frame by mere millimeters, as though nodding at him. And right in that moment he feels a force pulling him from behind the glass, a gradual but insistent tug that draws him in, sucking in his flesh, moving up his forearm, inch by inch. He opens his mouth to yelp, but no sound comes out. The strange substance seems to ooze out from the mirror, the silver coolness covering his arm and traveling quickly up to his shoulder, neck, and the edges of his face. His vision dims at first, then grows completely dark as the mirror envelops him in a balmy cold not unlike that of a spring night. Fear and surprise are overtaken by a realization that the void in which he finds himself is not so terrible. It is even soothing, in a way, this space between worlds where nothing has been born but everything remains possible. A place to rest his weary head, for a night or an eternity.

4

WITHIN TWO WEEKS OF DATING DIEGO, MEADOW DECIDED
he was in love. The world was in riotous bloom around him, the
days growing warmer and longer. He woke feeling light as a
feather each morning and was swooning and spiraling, tracing
wild and joyful arcs as he careened through the fantastic softness of spring. Things with Diego developed so naturally and
expediently that he barely had time to second-guess himself.
They went on full-day dates that transitioned seamlessly into
evening escapades. A bike ride to the Noguchi Museum, then
Polish food in Greenpoint, followed by a screening of *Mulhol-
land Drive* at BAM and cheap whiskeys at a dive bar. Dim sum
in Chinatown segueing into coffee and dessert, used bookstores
and flea markets, afternoon beers in the East Village and Indian
food for dinner. Diego dropped by Barley more than once, kissing him over the counter and asking about his plans for after
work or the next day. They'd go out for pizza or cook pasta in
Diego's tiny kitchen, drink beers and watch movies on his laptop, take a stroll to Gowanus or South Slope at night for a few
cocktails, lie down in a quiet corner of Green-Wood Cemetery.
On these long journeys through the city, Meadow could feel
himself easing into a nearly meditative state as he and Diego
talked about most anything that crossed their paths or minds.

They ruminated on foliage in the park, the façades of buildings, the unexpectedly bold fashions of the elderly or very young. Every seemingly ordinary person, place, or object began to glow with a significance that one of them would seize upon and the other would draw out, culminating in meandering, associative conversations about everything from the ubiquity of death in public spaces to the erotic appeal of food media.

"I mean, it's so obvious," Diego said once while they were at a downtown Brooklyn diner. "Everyone knows food is sex, sex is food. There's more to it if you dig a bit deeper, but most people don't bother or are too scared."

Meadow smiled at the earnest, impassioned look on his face and took a swig from a bottle of lager. "Sure, sure," he said. "But like, what are you getting at? We all have bodily cravings that we satisfy in our individual ways?"

"Yeah, something like that." Diego paused to take a bite from his BLT, his gaze drifting down to contemplate the sandwich. He chewed thoughtfully, then added, "Like, celebrity chefs each sell a particular brand of carnal consumption, right? Whether it's the wholesome, nourishing vibes of the Barefoot Contessa or the unhinged, chaotic Americana of Flavortown."

"Mm, yes." Meadow laughed, stabbing at the pickle next to his Reuben. "Go on."

"The same could be said of anyone. Your style of prepping, cooking, and even serving food alone says a lot about how you express yourself sexually. Let alone eating, which is a whole other layer. God, there's so much you can tell about a person from the way they eat."

A waitress came by and asked if they needed anything else. Meadow said they were all good and asked for the check. The waitress slid them a rectangular black clipboard, then strolled off smacking her gum. "Have a good night, boys. Pay at the register."

"Well," Meadow ventured, "what do you read in my relationship to food then?"

Diego thought about this seriously, his dark brown eyes darting upward as though searching the ceiling for the answer. Then he fixed his gaze on Meadow again with a mischievous smile. "You're straightforward about what you like," Diego declared, "and pretty easy to please."

"Oh."

"But you make surprising choices sometimes."

"Is this about the habañero I put in the pasta sauce . . ."

"You enjoy satisfying your hunger," Diego continued, leaning in. "But you also let yourself indulge. I like that about you."

Diego spoke so solemnly that Meadow stifled the urge to laugh again. Instead, he tipped the beer bottle to his lips and drained the rest in one gulp. "What can I say," he said. "I like a snack."

That night they went back to Diego's place as they always did, in tacit agreement that the privacy of his studio was preferable to Meadow's rented room. Diego had been there for less than three months, so the studio was still sparsely decorated. A single snake plant that they'd bought together sat on a bookshelf next to the closet. Two windows looked out onto the gray brick of a neighboring building, so that it was almost impossible to tell the time of day based on the quality of light. Meadow didn't mind drifting through lazy mornings together, spooning in bed until one of them mustered up the energy to make coffee. He was in the midst of packing up his sublet, trying to figure out what to bring to Selma's, what to throw into storage. This new romance felt like a solid, stabilizing force against the uncertainty of the next months. As Diego was taking a shower, Meadow lay in bed and pressed his face into the pillow, breathing in the faintly sweet scent of Diego's hair.

Diego was an inquisitive soul, so eager and giving, directing nothing but affirmations at Meadow when they spent time together. The way he looked at him, the questions he asked, these things helped Meadow remember who he was and where he'd come from. Tell me a story about Nashville, Diego would say. Tell me a story about Shanghai. And Meadow would close his eyes to conjure up the past, recalling heartaches long buried, mild blunders, happy coincidences. The loneliness and longing of a childhood adrift, transmuting into teenage angst and young adult shiftlessness in Indiana, California, New York. Meadow knew they were still in the honeymoon phase. But surely, with the way things were going, they would have a place in each other's lives in the months ahead—even with the short trip to Shanghai, the moving to and from Selma's. No matter how he tried to keep cool and take things slow, he could feel with grim certainty that he was falling headlong in love. How delicious and thrilling the descent was, the body tumbling head over heels, metallic momentum in his belly, so much air blasting upward into his mouth that he couldn't even scream.

HE AWAKENS.

It's less an awakening than a snapping into reality, a return from the void. One moment he is nowhere, adrift not in his own unconsciousness but the oblivion of nonexistence, there but not there, like an untold story. Now, back in the glare of light and awareness, he is embodied—painfully so. Must be morning. He's still fully clothed and on the couch. An involuntary groan escapes his mouth. Meadow tastes ash and liquor on his tongue, vague reminders of the night before.

A breeze wafts in and caresses his bare skin. He squints at the ceiling as it spins and throbs quietly above him. Hallucinatory flashes of last night's dinner come back to him in succession, the

Korean stews and plates of banchan, soju and bourbon, Whitney Houston. What happened after? He remembers getting home and pouring himself another nightcap of Suntory, rolling a joint. And then—the mirror. It must have been a dream, he realizes, grimacing at the empty glass on the coffee table next to him. "Fucking ghosts," he rasps.

Remembering he has an evening shift at Barley, Meadow pats his pockets and pulls out his phone. Not even eight in the morning. Plenty of time to recover, thank God. He lets the phone clatter to the floor with a weary sigh, blinking at his surroundings. Selma's apartment looks different in the morning light. He still hasn't quite gotten used to the silent, almost staid atmosphere, in contrast with his overlapping memories of dinner and cocktails or movie nights over the years. From the couch, he swivels his head just enough to glance at the hallway leading to the bedroom. A patch of powder blue is visible through the skylight above the front door, by which the gangly potted rubber tree and thin console table sit blankly. He remembers so vividly stomping his way over to determine the source of a strange noise, but now the whole apartment seems bland and benign.

He feels the dull weight of fatigue throughout his body. Probably best to sleep some more, he thinks as he covers himself with a thin woven blanket and closes his eyes. He imagines bobbing on a turbid seascape, his body juddering along with the waves, until finally he manages to relinquish himself to its gray depths.

HE DRIFTS IN and out of shallow sleep for the next several hours, flitting through a series of off-kilter dreams that seem to exist adjacent to reality. He passes seamlessly through the border between one and the next, a distant part of his consciousness aware of each shift. In one dream, he is running late for the airport again, but Diego is in Selma's apartment with him, helping him search for his passport. Meadow is frustrated by Diego's slow movements, how he doesn't seem to understand the urgency of his predicament. They rush to the bedroom, where Meadow desperately fumbles under the mattress. No dice. It's okay, Diego says, putting a hand on Meadow's shoulder. Maybe this just means you should stay here with me. I can't miss my flight, Meadow starts to say, when he hears a creaking sound. It's the cheval mirror jerking toward him, beckoning. Even from a distance, he can see the surprised look on the face of his reflection, his mirror-self.

The next thing he knows, he's in a parlor room with velvet-backed chairs and dark wooden furniture, staring into a gold-framed mirror on the wall. He wears a tuxedo jacket and a white mask on his face. The other guests are a blur of shapes behind him, their overlapping conversations impossible to make out. A perverse blare of trumpet sounds from a distant room, raising his hackles. He shouldn't be here. Meadow turns from the mirror and tries to locate an exit. In the midst of the faceless crowd appears a woman in an elaborate gown and sparkling mask, a jade clip tying back her cascade of hair. Selma, he calls out. How do I get out of here? She simply gives him a cold smile, baring her voluptuous shoulder as she turns and stalks away. He tries to follow her, but there are too many people in masks and full-body costumes in the way, a deranged parade of animals, monsters, jesters, and deities that block his path and cloud his vision.

The darkness dissipates. He blinks and finds himself looking at his own face in a mirror again. He stands in a gray enclosure, surrounded by hard plastic walls. His vision is bleary. Hard to make out the edges of the space. There's a gleam of metal on one wall, a white square with a red circle on it. When he draws near, he discovers that it's a No Smoking sign. I'm on the plane, he thinks. How long have I been asleep in here? Suddenly he feels a surge of embarrassment, imagining the long line of angry and impatient people who must be waiting outside the bathroom. No choice but to face the music. He turns to leave, then realizes that *The Masquerade* is sitting next to the sink. He must have brought it in to read, which explains the dream he just had. The green of the book cover seems to glow faintly in the monochrome environment, every letter startlingly crisp. Meadow bows his head when he exits the bathroom, preemptively averting his gaze from the other passengers, who must be livid. But there's nobody in the aisle. Beyond the pool of light in the galley by the bathroom, the entire plane is dark. It dawns on him that he is the only passenger, that he has been flying alone for a godless eternity. A chill passes over him, the weight of solitude so immense that he loses his balance and stumbles into a seat back. Or maybe the plane is banking, changing altitude, setting a new course—

Meadow gasps and flails upright, eyes wide open. A darkness lingers at the edges of his vision, receding like a gentle tide. He slows his heavy breaths, curling his toes to feel the fabric of the couch. A June day, Selma's apartment. He's still wearing last night's clothes, which are now damp with sweat. Shift at Barley. He picks up his phone from the floor and finds that it's past noon. A mirror on the wall by the inoperable fireplace reflects a rhombus of light onto the ceiling. As Meadow watches the light wink at him, a gurgle from his stomach reminds him that he hasn't eaten anything all day. It's high time to get a move on. He shambles off the couch and goes to brew coffee in the French press as a first order of business. A short while later, he examines the groceries he accumulated yesterday while sipping from a mug of piping hot coffee. For lunch, he whips up a batch of mapo tofu and a bowl of smashed cucumbers and minced garlic drizzled in sesame oil and chili flakes. He eats these with a bowl of steaming white rice, drinking more coffee all the while. Then he takes a long, hot shower in Selma's claw-foot tub, imagining the hangover sloughing off him, until he emerges anew, fresh and pink and ready to take on the world.

Weird fucking dreams, he thinks as he towels off. The memory of the desolate airplane disquiets him especially. And what is it about mirrors? He recalls that there was a mirror in each dream segment, at least the ones that he can remember. But then—the book. Though he hasn't so much as glanced at it since coming back from Shanghai, it seems to have wriggled into his consciousness. Meadow crosses back into the bedroom to get dressed. He remembers how crisp the letters looked on the cover of *The Masquerade* in his dream, more palpable and potent than anything else, and has an urge to find the real book and verify that the cover looks the same. After throwing on a shirt and shorts, he roots around in his backpack for it. He has never attended a masked ball himself, but the setting strikes him as so incredibly familiar for some reason. Could it be a subliminal effect of knowing the book's author shares his name? Then again, for all he knows, the author's given name might be *tian* for "sky" instead of "field."

His heart drops when he discovers the book is not in his backpack at all. He is certain that he stashed *The Masquerade* in there when he was packing up in Shanghai. It had been on the nightstand where he usually put his wallet and phone, so it's unlikely that he would have overlooked it. Or did he do such a thing in his haste? He checks the pile of rolled-up clothes in his suitcase. No book in there either. The disappointment that comes over him is swift, and surprising in its intensity. He must have left it at his parents', he thinks. Maybe he can ask Selma to drop by to pick it up before she comes home in August.

He fritters away the next few hours by unpacking a larger suitcase he'd brought from his sublet before going to Shanghai.

As he hangs a few shirts and puts underwear and socks into a dresser drawer Selma cleared for him, Meadow considers how few physical possessions he has to his name after almost ten years in New York. Apart from the suitcases, there are just a few things crammed into a sad storage unit nearby. He has never considered himself an ascetic, but surely this sort of accidental minimalism must mean something. His existence here is still so contingent, almost laughably flimsy. Were it not for the kindness and friendship of Selma, Peter, and others, he would cease functioning altogether, he thinks. By the time he finishes this task, the afternoon sun has started to wane into the more dramatic hues of early evening. Soon he'll have to get ready for his shift. He orders a fried chicken sandwich from a neighborhood restaurant, puts on an Aaron Neville record, and smokes the leftover roach from last night, easing into the familiarity of routine and expectation.

While lazing on the couch again, he checks his phone and sees he has a few dozen notifications on WeChat. The messages are usually advertisements, spammy promos, or viral videos that distant relatives and acquaintances like to share in group chats. He taps out a quick note to his parents, who ask him how he's been spending his time since returning to New York. Just as he is about to close the app and put his phone away, he sees a few messages from Anya, the director of Gallery Potemkin.

Sorry to bother you, Liu Tian, she writes in Chinese. *It was nice to meet you in Shanghai. I think you're back in America already, but have you talked to Selma recently?*

Selma? Why would Anya ask him about Selma? She still has another two months or so left in her residency. Meadow replies, letting her know that he is indeed back in New York and no, he has not seen Selma since the night of her opening at Potemkin, when they all went together to Douglas Koh's and—

He isn't sure when she left the party, but thinking back to it now awakens a mild sense of shame, the remembrance of a long night of unexpected indulgences. He has made efforts to cut back on drinking in recent years. Ironically, working at Barley has helped him scale back simply by virtue of placing him on the other side of the transaction. Lying on Selma's couch, he suddenly can't stifle images of the tryst with Douglas and Cotton, the banality of this convergence of desire, their bodies reduced to a mechanical cycle of stimulus and response. For him, the physical act of love has always been about intimacy, if not transcendence, offering oneself in service of pleasure or communion. And yet there was nothing sublime about the dusty morning in Shanghai as he tumbled over Cotton trying to coax the flame brighter, the slick sweat of his arms and chest more animal than erotic, while Douglas sat nearby, rasping quiet commands and fondling himself vacuously—

Meadow sighs. He checks the time and decides to start getting dressed for work.

It's a nearly forty-minute walk from Selma's apartment to Barley, but this route is preferable to taking a bus or transferring several times on the subway. He loves this part of Brooklyn, particularly the long stretch of residences on Nostrand Avenue interspersed with restaurants, churches, nail salons, and bodegas. And the summer sun sets late these days, which affords him some delicious views of dusky light cascading over the neighborhood through the treetops, onto the pavement, and illuminating the spaces between his fingertips. As he walks, he smokes a Chunghwa cigarette from a duty-free carton he bought at Shanghai Pudong. By the time he reaches the bar, his hangover from the morning is but a distant memory.

He first started working at Barley after quitting his office job, which he'd sought in the first place as an excuse to drop out of grad school. Originally he thought he could bartend for a while, gather his thoughts about career or existence or whatever, and figure out his next steps. But it's been easy to coast, one year turning into two, and now almost three. These days it seems like everyone takes one of two routes for pivoting careers: either you go to coding school or become a yoga instructor. Both options are out of the question for Meadow, a big tech skeptic with stiff limbs. Bartending actually suits him just fine, for the time being. But he can't shake the nagging compulsion or internalized shame to identify a supposedly more gainful vocation and start drifting in that direction. He can't deny that external pressure plays a part, as well, especially those demoralizing conversations with his parents, who find it unconscionable that their only son serves alcohol for a living when he could have amounted to something more, or something else.

Nonetheless, bartending sure beats sitting in an office and staring at a computer. He much prefers the physicality of being on his feet, mixing cocktails, pouring beers from the tap, moving up and down the length of the bar all night. He feels far more useful than he did when he had to wade through soul-crushing emails and meetings all day long. And making someone a drink certainly is a hell of a lot more substantial and grounded, more real, than trying to parse an awkward translation of some dead European philosopher's views on modernity. At the bar, there are usually enough customers or tasks to keep him happily distracted and the hours flit by with amazing speed. He likes to keep a low-key social life, but he doesn't mind shooting the shit with the clientele while slinging drinks. The small talk is even energizing, in its own way. It's part of the job, building that trust with someone in a single transaction, or over the course of many visits. Peter was endlessly amused the first time he came to the bar and watched Meadow in action. "You're a regular Chatty Cathy." He guffawed. "It's kind of hilarious."

"It's performance," Meadow said nonchalantly.

Barley Elixirs is a local watering hole at the edge of Crown Heights, just past the noisy thoroughfare of Atlantic Avenue, sharing a street corner with a Congolese restaurant and a shipping store. Duplexes line the block on one side, while prewar residential buildings loom across the way. The bar is just a touch bigger than your average studio apartment in the neighborhood. It's a cozy little place with diamond-checkered floor tiles and mismatched wooden furniture. Maidenhair, pothos, and philodendron in glazed planters form a verdant tableau by the south-facing windows. On the wall behind the bar hangs an oversized mirror, a gigantic stalk of golden wheat emblazoned across its length. The same art in shiny foil adorns the matchbooks stacked next to the cash register.

It's a typical Saturday night, buzzy but mellow, a dozen or so patrons scattered throughout the space. Meadow presides over his kingdom alongside Monique and a new barback named Quinn, who just graduated from art school. The three of them huddle around Monique's phone to review the playlist she is feeding into the speakers. "Mm, I love it, Momo," Meadow says. "You always know how to set a mood."

She giggles. "Thanks, baby. Let me know if you want to add any tunes or switch it up."

While Quinn returns to slicing the remaining limes on the counter, Meadow and Monique glide to opposite ends of the bar and greet customers to the beats of *Midnight Marauders*, taking orders for vodka sodas or draft IPAs, swiping credit cards and accepting fistfuls of cash. Meadow starts to get hot in his T-shirt, the familiar exhilaration setting in as a steady stream of people approach the bar, their gazes hopeful or imploring or indignant as he goes down his mental checklist of who's been waiting longest. He finds that his interactions on the job are more or less a microcosm of humankind. At the bar, as in life, all kinds of people demand his attention as their paths converge. Some are immediately friendly, full of conversational ease and eager to strike an earnest but fleeting intimacy. Others treat him with indifference, or thinly veiled contempt. It's all just a play, Meadow tells himself. Play and let play.

The faces swarm as the evening goes on, the bar thrumming with more energy and chatter. Donna Summer serenades them, injecting a bit of frantic disco energy into the atmosphere. Meadow and Monique dole out shots and cocktails and beers on tap, sneak in short conversations with the regulars, who ask about their weekends or summer plans. Quinn dutifully rounds up empty glasses, loads and unloads the dishwasher, sprays and wipes down the bathroom. By the time Monique leaves at midnight, the pace is already petering out with just a few couples on dates, a gaggle of commiserating girlfriends, and a middle-aged man nursing a beer. Quinn takes off around two due to their early morning plans, leaving Meadow to fend for himself and close up shop.

Past three, Meadow is zoning out to Herbie Hancock on piano. He wipes the countertop absentmindedly with a rag while his only customers, a lesbian couple in jeans and work shirts, canoodle by candlelight at a back table. He tries to ignore the physical aches throughout his body, and the despair and self-pity that offer themselves as company now that no one else is around. He hates to admit that a part of him was holding out hope that Diego might still show up at the bar. That he might waltz in and explain himself, asking for forgiveness and a cocktail—a pathetic fantasy, at best. But the heart is a recalcitrant creature that refuses reason. The heart clings to its pride.

At some point, he checks his phone and sees that Anya has replied to him.

I haven't been in touch with Selma since that night either, she writes. *She missed a few meetings I arranged this week. Typical forgetful artist, I guess. It's probably nothing to worry about, but can you let me know if you hear from her? Thanks.*

Meadow furrows his brow and reassures Anya that he will let her know if he hears from Selma. Selma going incommunicado is not completely out of character, but it strikes him as strange, given the seriousness with which she approaches her professional practice. She's probably just working too intensely at the studio, keeping odd hours and developing a fixation on whatever new project she has started. Still, Meadow feels a mild disquiet over this message from Anya, verging on an irrational guilt—as though he is responsible for Selma's disappearance, having subconsciously masterminded and executed some plan to displace her and claim her home as his own.

Meadow's thoughts are interrupted when the lesbian couple come to close out their tab. They thank him for the drinks as they saunter out of the bar, arm in arm. Then he's the last person on the planet again.

Time flows differently late at night. The silvery current that whisks life forward during daylight hours starts to grow murky and dark, the waters slowing to a confused churn. This darkening also reveals other aspects of reality that are not so apparent in the glaring white noise of the everyday: subtle textures and gradations, a porous quality to things that are supposedly solid. Even music sounds different, Meadow thinks as he wipes droplets off a glass with a dish towel, his back to the counter. Herbie's piano feels at once whimsical and resigned, tracing the shape of solitude with every keystroke. An empty bar at the witching hour is a strange place to be. For all Meadow knows, nothing exists beyond the doors of Barley. He is a single man holding on to the light, tending to the small space he calls his own.

Meadow snaps out of his reverie when the heavy wooden door to the bar creaks open. His first instinct is to look into the mirror hanging above him. In it, he sees the cast-iron planters hanging near the entrance sway gently as a tall and shadowy figure comes inside. The bar's illumination, at least in the mirror, seems so dim that at first he can't determine anything about the figure besides its silhouette. Then the figure sharpens into a bespectacled man in a dark jacket and hat. Meadow turns around as the man makes his way over to the bar with slow, plodding steps.

"Hey there," Meadow calls out, trying to affect a business-as-usual tone. The man nods stiffly in greeting as he sits down on a stool. He takes a moment to settle his frame, leaning forward on his elbows to examine the menu before him. He wears thick, round eyeglasses that partially obscure his long nose and gaunt face. In his black linen blazer and porkpie hat, he has the look of a down-and-out playwright or avant-garde composer, the kind of benign eccentric one might find ambling around the West Village. Meadow wonders if he's seen him somewhere before, maybe busking in Washington Square Park or giving an impassioned speech on Sixth Avenue. He sets the dish towel and glass down on the counter.

"Excuse me," the man says.

"What can I get for you?"

"I was hoping you might have some red wine, in fact. I don't see it on the menu." He speaks with a lightly German intonation, Meadow thinks. Or could it be Dutch?

"We do keep a few bottles on hand, actually." Meadow retrieves a laminated card from the cash register and sets it in front of the customer. "Here's our wine list."

"Ah, very good. Thank you kindly." The man furrows his brow and adjusts his glasses, peering down at the card. "A glass of the Tempranillo, if you please."

"Sure."

Feeling pleased to have a minor task, Meadow roots around in a cabinet beneath the bar, pulling out an unopened bottle and setting it on the counter. He removes the foil from the bottleneck, then deftly swivels the metal spiral of the wine opener into the stopper until he feels the meaty grip of the cork. In one smooth motion, he uncorks the bottle with a satisfying pop. He grabs a wineglass from a rack by his waist, places it on the counter, and gives the man a healthy pour.

"Here you are," he says, sliding it over.

"Much obliged," says the man with a nod, the white whiskers on his face shining faintly in the honeyed glow of the bar. "You're quite good at that, you know."

"At what?"

"Opening a wine bottle with nonchalance. Pouring with intention."

"Ah, thanks. Practice makes perfect, I guess."

The man grins, revealing a row of grayish teeth. "Cheers, young friend," he says, lifting the glass. "To your health."

"Cheers," returns Meadow. "Enjoy."

The hatted man is probably just a lonesome soul who wants someone to talk to. Meadow decides it's better to busy himself, though, so he wipes his hands on a towel, slips out from behind the counter, and starts to pick up the stray drinks around the room. It's amazing how much trash people leave behind, Meadow thinks as he grabs a pint glass filled with a crinkly wrapper and potato chip crumbs. A glint of white catches his eye. He squints and moves closer. There's an oblong shape on the black Formica table, just outside the halo of a tea candle. He's discovered his fair share of abandoned lighters at Barley, but this object is longer and thinner, a smooth white case with a beveled edge and a faint pattern engraved across its length. Meadow picks it up and feels its cold weight across the palm of his hand. The metal edge flashes again as it catches the light, and Meadow starts with the realization that it's a pocketknife.

There's a grunt from behind him. Instinctively he slips the knife into his pants pocket and spins around. The hatted man is hunched forward, a napkin pressed to his lips. He wheezes for a spell, then begins to cough with such ferocity that the entire bar seems to tremble.

"Sir, are you okay?" Meadow asks, striding over.

The guttural rasps continue for a good ten seconds. Then the man rises in his stool with a dramatically long inhale, his back straightening, the shape of the black blazer becoming sharper, more clearly defined. He exhales with a similar theatrical flourish, crumpling inward and downward until he reverts to his previous unassuming guise. He clears his throat.

"My, my," the man rasps, turning to face Meadow at last. "My deepest apologies for startling you. These lungs sometimes get the best of me."

"I'll get you some water." Meadow goes behind the bar counter again and begins filling a glass.

"That's awfully kind of you," the man says as Meadow hands it to him. Seeing how he drinks it in no time flat, Meadow refills the glass and slides it back his way. The hatted man sighs. "I so appreciate it. You know, while I was savoring the Tempranillo you poured, I was just beginning to think to tell you something. What timing, with that fit of wretched coughs."

"You were going to tell me something?" Meadow repeats, unsure if he heard correctly.

"Yes," the man says. "But first I would like to ask a question, if that's all right with you."

"Um, sure." Meadow folds his arms across his chest and wonders where this is going. His stomach tenses with a twinge of suspicion. Is this guy hitting on him, or is he just an oddball? He doesn't seem threatening by any means, but Meadow immediately remembers the pocketknife. The weight of it presses against his left thigh with a dull reassurance.

"Do you believe in symbols?"

"I . . . What kind of symbols?"

"What kind?" The man laughs. "Oh, just about any kind at all. Musical notation, Arabic numerals. Shapes imbued with power by mankind, or perhaps divinity: the perfect circle, the golden rectangle. Alphabets, hieroglyphs, ideographs. Names. Those are important symbols, are they not?"

"Well," Meadow says slowly, "I guess it would be stupid *not* to believe in symbols, when you put it that way."

"Now, now. I'm not trying to sway you one way or another." With an impish smile, he picks up his wineglass and takes a sip.

"I believe in them. Without a doubt." Meadow leans back against the wall-mounted cabinet above the cash register and credit card machine. A car whooshes by on the street just outside the bar, reminding him of their relative isolation. "So, what were you going to tell me then?"

"Ah." All of a sudden coy, the hatted man looks vaguely like a turtle retracting into its shell. Meadow tilts his head quizzically. "Well, my lad," he begins, "maybe it's less telling, and more of a suggestion."

"I'm all ears," Meadow says, now more annoyed than unnerved.

The hatted man leans forward and gazes upward at Meadow. "We live in a forest of symbols, in the modern world. Indeed, one can choose to interpret them in any number of ways. It is all too easy to forget the precession of the symbol, to flatten the signifiers with the signified. A name, a number, a note of music, they all have their own solitary power detached from the things they represent. They exist as shapes and sounds in primal, elemental form. This essential form is their meaning, to put it simply.

"Water is water, whether you contain it in a glass or pour it back into the ocean, no matter the language you use to name it. By the same token, you mustn't overlook the locus of possible interpretations affixed to a single symbol, like the petals of a flower fanning out from its center. The saxophone's B-flat is no more or less valid than that of the piano or mandolin. Everything converges in, and retains unity by virtue of, the symbol."

The lights of Barley dim ever so slightly as the man locks eyes with Meadow. His gaze is like a whirlpool spinning in a dark sea. Meadow hears the sound of distant waves as the music of the bar fades into the background. There is a tingling sensation in his fingertips as though hundreds of tiny fish are nibbling at him, silently entreating him to give of himself.

"Pay attention to symbols," the man says. "In them you will find the answers to all that you seek."

PART II

In Bloom

5

HE FIRST MET SELMA A LIFETIME AGO WHEN HE WAS STILL muddling through grad school, a tender twenty-three years of age. Meadow didn't know how the hell he'd bamboozled anyone into thinking that he possessed the intellectual capacity to pursue a PhD. In retrospect, he owed this state of affairs to a particularly supportive professor he'd had when finishing undergrad in the Bay Area, someone who helped him finesse his application materials enough to make him sound like a sensible young man with scholarly potential. The economy was crashing and burning, and staying in school was the easy way out, truth be told. The mythologies and circumscribed world of his young adult existence were no longer impenetrable, or even as sturdy as he'd wanted to imagine. He also needed to move on from his boyfriend at the time—though this was something he couldn't admit until much later.

A few months after graduating from college, he moved across the country without so much as a backward glance and landed in a gut-renovated walk-up apartment on 160th Street with his new acquaintance, Peter. They settled quickly into that space, hosting occasional dinner parties and growing herbs on the kitchen windowsill, sprawling out in different corners of the living room while sipping whiskey and reading Lefebvre or

Baudrillard. The first year went by blindingly fast, a time-lapse sequence of library books and cigarettes, disjointed seminar papers, fried plantains and pollo guisado, frantic nights drinking and dancing in Lower Manhattan, oceans of coffee. Meadow intuited almost immediately that grad school wasn't right for him, filled as he was with frivolous desires and unnameable aches. He just couldn't imagine what the alternative might be. So he pressed on, trying to walk the walk in as convincing a manner as possible, and before he knew it summertime was in full swing in New York, which only underscored his loneliness. He'd been single for almost a year then, during which time he'd been practically celibate and frothing with angst. There were any number of ways to meet men, but somehow he couldn't muster up the energy to even try. A coldly rational part of him suggested that he was too timid, or wounded in some way, afraid of rejection and thus preemptively consigning himself to solitude. The truth was that he was waiting for the hand of fate to work its magic. He wanted someone to simply waltz into his life with consummate grace, move him, love him, change him for the better. If this was an unattainable ideal, then so be it. Anyway, there was plenty to be grateful for: companionship, if not love; steadiness, in lieu of satiation.

All of a sudden his second winter in New York came. One weekend in January, before the new semester began, Peter invited him to a gallery opening in Chelsea. He'd met a girl from the fine arts department in the library a while ago, Peter told Meadow, and she sent him this thing on Facebook. Why not scope it out? At the very least, there would be free wine. In truth, Meadow had been enjoying these quiet weeks at home with little to do but tend to his mental garden. He'd spent Christmas in Shanghai with his parents, returning to New York just in time to host a college friend who came to ring in the new year. The weeks since then had been a remarkable oasis of peace, a time for catching up on reading, putting in half days at his work-study job, and chipping away at a draft of his dissertation outline. He'd even picked up a weekly jogging routine, in spite of the cold.

"You're not going to meet anyone flopping around the house by yourself," Peter reminded him. Instead of a droll rejoinder, which sounded too cynical before it even left his mouth, Meadow just hummed in agreement. So they bundled up in their winter gear and took the 1 train down to Twenty-Third Street. The evening sky was already blue-black when they emerged from underground, but the quality of light still felt different from a week or two earlier. Fugitive wisps of daytime were accruing as time marched ahead, wearing away the hard edges of winter's long nocturne.

The gallery was inside a nondescript building on Ninth Avenue. They ducked into the lobby, strode past the empty security desk, and took the elevator to the sixth floor. Several doors were open along one narrow hallway, warm light spilling out into the metallic fluorescence. People ambled by with plastic cups of wine, chattering and red-faced. Peter looked at the address on his phone again, then led them through one of the doorways.

There was a whiff of fresh paint in the air. Crisp black letters adorned the wall directly facing the entrance. "Selma Shimizu," Meadow read aloud. "*Infinitesimal Intimacies.*"

"Just where we wanted to be," Peter said, patting Meadow on the shoulder. "Come on, let's get a drink."

Soon they were circulating the room with cupfuls of merlot. It was overly warm inside the gallery, so they shimmied out of their coats and slung them over their arms. There were about two dozen works of varying sizes and media on display. One wall featured a Japanese Noh mask encircled by a series of progressively smaller masks that formed a loose spiral. Some of the masks were fox-like in appearance, while others looked vaguely humanoid, adorned with snouts and horns or grotesque teeth jutting from the mouth. The smallest could fit in a person's palm.

A massive framed photograph dominated a corner of the gallery. It was a sensual black-and-white photo of a woman's back, from the sweep of hair resting on her shoulder blade to the curve of her left hip. Her skin was pale and unblemished except for the moles that formed a constellation along her spine. On the opposite wall was a series of remarkably lifelike graphite sketches, depicting body parts in tension: a constricted throat, a long-nailed hand contorted into a fearsome claw, two surprisingly expressive nipples that telegraphed a kind of resignation.

Another framed work featured a grid of watercolor paintings the size of postcards, each of them showing the same room, with a bed and floor lamp as the only constants. The play of light was dramatically different in every painting, the room alternately saturated in daylight, cloaked in somber shadow, or somewhere in between. Meanwhile, the contours of a naked but faceless woman appeared in different positions in each scene: kneeling on the ground, one leg wrapped around the lamp, asleep in bed, making love to a male figure against the wall. There were probably at least thirty of these paintings.

At one point, Meadow looked up and realized Peter was waving at him from across the room next to a girl in a leopard-print coat. "This is Rebecca," he said after Meadow made his way over. "She's the one who invited us."

"I'm Meadow," he said, extending a hand.

"Nice to meet you!" Rebecca exclaimed while shaking his hand, eyes widening behind her cat-eye glasses. "What a cool name."

"Er, thanks. So how did you find out about this opening?"

"Oh, Selma was a guest speaker during crits last semester. I've been following her work ever since. What do you think?"

"She's very . . ." Meadow struggled for the right word. "Meticulous," he concluded.

A peal of high-pitched laughter escaped from between Rebecca's cherry-red lips. She turned to Peter. "Your roommate, right?"

"The one and only," Peter smirked.

Rebecca's eyes scanned the room. "I think my friends have already moved on to the other galleries. Are you guys up for checking out a few more? Have you had dinner? We were talking about hitting up the East Village later for some ramen. Doesn't that sound good? I'm telling you, some motherfucking ramen is what you need to warm the soul on a night like this. I'm so over winter, this postholiday slog is the worst. I guess I'm just glad we don't have to trudge through more disgusting sludge for now. That last snowstorm almost killed me . . ."

On and on she went, with Peter and Meadow involuntarily magnetized by her monologue, moving in sync with her as they drifted toward the wine table for a refill, then toward the hallway. Meadow tried to catch Peter's eye to gauge how interested he was in tagging along on Rebecca's outing. Suddenly it occurred to him that maybe Peter was into Rebecca and that this, in fact, had been the whole reason for them to come down here. Despite living with him for a year and a half, Meadow still hadn't quite pinned down his taste in women.

Just as they were about to cross the threshold of the entrance to the gallery, Rebecca let loose a theatrical gasp. For a moment, Meadow was uncertain what they were witnessing. Rebecca had someone new in her clutches now, a tall Asian woman in an austere black dress. She wore just a touch of eyeliner, which brought her light freckles, slender nose, and high cheekbones into relief. She gazed at Rebecca with cool detachment, the barest hint of a smile on her lips.

"My friends," Rebecca announced dramatically, "the artist is present. Please meet Selma Shimizu."

Only then did Selma turn to face Peter and Meadow. She was really quite lovely, Meadow thought. He was struck by the symmetry of her features and the smoothness of her skin, both of which lent her a statuesque quality. She looked like a woman that an artist of yesteryear would have made his muse. But clearly she had inverted that role, turning the gaze inward to produce the permutations of self on display in the room. Meadow realized he was a bit flushed from the wine. There was a cloudiness in Selma's eyes. Even as she looked directly at them, her gaze was distant, roaming, as though there were a translucent curtain between them.

"Congrats on your opening," Peter said, smiling nervously. "I'm Peter."

"My name's Meadow. Great work." He regretted saying this almost immediately. Selma's tight smile seemed to falter for a second. It had been a slip of the tongue, so casual and vapid an utterance, and perfectly ill-suited for this exchange. Meadow didn't know what to do with his hands. He took another sip of wine.

"Thank you for coming," Selma said finally. "I'm glad you enjoyed it."

Rebecca began to say something but was interrupted by a man in an expensive suit who materialized by Selma's side. He looked Middle Eastern or South Asian. His thick mane of hair and well-trimmed beard were both flecked with patches of white, and he wore stylish wire frames that gleamed in the lights of the gallery. He leaned in and whispered something in her ear, which elicited a more natural smile from her. In the blink of an eye, he was guiding her away from them with his hand on the small of her back.

"Well," said Rebecca, "I guess that's that."

Peter and Meadow trailed after her as they exited into the hallway, where it was considerably cooler.

"Must be her husband," Rebecca continued to no one in particular. "I hear he's an art dealer from Dubai."

In the end they did go out for dinner with Rebecca's crew. ("Ramen sounds good, doesn't it?" Peter prodded.) After ambling through the other galleries on the floor, they gathered in the lobby, decided on where to eat, and hailed taxis to an izakaya near St. Mark's. Miraculously, their large group was able to get seated without too long of a wait. The narrow restaurant was positively ablaze with activity. Servers circulated with trayfuls of agedashi tofu, blistered shishito peppers, and chicken-skin skewers. Raucous parties of college kids hooted with laughter over their pitchers of draft beer. "*Irasshaimase!*" roared the kitchen staff as they followed the host to their table like penitent children.

Rebecca's friends were mostly her classmates from the visual arts program. "I feel like I've seen you on campus before," one of them said to Meadow. With his bleach-blond curls, nose ring, and mischievous smile, Bobby reminded Meadow of the skater boys he used to crush on in high school. He was mildly intrigued. Maybe some unexpected goodness would come of this night, after all.

"Oh, really? I guess I do hang out at the library a lot."

Bobby picked up a piece of edamame and tentatively dabbed it in a shallow dish of soy sauce. "You're not in our department, though?"

"Nah. I'm in comp lit."

He whistled, then popped the soybean into his mouth. "That's pretty cool, man. What's your thesis about?"

"Travel writing in early twentieth-century China," Meadow said, shifting uncomfortably in his seat. "What about you? What's your medium?"

"I do collage and found objects," Bobby said. Meadow didn't know how to interpret the sly but blasé expression on his face. "I'm trying to branch out, though. Want to paint more. Learn how to blow glass, shit like that."

The two of them fell into easy conversation throughout dinner, which was the perfect diversion from Rebecca's shrieking repartee at the other end of the table. Bobby had grown up in rural Pennsylvania among verdant expanses of wheat and pastures full of cows. "No place for a German-Filipino faggot who liked to wear fishnets and paint his nails," he lamented, pursing his lips. "I got the hell out as soon as I could."

Meadow could relate. After elementary school in Tennessee and a couple years in Shanghai, suburban Indiana turned out not to be the friendliest environment for his budding adolescence, Auntie Marilyn's lenient household notwithstanding. The reverse culture shock was compounded by his grappling with sexuality and general teenage malaise. He was lucky enough to fall in with a rowdy crew that included aspiring pagans, suburban spelunkers, goth-adjacent metalheads, and retro-nostalgic greasers. But he was the only Asian among them, of course.

Marilyn's town house became the de facto launchpad for many of their excursions, since she wasn't often at home and, even when she was, didn't care to pry. Newly divorced and full of laissez-faire energy, she would simply drink wine in the kitchen and munch on almonds, occasionally asking Meadow and his friends if they wanted any soda or snacks. By sophomore year, they had access to quite a few cars among the lot of them, so they often drove out to the nearby state forests to drink beers and smoke cigarettes or conduct séances, or to Indianapolis and Cincinnati for concerts. In spite of it all, the Midwest remained far from an ideal place for his actualization. He began to carry the dull sorrow of imagining that maybe there was no place for him at all in the world—too much of one thing, not enough of the other, doomed to drift in a realm of the unknown and unknowable.

"You see yourself sticking around New York for the long haul?" asked Bobby, wiping the foam from his lips after taking a healthy gulp of Sapporo on tap.

"I have no idea," Meadow blurted out. In the year and a half he'd lived in the city, no one had asked him that question. "I guess we'll find out if it's meant to be."

After they devoured their bowls of shoyu and tonkotsu ramen, a few members of the group peeled off into the January night. Bobby and Meadow stood on the corner smoking Lucky Strikes, hobbling from leg to leg to keep warm. Once Rebecca had bade farewell to those headed to the Third Avenue subway, she came back with a conspiratorial glint in her eye. "Boys, what do you say to some more drinks?"

They were all game.

The rest of the evening was spent in a dimly lit dive bar where the sour scent of many a beer spilled hung in the air. Rebecca wasted no time in getting to the pool table, taunting and flirting her way into a few rounds with a group of bearded men. Meadow and Peter huddled at a nearby booth with Bobby and his classmate Daniela, a sardonic sculptress from Bogotá.

"If there's one thing I've learned since coming to New York," Daniela offered, gazing out at the pool game unfolding before them, "it's that mating rituals are the same everywhere in the world."

They took turns buying rounds, and soon it was past midnight, everyone sloshed and on their third or fourth drink, not counting the beers at dinner and the gallery wine before. Peter and Daniela seemed to be getting cozy, Meadow thought, watching her pepper him with questions about architectural theory and famous buildings in New York. Then there was Bobby, who circulated through the entire bar and talked to almost everyone he passed. He'd disappear for stretches of time, then come back to offer Meadow another cigarette, and the two of them would clamber back into their coats and brave the black wind of a winter's night in Manhattan to puff and blather about grad school and the city and past relationships and when they were going to quit smoking.

"I have a feeling," Bobby said at one point, leaning in, the nub of a Lucky Strike still dangling from his lips, "that we're going to be friends."

Meadow sucked on his cigarette, the smoke a pleasing warmth in his mouth and nostrils. He blew out of the corner of his mouth, tilting his head at the impishly handsome boy before him. "We better be," he said simply. "Nightcap?"

"You read my mind!" Bobby exclaimed.

As they entered the bar again, Meadow caught a glimpse of a woman with black hair at the far end of the room, partially silhouetted beneath a blue overhead light. His mind flashed back to the gallery, which seemed so long ago already, and the face of the artist that he'd chanced to meet in that awkward space by the entrance. Could that be Selma Shimizu? For a second, he truly thought it was her, that Rebecca had orchestrated it somehow, that fate had ordained this encounter because the first meeting had borne no fruit. But then as his eyes adjusted to the room, Meadow realized that it was someone else. Of course. Hard to imagine a person as self-serious as Selma hanging out in a bar like this, really.

I wonder if I'll see her again, Meadow thought as he sidled up to the bar, fishing for bills in his pocket. I wonder.

IT WAS SPRINGTIME when he did see her again. One Friday afternoon, after lolling about the apartment trying to write a paper, Meadow decided he needed to get out of the house. He packed his bag with all the essentials—laptop, library books, cigarettes—and took the train down to Broadway-Lafayette, where he was just a hop, skip, and a jump away from his favorite coffee shop within a bookstore.

At the bookstore, he landed a seat at one of the coveted second-floor tables, where he could overlook the comings and goings below in relative seclusion. While poring through piles and piles of notes, he felt an increasing dread over his capacity to formulate a sensible argument out of the work that he'd already done, to say nothing of how this current project would connect to his dissertation, ostensibly about cosmopolitan enclaves in Shanghai during the Republican period and the well-documented realm of luxury and indulgence that existed parallel to the simmering politics of the day. The era had fascinated him in his undergrad years for reasons he couldn't quite name. Now he was beginning to realize that it was not the political intrigue that spoke to him, but rather the intense strain and excitement of an ancient civilization trying to express and redefine itself in the modern world order. That cultural identity could be so extravagant, malleable, and even contradictory stirred something in the depths of his being.

But this trifling affinity was completely beside the point, Meadow lamented. It had nothing to do with his capacity to produce fresh scholarship, let alone make a full-on career out of such niche interests. What was the purpose in laboring over this paper or dissertation, he thought, when surely no one but his advisor would read it. He couldn't help but entertain the fantasy of deviating from this academic path entirely and striking out anew. It was a thrilling and thoroughly vertiginous thought, that he could make a major pivot and create a different life for himself. And do what, interjected the skeptic inside him. What skills do you possibly have to offer the workforce? Stringing together bullshit sentences?

Meadow pressed his eyes shut and closed his laptop. He decided to take a breather and watch the flow of people downstairs. It was rhythmic after a while, even therapeutic; he couldn't help but form split-second impressions of everyone entering or exiting the store. A frazzled Upper East Side mom with too many shopping bags to manage her bleating children. A retired professorial type thumbing through the bargain bin. A power couple leaving in a huff, probably for a cocktail reception at some fancy hotel.

The power couple paused by the door. They were saying something to each other. The man wore a royal-blue suit that was quite becoming on him. Even from a distance, Meadow could admire his dark features and sartorial elegance, the leather shoes glinting below. The man looked unhappy, though. He reacted sharply to something the woman said, his face twisting with indignation. Before their exchange could continue, they had to move out of the way for someone else to exit.

The woman had her black hair in a tight bun and wore a slim gray trench coat over a wine-colored dress. She suddenly turned her back to the man and crossed her arms, shooting a fiery gaze away from him. A flicker of recognition danced through Meadow's mind. Had he seen this couple somewhere before? The woman, in particular, seemed awfully familiar. Maybe they'd crossed paths on campus.

The man in the blue suit looked at her blankly. "All right then," he spat, with a British inflection. "If you're going to be a child, then I'm done. You can fuck right off, you hear me?" With that he threw open the door with great force, the handle bashing the wall, and disappeared into the street.

A hush descended on the store. The cashiers were whispering into each other's ears, making no attempt to conceal their glee at witnessing this domestic dispute. The woman remained where she was, staring stonily ahead. She stayed that way for a full minute or two, arms crossed and still as a statue. The atmospheric white noise of the store returned quickly. People averted their gazes and maneuvered around the woman as though she were just another display shelf. Then in one fluid movement, she released her body from its state of constriction, spun around gracefully, and strode out of the store with confidence, her heels clopping on the wooden floor.

Moments after she disappeared, Meadow realized where he had seen her before. "Selma Shimizu," he said under his breath. "We meet again."

THAT SUMMER, Meadow found himself sinking deeper and deeper into a quagmire of existential anxiety while serving as a research assistant to his advisor, who was in Taiwan for fieldwork. Their last meeting had put the fear of God in him about the oral exam he would be expected to take within a year, to say nothing of the Sisyphean task of writing an actual dissertation before subjecting himself to further tortures at the hands of the academy. He commuted to the library several times a week to scan book chapters and locate archival documents for his advisor, sometimes formatting and cross-checking an absurd number of footnotes and endnotes. Before, after, and in between these tasks, he parked himself in the stacks with piles of books, taking copious notes on continental philosophy and poring through several decades of monographs on the culture and media of Republican Shanghai. Luckily for him, every time he came close to blowing a gasket, it seemed, Bobby would text him and convince him to meet up for dinner downtown. *Bitch, I can tell u need a night out.*

Since their initial meeting in January, in fact, Bobby Feuer Flores had quickly become Meadow's go-to drinking buddy.

They usually hit up the same few dive bars in the East Village, but occasionally wandered over to Williamsburg when the mood struck. Bobby had a boisterous, buoyant presence that could ingratiate him to most anyone they encountered or any place they entered. When they went out together, Meadow softened into the embrace of a camaraderie that he'd long craved and hadn't been able to name.

From the beginning Bobby treated him with compassionate nonchalance and playful intimacy. As a result, Meadow eased into New York's queer nightlife in earnest and found himself playing a role he'd long felt ill-equipped for: that of a single man on the prowl, blossoming in midnight hours to the buzzing potentiality of connection. Looking back, he decided his world in college had been too self-contained. Despite living in San Francisco, he'd been too dependent on a nest of friends, not to mention his first relationship, to grow truly comfortable in his own skin or as an autonomous being. No wonder he'd been floundering in New York for the past two years. Now, with Bobby as his guide, Meadow felt that he was coming of age again—how often did this happen in a lifetime? He was emerging from his chrysalis to test the capacities of this new incarnation and glide into the dawn of a wayward spring.

It was so effortless, the way they strolled into any old bar like they owned the place and spent the whole night talking up a storm while leaning against an ATM machine or pool table, or squeezing onto an ancient couch when they got lucky. The cogs were undoubtedly greased by plenty of alcohol, as well. Round after round of whiskeys neat, cheap cans of PBR, tequila shots when the night needed some enlivenment, gin and tonics or vodka sodas just because.

The first time they hit the town together, Bobby asked what his deal was.

"What deal?"

"As in, are you looking? Or just here for shits and giggles?"

They'd talked about Meadow's ex-boyfriend in California before, but not in great depth. Now Meadow was prompted to affirm that he was indeed single, painfully so, and would not be averse to meeting a fine gentleman or two. Bobby grilled him to recount the whole sordid tale of his last relationship as they polished off two Jamesons each. He listened impassively, waiting until Meadow was finished. Then he leaned back and issued his grim appraisal. "Your ex was a rice queen, and you deserve better."

Meadow cringed. "It was my fault, too," he muttered, "for letting it drag on."

"No more talking about the past!" roared Bobby. "We need to get you laid. What kind of guys are you into? And don't tell me you don't know."

Meadow really didn't know. Thus Bobby set out to become wingman extraordinaire and figure out his taste by trial and error. They spent most of July getting acquainted with the West Village after Bobby found a part-time job at a flower shop on Sixth Avenue. It was an older and more staid neighborhood, in their view, but still better than the gym bunnies and preening dolphins that dominated uptown. To his delight, Bobby discovered that his place of employment was also the perfect vector for community gossip. He began to recognize customers when they went out drinking, white-haired veterans of the Stonewall generation, muscle-bound lawyers in overly tight shirts, and even some local artists and musicians moonlighting as bartenders and servers. Sometimes they'd get a round on the house or a complimentary appetizer, or at the very least an affectionate hug and a song's worth of sly banter.

The weekends would begin on Thursday or sometimes earlier, half a day's academic work unceremoniously abandoned as

Meadow burrowed his way southward across the isle of Manhattan, from Washington Heights all the way to the tiny flower shop on Sixth Avenue. He'd wait for Bobby to wrap up and hand things off to the next part-timer or recap the day's customer interactions with Sarita, the Honduran matriarch who owned the store. For whatever reason, Bobby could do no wrong in her eyes, and she depended on him for intel about the regulars. From the shop they would move on to happy hour, and then maybe a slice or two from a hole-in-the-wall before heading to the next establishment. On occasion they sat down for green curry and pad see ew or mediocre Mexican food, dropped in on friends' birthday gatherings, or even wandered over to Chelsea to check out a few gallery openings for the free wine. By nightfall, they were prowling the streets of Lower Manhattan, ducking into one dark bar after another where they talked up some nonsense, drank heavily, and commiserated with strangers about politics and capitalism while pop music blared in the background.

Time would melt into a golden pool, both of them settling into attitudes of grinning insouciance, eager and open to how anything might play out. Hours past midnight, there would sometimes be a proposition. Meadow usually had difficulty the next day recalling how it had transpired. One minute he was in a bar, leaning in close to someone to hear and be heard, eyes swimming and heart coasting with the current, Bobby by his side or maybe out of sight. Impressionist fragments of these nights would stay with Meadow for years: the shape of a man's lips, a stubbly smile, teasing electricity or languid ease. They would agree to something in words or gestures. Then suddenly they were in a cab, and he was jamming unintelligible words into the brightness of his phone screen. They were going to Fort Greene or South Williamsburg, or maybe the Lower East Side.

Or maybe he'd talked the man into coming uptown, where they might barge in on an unsuspecting Peter watching *Mad Men* in sweatpants or sawing wood in the living room.

These were nearly perfect nights. He had no expectations for himself or anyone else. They could simply be lovers, breathe the air and taste the salt of each other's bodies. It was not even carnal impulse that drove him, but a yearning, clarified and sharpened by liquor, for human touch and the simple intimacy of sharing a bed, if only for a night. Sometimes they would kiss and laugh and fumble around for a while before simply falling asleep as day was beginning to break. The morning after he might feel self-conscious while scurrying to collect his clothes, get dressed, and slip out the door. Or maybe he'd wake up early with a hangover, decide to make coffee, offer toast and fried eggs to his houseguest. They'd ruffle his hair, nuzzle against him, bite his shoulder with teasing affection to stave off the awkward sobriety of daylight. At least they could still share a moment of tenderness in what was only ever meant to be a temporary affair.

By the time fall semester loomed again on the horizon, Meadow had made up his mind. A debacle and a half it was, this whole enterprise. He was simultaneously mystified by his motivation to enter grad school in the first place, and appalled that it had taken him two full years to realize he could no longer continue the charade. Now, during his trips to the library, he spent hours trawling job boards for anything that could unshackle him from dependence on the tiny stipend he was receiving. Rather than wallow in despair and mentally flagellate himself any longer, he reformatted his CV and combed through the internet for a lifeline, practically whimpering with distress, legs jittering ceaselessly beneath the table. He was leaving the library in a huff one day when he saw a job posting on a bulletin board in the hall for a full-time administrative position in the history department. The details were scant, but he made a mental note to look up more information online.

"I'm thinking of quitting school," he told Bobby at the flower shop that night. The words had slipped out of him, seemingly of their own volition. Though the sentiment had long been building, it was the first time he'd vocalized the desire aloud.

"Girl."

"Do you think that's a bad idea?"

Hunched over the cash register, Bobby pursed his lips and examined Meadow's face. "I wouldn't say it's a bad idea at all," he said carefully. "To be honest, you've never seemed very excited about doing what you're doing. Where do you want to go instead?"

Meadow sighed. "That's the clincher, isn't it? I need a viable alternative." He told Bobby about the job posting he'd found that afternoon, the hundreds of opportunities he'd looked at, some of which he'd even applied to, imagining himself at the front desk of a nonprofit, coordinating events for a media agency, filing papers at a law firm, anything at all. There were so many ways to exist in the world and exactly none of them seemed to be right. As he spoke, Bobby picked up a snapdragon from a bucket behind the counter and twirled the stem in his hand. He lifted the pink petals to his face, taking a deep breath, then thrust it right under Meadow's nose mid-sentence.

"It's good to let it out," Bobby said, "but you don't have to decide your life tonight, you know. Shit gets overwhelming once you start spiraling out into all the what-ifs."

A jingling sound alerted them to the entrance of a customer. Meadow blinked as though seeing Bobby for the first time, a thoughtful-looking young man with a nose ring standing against a floral profusion, shiny green leaves, brown stems, and wild explosion of colors barely contained by the receptacles of glass, plastic, and wood all around the shop. Bobby was full of aphorisms like that. They were usually about men, but sometimes he would offer an utterly simple statement about making it in New York or figuring out the purpose of one's existence that struck Meadow like a revelation. "So where do I begin then?" Meadow heard himself asking.

"Gimme a sec, girl," Bobby said with a wink. "Gotta help this customer. Why don't you start by figuring out where we're going for dinner tonight?"

6

MEADOW AWAKENS CLOSE TO NOON AFTER TUMBLING
through dreams of hidden passages, boxes nested within boxes,
mirrors that dissolve at a touch. The first thing he becomes aware
of is a dull tension in his body, almost a physical itch, scalp tingling and stray hairs standing upright. Before he even glances
out the bedroom window, he can tell something is different by
the milky light in the room that renders his surroundings in a
soft, soporific haze.

It takes him a long, long time to get out of bed. Clouds
gather fat and heavy in the sky, letting loose an occasional rumble that vibrates in the apartment walls. The grayness seeps into
the air and weighs on his chest like a small animal. Monochrome
and tasteless, the world is a can of soda gone flat. The only thing
that inspires him to get dressed at all is a desire for coffee, which
he eventually gets around to making with slow, plodding movements in the kitchen.

When he turns on the range hood light, the sleek and
pearlescent pocketknife he found at Barley winks at him from
the counter. Seeing this object again gives Meadow a start. He
deposited it here after returning from his shift and more or less
forgot about its existence. In some ways, the knife looks like it
belongs in Selma's apartment, as though it has always lurked

among her figurines and art books, her boxes of jewelry and drooping vines. But the presence of the object is also an affront, its appearance inextricable from the visitation of that strange character last night. *Pay attention to symbols*, the hatted eccentric said. *In them you will find the answers to all that you seek.*

After the man finished his wine and left the bar, Meadow breathed a sigh of relief. He wondered if he was some kind of fringe academic, one of those part-time philosophers or full-time kooks that abound in the crevices of New York, trawling bookstores and bars like restless spirits. Now, as he waits for water to boil, Meadow picks up the knife and clasps the length of it in his palm. The handle is smooth and cold to the touch. Holding it above his eyes, he examines the pattern on the handle, the texture a faint, somewhat uneven imbrication that recalls scales or feathers. The gold button on the end of the handle is triangular and beveled, like the handle itself. Such a minor design detail, odd and elegant. He pushes down on the triangle with his thumb and hears the spring snap as the blade of the knife swings out. He runs his finger along its spine. It's a beautiful object, endowed with primal energy, the power to sunder. Meadow folds the blade back into the handle and sets the knife down carefully as the kettle begins to whistle.

Something feels off today, he thinks as he pours hot water into the French press. He hates to think of it as a premonition. Oftentimes this sense of foreboding is just his overactive imagination or jumpy disposition, as someone who is perpetually and painfully attuned to the world around him. He wants to chalk it up to the impending thunderstorm, but gut instinct tells him it is a different unease that has poisoned the atmosphere of Selma's apartment. Symbols and ghosts dance through the murk of this darkened day. A flash lights up the living room, casting a frenzied, expressionist ambience onto the space. The white fox mask on the wall remains stoic as ever, while the wooden demon next to it exudes glee and sorrow at once.

Meadow sighs and pours himself a cup of coffee. Thunder growls through the concrete and resonates in his bones. Wary of this sensation, he decides to turn his attention to something else. He crosses over to the shelf where Selma keeps her records and a few stacks of books. Sipping from the mug, he lets his eyes wander across the spines and album covers until he spots a thin green book leaning against a succulent. It's *The Masquerade.*

"What the fuck?"

He picks up the book with his free hand and squeezes it between his thumb and index finger. The gold letters shine faintly in the washed-out gray light of the afternoon, nowhere near as crisp as they appeared in his dream. After failing to locate the book in his backpack or suitcase, he'd all but resigned himself to the fact that he'd left it in Shanghai. Could he have unknowingly recovered it at some point in the past few days? Did he take the book out of his backpack and put it away after drinking with Peter the other night? Meadow wracks his brain for an answer that doesn't come. In the end, he gives up and decides to go with the flow. He sets the mug on the coffee table, releases his body to the couch, and begins to read.

Spring splendor this garden cannot restrain,
A branch of red blossoms yearns past this domain.

The party is in full swing once more as Du Kuo-wen removes his cape, handing it to an attendant, and steps into the throng of socialites and sycophants that gather around him, their masked faces bobbing in exaltation. It's a bit of a monstrous scene, Mizuno thinks as he observes Du in his pig mask surrounded by men and women in glittering finery and ornate facial coverings.

"Boss Du, is this an homage to *Journey to the West?*" coos a woman with a band of black lace over her eyes, stroking the pig mask with her gloved hand.

"It's his zodiac sign," declares a man with the lazy fronds of a jester cap protruding from the white resin mask on his brow.

"You are both correct," says Du, laughing heartily. "I am but a pig who has lost his way from the stalwart Tang Seng. No sacred scriptures for me, only indulgence and dissipation. And indeed I was born in the Year of the Pig. A swine is no brute, my friends. I ask you, what greater expression of patriotism is there than offering pleasure to your fellow man?"

Mizuno is hoping to secure an audience with Du this evening, in regard to a feature he has been planning on Wonderwood Studio, the production company that Du has recently begun financing. The herd of people around Du in the garden, however, has made it all but impossible to reach him. Mizuno decides to try his chances later, turning his attention instead to Orchid and Peony, the two women in identical dresses and masks, who banter demurely with a group of Western men nearby. Du mentioned something about the film business when introducing them. Mizuno surmises they are aspiring actresses, perhaps under contract with Wonderwood Studio. They are nearly indistinguishable, not only adorned in the same clothes but also possessing strikingly similar physiques and even hairstyles. A flicker of recognition dances in his mind, but his train of thought is interrupted by the blare of a jaunty tune beginning again inside the house. Setting down his cocktail glass, now drained of the frothy drink that Du Kuo-wen announced as the Phantasm, Mizuno makes his way out of the garden and back into the lounge.

For a while he simply meanders through the lavish rooms of Du's estate as though on an inspection tour. Some corners of Shanghai are wretched indeed, but the fabulous ambience of tonight's party could exist in no other city, Mizuno thinks. Part of him feels as though he conjured it up for himself: this house and all these people are almost the exact image of the glamorous world he once dreamt of as a young man, the fantasy that originally enticed him to leave his country and rush toward continental adventures and this cauldron of modernity. Only in Shanghai could he rub shoulders with rakish Chinese men just returned from Hong Kong or Malaya, fervently offering their opinions on tropical temperaments and cookery, or an American dowager with enormous jewels gleaming on every finger, holding court on the latest talkies that have yet to be released locally. Mizuno slips past them and toward the red-carpeted staircase, pausing to admire the jazz band's redoubled efforts in the grand foyer, the manic energy they manifest through a wailing trumpet and spritely clarinet matched by the slickness of sweat on the musicians' brows. He ascends the staircase languidly, following a couple with matching Peking opera masks painted in florid strokes of red and black.

Upstairs, he finds a handful of guests making themselves comfortable in another dining room, attended to by more masked waiters ferrying canapés of caviar, smoked salmon, and cured ham on crackers and thinly sliced bread. He walks past a number of people bustling in a tiny kitchen, a woman with permed hair and a mask with star-shaped eyes smoking a cigarette in the hallway, and a portly man with a Charlie Chaplin mustache. At the end of the hallway is a dimly lit room that turns out to be a study. Illuminated by a single oil lamp atop an oversized desk of burnished wood, the study stands in stark contrast to the frenzied vitality of the rest of the house. Mizuno steps in and curiously examines the bookshelves, which are filled with tomes in multiple languages, their spines glimmering faintly in the light. He knows that Du Kuo-wen, in addition to being a film financier, has business activities in the realm of publishing. It is no surprise then that he appears to be such an avid reader. Charles Dickens, Mizuno reads to himself, brushing a hand against the leather and cloth covers. Voltaire. *Dream of the Red Chamber*. Lewis Carroll.

"Good evening."

An inadvertent gasp escapes Mizuno's lips as he spins around. A figure stands in the doorway, blocking the light from the hallway and darkening the study even further. As his eyesight adjusts, he makes out a man of average height wearing a long black cloak, his face entirely obscured by an ivory-colored mask. But this mask is unlike the sartorial adornments of most everyone else at the party. The eyes are simply two round holes, while a curved beak protrudes from where the mouth should be. Although it's impossible to make out any of his features, Mizuno senses those beady eyes watching him with a fiery intensity.

"Are you alone, sir?" the stranger asks in English.

The man speaks with an odd accent. One of the European guests, Mizuno assumes, collecting himself. "Yes, I am," he says evenly. "I was admiring Master Du's library."

"Ah," the stranger replies. He takes a step closer. "So you are interested in literature, it seems."

"In a way," Mizuno says, crossing his arms and leaning against one of the sturdy shelves. "Where do you come from? If I may be so bold."

The man in the beaked mask raises his chin. "My name is Spiegel," he says flatly. "Siegfried Spiegel."

A cool wind blows in from a window that Mizuno hadn't noticed was open, causing the flame of the oil lamp to dance in its glass encasement. "That name," he says with a shiver. "You must be—"

"German. Good sir, please allow me to convey a message, for I have other matters to attend to."

A message? Mizuno stands silently with his back to the open window. He hears a distant commotion as the jazz band ends another number and a cheer erupts in the foyer. Alone in this study with the man in the beaked mask, he feels as though he has unsuspectingly wandered into a Buddhist underworld. "You mustn't forget," continues the German in lilting, almost musical speech, "the five phases that constitute all earthly existence. They offer clues as to the patterns of creation and destruction in human affairs. The modern world is built atop the primitive plane of existence that our ancestors knew. Modernity is merely a cloak and cannot contain or obstruct the elemental nature by which the universe orders itself and all its beings. You may take these qualities to be mere symbolism now, but be aware that all symbols invoke a fundamental power that cannot be stifled by man or machine. I hope my words will be able to guide you in some way when you are most in need. Do not fear the symbol, my lad, but do not overlook it either. All is contained in its simplicity, and its simplicity gives rise to all things."

DIVINE LIGHT SLICES through the curtain of gray and casts a manic brightness on the living room for a split second. What in the world? Meadow blinks and sets *The Masquerade* down. It has to be a coincidence. His face grows hot as he remembers the words of the hatted man who visited him at Barley the previous night. What a fluke of timing, this scene in the novel and the late-night conversation at the bar. It's as though the book is echoing what just happened to him. But that doesn't make any sense. The book is just a book, a fully written novel, printed and bound. The fictional world of Liu Tian, translated by Barnaby Salem. Meadow flips to the end just to double-check. Sure enough, every page is filled with text. Meadow shakes his head.

Now you're starting to sound like Selma, he chides himself. Head full of ghosts and superstitions.

Out of nowhere, the heavy atmosphere gives way. Rain batters the windows as a warm wind whistles through the streets, whipping into the living room and sending a spray of droplets through the screens. The crash of thunder that follows sounds like a castigation from the sky directly above, the entire building shaking beneath its fury. Meadow feels energy crackling in the air, seeping into his pores, and tunneling under his skin. The current pulses in concert with the storm that rages outside, a storm that demands nothing less than full release. He gets up from the sofa and lowers the windows, then crosses into the kitchen to pour himself another cup of coffee. A warmth throbs gently behind his eyes. Returning to the couch, he sits back down and, for lack of anything else to do, continues to read.

AFTER THE ENCOUNTER with the man in the beaked mask, Mizuno descends to the first floor again and wanders through the party in a daze. The masks worn by the party guests seem to become disembodied, leering at him from states of repose on scarlet divans or floating silently in shadowy nooks. What could the German possibly have meant? Mizuno can't make sense of it. Perhaps the speech is simply part of another game that Du is orchestrating for this evening. He is still lost in thought when he arrives in a parlor where a group of people are playing cards. A stout man in a Noh mask interrupts his reverie. "Mizuno-kun," blares a familiar voice in Japanese. "Is that you?" It turns out to be director by the name of Kobayashi, a womanizing boor whom Mizuno interviewed a year earlier, on the occasion of his latest film's release.

Mizuno is startled by how easily Kobayashi recognized him. The Japanese theater mask he wears is a pale face with minimalist features wrenched in permanent anguish. "Kobayashi-san," Mizuno greets him. "What a sharp eye you have. Back from Manchukuo already, I see?"

"It was a bloody nuisance getting back," Kobayashi groans, "but what an incredible trip it was. The film studio up there is something else, to say nothing of the streets of Shinkyo. I tell you, it's leaps and bounds nicer than any city you've ever seen. Forget Europe or America. The future lies with us here in the East! What an amazing time to be alive." As Kobayashi chatters on, servers bearing more food and drink thread through the guests and replenish their empty glasses. The card players roar with laughter and shout excitedly at the conclusion of another round. Another staff member of the Du estate announces that a dance performance is due to begin in the ballroom and invites the guests to partake.

Kobayashi suggests that they go watch the dance and beckons Mizuno to join with a flutter of his plump hand. Before Mizuno can follow, a woman in a damask dress plants herself in his path. "*Spring splendor this garden cannot restrain,*" she recites in English.

Mizuno flushes as he tries to recall the rest of the lyric. "*A branch—*" he begins. "*A branch of red blossoms . . . yearns past this domain?*"

"Well done," the woman coos. "As for my name?"

He struggles for a minute, then ventures a blind guess. "Orchid?"

The masked woman says nothing, the edges of her painted lips upturned coyly. She drops a hand to the sash around her hips, where a number of red roses with short stems are pinned. With a series of deft movements, she removes one of them and brings the flower within inches of Mizuno's nose. "Savor this sweet scent," she says. "Your reward for winning this round." Before he even has a chance to react, she places the rose against his breast pocket, piercing the fabric with a pin and affixing the flower to his jacket.

AS THE THUNDERSTORM rages outside, Meadow finds himself growing increasingly antsy and eventually sets down the book. He tries unsuccessfully to take a nap, then stomps around the apartment putting away clothes, washing dishes, playing with the pocketknife. He practices slicing the air with the blade, a horizontal slash followed by a vertical, a sudden thrust, a parry. He puts on a Josephine Foster record and cleans some of Selma's baubles on the credenza, flicking a duster over figurines of glass and ceramic, brushing the bindings of the books lined up on the nearby shelf.

Later in the afternoon, the storm relents and the sun comes out again, rendering a warm familiarity to the living room. As he stares at the few droplets that still fall from the rain gutter, Meadow remembers that he ought to water the plants again. He fills the watering can and makes the rounds in the bedroom and bathroom. When he stops to water the rubber tree by the front door, he notices something inside the glazed pot that gives him a mild surprise. He stoops to take a closer look. The skylight above casts a square of bright light on the wall, while deep shadows envelop the rest of the hallway, so that Meadow feels for a moment like he is on a strange stage performing for an audience of no one. There's a sprout growing out of the soil in the pot, right next to the sturdy trunk of the rubber tree. He wouldn't have looked twice, except the green bud is markedly different from the lanky rubber tree next to it. It's clearly a flower, though when and how such a seed took root is hard to imagine. He doesn't recall seeing it in the pot before.

From his pocket, a buzz from his phone draws his attention. Meadow sets down the watering can and looks at the notification. It's a long message from Anya.

Liu Tian, it's been almost a week since anyone has seen or heard from Selma. Given the circumstances, we decided to file a missing persons report yesterday. I have just been informed by the investigating officer that they were able to gain entry to her residence and nothing appeared to be suspicious. In fact, CCTV footage shows her returning in the early morning after the show at Potemkin. It seems she got in a cab just several hours later, around seven. The officer is now checking to see if there is a record of her on any flights or trains out of Shanghai that day. Since there is no evidence of foul play, her case has become less of a priority, I'm afraid. It is my duty to inform you of this matter because Selma listed you as her emergency contact. Please stay in touch and let me know if you manage to talk to her, or find out where she might have gone. Take care, Liu Tian!

"Fuck." Meadow goes to sit down, stomach sinking. Emergency contact? He can't recall Selma ever mentioning this to him. At the same time, it's not a complete surprise. Selma is an only child, and he has known her to be all but estranged from her immediate family. He taps out a note of appreciation for the update and asks Anya to keep him posted on any developments. He promises that he will try to reach Selma, too.

It seems ridiculous to write such a message while comfortably ensconced in her home in Brooklyn. An inordinate amount of guilt cascades over him. Was it something he did or said that could have triggered this? He shakes his head. No. Completely illogical, no matter the mild shame he still feels about the tryst with Douglas. In any case, why would that set Selma off in any sort of way? He writes a quick message to her on WeChat, then via email, conveying to her the urgency of what he has just learned from Anya. He even checks her social media pages, which he has to search for one by one since he doesn't use any platforms himself. The last updates are all from June, snapshots of Selma installing work at Potemkin, a motorcyclist careening beneath plane trees, a Chinese porcelain in striking amber and white on display in a museum. "Fuck me," Meadow murmurs quietly. "Selma, where have you gone?"

Shiftless and uneasy, he takes a shower and pops a melatonin after dinner in order to catch an early bedtime. In the end, he manages to sleep only for a few hours and wakes up around three in the morning, heart pounding from an anxiety dream that had something to do with a mirror maze, and chasing after an apparition he was desperate to catch but could never reach. The figure eluded him by turning down hallways and disappearing, only to resurface on the opposite side of the room. No matter how he tried, he could never catch sight of its face.

A heaviness lingers in his limbs. As he squeezes his eyes shut and tries to contemplate his breath, thoughts ricochet in his head like bats fluttering in a cave, summoning images and half-formed ideas from even darker recesses within. Selma on a grainy security camera, getting into a taxi. Selma smoking a cigarette, walking alone on a dark Shanghai street. *You fall easily into this kind of story*, Meadow hears her whisper in his ear. *Invent a new one and start over.*

After tossing and turning for half an hour, Meadow resigns himself to being conscious. He switches on the bedside lamp and blinks grumpily at the wall. A surprisingly strong gust of nocturnal wind howls outside, sending a shudder through the building. He throws on a T-shirt and pads over to the kitchen in his underwear. For a long and stuporous moment, he peers at the contents of the refrigerator, unable to decide whether he wants to snack on something or have a beverage. He opts to uncap a bottle of Jamaican lager, then shuffles back into the bedroom.

Rather than lounge in bed, he decides to sit at Selma's writing desk, an antique Victorian-style escritoire with brass handles on the drawers and shelves on top. Turning on the desk lamp, he sets the lager down on a marble coaster and stares blankly at the few books stacked in one corner, a collection of vintage paperbacks by Ionesco, Ernest Hemingway, and Yasunari Kawabata. Meadow wonders if she got any of these at the same place she picked up *The Masquerade*. A few pieces of jewelry are on the shelves, beaded bracelets and sterling silver rings with shiny elliptical gemstones. He takes a swig of the beer. Selma has always kept her household pretty organized, he thinks as he opens the left drawer and finds a stack of blank envelopes next to a row of fine-point pens. When he opens the other drawer, he discovers a few papers and knickknacks arrayed inside, but what catches his eye is the gleam of a golden pendant shaped like a hummingbird. The bird's feathers are remarkably detailed and encrusted with tiny crystals. Meadow gently lifts the pendant and places it in his palm, surprised by the weight of it.

As he examines the hummingbird under the lamplight, he remembers Selma's brief and intense fixation on birds a while ago. It must have been the previous year, when she was reading and researching pretty broadly, paying visits to aviaries and finding bird-watching groups to infiltrate. He never got the full gist of what she'd been planning to undertake—she was always someone who liked to have multiple projects going in parallel—but now, looking back, it occurs to Meadow that her acceptance to the Shanghai residency probably derailed whatever she'd had in mind. Too bad, he thinks. He wouldn't be surprised if this tiny hummingbird pendant was something she'd made herself, its fearsome exactitude and unsettling beauty recalling some of Selma's other work.

Meadow takes another drink of beer. He deposits the bird pendant back into the drawer and is just about to close it when a few printed words catch his eye. There's a piece of paper folded into thirds, a letter of some kind next to where the pendant was. He wouldn't have noticed anything, except the top flap of the paper is open, while the other two-thirds are folded into each other. It's the name on the letterhead that triggers a spasm of recognition in him. *Barnaby Public Library* is printed in the header. Why does that name ring a bell?

He carefully takes the letter out and unfolds it. It appears to be a letter from a library staff member in regard to a request from Selma. "Dear Miss Shimizu," Meadow reads under his breath. "Thank you for your inquiry about accessing the journals housed in our library's Augustin Collection . . ." Scanning the letter, he surmises that the journals belong to a famous ornithologist whose personal effects are stored at an archive in the library. This is reasonable enough and aligns with what he remembers of Selma's unconsummated project. But why does the name Barnaby seem familiar? He's about to put the letter away and shrug it off when he notices the full address printed on the letterhead.

"What the fuck," he says out loud. The library is located in the town of Salem, Vermont. The moment this second name clicks into place, Meadow is awash in a sickly feeling of unreality and disbelief. He puts the letter down on the desk and dashes into the living room to retrieve *The Masquerade*. Back in the bedroom, he flips to the title page of the book to confirm that he is remembering correctly. "By Liu Tian," he reads. "Translated from the Chinese by Barnaby Salem." He knew something felt off, and now the fact of it is staring him in the face. The translator's name seemed a little outlandish when he first saw it, but at the same time it was plausible enough. Meadow imagined the guy as some old China hand, most likely a Brit who'd picked up passable Chinese while cavorting around the Orient, fraternizing with people of intrigue: journalists, literati, tycoons, the very people who would be in attendance at the book's masquerade ball. But now he finds himself confronting a glaring indication that the translator's name is most likely bullshit. Which means *The Masquerade*, by extension, is probably fake as well. And, given the circumstances of his finding the book in the first place, the likeliest suspect behind this whole scheme, the only person who could feasibly pull it off, is none other than Selma herself.

7

HIS FIRST ENCOUNTER WITH SELMA HAD BEEN AT HER SHOW in Chelsea on a frigid January night; the second time was the voyeuristic episode in the SoHo bookstore in the spring. Years later, Meadow would recall these glimpses from before he actually got to know her and feel a mild bewilderment at how skewed his impressions had been. In the end, it took a third meeting for them to truly enter each other's lives, like magnets that simply needed to be maneuvered into the right position to snap into place.

It was in September that same year. Meadow and Peter had just traded their sunny Washington Heights digs for an apartment in Greenpoint. The new place was a block away from McGolrick Park and a fifteen-minute walk from the most viable subway station. The building's stairs were narrow and decidedly crooked, so much so that Peter lost his balance and almost fell backward to his doom while they were hoisting the sofa up. It was a railroad-style unit with doors on either end of a corridor opening into the two bedrooms. The kitchen and common area had no windows, and damp air was almost always swirling listlessly in the bathroom. But for the rest of their twenties, it was home.

Time passed strangely in New York. Meadow couldn't understand how two years had evaporated already. He still felt wide-eyed and artless, no idea about what kind of life lay ahead. Though he often bemoaned that he'd accomplished little to nothing, it was true that his material circumstances had changed. Brooklyn was a reminder of that, another new beginning in a city of constant reinvention. Just weeks earlier, he'd miraculously landed a desk job at the university and sent a long-winded, apologetic email to his advisor. The act of finalizing his withdrawal from the PhD evoked a feeling close to pure elation. Full-time work turned out to be dull and involved spreadsheets in disarray, scheduling meetings, and placating various senior faculty members. Yet he couldn't have been happier to work a prescribed set of hours and take home a steady income.

His social life was going strong. He still regularly went out with Bobby, who had decamped to a questionably legal tenement in Bushwick. Peter was dating Daniela, Rebecca's sculptress friend, who lived in Prospect Heights. That their collective lives could progress in tandem brought Meadow a reassuring sense of solidity. The weekend after they moved to Brooklyn, Meadow and Peter invited everyone over for a party. It had been blazingly hot all day, summer unwilling to relinquish its muggy hold on the city. The guests started to arrive around nine, languid and lackadaisical from the day's punishing heat. Daniela was the first to show up, with a potted fern and an aluminum trayful of brownies. "Hello, my loves," she chirped, kissing Peter on the lips and Meadow on the cheek. "Happy housewarming." She'd made two batches of brownies, one with weed butter and one without. "Shall we have a sample of each?" she offered. They were all too happy to partake.

Peter was doling out frothy aguardiente sours from a pitcher he'd made, Smokey Robinson playing in the background, when the buzzer sounded again. Meadow pressed the button to let the next person in. And so arrived, one after the other, their grad school classmates, neighbors they'd met while moving in, acquaintances from work, and newly transplanted college friends, bringing with them six-packs of cold beer, bottles of bubbly, and bags of chips or the occasional pie. At some point Bobby appeared in a drapey tank top, a bottle of mezcal tucked under his arm. He poured two enormous cupfuls in the kitchen and handed one to Meadow. "Cheers, bitch," Bobby said, wiping sweat from his forehead. "Welcome to Brooklyn!"

As they sipped their mezcal straight, Bobby grilled Meadow about Caleb, the bassist that he'd been seeing for a few weeks. This dalliance had been facilitated by Bobby one night, when he and Meadow were stumbling down Avenue C at two in the morning and came upon a tall guy smoking outside a bodega. He was darkly handsome, with a mane of chestnut hair that fell to his shoulders. Already three sheets to the wind, Meadow later couldn't remember how it all happened. Bobby had accosted Caleb for a cigarette, asking about the instrument case leaning behind him. Somehow a cigarette became a nightcap with the two of them, and then it was closing time at the dive bar, Bobby had vanished, and Meadow was lurching up an Alphabet City staircase with this beautiful stranger. What surprised him most, in retrospect, was that Caleb had asked for his number the morning after.

"I knew Jazz Man was going to be a good lay," Bobby said breathily at the housewarming. He and Meadow had drifted into the living room, where Peter and his architect friends were doing impressions of their professors and dissolving in uproarious laughter.

"Ugh," Meadow exhaled. "He's so sexy, I could die. We went out for Indian last week. Only thing is, he's kind of a space cadet. I'm not sure we have much in common."

"Well, he's part Chinese, isn't he?"

"Yeah. His dad's from Beijing. Ended up going to school in Florida and marrying a local socialite. Super random."

A whoop pierced the air. "Happy housewarming, mother-fuckers!" cried someone from the door. Meadow and Bobby turned to look. A woman in a hot-pink dress and cat-eye glasses stood triumphantly with a bottle of prosecco raised in the air. Rebecca. There was a round of applause when she popped the cork. She strode over to Peter, commanded him to open his mouth, and tilted the bottle above him. Moments later, he was wiping his chin, coughing and belching at the same time. "The goddamn bubbles!"

"Now where's Meadow?" Rebecca demanded, scanning the room.

"Oh shit," Bobby whispered. "Here she comes. Better accept your fate."

Meadow put down his mezcal and dutifully opened his mouth as Rebecca approached with the bottle, a predatory glint in her eyes.

Half an hour later, Meadow realized he was pretty drunk. Rebecca was somehow hilarious tonight, a fast-talking caricature in flashy colors: hot-pink dress, shiny pearl bracelet, tropical-green eye makeup. She could have been the frantic female lead in an Almódovar film. She was talking about waste treatment for the longest time, then something about dioramas. Meadow was having a hard time following.

Eventually he orbited back into the conversation. He realized he was standing with Rebecca and a guy with a goatee he didn't recognize. "Did you say something about dioramas?" Meadow asked, blinking blearily.

"Yeah, dude, I've only been talking about it for like ten minutes!" exclaimed Rebecca. "But don't worry. You can ask her yourself when she gets here."

"Who?"

"Selma Shimizu, that's who!"

Turned out Rebecca had run into her on the street walking over to the party. Selma lived in the neighborhood as well—a somewhat recent relocation—so Rebecca had taken the liberty of inviting her to their housewarming. Selma said she would come by. Rebecca grabbed Meadow by the arm all of a sudden. "Look into my eyes," she commanded. As she leaned closer, her face filled his field of vision until she seemed to frown down at him from the heavens. A supreme being with eyes wide in incredulity. "Are you high? You're high as shit, aren't you?" She let go of his arm and looked around the room again. "Dani!" she barked. "You better have saved me a brownie!"

Meadow lost track of the sequence of the following hours. Time became viscous and warm, a translucent jelly through which he oozed from room to room, where he found familiar faces huddled together talking over cupfuls of wine or whiskey. A woozy hedonism came over him, or maybe that was just the effect of George Michael and Erasure belting their hearts out from a decade long past. There was a fat blunt circulating, and a few puffs in, he found himself beyond the stratosphere, slouching in a corner of Peter's bed, face hot and barely paying attention to what was going on anymore.

He was drifting in that happy haze when, for the second time that evening, a face suddenly loomed before him. This time it was a man with wavy hair, brown eyes, beautiful eyelashes. "Oh, shit!" Meadow heard himself say. His voice sounded strangely muffled, like it was coming from the bottom of a pool. He struggled to an upright position, threw his arms around the man, and pulled him back down onto the bed, to much laughter. Caleb had arrived.

Soon he was in the kitchen again, having insisted on making Caleb a drink. The aguardiente sours had long been depleted, so

Meadow decided to mix a quick gin and tonic or something like that. It was a much harder task than anticipated, and he kept losing his train of thought mid-action. At one point he realized he was wielding a butcher knife over the sink, looking down at a bag of ice and not sure what he should do next. By the time he had a few solid chunks of ice for the drinks, he didn't know where the cups were.

The whole time he had been mumbling to himself, apparently. Two clean glasses emerged on the counter next to him, then a bottle of Hendrick's. "I think this is what you're looking for?" came a woman's voice.

"You read my mind," sighed Meadow gratefully. His hand pulsed with cold where he was clutching the ice. "Thank you."

"I wanted to say happy housewarming," the woman said as Meadow poured the drinks. "Such a coincidence that I saw Rebecca on my way home. I live just around the corner from here, actually. Anyway, I hope you don't mind me crashing your party tonight."

"Oh, it's not a thing," he replied casually. "Glad to have you!"

It was only after he made both drinks that he realized it was Selma. She was leaning against the opposite counter in a white cotton frock. Her lips were the bright red of a summer strawberry. Standing next to her in the kitchen, Meadow saw they were around the same height, and she was neither as tall nor as intimidating as he'd registered from previous encounters. She had a relaxed smile on her face, a glass of brown liquor in hand.

"What are you drinking?" Meadow asked.

"Four Roses," she said. "Hope it's not gauche to crack open the bottle I brought."

"Not at all. Cheers."

They clinked glasses and fell into easy banter in the soft glow of the kitchen. The party had dwindled somewhat from the earlier chaos, reaching a warm pliancy that still whirred with weekend energy. Selma told him she'd moved to the neighborhood just a few months ago, from the West Village. It was a welcome change, though she still needed to acclimate and make friends.

Meadow admitted he wasn't too familiar with the area, either. His knowledge of Brooklyn nightlife was mostly limited to a few dive bars off the L train. But he was looking forward to recentering his social life, even though he still worked all the way uptown. The commute would give him a chance to read for pleasure, anyhow, something he'd barely been able to do in the past two years. They were in the midst of talking about his grad school experience when Caleb appeared in the kitchen.

"Oops," Meadow said. "Here's your gin and tonic!"

"Ah, thanks," Caleb smirked as Meadow handed him the drink. "Don't mean to interrupt."

"Not at all," said Selma. "I was just prying into his past life."

"Caleb, this is Selma," Meadow added hastily. "She's . . . an artist friend who lives in the neighborhood."

They exchanged pleasantries for a bit before returning to the topic of academia. Selma revealed that she had just started teaching a few studio classes herself. "Art school is so special," she mused dreamily. "Everyone wears their heart on their sleeves. It's such a vulnerable place."

"I guess I wouldn't know," Meadow said, thinking about the stodgy, rarefied atmosphere of the classrooms that had defined his education. "I've gotten a lot from being in school, but it feels so good to be done with it, too. Like, I can finally just be a human in the world."

"Of course," Selma replied. "It's important to learn how to exist on your own." She turned to Caleb and said she'd heard he was a musician. Meadow had no idea how she'd gleaned that information. But with consummate ease, she went on to ask Caleb who his creative inspirations were, whether he came from a musical family—things that Meadow hadn't yet uncovered during their stilted dinner conversations or nocturnal revelries.

Caleb said his maternal grandfather had been a jazz pianist and used to play with Ahmad Jamal in Chicago back in the 1960s. It was his grandfather's influence that led him to take up music before he even entered elementary school. He never received a formal education in music, but moved to New York with the express purpose of going to as many gigs as he could to meet as many people as he could. Meadow was stupefied by this whole narrative, the most he'd ever heard Caleb speak. Before he could say a word, Selma cut in and shared how much her father had loved Ahmad Jamal. He had left her his enormous record collection when he passed away a few years ago. Most of it was still stored at her parents' home in Boston, but she was trying to sift through the stack to decide what to keep. She'd have to finish this project soon, since her mother was paring down all their remaining worldly possessions to return to Japan.

Meadow sipped his drink as they talked, quietly stunned at how effortless Selma was in coaxing out conversation—not at all the stiff and unfriendly person he'd imagined. Thanks to her, Caleb opened up with seemingly little effort, speculating on the value of this vinyl collection that now belonged to Selma and inquiring about the state of Japanese jazz. They talked freely and easily until Selma excused herself to find a nibble in the next room.

The party wound on and on into the early hours of morning. Bobby was trying to convince people to go to a bar, but everyone was too stoned or complacent to budge. Another spliff was making the rounds in the living room, where someone had put on a Busby Berkeley film on mute. Rows upon rows of bodies were gyrating in formation, elaborate plumes bursting forth from headdresses with a glossy shimmer like palm fronds. Hypnotized, Meadow curled up on the couch next to Caleb. Across the room, he saw Daniela talking animatedly with Selma while Peter was gathering up empty bottles.

The next thing he knew, the apartment was mostly empty and dark and he was shuffling into his bedroom. He opened a window to get some air, the sound of night insects and faraway trucks immediately infiltrating the apartment. He felt someone put their arms around his waist, hands caressing his stomach, then stroking lower with firm intention. Turning around, he let his mouth join Caleb's in a warm, sloppy kiss. Without a word he led Caleb to his bed, where they undressed in the darkness. Caleb's skin was taut and hot to the touch, his musk tinged with a trace of tobacco, a hint of lime and juniper on his lips. The shadows of tree branches trembling in a night breeze danced on the wall next to them, the pale shards of light between their snaking boughs winking like fragments of a dream.

MONTHS PASSED. In the dead of winter, early in the new year, Meadow received an invitation in his mailbox. Addressed to Meadow Liu and Peter Kim in careful penmanship, the square envelope was a robin's-egg blue that seemed to glow faintly in the vestibule. Tucking the junk mail under his arm, he had made it only halfway up the stairs when he turned over the envelope and saw the gold foil sticker with the initials *SS* embossed on it.

The invitation itself was a single off-white card with speckles of maroon and gray. On the cover was a minimalist drawing of a martini next to a plate of steak. Inside, it stated simply:

DINNER PARTY
136 Russell Street, #3
Saturday, January 7, 2012
7:00 PM

Yours,

A voluptuous ink signature completed the salutation, the curve of each *S* flowing smoothly into a sharp scrunch of lines resembling a cardiogram.

A few days later, Meadow donned his jacket and stepped out into a damp and overcast evening, clutching a bottle of Maker's Mark in a plastic bag. He was flying solo that night, as Peter was still in Costa Rica with his parents on a new year's vacation. The sky was a black chasm without any visible stars. Selma's street was on the opposite side of McGolrick Park, less than a five-minute walk from where he lived. From the outside, her building looked just like his own, maybe a touch fancier: a squat three-story townhouse with bay windows, curtains drawn and blinds lowered at the windows reflecting the cold glow of streetlamps. The park was deserted and forlorn at this hour, he noted, but surely this would be a pleasant scene in the summer.

He thought back to the day Selma had shown up at his house-warming party. It had been so hot, then. What compelled her to come by? Especially when the invitation had been extended by Rebecca. Boredom? Curiosity? He couldn't figure it out. For all of Rebecca's eagerness, he knew that she and Selma were not really friends—at least this was what he'd heard from Peter, via Daniela. Still, a part of him wondered if he would walk into this dinner party and find Rebecca there holding court, prattling on to everyone and anyone who would listen. A dazzling gibbous moon hung in the sky above the treetops, a ceramic marble floating in the black of night. Something about the stark edge of shadow on the moon made him feel very lonely, out of the blue. He turned and rang the buzzer.

The door was already ajar by the time he trudged up the steps and reached the third-floor landing. A warm, savory aroma wafted into the hall along with the honeyed melodies of Aretha Franklin. Meadow knocked gently, then stepped inside. A brass floor lamp illuminated the narrow hallway, which was painted a dark teal. Down the corridor, a woman in a black sweater appeared and walked toward him. "Hello," she said with a nod. Something about her wide blue-gray eyes and the golden ringlets tucked behind her ears made her seem childlike and somewhat timid.

"Hi," he said. "I'm Meadow."

"Yulia. Pleased to meet you. May I take your jacket? And please take off your shoes, if you don't mind." Her accent was mild and lilting, like the gentle stir of a silver spoon.

"Uh, sure." He slid one arm out of the jacket, then the other, and handed it to Yulia before bending down to remove his boots.

"I will place it in the closet," she said, gesturing at a door farther down the hall.

"Are you Selma's roommate?" he asked.

Yulia laughed. "No, just a friend who likes to cook."

Once his boots were off, Meadow took a second to examine a framed photo hanging just outside the light of the brass lamp. It was a black-and-white studio portrait of a young man, presumably a relative, dressed to the nines in a vest and suit jacket. He sat on a stool with his body angled away, but his head faced the camera directly. The smile on his lips somehow carried a hint of somberness. Meadow blinked and shuffled down the hallway toward the light.

"You're here!" Selma called when he entered the living room. "So punctual. Welcome." Hair in a loose ponytail, she was tending to a sizzling pan in the adjoining kitchen, an elegant space with marble countertops and shiny black tiling.

"Ah, thanks," said Meadow, surveying the apartment. Yulia was in the kitchen hovering before an enormous bowl of salad. In the living room, an enormous Chagall print hung between two windows that looked onto the bare treetops of the park. Books and records spilled forth from a shelf next to a fig tree. There was only one other guest, a bearded man in a striped shirt who nodded in greeting from the burgundy couch.

Meadow moved toward the kitchen, taking the bottle of Maker's out of the plastic bag. "Brought some bourbon," he offered, placing it on the counter. "Peter's out of town, by the way, so he couldn't make it. Thanks so much for inviting us, though."

"Thanks for coming!" Selma set the wooden spatula in her hand on a plate. She pranced over to him and kissed him lightly on the cheek, to his surprise. "What would you like to drink? We have a bottle of pinot open. There's also beer in the fridge, and of course, your bourbon."

"The wine's excellent," the man in the living room called out. "Highly recommend it."

"I'll take some wine, then," said Meadow. "Can I help you guys with anything?"

Selma laughed melodiously, waving him away. "Not a thing." She swiftly procured a wineglass from a cabinet, uncorked a bottle sitting by the fridge, and filled him up. "Here you are," she said. "Why don't you go keep Edward company over there?"

Edward was about forty, with flecks of silver in his close-cropped hair and well-groomed beard. Meadow settled into the couch and took a careful sip of the wine. He looked sheepishly around him. "So do you live around here, too?" he asked Edward.

"No, I'm farther west, about fifteen minutes by car," he said. "Hasidic territory, rather than Polish. Quiet neighborhood, which

I like. It's nice to have a liquor store on every block here, though." Edward turned out to be the managing director of an imprint specializing in translated literature and academic monographs. He had come late to this career, after vagabonding in North Africa and Eastern Europe for a decade. "Ostensibly as a journalist," he said, tilting his glass of wine at Meadow. "But I lost my passion for that life a long time ago. It just took me a few years to part ways with it."

He asked what Meadow did for a living, how he found himself in that role. "The desk job gave me an out that I desperately needed," Meadow replied. "I guess I'm taking some time to decompress."

"Decompressing is necessary," Edward declared, fixing his gaze on Meadow. "But surely you have some other ambition, a calling that the full-time job supports. Jobs are sometimes nothing more than stepping stones."

Meadow took a sip of wine, the smooth velvet coating his tongue as he pondered Edward's question. "I've always been interested in stories," he said at length.

"So you're a writer, then."

"No. I just . . . think about the story, as a form, a lot. How arbitrary it is. It's a coping mechanism, no?"

"What do you mean?"

"We use stories to make sense out of the senseless. Not just in books and movies or whatever, but in the way we imagine our lives and how we relate to other people. Everything that happens to us individually, or larger events that impact an entire country, even the whole world—there's no rhyme or reason to it, or any meaning, unless we string together those events into a narrative. We impose this kind of logic as a means of survival, right? I don't know if that's reassuring or unsettling."

Edward raised his eyebrows and laughed. "That's quite a burden to carry," he said. "Are you sure you don't want to face this nihilism head-on and—who knows, maybe even vanquish it—by writing?"

Hell no, Meadow wanted to say. He didn't see any point in it. He'd lived with stories his entire life, taking refuge in them, learning from them, looking to them for guidance or some semblance of meaning. For a while, it had felt like he was on the trail of something important in his grad school research, peeling back the gauze of accumulated time to ponder his origins, as if the misadventures of dilettante foreigners and flighty artists from the last century could explain something about his own life. Then, after he dropped that whole enterprise, he was relieved to be able to get back to leisure reading, movies and TV shows, anything that struck his fancy. But he had realized with equal parts horror and resignation that nothing moved him anymore. Perhaps it was simply a symptom of growing older and acknowledging the vacuum of meaning at the core of this worldly existence. Still, he found himself yearning to understand something about the people in his life, the separate realities they inhabited, through these memories of stories still layered thick in his mind.

All of this flashed through Meadow's head in the span of a few seconds. Before he could say anything, there was a high-pitched buzz from a panel in the hallway. "I'll get the door this time," said Edward. "Excuse me one moment." He sprang to his feet and shuffled down the hall.

There ended up being a total of seven people at the dinner party. It was an intimate affair, the lot of them encircling the table where Selma and Yulia had set out dishes, cutlery, and serving utensils for a beautiful radish and green bean salad, strip steak with fried potatoes, and an assortment of olives and pickles. A cheese board and a jar of berry compote sat next to a crusty baguette. Selma poured the remaining pinot noir from the bottle into their glasses and offered to make cocktails.

"Martini, anyone?" she asked, looking around.

Meadow raised his hand along with several others.

She had changed outfits at some point between cooking the steaks and setting the table. Now she wore a mustard-colored cashmere top that draped her shoulders loosely, along with a gray pencil skirt. Opal earrings hung close to the nape of her neck. "They're by Yulia," Selma explained when someone complimented her. "Aren't they fabulous?"

"Just some old merchandise I off-loaded," Yulia said. "She makes them look good."

Besides Edward, Yulia, and Meadow, the other guests were Wei-Ning, a dancer from Taiwan with a gentle smile; Brigitte, a textiles curator with a shock of white hair and red eyeglasses; and Simon, a slick-haired restaurateur whose Long Island accent infused the intimate party with a tinge of raucous cheer. Meadow suspected he was the youngest among the group by far. They were a motley crew, but he gathered from their conversation that they had all known one another for some time.

Selma urged them to start eating as she returned to the kitchen to make the martinis. "I'm making these dirty," she said. "Speak now or forever hold your peace."

"That's how we like it, baby," assured Simon.

They tucked into their meals with gusto, compliments to the chef ringing out with every forkful. Yulia went to put on more music once the Aretha Franklin record ended, and soon the sentimental croonings of the Bee Gees filled the room. Selma's eyes crinkled with fondness as she glided back in with a trayful of martinis and began to deposit them on the table. "Brings me back," she sighed.

Yulia gasped. "Oh my goodness, I totally . . . We can change it if—"

"No, no," Selma said. "Don't worry about it. I'm in the process of reclaiming musicians, books, movies. I'll be damned if I let him soil it all for me." She looked at Meadow. "We danced to this album at my wedding," she said, setting the tray down on the windowsill and taking her seat at the table. "Ancient history!"

Brigitte raised an eyebrow as she chewed her steak. "Good riddance," she said. "May he languish in the dustbin of history."

"You know, I'm pretty sure I ran into ol' Fawaz a few weeks ago," Simon piped up. "I was tryna catch a taxi in Midtown around Christmas—a nightmare if there ever was one—and thought I saw him come around the corner and slink into the Carlyle. Looked like he'd lost a few mil on horse racing that morning."

Selma rolled her eyes. "It definitely was him. He loves that hotel."

Fawaz, it turned out, was her ex, an Anglo-Syrian investment banker who lived between New York and London. They were in the process of getting divorced. Meadow thought back to the public spat of theirs he'd witnessed, at the bookstore last spring. The timing of it all made sense now, as well as the reason why Selma alone lived in this apartment.

He found out over the course of the evening that Selma was twenty-nine years old, turning thirty in May. She and Fawaz had gotten married five years ago in England. Yulia had designed their engagement rings. Fawaz had always been supportive of Selma's art, and even introduced her to a few gallerists when they moved to New York. But his possessiveness had gotten out of hand recently, made worse by an addiction to uppers and a fixation on amassing obscene amounts of money.

Wei-Ning and Selma had done a residency together in the Black Forest a few summers ago. "We danced under the moonlight almost every night," he said, smiling across the table at Selma. "It was a special time. I wished we never had to leave."

"We cultivated a serenity of mind over two months," proclaimed Selma, "and destroyed it over the course of one weekend in Berlin."

Edward had met Selma when he lived in Algeria and she'd participated in a group show organized by a French corporate sponsor. Brigitte was a friend of Selma's cousin, an art professor in Rhode Island. And Simon owned a bistro around the corner from where Selma used to live, in the West Village. "Tiny place, good food," he said with a wink. "Between Christopher and Tenth. I've had it for . . . what is it, almost a decade now?"

"Good place to celebrate a birthday," laughed Brigitte with a conspiratorial wink.

Wei-Ning spoke up. "Meadow, what about you? How did you meet each other?"

Around the table their faces, rosy with drink, peered at him expectantly. "Oh," said Meadow. He hesitated. "Friend of a friend, I guess. I saw Selma's solo show last year, and we . . . sort of met then."

"I chanced upon his housewarming party a few months ago," Selma offered casually. "So nice to have a friend in the neighborhood."

A sweet smell gradually filled the apartment as they finished their steaks and martinis and continued to pick at the cheese board and pickles. "Is there something in the oven?" exclaimed Brigitte.

"Of course," said Selma. "It wouldn't be a full meal without dessert."

"The consummate hostess," Simon said, shaking his head. "What's cooking?"

"It is a winter fruit pie," Yulia replied. "Berries and pears, that kind of thing. We also have a Polish digestif from the liquor store on Norman."

"I'm going to need a ciggie before we get into that," said Brigitte, sliding her chair back from the table. She caught Selma's eye. "Do you mind?"

"Of course not. But let's crack open a window."

What a strange assortment of characters, Meadow thought, watching Brigitte cross the room in her polka-dot sweaterdress while Edward and Wei-Ning talked about the best spots for hiking around Taiwan. Yet there was something endearing about the group of them, the ease with which they performed their social identities, at once cosmopolitan and unpretentious. He wondered how he might be viewed by an outside observer, whether he truly could fit in with this lot. "Meadow, would you care for a cigarette?" Selma asked, rising from the table.

"I'd love one."

As they crouched by the windowsill with Brigitte, Meadow realized he had never pictured Selma as someone who smoked. She had simply seemed too dignified for this habit, as though she inhabited a realm where cigarettes didn't exist. But now as he watched her light up a Seven Stars, inhale, and tilt her head back with great pleasure, he found that she smoked with considerable poise. The cigarette appeared dainty between Selma's middle and ring fingers, while a sweep of dark hair dramatically framed her face as she exhaled out the window. He accepted gratefully when she handed him the pack.

"I'd sooner swear off alcohol than cigarettes," declared Brigitte, "but the both of them are a divine pair, don't you think?"

"I couldn't bear to live without either," smiled Selma.

The evening turned out to be a parade of delectable creature comforts for a cold January: steak and wine, martinis, pie, good music, Japanese cigarettes. Meadow wondered how Selma was able to pull it off so seamlessly. A far cry from the chilly mien she had shown at first encounter, her several other faces as a skilled home cook, charming hostess, and convener of creative souls were now apparent to him. But who was he, to her? What role could someone like him, a half-hearted itinerant drifting from station to station, possibly fill in the universe she governed?

It seemed like an unlikely friendship from the beginning. Yet as the dinner party lasted late into the night, the flow of conversation between them was effortless, even energizing. Meadow discovered that they shared similar tastes in music and film. Selma had also lived in Hayes Valley for a spell when Meadow was bumbling his way through undergrad. He wondered if they'd ever passed each other in Chinatown or Dolores Park. Talking with her reminded him of a simpler time, a time before New York, perhaps, when he was still overly impressionable and yearning to sink his teeth into adulthood. His mind drifted to his tribe back in California, how he'd believed they could persist forever, and how quickly they ended up scattering to the winds—for money, love, or grad school. Then he was coaxed back into the present moment by Selma handing him another drink or cigarette, at once empathetic and studious as she gently interrogated the boundaries of his personhood. She'd had so many wild, colorful experiences, and yet didn't seem to tire of asking him questions, about his romantic history, his family, his bifurcated upbringing between Shanghai and Middle America. She'd regularly visited Japan since childhood, with even more frequency after her father's death. The fractured self, the incredible distance and mundanity of that journey across the ocean—these were things Selma knew all too well.

Though he tried not to overthink it, Meadow was secretly pleased that he had earned a spot at Selma's dinner table. She'd materialized at just the right moment, offering a dash of caprice and an element of the unknown to liven up his social world. Things with Caleb had fizzled out in the fall, the two of them mutually ghosting each other. Since then he and Bobby had been barhopping every weekend again, but without the same zeal as during the warmer months. Meadow felt like he was standing in place in an open pasture, surveying the expanse of life on all sides. He assumed he would eventually discover a vague but intuitive sense of direction, an image of a destination in mind. But in truth he was floundering in the undergrowth, spinning around and around until the scenery blurred and he didn't know which way was which anymore. He was almost a quarter-century old. The scholarly life was not for him, he'd determined, and for now it didn't bother him to be a cog in the machinery of academia. He could putter along with a lover, or without. In spite of the occasional bout of loneliness, he felt no urgency around finding a partner. But still. He yearned to give shape to his existential desires, explain in words what the pulsing, vital mass within him was driving at. He sensed that Selma saw this hunger in him, felt its heat emanating from his core. Or perhaps he was projecting this onto her—his longing to be not just understood, but comforted and fortified. He could tell somehow that she was looking for the same.

After the dinner party at Selma's, Meadow was invited to a Lunar New Year party by Wei-Ning, the Taiwanese dancer. Selma was there, naturally, along with Brigitte, who wore an elaborate black cheongsam gifted by a designer friend from Hong Kong. Together they folded dumplings in the living room while listening to Mandopop ballads from decades past, making frequent trips to the stoop to smoke cigarettes, where they shivered and hobbled from leg to leg while talking about astrology. That spring, as the city thawed out, Meadow found himself joining Selma for picnics, cocktails on bar patios, and walks along the East River. Yulia was usually by her side—she lived nearby in Williamsburg—or sometimes Edward, who would meet them late after a long day in the office in Dumbo. Selma had an endless coterie of other interesting characters that Meadow met in passing, over time. Sometimes he felt out of his depth among the people she introduced him to, painters and experimental musicians, poets and video artists. But she always seemed to know how to draw him into the conversation, treating him with whimsical affection as though he were a long-lost younger brother. On occasion, Meadow invited Peter to these outings, as well, and he and Daniela would surface and knock back a few drinks with them, Daniela plying Selma with questions about the artist's life: how to hobnob with gallerists, find a studio, and so on. She wasn't sure if she would be able to stay in New York after she graduated.

In May, Selma invited them all to her birthday. Thirty seemed impossibly distant to Meadow at the time, an undeniably adult age that was respectable in its solidity, even conferring a measure of worldliness or artistic maturity. Of course these notions could not be disentangled from Selma herself, who moved briskly through life with unflagging charm and composure. This much alone Meadow found admirable, the sense of purpose she exuded in constructing a social world to her liking. There was something to be learned from her self-assured manner, he felt, even if he lacked the same conviction about his creative or professional goals.

Selma deemed it absolutely necessary to have a party on a grand scale to celebrate the closing of one decade and beginning of another. She also proclaimed that she didn't want to cook, much as she enjoyed entertaining at home. For that reason, she rented out an entire bar on Manhattan Avenue in Greenpoint. She received permission from the manager, an acquaintance of hers, to transform the walls into a lush tableau of gold and green, vines snaking down from the ceiling, streamers shimmering above leather booths and garlands of lily, safflower, and lavender on every table. For the music, she enlisted a friend from Oslo to DJ at the event, even paying for his round trip to New York. She was expecting more than fifty people, including curators, critics, colleagues from the universities where she taught, and fellow artists from London and Tokyo. A solo show overseas was her next big target.

That night, Meadow, Peter, and Daniela dropped by the bar after tacos and margaritas up the street. Once the bouncer checked their IDs, they stepped inside and gave their names to a frazzled woman hunched over a clipboard in the corridor. They could hear the music thumping from down the hall. The woman waved the three of them in and they proceeded to the back room, where a light fog lent a primal air to the vines draped along the walls and floral embellishments spilling forth from tabletops. Party lights strobed and shifted from deep purple to emerald green to bright topaz as the DJ, a preposterously tall man with a shaved head, gyrated onstage to Beach House.

A handful of people were on the dance floor, but it looked like most were congregating around the booths. Peter offered to buy a round from the bar on the other side of the room. "I wonder where the birthday girl is," Daniela said, folding her arms and scanning the area.

Just then a person emerged from the dance floor and stood next to them. When the fog had dissipated a little, Meadow recognized the woman in the black dress and braided hair. "Yulia!" he called.

Yulia turned, squinting in his direction. Then her face lit up. "Meadow!" she said, reaching over for an embrace. "It's so good to see you."

"Where's Selma? Is she in the back somewhere?"

"Mm, well, I'm looking for her, actually. We were sitting together, her and Simon and me, and then she got up to talk to people who had just arrived. The next thing I knew, she was gone. I thought maybe she went to get a drink, but she's been gone for, like, half an hour?"

"Maybe she went to get some air," Meadow offered. "Although we didn't see her outside. We just got here. You've met Daniela before, right?"

"Hi," said Daniela.

"Yes," replied Yulia. "Nice to see you again."

Yulia told them there was plenty of room at her table if they wanted to join. She led Daniela and Meadow to the back, where Simon was slouched against the leather booth with a half-drunk pint glass before him. Daniela dropped off her jacket and said she was going to help Peter bring over drinks from the bar.

Simon rose from his seat. He wore a striped blazer that was short at the sleeves, hair slicked back like a young Al Pacino. "My man Med!" he said, clapping Meadow on the back. "Still no birthday gal, huh?" he asked Yulia. "She ain't answering my texts, either."

Yulia shrugged helplessly. "I checked the bathroom, circled the dance floor and all the tables. Maybe she decided to run back home for something? This wouldn't be the first time."

"What a pain in the ass," Simon grumbled.

Peter and Daniela returned to the table a short while later. Meadow introduced them to Simon, whom they hadn't met before. Then the group sipped their tequila sodas and whiskey sours as they surveyed the room and got Yulia's scoop on the various partygoers in the vicinity: ex-classmates, rivals, old flames, and hangers-on.

It was Meadow who eventually found Selma. On the way back from the bathroom, he stopped to admire one of the dense lattices of vines that hung against the walls. Rather than haphazard clumps, the vines were affixed with transparent tape in an intricate and clearly deliberate pattern, leaves draping languidly and opening into delicate bursts of lavender and orchid. He remembered Selma talking about how she planned to decorate. It was amazing she'd managed to pull this off in the span of an afternoon with only Yulia's assistance. In the corner of the room, there was a storage area where a row of leafy plants stood sentry on a counter, behind a massive lemon tree that nearly reached the ceiling. Running his hand along the bark of the tree, he wondered if this was part of Selma's scheme as well. He wouldn't have been surprised if the lemon garnishes for the cocktails were being plucked straight from this plant.

As he leaned in to inhale the scent of a lemon, Meadow thought of the approaching summer and the feeling of lightness that the season instilled in him. Summer meant long hours of daylight, carefree wanderings around Manhattan, movie screenings in the park, street fairs, and beach getaways; it was the stuff of life itself.

Meadow opened his eyes. He was startled when he noticed there was a shape directly behind the row of plants. There was a person sitting below the counter, huddled against the wall with arms wrapped around her knees.

"Selma?"

He made his way around the lemon tree and knelt down. It was indeed Selma, her face turned toward the wall and partially hidden by a curtain of hair.

He drew closer. The music continued to thump as planes of light streamed pink and orange and then yellow. For a moment, as the room grew bright, he was able to see her more clearly. She was on the floor in a long dress, still as a statue until she turned her head slowly to face him.

Meadow was surprised. He'd assumed immediately that maybe she was having a panic attack, and expected her to appear distraught or agitated. Her expression was placid and neutral, however, betraying almost no hint of emotion. It was not the cloudy detachment that he had detected when they'd first met at her exhibition opening over a year ago. Instead, her gaze was cold and pellucid as a mountain stream in winter.

"Selma," he ventured weakly a second time, "are you okay?"

She was looking straight at him now, but still yielded no reaction, as though she did not comprehend what was happening. Meadow furrowed his brow and lowered himself to the ground. He gently reached a hand out and placed it on hers. Her slender fingers were icy to the touch. As he opened his mouth to speak her name again, he felt as though he were stepping into a shallow but swift current that he hadn't anticipated encountering. The cold water was a shock to his senses. He called out for Selma as he waded toward her, struggling to maintain his balance against the undertow.

8

JUNE SLIPS QUICKLY INTO JULY. AFTER CLOSING UP AT BARLEY
and bidding goodbye to Monique, Meadow walks home alone at
four in the morning. He stews in the silence and stifling heat of the
nightscape, trying to stave off the thoughts that have been cluttering
his mind for days. Monique assumed he was still melancholic
over Diego and spent the entire shift peppering him with distractions,
playing triumphant breakup anthems or talking shit about
politicians. But the truth is Diego has been far from his mind. It's
Selma—or rather, the negative space she has left—that fills him
with gnawing anxiety, or resentment, depending on the hour. And
he can't help but turn over the matter of *The Masquerade* again and
again, even though he has arrived at no new answers.

At this time, the witching hour, Brooklyn is completely still.
Meadow tries to focus on this instead, on how the entire city has
become a solipsist domain, a dreamworld through which he can
traipse while admiring its remarkable detail, every sidewalk and
façade layered with history. He passes a homeless man on the corner
of Atlantic, then a woman smoking outside of the Nostrand
Avenue subway station. For a long stretch thereafter, as he makes
his way north and west, it's just him and the occasional vehicle
whizzing by. A few bodegas still have their doors open. Otherwise
he's moving past one shuttered storefront after another, darkened

churches and elementary schools, a playground abandoned to nighttime. Leafy treetops flutter in the wind, bobbing in and out of shadow or pools of sickly orange light.

He thought he'd gotten over his jet lag relatively quickly, but his circadian rhythms have been thrown completely out of sync again in the past few days. At first, he figured it was fine to wake up in the afternoon or take long naps in the middle of the day, as the only commitments he had were a couple of late shifts at Barley, stretching from eight to four in the morning. But now, even on his days off, he finds it practically impossible to fall asleep before dawn, no matter how he tries to wean himself off this vampiric schedule via melatonin, meditation, or marijuana. Every time he's given up on trying to sleep, he inevitably finds himself puttering around Selma's with a record on, testing the soil in all the plant pots or scouring her cupboards for a snack. He has also spent time contemplating the strange flower blooming next to the rubber tree, the single stalk having grown several inches now, with new buds appearing around it. The petals of the flower appear to be whitish green, almost like the celadon glaze of traditional Chinese pottery. It's a wholly unnatural color for a flower, Meadow has decided, the translucence recalling the ghoulish pallor of the undead.

He blames the book for this state of affairs, at least partially. Since discovering that the name of the supposed translator appears to correlate with that of a Vermont library, he has been more or less convinced that *The Masquerade* is not a real book. Or rather, it is not what it appears or purports itself to be, a translation of a Chinese novel. The likelihood that everything is simply a coincidence seems preposterous: that a man named Barnaby Salem would translate a book written by someone with his Chinese name, Liu Tian. But if his suspicions are well-founded, does it mean that Selma concocted the book herself?

Did she intend for him to find it at her apartment? And what, if anything, does it have to do with her disappearance in Shanghai?

The plot of the book contains some kind of riddle, Meadow is sure of it, but he is frustrated by his inability to parse exactly what question is being asked, let alone produce the answer to it. That hasn't stopped him from continuing to read in fits and starts. Snatches of the fictional world of 1930s Shanghai occasionally surface in his mind like false memories or folktales heard long ago: the opulent mansion bathed in the milky glow of the full moon; Du Kuo-wen in a pig mask, surrounded by admirers; the woman known as Orchid reciting a line of poetry to Mizuno. *Pay attention to symbols.* In these liminal hours as night transitions into day, Meadow is often so stoned that the border between his life and that of the book seems to start to dissolve, or become permeable. He scours the text for a hint or clue, but remains empty-handed.

The masquerade ball itself feels like an allegory, one that he's somehow missed from the beginning. A long time ago, when he first met Selma, she was indeed going through a phase in which masks were one of her central thematic preoccupations and mediums; there was a whole wall of them in the exhibition where Meadow had seen her for the first time, the night he went out with Peter and met Rebecca, Bobby, and the rest. He remembers Selma eventually telling him about why she became interested in making masks, sharing some backstory about her investigations into folkloric traditions and ancient mythology. This detail, like many other facets of her, simply faded into the background as he got to know her more and began to construct a new narrative of their friendship. Now the memories of other works of Selma's bubble up in his mind, pieces he has glimpsed in her studio or at other shows: oblong faces made of wood, with protuberant noses and sneering lips; metal figurines with expressionist slits for eyes; rubber grotesqueries with painted brows, mouths agape in permanent surprise; an inverted triangle painted the sallow whitish yellow of a newly hatched larva, features etched in charcoal.

All these things are churning around the back of his mind like a pool of debris as he navigates Brooklyn at four in the morning, completely on autopilot. The masks, the masked ball, *The Masquerade*; the fact that he might as well still be on Shanghai time given his sleep schedule. Selma told him she was rising early and going to the studio in Jing'an district around five in the morning each day. He wonders if they may be synchronized while thousands of miles apart, if she's still getting up at this hour—wherever she is. Part of him wants to reach out and ask Anya if she's heard anything new, or even try harder himself, somehow, to determine where Selma may have gone. He was on the verge of emailing Yulia until he remembered she had gone back to Ukraine a few months earlier for a family emergency. Another part of him is glad to have an excuse to look the other way, telling himself that he has already done all that he can. He also knows that Selma can be intensely private, surprisingly so, based on his experience of her past crises. Among the difficult truths the situation forces him to confront is that Selma's disappearance is, ultimately, not out of character.

Meadow turns onto a residential street lined with brownstones and some uglier buildings, squat and unhappy like children in mismatched outfits. The street is mostly swallowed in darkness. He hears a dog barking, a faraway siren droning before fading altogether. In moments like these, he feels as though he has unwittingly slipped into a realm of profound solitude—as if the brick and concrete, the metal and glass, the mess of gnarled branches, trash bags spilling out of bins, crushed cigarettes and Styrofoam scraps in the street, all these are simply elaborate props for a stage occupied by him and him alone. He pushes out a quick, short breath. Even this sound seems flat and unreal, muffled somehow.

A noise from behind catches his attention, like something kicked off a curb, a metal can, rolling for not even a second. He's halfway down the block at this point, walking beneath the canopy of leaves. Meadow glances back: not a soul in sight. Nonetheless he quickens his pace. It may not have been the best idea to turn off the main thoroughfare. He's been savvy, or lucky, all this time in New York. Never been mugged or had an encounter that felt close to any modicum of danger. No excuse for complacency, though. He grits his teeth and reaches a hand into his pocket to feel for the solidity of the switchblade, which he has begun carrying with him for some measure of reassurance.

He could swear he detected another sound coming from behind, this one even fainter—the padding of footsteps on gravel. Or maybe it came from the opposite side of the street. Meadow keeps moving as he swivels his head to look around, but nothing is out of the ordinary. Orange and black, darkened windows, the pale glow of fluorescent entryways. His breath catches as he sees something tall standing by a metal fence, enveloped in shadow. But it seems, as his eyes adjust from a distance, to be a rolled-up rug.

He turns right on Classon Avenue, grateful to be on a somewhat more trafficked street, even if there's no one else around at this hour. More than halfway home. A yellow cab rolls by, slowing down as if inviting him for a ride. He keeps walking. The cab speeds past and turns at the next light. A few blocks later he approaches the entrance to the Bedford-Nostrand subway station. No sign of anyone coming or going, just eerie silence. He makes a fist and knocks on the painted metal banister at the mouth of the subway as he walks by.

Once he reaches the opposite side of the intersection, he notices what appears to be a person sitting on a bench at the bus stop ahead. The person is mostly cloaked in shadow and covered head to toe, a hood obscuring his head. Probably someone waiting for the bus, Meadow thinks. But tonight feels different from other nights. Though the world that he has been traversing may look ordinary enough, something is not right. Meadow's breath becomes shallow as he draws closer to the man on the bench. So far he has remained completely still—unnaturally so. He can't be asleep, not with that perfectly upright posture and straightforward gaze. Stay away, a voice inside Meadow's head says. Don't wait for something to happen.

Less than ten feet away, Meadow abruptly swerves from his path and steps out into the street. He crosses in haste, then continues walking north, only daring to glance from the corner of his eye at the figure on the bench. The man hasn't budged an inch. What if it was a dummy this whole time, he thinks. Some art student's idea of a joke. He doesn't want to test that hypothesis, though. He speeds up, adrenaline pumping. The next thing he knows, he's bounding up the stoop and fishing the key from his pocket.

Once he gets into Selma's apartment, Meadow locks the door securely behind him and exhales with relief. He flicks on the hallway light and hangs his jacket in the closet. Moving into the kitchen, he sets his phone on the counter and sees that it's not even half past the hour. Strange. The walk to or from Barley usually takes a solid forty minutes. He's timed it often enough to know this. He was certain he and Monique had wrapped things up shortly after four. How could he have made it back so quickly?

"You were speed walking the whole time," he says out loud, shaking his head.

He turns on all the lights in the apartment and then takes a long, hot shower. Selma's bathroom is luxuriously big, with a claw-foot tub and a high window that looks out onto a neighboring courtyard. A light fragrance of verbena lingers from a scented candle on the counter, while a few moisture-loving ferns sit on a shelf above the toilet. As steam rises around him and grazes his shoulder blades, his throat and cheeks, he closes his eyes and steps directly beneath the showerhead. He imagines the tension in him like a tightly wound spring and sighs unconsciously. Let the whole thing uncoil, grow slack, fall limp to the ground.

His nerves already frayed, Meadow opts for a beer over a joint after getting out of the shower. As his mind eases into the familiar lucidity of this hour, he decides to forgo music as well and simply plops onto the couch in a fresh shirt and underwear. He opens *The Masquerade* to where he left off and reads for a while in between swigs of the cold lager. At one point, though, he looks up and remembers the white kitsune and wooden demon masks hanging in the corner of the living room. The eyeless eyes stare at him, seemingly observing his every move. For a second, the texture of shadow changes in the eyeholes, a flicker of movement or something flitting by, like an insect. "Fuck that," he says. He turns off the lights in the living room and kitchen and goes to read in bed.

THE PERFORMANCE HAS already begun by the time Mizuno arrives in the ballroom with the rose newly affixed to his breast pocket. Everyone is thoroughly enraptured by the bevy of Javanese dancers in their golden vestments and robes of scarlet silk. The assembly of masked partygoers stands stiffly in the shadows, spectating on the ethereal movements of the performers while a group of vocalists and musicians at the edge of the inverted stage continue their ominous song. Head swimming from drink, Mizuno finds the whole display discomforting, even nausea-inducing. He decides to search for a different environment where he might make better use of his time at the party.

At thirty years of age, Mizuno has spent a quarter of his life in China. A family friend offered him a job at a Japanese-run newspaper right around the time he was completing his studies at university. There was no reason to refuse. Not only could he bask in glorious freedom, deferring the pressure to marry or otherwise settle down, as would be expected had he stayed in Yokohama, he could also embark on the adventure of a lifetime in the huge, fathomless nation that was China. Setting off by steamer was perhaps the most exciting moment of his life. Thanks to the considerable network of Japanese compatriots, he had little problem adjusting to his new life in Shanghai's Hongkew district. But beyond the familiar rhythms of this residential enclave, the city is a wholly alien landscape filled with treachery and glamor, neon and sludge. Beautiful men and women in expensive imported fashions stride briskly through the foreign settlements, while just a stone's throw away are hovels where whole families sustain the drab activities of daily life within a single room.

With his facility in English, Mizuno mostly covers the social world of the Americans and Brits in the city. He fraternizes with traders and diplomats, curries favor with flappers and traveling jazzmen, shadows the movements of alcoholic poets and actors on tour. As for the locals, Mizuno regards them with a mixture of pity—for their cultural stagnation and social backwardness, the vast resources squandered by the late empire, the mismanagement and ineptitude of the Republican government—and grudging admiration for the capacity of some individuals to rise above it all. The Chinese who are savvy enough to play the game of modernity tend to be like Du Kuo-wen: beguiling, whip-smart, and ruthless. If they should all rise to this level of competence one day, the balance of world power would most definitely be disturbed. Though he considers himself to be but a neutral observer, Mizuno maintains the belief that China needs the Japanese, that they share a common goal and simply different stratagems. The rejuvenation of China would mean the rejuvenation of Asia; the only way to achieve this glory is to make offerings at the altar of self-determination and pry the continent from meddling Western imperialists.

Away from the ballroom, Mizuno finds that the rest of the house is almost disconcertingly empty now. Only a few household staff members are collecting empty dishes and glasses. The American jazz musicians are packing up their instruments in the grand foyer. He reaches the staircase leading upstairs just as a woman in a damask dress is descending. She pauses there, a few feet away, a smile upon her lips. "*Spring splendor this garden cannot restrain*," she proclaims, looking straight at him.

Mizuno pushes the mask up on his nose, his hand drifting inadvertently to finger the stem of the rose against his breast pocket. Surely Orchid wouldn't invite him to play this game again so soon? But if it were indeed Peony, the other woman, shouldn't she see that he has already won the prize pinned to his tuxedo jacket? "*A branch of red blossoms yearns past this domain*," Mizuno answers dutifully.

"Well done," the woman says. "And my name?"

"Peony."

She takes several steps down the staircase, approaching Mizuno and leaning forward to speak directly in his ear. "Wrong," she says somewhat ruefully. "I am Orchid. Now this time you'll be punished." A slender hand clasps Mizuno's wrist. Orchid's grip is surprisingly firm, her fingers cold as she swivels around and begins walking up the staircase again.

"Wh-Where are you taking me?" Mizuno sputters.

"Relax," Orchid says, the smile never fading. "There's a mahjong table waiting. It's just a game, remember?"

When they reach the top of the stairs, Mizuno hears murmuring voices and the sound of tiles clacking from a nearby room. Orchid takes him down a corridor he didn't notice earlier and ushers him into another parlor, where two groups of people sit around tables on opposite ends of the room. On the wall hangs a massive portrait of Du Kuo-wen in the style of the European gentry of old. The warbling voice of a Chinese songstress coming from a brass gramophone by the window imbues the parlor with a hint of melancholy. A game seems to be well underway at the far table, where a man in a Venetian carnival mask frowns while peering at a tile. "Six of sticks," the man says in Shanghainese, slapping the tile into the center with a gloved hand.

"Aiyo, why couldn't you have thrown this one out two rounds ago?" complains a woman to his right with a black lace mask that covers almost her entire face.

A woman dressed identical to Orchid presides over the game, her arms folded as she observes the proceedings. "Maybe you need some more liquor for luck," she chuckles.

Mizuno barely has time to take in the surroundings as Orchid leads him to the other table, where three people are apparently waiting for him to complete the square. "Finally, we can start!" sighs a blonde woman in a sapphire-colored dress and matching mask. She looks Mizuno in the eye. "I've bored myself to bloody death waiting for Peony here to assemble enough players. Excuse me, Orchid, that is. Let's go!" She reaches her pale arms into the center of the table, where the orange-backed tiles are amassed, and begins to scrabble them together with force.

Orchid laughs. "Lady and gentlemen, please welcome Mizuno-san to the table. Would anyone care for another Phantasm cocktail?"

Mizuno looks from the woman in the sapphire dress to the other players. Directly across from him is a man with a head of curly hair who wears a rawhide mask and a brown vest over a starched white shirt. "Perhaps we should make introductions before we begin," the man says, baring his teeth as he gazes at Mizuno. "Luigi Luna of Napoli, at your service. And yes, Signorina Orchid, another cocktail sounds fabulous."

"Ah, right," says the woman in sapphire. "Dahlia Derby. Call me Dahlia."

Only then does Mizuno notice that the third player is a man in an ivory-colored mask with a curved beak. "My name is Spiegel," says the man in the beaked mask, betraying no hint that he spoke to Mizuno earlier.

"And I am Masatoshi Mizuno," Mizuno says, steadying himself. Glancing at Orchid, who gazes at them like a schoolteacher satisfied with the work of her pupils, Mizuno stammers, "But how is it that you already know my name, Miss Orchid? I don't recall telling you earlier."

"My dear man," Orchid begins dramatically, "that's because tonight is not our first meeting. But let me fetch you drinks first. And please do get this game started. Miss Derby here is most impatient."

"DINNER TWO TIMES in a week? It's like we're roommates again." Peter is all smiles when Meadow meets him in Chinatown, outside one of their favorite Cantonese places by East Broadway. He grows serious as he takes in Meadow's sullen expression. "I figured from your texts that you had something pretty heavy on your mind. Med, what's going on? Are you okay?"

"Well," Meadow mutters glumly, "I'm not sure where to begin. Can we talk about it over some food?"

"Sure, sure," Peter says, opening the door and gently pushing Meadow inside. "Let's grab a table."

Peter's face is hard to read as he listens intently to Meadow, both of them spooning at their lobster fried rice and pork and sour cabbage soup. I must sound like a maniac, Meadow thinks. He tells Peter about *The Masquerade* and the weird coincidences that just keep piling up: Liu Tian, the name of the Vermont library, the conversation about symbols. Then there's Selma's disappearance, or intentional absence. Getting into a cab going God knows where, and totally incommunicado ever since.

"Listen," Peter says finally, taking a swig of Tsingtao. "One thing at a time. I think it's natural to be worried and confused. First off, Selma going away somewhere unexpectedly seems like it's really got you on edge. So I'm glad this Anya woman is looking into it. That said . . ." Meadow waves his hand impatiently, gesturing for Peter to continue his thought. "You're not responsible for her, right?"

"Huh?"

"From what you've told me, it sounds like everything that has happened so far has been a deliberate action. She wasn't coerced into a cab, as far as we can tell. She left of her own volition. Besides, hasn't she gone incommunicado before?"

"Yeah, but usually it's intentional, and—"

"And nothing about this time suggests otherwise. So let's set Selma aside and presume she is safe and doing whatever it is that she does. That leaves you here in Brooklyn, in her house, reading this book that you think she made, or had someone write for her."

Meadow stares at the tablecloth, where liquid from the different dishes has dribbled into orangey and yellow-green splotches. He pokes at the garlicky greens on another plate with his chopsticks, lifting a clump to his mouth. "That leaves me here," he parrots while chewing.

"I dunno, man. And what if all of these things about the book are just a coincidence? Would that make you feel better?"

"You mean, if the book is actually what it says it is? That there really was a translator named Barnaby Salem and a writer with my name. And I just happened to run into a weirdo who wanted to give a speech . . ."

"Yeah."

"I would say that's even more fucking bizarre. What about Occam's razor?"

"You know Selma better than me, obviously. It sounds like you're pretty convinced that she's capable of pulling off some convoluted plot like this."

"Well," Meadow concedes, "I don't know. She's always been a bit outlandish. When we were at the party in Shanghai, she mentioned having a few other major projects coming to a head. Not that it means anything. But I feel like all the clues so far point to this idea that maybe the book is part of some . . . some elaborate, fucked-up performance."

"Does everything fit so neatly though?"

Meadow takes a sharp inhale. He tries to consider objectively the other things that have befallen him of late. The dream he had about getting pulled into the cheval mirror, the feeling of being followed on his walk home from Barley. The ghostly, unsettled quality of his daily life in Selma's apartment. The hatted eccentric spouting weird philosophies.

Peter continues, "Look, I've never been close with her like you, but I think we can both agree that Selma is a woman who lives in her own world and does what she wants. We might describe this behavior differently"—he pauses, choosing his next words carefully—"but the principle is the same. In spite of all that, I don't see what she stands to gain from involving you in some kind of devious performance."

Meadow sighs. "I don't know either. Maybe I'm just grasping at straws."

Peter tilts his head to the side. "Don't take this the wrong way, Med. I think this house-sitting thing is putting you in a weird headspace, more than you want to admit. That, and you just got your heart broken, right?"

"Yeah, that one still stings. But what does that have to do with anything?"

"I've known you for how many years now? I know you put so much of yourself into every relationship. At least every one that seems worth your while. You're going through a period of mourning. And it seems to me that maybe your subconscious is searching for some kind of meaning. A way to connect the dots. Because you've been left in a vacuum after whatshisface ghosted you."

Meadow bites his lip, face wavering into an uncomfortable smile. "I mean . . ."

"Believing that Selma has orchestrated all this also implies something else to me."

"What?"

"That you've renounced a sense of control or responsibility over your own life."

Peter is one of the only people in the world who has ever spoken so bluntly to him. For that, Meadow is grateful, even when he finds himself put off by Peter's words, unwilling or unable to acknowledge the reason behind them. Of course Peter would interpret the situation like this, Meadow realizes, with his utilitarian and unsentimental approach to puzzle-solving. Maybe that's even why he sought Peter's opinion in the first place: to hammer at his existential crisis with cold rationality, solid and sturdy as a hunk of metal.

"Well," Meadow acquiesces, "I guess I have been fumbling in the dark for some time."

"It sounds like you need a change of scenery," Peter offers gently. "I know you just got back, but maybe we can go on a weekend trip sometime."

They haltingly shift the conversation to lighter topics as they order more Tsingtao and finish dinner. As they're waiting for the check, Peter tells Meadow that he's hosting a barbecue next weekend. Apparently Annika's pescatarianism is forcing him to explore new culinary frontiers and get to know his neighborhood fishmonger. "But don't worry," Peter says with a chortle. "There'll still be plenty of meats for the rest of us. I hope you can make it." When they leave the restaurant, Peter embraces Meadow at the mouth of the subway station as a roar from underground sends sour gusts of hot wind whipping around their bodies. "Take care of yourself, man," Peter tells him. "Hope you can start sleeping normally, too. Staying up until five is probably not doing wonders for your mental health."

"Thanks, Peter," Meadow says. "I think you're onto something there."

After Peter bounds down the steps to the subway, Meadow decides to take a walk before heading back to Brooklyn. It's a stuffy July night, but he feels the restless energy of the city around him in the roving groups of tattooed hipsters, the teenagers hanging around the basketball court, even the elderly Chinese women walking their yappy dogs. With his odd sleep schedule, it's only now, between eight and nine at night, that he begins to feel truly awake. A candy-colored crepuscule sets the skies aflame as he traipses mindlessly through the Lower East Side, peering into the boutiques that are still open and breathing in the sweet scent of a summer evening. Alfresco diners jabber happily over carafes of wine while middle-aged couples and throngs of college kids amble along the sidewalk.

Eventually he crosses Delancey, which is clogged with traffic heading to and from the Williamsburg Bridge. He strolls on in the night's warm embrace, moving north on Ludlow, thinking about all the messy adventures he's had around here with Bobby and sometimes Selma, layer after layer of implacable memory, cumulative and invisible at once. He decides to walk west, away from this stretch of bars and toward the relative quiet and green of the park between Forsyth and Chrystie.

He has worked up a good sweat by now, and is about to sit down on a bench in the park when his neck suddenly tenses. The intuitive discomfort recalls his walk home from Barley when he thought he was being followed. Meadow spins around but spots nobody in the immediate vicinity, only people walking between the scattered bars on Chrystie. Odd. Turning back to face the other side of the park, he gasps when he notices that there is a figure standing by a tree about thirty feet away from him. Though he can't make out his face, Meadow can tell that the man is staring straight at him across the shadowy expanse of the park. Before Meadow can even register an emotional response, the man sets off to the north in brisk, even steps. Meadow follows after without hazarding a second thought.

The man is dressed simply in shorts and a white T-shirt. He's of average build, the back of his head shorn close, although the top of his head is a dense swoop of longer hair. There's something familiar about his posture and gait. Even from afar, without any view of the man's face, Meadow has the sense that this is a person he knows. He quickens his pace, taking long strides forward to close the distance. The man was looking at him, no doubt about it. The initial jolt of awareness transforms into curiosity tinged with indignation. Who the hell could it be?

When he reaches Houston, the man turns left, crosses the width of the park, and comes to a stop on the corner of Chrystie. Meadow hurries after, squinting to make out a few details of his appearance. Yes, that sauntering gait, even the shape of his legs—it's definitely someone he knows. He is still a good twenty or so feet away. At this point, Meadow thinks about pretending to be in a rush and sprinting ahead so he can turn back and steal a glance. He stuffs his hand in his pockets while weighing this idea. The man turns to face him right as Meadow feels something flat and hard behind his wallet.

The switchblade. He forgot that he still had it in these shorts. His hand is sweating. His whole body is emanating heat. He can feel the grooves of the pearlescent case against his fingertips. His breathing becomes staggered, rasping. But not because of the blade—rather, the profile of the man is what strikes Meadow almost completely still, rooting him to the sidewalk. He recognizes that profile. He should be able to recognize it anywhere.

It's his own profile. Is it the angle? The man standing on the street corner looks almost exactly like Meadow himself. Same height, same posture. Same build, same face. The man moves into the crosswalk at Houston. Meadow rushes forward, still fingering the switchblade in his pocket. The man is moving faster now, as though aware of being followed. He passes First Street in a rush. Meadow is drawing closer and closer, but then a bicyclist followed by a honking taxi cuts him off. Fuck. He sees the figure of the man recede, then turn left onto Second Street. What the fuck, Meadow thinks. He pulls the switchblade out of his pocket.

When the taxi passes, Meadow dashes across the street. The switchblade feels heavy and hot in his palm, slick with sweat. He finds himself walking faster, then breaking into a run, to catch up with his double. He needs to know. He needs to see for himself. But it's too late. There's nobody on Second Street except for a mother pushing a baby stroller on the sidewalk. Meadow breathes shakily as he spins around in place. A summer breeze rustles the treetops and caresses his body like silk. The switchblade in his hand is a dull, egregious weight.

He slides the knife back into his pocket and tries to take deep breaths. He walks down the street dumbly, looking at the nondescript buildings on both sides, the windows full of whirring air-conditioning units, laughter and music drifting out from somewhere. The man could have entered any of these buildings and he would never know which one. Meadow blinks as he moves past a used bookstore, café, and dry cleaner, unsure of what has just happened.

He arrives at a gate with a display case. *Embarcadero Theater*, a sign reads, below which is a letter board with the dates and times of some upcoming productions. Meadow looks at the theater behind the gate. It's an art deco building that looks like it belongs in Chelsea rather than this part of the East Village, with an elegant arched doorway and geometric patterns etched into the stone. He's about to keep walking when something else in the display case catches his eye and makes him do a double take.

Beneath the letter board with the list of upcoming events is a poster with photographs of the talent. There are two rows of four headshots, printed on glossy paper that gleams beneath the display case's light. It's the picture on the bottom left that sends his heart pounding again. He feels electricity crackling inside, his nerve endings frying as he stares at the headshot, then the name, then back again. Over and over and over. It's Diego's face that stares out at him from this photograph, no question. Diego with longer hair, a few tufts curled behind his ears, and no glasses. Rather than mysterious, he looks open and earnest in this photograph—a true theater kid with sparkling eyes and a wide-set smile.

Beneath his picture there is an unfamiliar name printed. It takes Meadow a minute to register. He feels his mind short-circuiting, the night air suddenly thick and hard to breathe. "Matthew Morales," he reads aloud, staring at the type. "Who the fuck is Matthew Morales?"

As the blood swirls wildly through his body, a wind lifts the edges of his shirt and whips into the sky. Residential buildings line the block on either side of the theater, with warmly lit windows where a matrix of human dramas plays out in parallel: a couple dining by candlelight, an old man watching television, a schoolgirl practicing piano. Frozen in disbelief, Meadow's first instinct is to raise a hand to his face and press fingers against his cheek. It's all a sham. The words froth against the edges of his mind. And then: *You fall easily into this kind of story.* A world of flagrant falsehood envelops him while he stands dumbstruck, dissolving into the Manhattan twilight.

9

BOBBY GREW OUT HIS BLOND CURLS AND DYED HIS HAIR PINK
shortly before graduating from art school. Around the same time,
he got into the habit of affecting a Valley girl persona with his bubble gum and vocal fry, high-pitched laughter slicing through any
commotion, no matter how loud, so that Meadow could always
locate him at an outdoor festival or crowded bar. He was ever eager
to be Meadow's partner in crime, barreling through the weekends
with throat-burning shots of liquor, screeching karaoke sessions,
garish prints and booty shorts. Together they went to warehouse
parties in Gowanus and dance floors in Bushwick, took long, confusing cab rides to the homes of acquaintances in Midwood or
Dyker Heights, made friends with everyone waiting in the bathroom line or picnicking within a ten-meter radius of them.

Rebecca and Daniela finished their programs as well. Like
Bobby, they scrambled to figure out their next steps while complaining about classmates who were going on to fancy residencies
in Europe or mountainside ashrams for a spiritual realignment.
"This is my lot in life, I suppose," Bobby grumbled about his
part-time gig, "to just twirl among these fucking flowers all day."
In the years to come, he would eventually dabble in other realms
of employment as a courier, cashier, dogwalker, nude model,
museum guard.

With her student visa expiring and no company to sponsor her long-term stay, Daniela decided she would go back to Bogotá and regroup, reconnect with artist friends, maybe apply for some grants. Meadow heard from Peter that they were going to try a long-distance relationship, though he spoke of it with the same enthusiasm as one might describe dental surgery. He had finished architecture school barely a month ago and already landed a job with a firm near Union Square. The internal politics were a minefield, but he had to stick it out for the sake of his résumé while keeping his eyes peeled for the next opportunity.

Now, before every weekend rolled around, Peter would ask Meadow what was on the agenda. He didn't want to spend any time at home. He had other friends he saw on occasion, architecture school classmates who lived in the East Village or Chinatown, but mostly it was the Peter and Meadow show again, as it had been when they first met, with recurring guest stars Bobby and Rebecca. That summer they drifted from one bar backyard to another, polishing off whiskey sodas and cheeseburgers in between spritzes of insect repellent. They rustled up other friends to go to Brighton Beach or the Rockaways and spent long, lazy hours baking under the sun, treating themselves to beers and tacos when they got back to the neighborhood, or soft serve and iced coffee, stopping at home to change clothes and take power naps or smoke a spliff before whatever lay ahead for the evening.

What Meadow cherished most, though, were the quiet nights they spent at home, smoking a bowl to Charles Mingus or sipping aromatic sencha in the living room. It was a continuation of their grad school rituals in Washington Heights, when the two of them would convene at ungodly hours to complain about the week's readings and their work-study jobs while assessing each other's haggardness, then get stoned and giddy and watch weird videos from the internet, *Twin Peaks*, or some obscure movie that Meadow's classmate or professor had lent him.

Now, as working adults, the contours of their lives had become more solid—or they wanted to believe as much. That they could share this Brooklyn apartment, and listen to jazz and talk about life as a night breeze rustled the edges of a magazine on the coffee table, suggested to Meadow a maturity that seemed both tenuous and irrevocable. He still had so many lingering questions about how to exist in the world, who or what he could become. He was grateful that he never felt a need to put on pretenses with Peter. They could stew in comfortable silence with late-night takeout and good music, letting their bodies slacken and melt into the darkness and comfort of home. He'd heard so many horror stories from Bobby and others about nightmare roommates who made people's lives a living hell, withholding rent, leaving trash or dirty dishes everywhere, bringing all manner of shady business or people into the home. He and Peter simply never had those kinds of conflict. They had been on each other's wavelength from the beginning. How funny and strange, that the whims of others—in this case, their original connection via a mutual friend—could alter one's life like that. For the better, Meadow told himself. Always for the better.

HIS LIFE AND SELMA'S continued to intertwine as though by the warp and weft of a loom. One April she asked him to dinner at a Japanese restaurant in Murray Hill, of all places. She'd just returned from Los Angeles, where she was exhibiting at a gallery in Echo Park. She mentioned over text that there was something she wanted to talk to him about. Nothing serious, but it would be good to catch up in person, anyhow. So they picked a midweek evening for their dinner date.

Selma had shorn her hair just above the shoulders since the last time they'd hung out. It was a perfectly symmetrical frame for her face, which had a bit more color than usual from the California sun. She wore an onyx pendant on a gold chain and a bright green taffeta shirt, which gave her the appearance of a genteel lady from a Kurosawa film. As they ate, Selma told Meadow that she was moving. She had found an ideal spot in Clinton Hill that was considerably larger than her current home. It was closer to her studio anyway, and she thought it would be good to start fresh. Greenpoint was fine for the most part, but it skewed young for her tastes. "A bit homogeneous after a while, don't you think?" she offered.

"Hmm," Meadow said. "You might be right. Good for drinking and cavorting within a certain radius. But it gets old."

Selma admitted that part of her desire to move was that she and Fawaz had often spent time in Greenpoint, even though they'd lived in the West Village, and the neighborhood reminded her too much of her failed marriage. Street corners, restaurants, even grocery stores—when they'd separated initially, she thought the familiarity would be comforting. But now she realized she was all too eager to extricate herself from any reminder of this past life. A new home would be a brand-new canvas for her. She hoped Meadow might have some time to help her pack the following weekend. Yulia and Brigitte would also drop by, time allowing. Dinner would be on her, naturally. And she had quite a store of expensive booze that she didn't feel like hauling to a new apartment.

"Count me in," said Meadow. "Let me know what time."

The afternoon they spent packing up her apartment was so mundane and yet almost shockingly intimate. Selma looked more casual than he'd ever seen her before, in high-waisted black pants and a faded zebra-print shirt, her hair swept up in a bun. With Yulia, they stacked books and records into boxes and decided which clothes to keep or donate. When Meadow asked why Brigitte was absent, Selma casually said that they were feuding over an inconsequential matter, something to do with art supplies in a shared storage unit. Though her tone was light, he had the distinct impression that this wasn't a topic for further discussion. Even Yulia seemed to avert her gaze, humming to herself as she wrapped glassware in the kitchen. Selma had a tendency to divulge information in an offhand fashion like that, treating quotidian anecdotes and startling disclosures with equal nonchalance. To Meadow, news of her conflict with Brigitte was on par with finding out she had tattoos: her family crest, a circle with a stylized array of petals in water, on the small of her back, and something more intimate on her inner thigh, which she refused to talk about.

She'd shared other, more disquieting proclamations over time. That she suspected her father had been murdered during a trip to Kamakura, his hometown. The official cause of death was noted as a heart attack, but Selma insisted, without elaborating, that she had evidence that foul play was more likely. As a teenager in Boston, she'd almost been drawn into a local doomsday cult by a boyfriend. She seriously considered running away from home to join them in the prairies of Iowa. In the year and a half that they'd been friends, Meadow had discovered that Selma was fascinated by the fantastical and the occult. She didn't care much for Western astrology, but she was interested in esoteric East Asian cosmologies and the spirit worlds of antiquity. The nature of time and the fabric of reality were both porous and malleable, in her view. Though she didn't consider herself a performance artist, she was interested in the potentiality of viewing everyday objects, places, and even people around her as a conduit to artistic expression, if not the medium itself.

Most impressive and unsettling of all was how much of a shape-shifter she was. With a simple haircut or change of clothes, Selma could affect a whole new aura or personality. At times she embraced a demure mid-century femininity with long skirts and permed hair, bright red lips, pearl adornments. Then she might show up as an austere white-collar worker in a suit jacket and tie, a pencil skirt hugging her hips. For a few months, after she'd gone on a pilgrimage to Morocco, she cycled through a wardrobe of flowing robes, open-toed shoes, elaborate headpieces. Occasionally she reverted to another incarnation as a femme fatale, with short hair and severe makeup, black dresses and high heels, a gleaming black clutch.

During the more intimate intervals of their friendship, Meadow saw her at least once a week. They were so different on the surface. Selma was a woman of incredible poise, a wry and self-possessed jet-setter and chameleonic artist who cultivated serious, quasi-philosophical relationships with her closest friends. Meanwhile, though he was gainfully employed and getting by, all things considered, Meadow spent years simply treading water. He had no desire for upward mobility, and felt complacent enough about his social circle. Lacking the agency to define his own narrative, he drifted along at the mercy of his fickle emotions and fixations, strung along by the movies he saw or the books he read until he could indulge once more in the flickering shadow play that was romantic love. In this he was like Selma, he thought. They both thirsted for intimacy in all forms, which included a knowledge of the inner self and a finely tuned sensitivity to the world they inhabited.

Over the years, he would discover that sometimes Selma withdrew into herself without warning, veering away from him and all others like a rogue planet. There was usually the pretext of another activity or responsibility that demanded her time and concentration, an upcoming residency in New Hampshire or Paris, a research trip to Cambodia, a book project with an artist collective in Portugal. But then weeks would pass, the supposed engagement come and gone, and still she would not resurface. When he finally managed to wrench a reply from her or corner her into catching up, he would learn that the real reason for her hermitude was that she had switched medications again, discovered some unspeakable truth about a past lover, or overexerted herself in the months prior.

And then there were the times she reverted to a state close to catatonia, like at her thirtieth birthday party. It had taken her a minute to snap out of it, even after Meadow found her in the corner of the room. He eventually coaxed her into the bathroom and texted Yulia to come find them. Selma could barely speak, at first. When she was fully responsive again, all she could say was that she had been exhausted from organizing the event. She apologized for worrying them, but insisted she was fine. She drank a few cups of water and set out to greet her guests as if nothing at all had happened.

Meadow would come to realize that these ebbs and flows of her emotional tides were tied to the slipshod way in which she managed her mental health. She could be exacting and unpredictable in her demands or expectations—never of her friends, but of herself, her creative practice, and enterprises or institutions intended to facilitate her existence in this world. She oscillated between supreme confidence, or self-sufficiency, and scrabbling desperation for something to salve the pain in her life, of which she spoke little to anyone. Over time she cycled through a number of therapists and psychiatrists, trying out new medications until she would inevitably decide to unceremoniously rip up their prescriptions. Microdosing MDMA seemed to even her out for a while. But the unnameable sorrow always came back, roiling and tumbling and accumulating angry force, like waves crashing against the shoreline of her mind. She sought peyote in the Southwest, then went on a pilgrimage through the mountains of southern Japan. She found indigenous healers who promised her transformation, if not enlightenment, through sweat lodges and ayahuasca ceremonies.

But these were things that had not yet come to pass. Selma of this season, in this year, with her bobbed hair and zest for life, seemed almost mischievous in her eagerness to ditch her current living space and start anew. She was also, Meadow realized, never hurting for cash. He knew that she had received a sizable settlement from Fawaz, or that he had agreed to fund some of her ongoing endeavors, or perhaps both. She seemed to come from money, anyway, from the way she spoke of her childhood in Boston. Though her parents both had humble origins, her father became the head of a pharmaceutical company, while her mother had an import-export business that had to do with fine gems. It meant, in the end, that she could do what she wanted with her time, which was mostly dedicated to her craft, apart from teaching the occasional class and writing for art publications.

Though their friendship was still relatively new, Meadow felt it was somehow more solid and deeper, or at least different, than what he had with the other people in his life. In the months after he helped her pack up the Greenpoint apartment, he and Selma spent many late nights together, waxing romantic about the cruel and inexplicable whims of love, each of them somehow finding in the other the ideal interlocutor for understanding their own romantic foibles. She eventually divulged to him some of the affairs she'd quietly entered into since separating from Fawaz. Nils from Oslo, who'd been the DJ at her thirtieth birthday, was an old flame. She had hosted him in an attempt to rekindle things, but it had been an utterly exhausting effort that had in part contributed to her breakdown at the party. She'd also been deepening her relationship with Simon, the restaurateur from Long Island, but she knew already that it was a messy situation. He had a tumultuous relationship with his ex-wife, from whom he couldn't make a clean break, and there were two young daughters in the picture on top of that.

There were other dalliances, too, besides Nils and Simon, but Selma never mentioned too much about them apart from the barest sketch of an outline. A man I know wants to take me wine tasting next weekend, she'd say. My paramour says this is his favorite author, she'd mention breezily, thumbing a paperback at a bookstore. But I've never even heard of this writer. Have you, Meadow?

Walking with Selma in the Village, having oysters together at a bistro in East Williamsburg, grabbing her raincoat from a museum locker room—Meadow telescoped out of his body in these moments and understood suddenly why they always seemed to draw attention when they were out as a pair, old women offering Meadow breathy, misguided compliments about his wife's sense of style or the furtive appraisals he felt sweep over them on the subway. Meadow didn't flatter himself to think it was anything about him. It was Selma's presence by his side that attracted curious gazes from all around, whether they were at a rest stop in the middle of nowhere or a Midtown hotel bar. Her presence was magnetic, undeniable; she was an organism that kept evolving for the pure pleasure of transformation.

HE WAS NO STRANGER to love in his late twenties. He found some semblance of it, again and again, in the men he met at closing time in dive bars, chopping zucchini at a dinner party, smoking a cigarette outside a bookstore. Whether in a night or a year, the fantasy always fell apart and they would go their separate ways. One after another, Meadow fell in love with narcissists and social butterflies, party boys and poets, sloppy kissers, prodigal sons, ardent dreamers, broken men. Even the darkest, most spiteful creatures he came to know were reflections of him, he thought. They hurt him in the same way they loved him: by showing him what he already knew about himself. What he craved more than bodily satisfaction or fleeting adoration was that spark of new desire, an attraction so natural as to be nearly innocent. He was reborn over and over in the span of a drunken cab ride or a shared glance across a dinner table. He wanted simply to hold someone's hand, feel substantiated in their gaze, as if it would help recuperate a part of him that had long been lost. In return, he hoped to give back the same kind of love, soothe someone's aches, and make him feel whole again. Love was a conviction he carried so strongly sometimes that he even surprised himself.

Bobby would always remind him that men of their kind all had trauma, and that it simply manifested differently for each of them. "I think I'm pretty well-adjusted," Meadow insisted. "Aren't I?"

"You're like elastic drawstring pants," Bobby replied without missing a beat. "You slide on real easy and can accommodate lots of different shapes and sizes. And girth." He took a coy sip of his cocktail. It was springtime again, and they'd decided to check out a newly opened bar in East Williamsburg. The space used to house a fancy omakase restaurant, and there were vestiges of an open kitchen area that was now lined with several large fish tanks instead. It was relatively early for a Saturday night, so they were able to find a table against a wall beneath fluorescent hues of coral, undulating clumps of seaweed, and a swarm of banana fish.

"Elastic pants?" Meadow frowned. "That's not very flattering."

"Yeah, and let me finish. You fit so many different kinds of people that it's easy for you to lose your own shape. That's your tragic flaw. You have to decide who's best for you, who deserves to stick his feet down your holes."

"Umm . . ."

"Are you gonna be a loose fit on someone lanky and lean, or do you want to be snug up against thunder thighs? Emotionally, that is."

Meadow thought about this, eyes darting back and forth. "I have no idea how to answer that."

"Exactly. Now do me."

"Like, what do you resemble spiritually?"

"Mm-hm."

Meadow drained the rest of his gin drink. "Easy," he said. "You're a tropical fish, like the ones in these tanks." He gestured at the watery scene right by their table. "Lovely to look at, but a bitch to maintain."

Bobby cackled. "Girl, you really know me, don't you."

"You need a beautiful environment to swim in. You might kill and eat someone if they're not your type."

Bobby raised his glass for a toast, seemingly pleased with this answer. Though he wore a carefree smile as always, there was a wince of something more brittle beneath. He'd shaved the pink curls he'd been sporting and seemed to have lost weight. When Meadow prodded him about it, he simply shrugged it off. He'd decided to cast aside his older benefactors, he said by way of explanation, referring to the financiers and lawyers who'd been keeping him sexually satisfied and, more importantly, fiscally afloat—men who lived in Tribeca or on Park Avenue, had families on the Upper West Side, sometimes Jersey. Too messy, too much effort to schedule. He'd also been fired from the flower shop after getting into an explosive confrontation with Sarita, the owner. In order to make money, he was working double duty as a bike messenger and weed delivery guy these days.

"Are you painting?" Meadow asked later, after they replenished their drinks.

Bobby made a face. "Not so much. Honestly, I'm pretty exhausted by the time I get home most days. Usually just smoke a blunt and pass out."

Bobby looked older with his head buzzed like this. It brought out his jawline somehow, which in turn was offset by the curve of his lips and that affectionate, if world-weary, gaze. Sometimes when it was just the two of them, Meadow would find himself fantasizing for a spell. It usually only happened when they got drunk enough. But what if, just what if, the two of them were to give it a go—as more than friends? Had this been the answer all along? That a man he could love had been right under his nose for years, and they'd simply overlooked each other in the name of friendship? These confusing thoughts would cross his mind late at night when they leaned against each other in a bathroom line, or when they were sweating and twirling on dance floors. There were also those early mornings when they stumbled together to the train, saying goodbye at the top of the stairs, and he could envision angling his head to plant a kiss on Bobby's mouth.

Would it be the end of things, or a new beginning?

He always felt a bit foolish the next day, in the white light of sobriety. But lately Meadow had come to embrace the idea that it wasn't necessarily wrong to entertain this kind of attraction. Surely there was a purity to it, too. You were supposed to see the good in each other, in friendship, love someone in spite of their shortcomings, support them to become the best version of themselves they could be. Wasn't the fantasy about taking things further simply a natural extension of that? Not only acknowledging the present value of this person in your life but also seeing them even more fully—recognizing their potential as a lover and long-term romantic companion.

Objectively, he knew that Bobby and he would probably be disastrous as lovers. Best to leave it be. He let the thought circle around his head like an errant insect, then flit away with the breeze. Meanwhile, Bobby was asking him how Peter was doing since his long-distance relationship with Daniela had fizzled.

"He seems better now," Meadow replied. "He was really sad about it for a while, but I think the warm weather is helping."

"Spring fever," Bobby said. "What's his type? Does he go for older women? Bet there are some cougars that would love to get their paws all up on his tight bod." He bared his teeth with a wolfish smile.

"I've never been able to figure out his type, honestly," Meadow said. "But anyway, he says he doesn't want to date for a while."

"Perfect. Let's just dress him up and take him to Sotheby's to find a wealthy dowager."

The bar stayed at low buzz all night without frothing over. Most of the people who drifted in seemed surprised by the decor, which was decidedly a bit chichi for the neighborhood. The frenetic jazz music made the ambience seem livelier than it otherwise would have. Soon it was after midnight and they were plastered and garrulous, Bobby insisting on the evidence for the unconsummated lesbian tension he saw between Yulia and Selma.

"She's gay as fuck," he was saying of Yulia. "Don't let that prim femininity pull the wool over your eyes."

Meadow dissolved into a fit of laughter. "What about Selma, then?"

"She's the dom top in that relationship," Bobby said. "In any relationship. I can tell. You better watch out."

"Me?!" he yelped indignantly.

"She wants something from you," Bobby continued. "It's just a hunch."

Meadow snorted. "Like, my friendship or my immortal soul?"

"Selma Shimizu is grooming you," Bobby declared, gulping down the last of his vodka. "For what, I can't say. But you better watch your booty, boy."

Meadow rolled his eyes and stood up. "Can I get you another round? Vodka soda?"

"Yes, sir." Bobby snapped his hand to his forehead, offering Meadow a salute and a wink.

HE QUIT his office job shortly after turning twenty-nine. He'd lasted a respectable five years, and this was enough, in the end. Thanks to Selma's introduction, he was connected to Royce, an acquaintance of Simon's who was preparing to open a new bar in Crown Heights. That Meadow had no service industry experience to speak of, apart from a brief stint working at the mall in high school, was not an impediment to his being hired. Don't sweat it, kid, Royce told him when they met for a drink at a Senegalese restaurant in the neighborhood. My girl Monique is gonna set you up just fine. She'll give it to me straight if you can't cut it, too.

Working at the bar was amazingly exhausting and thoroughly edifying after years of email diplomacy, espresso machine banter, and bureaucratic vagaries. Ironically Meadow felt that he was doing much more good for the world slinging drinks than he had completing expense reports or coordinating committee meetings with professors who could barely conceal their rage toward the institution to which they were beholden for salary and reputation. The election that year was a shock and a somber reminder that humans were liable to align with the bombastic and the cruel, and Meadow wanted to believe that self-care was its own form of protest. That seeking relief, if not happiness, for himself was a worthy cause. He'd been mechanically going through the motions of his office job for a long, long time. This lackluster spirit was somehow mirrored in the man he had been with since the summer, a sociopath with a penchant for blow who alternately fawned over Meadow or treated him with indifference. He left both the job and the man in the same week, easy breezy, light as a feather.

In the next year, Peter moved in with his new girlfriend, Annika, and Meadow ended up in a sublet in Bed-Stuy, closer to Barley. Selma was gone for long stretches of time in Japan and elsewhere, vaguely alluding to family troubles connected to an inheritance. Meadow got in most of his socializing through bartending, whether gossiping with Monique about their respective love lives or lending a sympathetic ear to any patrons who wanted somebody to talk to. Bobby broke the news to him that spring that he was moving west. Rebecca had been living in Portland for a few years, working at an arts nonprofit, and her roommate was about to leave town. The rent for this room was ridiculously affordable compared to what Bobby was paying for his Bushwick hovel, and he already had an interview for a part-time job at the city's rose garden.

Meadow was happy for him, but he couldn't help but wince at the palpable contraction of his world yet again. It was nobody's fault but his own. He had cultivated a streak of solitude, after all. In spite of all the messy, dead-end relationships he wound up cornered in, he had never bothered to try harder to make more friends, complacent or just comfortable with the people who'd fallen into his life. Bobby told him he would stay long enough to celebrate one last birthday in April, then fly off to Oregon for a fresh start to his thirties. For Bobby's last weekend in New York, Meadow organized a dinner in Sunset Park at a newish Chinese restaurant that offered private suites where one could enjoy both hot pot and karaoke. There were ten or so of them, including Bobby's art school classmates, former coworkers from the flower shop, random girls he'd recently befriended at a club. They plowed through bucketfuls of beer and a few bottles of whiskey while belting out soulful renditions of Elton John, Sinéad O'Connor, and Teresa Teng, occasionally returning to the dinner table to pick at the remnants of the hot pot, dropping in more bundles of chrysanthemum greens or scouring the shimmering red broth for another fish ball or sliver of lamb.

Around one, the night was winding down and the restaurant clearly wanted them to get the hell out. Meadow was also ready to go home and sleep, his belly full of Sapporo and Dewar's, noodles and shiitake mushrooms and thinly sliced beef. Just as he had calculated the bill for the party and sent off a stack of credit cards with the waitstaff, Bobby came over and clasped his hand conspiratorially. "You can't say no, bitch," he whispered. "It's my birthday." When he withdrew his hand, there was a pill in Meadow's palm.

He couldn't say no, and he didn't. After most of the group went home, Bobby took charge and ordered a car for him, Meadow, and two girlfriends to go dancing. On the ride to wherever it was they were going, Meadow felt that familiar rush of euphoria course through his body.

"Oh, shit," he said with a laugh. "I haven't done this in years."

"Just relax, babe," Bobby said, patting his hand. His fingertips felt velvety and so deliciously warm. "We're going to have a great time."

Meadow couldn't recall how they got in or what the place looked like, whether it was a bar or club or some other venue. The next thing he knew, they were on a dance floor with colorful lights strobing all over. The music was pure, pumped-up '70s, Sister Sledge, the Bee Gees, wailing and beautiful. So earnest, Meadow thought as he spun around the room, feeling hot all over. So emotional.

The molly peaked at the perfect moment. There was a long intro into some kind of remix, a succession of beats and indecipherable melodies that seemed to go on forever as they danced in the dark to flickers of scarlet and purple. Then, finally, the DJ loosed Al Green's voice onto the dance floor crowded with bodies, and Meadow felt a surge of something close to pure joy in his heart. The lights flashed diamond white, a crispness thrumming with radiant color. Bobby was beside him, performing acrobatic moves, kicking a leg up, casting a sharp elbow to the right. Meadow realized that he'd been spinning in circles for a while now, or maybe others were spinning around him. He felt a prism of colors flood his brain as he looked at Bobby and thought about the years they'd known each other, their lives running parallel, twining and diverging, forming braids and complicated knots and yet separating, in the end. There was so much love surrounding him, he realized. It had been there all along, and he was foolish to constantly seek it elsewhere. The love that already existed was enough to sustain him, to nourish him. And he needed to look no further than the pulsing warmth of his own heartbeat to find all he could ever want.

They danced on and on until the hours melted away, as they so often had when Meadow was with Bobby, but instead of coagulating into darkness, time sublimated into an easy, effortless vapor that filled the room and infiltrated their pores, imbuing them with a weightlessness that continued for hours thereafter. Bobby's girlfriends had taken off at some point, and now it was so late, or early, six in the morning somehow, and they were among the few people still dancing when the lights came on and they fell into each other and all they could do was laugh and laugh and then kiss.

A haggard-looking man was cleaning up behind the bar, and he was kind enough to pour them two big plastic cups of water. When they tumbled out of the venue, Meadow didn't recognize where they were. Bobby was shivering, and instinctively Meadow put an arm around him. They both checked their phones and realized they were completely out of battery. Meadow began to ask, "Should we go to the su—" when Bobby kissed him again, for longer this time, a warm, full kiss that tasted pink and white like the morning sky that was lightening around the warehouses on the street.

It was such a simple, stupid, satisfying kiss. He didn't even want to think any harder about it, but now that the molly was wearing off, Meadow couldn't help but open one eye while they were still kissing as he became aware of what was happening. Bobby also opened his eyes and pulled away. A look came over his face. Meadow felt his insides tense up, but just then Bobby yelled, "Taxi!"

A yellow cab rolled to a stop right in front of them, the driver turning out to be a relaxed, heavyset man who sounded like he'd been making his rounds of Brooklyn clubgoers all night. Bobby offered his address and took Meadow's hand in his for the second time in one night. They didn't speak the whole ride, each of them watching the colors of dawn from their respective windows, their hands clasped in the middle of the car seat while the driver listened to Spanish radio and occasionally whistled a few bars to a familiar advertisement.

They didn't speak either when they entered Bobby's apartment in the pale morning, slipping past the closed bedroom door of his unsavory roommate with stifled giggles. Only when they had both sat down on his bed did Bobby turn to Meadow with a serious look and suggest that they take showers. He dug out a clean towel from the bottom of a pile of clothes and handed it to Meadow. For the life of him, Meadow would not be able to recall later on what he thought about in the shower, if he thought anything at all, or while he was waiting for Bobby to finish up. It seemed like one minute he was lying down alone, naked beneath the covers that smelled very much of Bobby, and then the next thing he knew Bobby was back in the room and on top of him, repeating that same, simple kiss, over and over, not only on his lips but also along his collarbone and down his stomach, on the tip of his penis, against his thigh, and then back up to his mouth, this time with a warm, sweet lash of tongue that quivered tensely with the compact energy of the last twelve hours.

Meadow spiraled out of his body and only returned to himself in the midst of the act. The first thing that came to mind, strangely enough, was a phrase from classical Chinese he'd learned about in grad school, a euphemism of carnal love as "a matter of cloud and rain." He couldn't understand at the time how sex could be abstracted as such, so poetic and pristine and seemingly detached from the messy reality of human desire. But now, he thought, as he and Bobby found their way together in this early morning in Bushwick, it made perfect sense, the unpredictable quality of a rainstorm and the range of intensity or emotion it could express so perfectly apt to describe the union of two humans at the mercy of elemental forces themselves, some easier to name than others.

And perhaps he had loved Bobby from the beginning, that very first night in January when they drank and smoked cigarettes together and talked openly about where they'd come from and where they wanted to go. He had played such a special role in Meadow's life all these years, his presence singular and irreplaceable. Yet there was a terrifying moment, too, when Meadow was inside him, their mouths pressed against each other as a sunbeam pierced through the cloud cover at last and warmed their shoulders, that he was so close, so, so close to Bobby, that he couldn't tell it was him anymore. He chalked it up later to being at the tail end of a long and sleepless night, but a pang of wonder struck him while they were making love and he realized that, in some ways, it felt no different than with anyone else, that Bobby was no different, that maybe he had always been chasing after the same man and found him, again and again, in different forms, that he ached for the same sparkling insouciance and secret tenderness, the same easy smile to soothe him and give him relief after all these years of searching and searching.

It was a faltering April sun that shone on them that morning, crisp as a fresh sheet of paper, then quickly cloaked again by wisps of cloud. A gentle rain began to fall while light streaked down from the heavens and Bobby pressed his weight on top of Meadow, clasping both of his hands, then leaning forward until they were cheek to cheek, his face to the pillow as Meadow stared up at the ceiling, locked in place but perfectly comfortable. They stayed that way for a long time, Bobby rocking gently to bring him closer and deeper inside that delirious warmth, that universe where the two of them were joined. He began to drowse from the past twenty-four hours of wakefulness, occasionally roused by a languid, sweet kiss or a sudden sensation of falling, his whole body tensing with fear and confusion, to which Bobby simply stroked his hair and whispered, It's okay, it's okay. We don't have to finish, he said with a yawn, his breath hot against Meadow's neck. It's better this way, he was mumbling. It's better if we never let each other finish at all.

10

WHEN ORCHID COMES BACK TO THE MAHJONG TABLE WITH
the Phantasm cocktails on a tray, she whispers a single line into
Mizuno's ear. The melody, and the fleeting moments they shared
in different seasons, flood his mind in an instant. He danced
with her several times at the Paramount, that favored establishment of Chinese magnates like Du Kuo-wen and the foreigners
they did business with. The first time had been almost a year ago,
on the occasion of a film release that Du had been involved in
financing. The lead actress of the film, who was also a singer, performed a full set of songs that night while couples paired up and
spun around the floor with their hands clasped together. Mizuno
had been watching from the sidelines for most of the evening
until one of Du's cronies clapped him on the back and declared
that he seemed lonely. *Some dance tickets for you!* he shouted. *Go
enjoy a round with one of these fine women.* In the end, Mizuno
danced for three songs with the same young woman, who had
the most bewitching eyes, a whiff of powder and persimmon on
her body. Whenever he heard those songs thereafter, he thought
of the romance of that early summer evening.

He saw her for a second time at the Paramount in the winter. The fighting had died down by then, a grudging acceptance
of the status quo having settled over the city. A number of

dignitaries had traveled from Manchukuo to bolster the newly formed country's ties with the city of Shanghai. Manchukuo was a utopian paradise where Japanese lived in harmony alongside Chinese, with sizable populations of Koreans, Mongols, and even Russians. All of them were united under Puyi himself, the last emperor of China, now the ruler of this new pan-Asian kingdom that would lead them toward a glorious future. Mizuno had always been curious about Manchukuo—there had been more than one opportunity for him to travel north and see it for himself, the wide boulevards of Shinkyo, the cathedrals of Harbin. But travel had proven treacherous over the years. Now Manchukuo had come to him in the form of cigar-puffing bureaucrats and enchanting young women of uncertain provenance. He was in the midst of talking to a female novelist, a Manchu herself of some pedigree who smoked Three Castles cigarettes in rapid succession, when a lace-gloved hand appeared on his shoulder. "Pardon me for interrupting," said the woman with a permanent wave and a face as radiant as the December moon. "But you are Mizuno-san, are you not?"

She swiftly and easily threaded her way into his endearment once more that night, this taxi dancer named Yueh-Lan—Moon Orchid. He had known many Chinese women during his time in Shanghai, but none commanded English, and even rudimentary Japanese, with the same ease, could dance the foxtrot and recite Tang poetry in the same breath like her. This time he learned that she was from Soochow, fabled for its Elysian gardens and cultural refinement. She'd come to Shanghai to study literature originally. They did not speak of why she now worked at the Paramount, a taxi dancer of local renown, as it were. Mizuno imbibed countless gin sours with Yueh-Lan that night until he couldn't tell his head from his toes. They talked about his work, his loneliness, his parents back in Yokohama.

The adventure he'd sought originally in coming to China, the tremendous amount of unspent energy that had pooled in him over the years from the humdrum rhythms of his daily existence. The next thing Mizuno knew, he was being dragged away from the dance hall and ferried off in a private car by a colleague. Much to his surprise, no one even reprimanded him over his careless comportment.

Now he has found Orchid again. Or rather, she has found him amid the revelers and raucous energy of Du Kuo-wen's party. Before the mahjong game begins, Spiegel, the man in the beaked mask, declares that they ought to gamble not with money, but something more interesting. "Whatever do you mean, my dear?" asks Dahlia Derby. "Isn't money the most fascinating thing in the world?"

Luna, the Italian, taps impatiently on the table as a rakish grin spreads on his face. "I would bet a good meal," he offers, "or perhaps a beautiful woman."

"Money is fleeting," says Spiegel, "but knowledge is not. I propose that the losers of this round offer the winner a piece of information."

"How dreadfully boring," Dahlia says with a dramatic shudder.

Spiegel leans in. Even without being able to see his face, Mizuno can sense a satisfied gaze from behind the mask. "Information about someone else at this party," Spiegel clarifies, "that could be exchanged for value."

"Fine, fine," Dahlia says. "I've spent enough time on Avenue Joffre to come up with a piece of juicy gossip for you. And I thought Luna here was the journalist," she mutters, glancing around the tabletop. "So are we agreed then? Mister Mizuno?"

Mizuno clears his throat. "I have no objection," he says, even as he begins to wonder what kind of light gossip he could come up with.

"Excellent," Dahlia says. "Now where are those dice?"

The game proceeds in swift order. Mizuno keeps glancing furtively at Orchid and Peony as they talk in hushed tones in the center of the room, occasionally looking over at the partygoers in their charge. Dressed as they are in identical garb, it is nearly impossible to tell them apart. Mizuno has the strange impression that he is looking at one person split into two, a reflection in a trick mirror or a woman's internal equivocation represented by some cinematographic technique. Behind them, the portrait of Du Kuo-wen gazes imperiously at the games unfolding in the room. The gramophone continues to play popular songs by golden-voiced Chinese divas whose sentimental yearnings quiver in the parlor space. When the round of mahjong at the other table ends, Peony—or so Mizuno presumes—returns to her group and ensures everyone is satisfied with their result. The winner is a portly, bespectacled Chinese man called Fatty Jin, who chortles happily as he consoles his fellow players. Peony sees them all out of the room and follows after, ostensibly to find guests to participate in the next round.

The pace of Mizuno's game slows, despite an early rash of moves by Dahlia Derby. She manages to form two pongs within the first few turns, proudly displaying the three-of-a-kind melds before her tiles. "Four of circles, now four of sticks," Spiegel says, leaning over to look at Dahlia's sets. "Ominous numbers indeed."

"I don't believe in that Chinese claptrap about four representing death," retorts Dahlia. "Four is my lucky number. Anyhow, the word *four* in English sounds nothing like *death* and more like . . . *fortune*!"

"Four for *forza*," adds Luna.

Luna eventually melds a set of his own with a discarded tile from Spiegel. But then, for many rounds, no one seems to progress. Mizuno makes a few lucky draws and completes several melds without having to show his tiles. Dahlia Derby moans theatrically when someone casts a wind tile she needed several turns ago. As play continues, Orchid flits around the table, adding teasing commentary and checking on their drinks. Without realizing it, Mizuno drains several more cocktails. By the time he draws the tile that he needs to win the game, his face is flushed and his head awhirl. He turns his row of tiles face up. "I have won," he says, somewhat uncertainly.

"I got off to such a good start, too," complains Dahlia as she and the other players reveal their hands. She launches into an intricate speech about the wrong moves she made that led her to lose this round, then heaves a sigh and stands up brusquely. "Well, at least I saved my pocketbook since it was information that we wagered. But it won't do to give Mizuno-san our precious bits of wisdom and whatnot in front of everyone." She grabs Mizuno by the wrist with a surprisingly strong grip, pulling him to his feet. "Let's talk in private, darling. Orchid, you see to it that these men hold their end of the bargain, as well."

The floor beneath his feet seems to undulate as Mizuno lets himself be led by Dahlia out of the room, Luna snickering behind them. In the darkened corridor, Dahlia glances from side to side, then decides to maneuver them toward a door on the right. They enter a quiet bathroom like all of the other ones in the Du household, fragrant and elegantly appointed, a vision of modernity in marble and brass. Dahlia flicks on a light switch, closes the door behind them, and presses a finger to her lips.

"Mizuno-san," she says in a much softer and more serious voice than he expected. "I'm glad it was you who won the game. If there's one piece of information that I know to be of any value, it's this: that German man, Spiegel or whatever he calls himself, is not to be trusted." She gazes at him meaningfully from behind her blue mask. "Do you understand what I mean?"

"Trusted?" Mizuno hiccups, leaning his back against the wall. "But I don't even know who he is."

"Good," Dahlia says. "You had better keep it that way." She opens the bathroom door and steps over the threshold. "Stay right here," she says, turning back to look at him. "I'm sure the others will visit shortly." She closes the door without a sound. Mizuno looks at his reflection in the mirror, his eyes blinking behind the white mask. He hears music and commotion downstairs, the sound of feet shuffling from another room, but he has the strange perception that the sounds are coming from the realm on the other side of the mirror.

Before Mizuno can further consider this illusion, the door opens and a head of curly hair pokes in. "*Scusi,*" says Luna, slipping inside and shutting the door again. "I was told it is my turn." He crosses his arms and smiles widely as he looks at Mizuno askance. "Bravo, Signor Mizuno. You are an impressive man. A newspaper editor, yes?"

Mizuno nods. "That is correct."

"Then I have the most useful piece of information to share," he declares, lowering his voice. "It concerns Signorina Orchid. She is close with Signor Du, so they say, and aspires to become an actress through his patronage. All this is widely known. But what I can tell you from my own observation is that she and the woman called Peony have grander designs on Du." Luna's voice is almost a hiss as he continues, "As you may know, Du is something of a philanderer, but he acts with great caution—or so he thinks. I have heard of a scandal brewing that may soon come to light. Pay close enough attention, and perhaps you will have your next story." He offers a curt bow. "*Arrivederci,*" he says before Mizuno can open his mouth, leaving the room as stealthily as he came in.

Orchid and Peony, conspirators. Spiegel, not to be trusted. What could it possibly all mean? Mizuno feels the coldness of the Phantasm cocktail oozing in his veins, sharpening and loosening him at once. A series of three raps on the door. Mizuno clears his throat. "Come in?" he says weakly. The bathroom door opens again to reveal the heavyset German man in his beaked mask.

"At last, my turn," Spiegel says, entering the room in plodding steps. "I hope I did not keep you waiting too long." Despite his relatively small stature, his silhouette in the doorway looms menacingly. Mizuno unconsciously recoils. Spiegel closes the door. "We have already had occasion to speak earlier tonight, Mister Mizuno. I believe it was symbols of which we spoke, was it not?"

Mizuno is frozen by the eerie sight of the beaked mask in such an enclosed space. He tries to speak but simply nods instead.

"Symbols have power. Names have power. This, I have shared with you already. Mister Mizuno, I do not mean to be presumptuous, but I take it you are not a speaker of German. Am I correct?"

Mizuno's voice catches in his throat again. "Yes," he manages to wheeze.

"Of course," Spiegel says. "You would have no way of knowing, then, the literal meaning of my surname. The name Spiegel, in fact, means 'mirror.' Fitting that we stand here now, together in front of a mirror." He gestures at their reflection, where a man in a tuxedo jacket and white mask, a red rose pinned to his pocket, grimaces at a beaked mask. "But the real piece of information I have to offer you is this: the Du estate is a place of ill repute. Perhaps you are not privy to all the rumors, but they say that Du's staff are sworn to secrecy about what unfolds here. For Du himself has not obtained his wealth through natural means."

"Natural . . . means?"

"Beware of your surroundings, Mister Mizuno. People here are not always who or what they seem. We think of mirrors simply as objects that cast our reflection back at us. But they can also be doorways, or instruments of deceit. The Chinese have a saying about the illusory nature of a flower that one gazes upon in the mirror. It is both flower and not-flower, just as the water's reflection of the moon is no moon at all. This is my final word of warning to you. I trust you will heed my advice."

THE LAST TIME Meadow had seen Diego was already over a month ago, in early June. He'd gotten off work at Barley around eight and gone over to Diego's apartment on Friday night, where they ordered Chinese food for dinner and watched a horror movie. When Meadow noticed that Diego had drifted off next to him, he gingerly lifted the glasses from his face and set them on the nightstand. He took off his shirt as gently as he could, closed the laptop, and slid it to the floor. They would still have to get up and brush their teeth and wash their faces in due time. But for the moment, he was content to lie by Diego's side.

He blinked in the dim light and looked at his surroundings. The first time he'd come over to Diego's studio apartment, he'd been too drunk to really notice how sparsely decorated it was. It struck him as minimalist, rather than bare, a deliberate design choice perhaps. Over subsequent visits, he realized that the lack of belongings was due to the haphazard circumstances of Diego's move. It had been a last-minute decision, Diego had told him, almost an impulse. He'd transplanted himself from LA with little more than a suitcase, found this tiny apartment thanks to a friend of his sister's, and gotten all the furniture for free by trawling Craigslist. On the one hand, the look of this home environment was familiar to Meadow, who'd just off-loaded or stored most of his own personal effects and moved from his subleased room to Selma's. Maybe it was Selma's apartment that made him feel vicariously superior in a way—as though the dignity of space, all those plants and tchotchkes, a full set of dishware and then some, suggested he was a full-fledged adult. But something about the austere nature of Diego's apartment bothered him, like he was looking at an inadequately designed set on a theater stage. There was almost nothing in the room that gave a clue as to who its inhabitant was. The fridge had a few utilitarian magnets that held takeout menus and a dry cleaner's business card in place. The walls were still completely bare. Besides the handful of secondhand paperbacks Diego had acquired from the Strand, the shelves served primarily as a place where he stashed his keys and wallet next to a bottle of cologne. Meadow told himself that none of this was objectionable, really, and he was just projecting his own insecurity and sense of rootlessness. He nudged Diego and whispered that they should wash up. It was getting late already.

When they awoke on Saturday, it was close to noon. They decided to go out for breakfast and coffee. It was a sun-soaked day in New York, right on the cusp of summertime. After eating their sandwiches of eggs, ham, and homemade hot sauce on a bench outside a deli, they clutched their paper cups of hot black coffee and meandered casually away from Boerum Hill. They peeked into stores on Atlantic Avenue, smiled at excitable dogs or gurgling infants in strollers. Eventually they found themselves at Brooklyn Bridge Park, wading through a bevy of tourists to claim a sunny spot on the lawn.

"Ah, too bad we didn't bring a blanket," Diego said once they sat down.

"Would've been nice!" sighed Meadow. "With a little picnic basket, an olive and cheese plate, a bottle of Lambrusco. I could be feeding you grapes right now."

Tugboats and ferries intermittently crossed their view of the East River and sent waves of blue and white rippling over the water. On the other side of the bridge, the towers of Lower Manhattan sparkled beneath the sun, the same buildings that they'd gazed upon on their first date just weeks earlier. The grassy lawn around them was dotted with couples and families. An older man in khaki shorts flew a kite shaped like a magnificent butterfly in neon pink and orange. A white Frisbee whirled back and forth between two middle-school-age kids in baseball caps. Meadow yawned, stretched his arms to the sky, and lay down on the grass by Diego's side. The momentary doubts that sometimes crept up on him were easy to allay when they were together like this, enjoying the ease of each other's company. What was blossoming between them was so simple and beautiful, he thought. It had been ages since it had felt this effortless to date someone.

And yet he could not deny there was a dull ache in his heart, acknowledging the gulf of unknowns that still separated them. They'd been in each other's lives for mere weeks. Meadow wanted to believe that love could be easy, that he could find a suitable man among the millions of souls in New York, someone who understood his inclinations and matched his temperament, who was willing to give and take in equal measure. But, he reminded himself, this was not the first time he'd felt this giddy about a new dalliance. In the past he'd been proven wrong, the perfect grace of the early stages of romance devolving into something more real and complicated, even sordid, with the passage of time. Perhaps that might happen with Diego, too.

Diego lay down next to him. They contented themselves against the scratchy grass, Diego's arm slung over Meadow's chest and nose nuzzled into his neck. Meadow grew sleepy, in spite of the coffee. He began to doze intermittently, a fantasy surfacing in his mind of the two of them years later, traveling in a distant land: an old European town by the sea, the town square with its ancient church, a rocky shoreline. They wade into the bracing cold water, skin still hot from the sun, hair drenched and mouths full of salt.

When Meadow awoke, he couldn't recall where he was. The sun shone directly into his eyes. A lone bird circled in the boundless blue. Murmurs and city noise surrounded him. By his side, he saw the profile of a handsome youth who was gazing out at the water. Meadow sat up. "Shit, what time is it?"

Diego looked over. He glanced down at his watch. "Getting close to three."

"Ah, I should head home and change. Gotta work the late shift today."

"Okay. Let's get a move on." Diego leaned in and brushed a few stray blades of grass off Meadow's head. "There you go. Now you're all ready."

They made their way out of the park and stood silently at a crosswalk, waiting for the light to change. "Hey," Meadow said at the same time that Diego began to speak. They both laughed. "You first," said Meadow.

"I was going to ask if you wanted to do something tomorrow," Diego said.

"Oh," Meadow replied, trying to sound nonchalant. The light turned green and they stepped out into the street in unison. "I think I could spare some time for that. Something in the afternoon? Mornings are usually a no-go for me when I work till close."

"I've been interested in the aquarium, actually."

"Down at Coney Island?"

"Yeah! Did I tell you about the dream I had last night?"

He'd been in a forest surrounded by fish, he said, that flew and flitted through the open air like butterflies. Their colors were so vibrant, flashing gold and green in the sunlight that streamed through the treetops above. Seahorses floated idly by and rested on drooping fronds, while schools of silver minnows circled the bases of ancient trees. He made his way to a clearing, where motes of pollen danced and swirled on an unseen current, entering through his nose and burrowing deeper until his lungs were tickling. The pollen was faintly sweet, and it was making him sleepy, he realized, but by then it was too late. When he opened his eyes again, he was in bed next to Meadow.

"That's pretty vivid." Meadow laughed. "I would have thought that it's more of a botanical garden dream, though?"

"Psh, been there, done that. Let's see some fishies and hit up the beach. How's two o'clock tomorrow for you?"

"Perfect," Meadow said. "We can have a late lunch at a Russian place down there." A short walk later, they approached the intersection on Atlantic Avenue where they would part ways.

Diego leaned in for a kiss—tenderly warm, sweet and soft. "See you soon, babe." He waved and turned to head toward his apartment.

MEADOW LOOKS UP the Embarcadero Theater when he gets back to Selma's apartment, the night of his run-in with the man who could have been his double. There are few relevant search results. When he does find the website, it's simply a placeholder with no real information on it, only a black background and the theater's name and address. He decides that he'll have to investigate further in person. Time and again, he looks at the photo he took of the poster with Diego, or the man who looks just like him. *Matthew Morales.* That he only made this discovery by tailing his own doppelgänger sets his brain ablaze with confusion.

It has to be him, the facial features a perfect match, down to the curve of the lips. Meadow feels tremendously certain of this.

But why would he lie about his name? In the time that they spent together, Diego mentioned nothing about being involved in theater. Was "Diego" just a character or some sick joke? Meadow shuts his laptop and sets it on the coffee table with a shriek of exasperation. He grudgingly decides to return to *The Masquerade*, scouring it for clues. But he stops reading after just half an hour or so. The mahjong game that Mizuno enters is claustrophobic to begin with, and made that much worse by the series of bizarre conversations that follow. *Mirrors can also be doorways, or instruments of deceit.* Meadow thinks back to the dream he had about the mirror in Selma's room. A sudden misgiving overwhelms him. How could Selma have engineered an experience like that? And the book itself is so dense with information, the specificity of a liminal world from the last century that would be nigh impossible for her to produce. She could have hired someone to write *The Masquerade*, he supposes. But to what end? What message could this possibly be intended to convey? There's too much weirdness going on, with his insurmountable insomnia, Selma gone to God knows where, and the clacking tension of *The Masquerade* marching onward. The doorway of the mirror he was pulled through, the vision of his own double on the streets of Manhattan leading him to Diego's double—

He snaps to attention and shakes his head. Enough of this bullshit, he thinks as he makes his way over to Selma's liquor cabinet. A stiff drink is what I need. Something to burn away all this anxious energy. He is pleased to discover almost a full bottle of Four Roses on the top shelf. Taking out a glass and filling it with ice, he gives himself a healthy pour and listens to the tiny whispers of the liquor settling over the ice.

"Fuck me," he sighs after a gulp.

He cycles through a few records while drinking bourbon, feeling the golden-brown liquid simultaneously warming his body and dulling it into a soft, smooth mass. Every so often he gulps down a glass of water to even things out, but he can still taste the sweet bloom of bourbon on his breath. He'll go back to the theater tomorrow, he decides. He'll buy a ticket to attend a performance and then intercept Diego, or Matthew, afterward. The idea is nauseating and exhilarating, at once. He can't even imagine what he would say to this man, what he could demand from him. But neither can he simply let go of this bizarre turn of events. Diego must be an invented persona. A character. But for the sake of whom, and to what end?

Meadow is mildly satisfied to have a concrete goal in mind. The next order of business is to get to sleep early enough so he can make it into Manhattan at a reasonable hour. Since his shift at Barley begins at four, this means he ought to return to the Embarcadero by early afternoon to be safe—a time these days when he is usually deep in slumber. An absurd idea comes over him, one that he can't help but laugh bitterly about. He can drink himself to sleep. It won't be the most restful evening, but it will guarantee a few hours of nothingness, at the very least. And nothingness is what he needs right now, no heartbreak or confusion, no fear or frustration. He wants to be swallowed into a dark, dumb void, a primordial soup of nothing.

He pours himself another glass of water, drinks it quickly, then sets a few cubes of ice in the glass and tops it off with Four Roses. By midnight, he's practically swimming in gleeful abandon, lying on his back on the couch with toes splayed toward the ceiling while listening to Björk's ethereal wailing. Ten years in New York, he keeps repeating in his head. It's been almost ten years. Could he have imagined when he first arrived that this was how things would turn out? Drinking alone in the home of a woman who has disappeared, living with her ghosts and her masks, while his own ghosts come back to haunt him.

Without realizing it, Meadow begins to doze off intermittently. Ten minutes here, fifteen minutes there turn into longer stretches of half an hour or more. Each time he dips below the surface of his consciousness, he finds that the waters beneath are so turbid as to be completely opaque. It is a realm that light cannot penetrate, where space and time don't exist. The next thing he knows, he is sloppily staggering to put on another vinyl or rummaging for a new cup because he can no longer find the one he was drinking from. He barely recognizes the room around him anymore. The kitsune and demon masks play tricks on him, causing some of the plants and furniture to change location. The cup he's drinking from keeps disappearing. Then there's a broken glass on the counter, a shard in the sink. At some point the music is completely gone. He's lying down in the bedroom. Something tugs at his memory, but all he can muster up is the image of a circle. He strips off his shirt and casts it to the floor, finding he has no energy to do the same with his shorts.

A rattling at the door. It's just the wind, he tells himself. But the sound continues and grows more urgent, beyond the clatter of the frame. He swears he can hear a metallic jingle in the hall, a hand testing the doorknob, someone trying to enter. A voice, an entreaty? An intruder. The pocketknife. He whirls to the ground. He's still wearing his shorts. The blade, yes, thankfully, still there. He stumbles out into the hallway. When did he turn off all the lights? Nighttime in the apartment is all too familiar, but never has the darkness felt so thick and expansive, at once. The knob of the front door jiggles again, and he plods toward it shirtless, one hand reaching to feel the switchblade in his pocket, another palm pushing against the wall that looms suddenly against him. He can make out a sliver of light beneath the doorframe now, a yellowy strip of illumination. Trying to be as discreet as possible, he creeps down the corridor, left palm and shoulder against the wall. Whoever is on the other side seems to have stopped trying to enter. A pregnant silence pervades the dark as he treads gently forward and approaches the front door.

There's a peephole through which he should be able to see. He doesn't want the person outside to know he's there, though. What if they're waiting for him to press his eye up against the glass? Meadow holds his breath and tries not to make a sound. He simply stands in the darkness and silence for an eternity, anxiously trying to ascertain who might be attempting to gain entry. When he finally has the fortitude to look through the peephole, he is startled to see neither a drifter nor a would-be burglar in the vestibule, but a woman with long hair swept over her face, her skin glistening like white sand beneath a moonlit sky.

Selma.

PART III

Seascapes

11

IT OCCURRED TO HIM NOW AND AGAIN, DURING THEIR YEARS of friendship, that perhaps he was in love with Selma. The idea was more layered and perplexing, and therefore terrifying, than anything he'd previously confronted. That such a feeling could exist seemed somehow beyond reason and propriety, unsettling the foundation of the person he believed himself to be. He knew it was not sexual in nature, more of an aesthetic attraction to the way she moved through life, the unspoken logic by which she ordered her universe. She was sheathed in an uncanny brilliance, almost too bright to behold directly. Then the light could vanish without warning, turning her dull, dumb, and cold. Though these episodes never lasted terribly long, they were irrefutably part of her, in the same way that the tenderness Meadow felt for her could not be effaced. It was no secret then, but a weary acceptance of something private and unnameable. Meadow stored it away in the recesses of his heart like a precious object of uncertain value.

She convinced Meadow to go on a trip one summer in his late twenties, when he was newly single again. He had been lukewarm to the idea at first, absorbed in the routine of his office job as a desperate ploy to focus on the straight and narrow. July was a ghost town at the university, most of the faculty away on research, tending to their families, and generally unbothered by their cluttered inboxes. After work, he'd been filling up his time with healthy, mundane pursuits: jogging, errands, maybe dinner and drinks—but always home by a reasonable hour.

One evening, he found himself at Selma's apartment in Clinton Hill. Even though she'd been living there for only a few months by then, the space looked homey already with the perfect array of plants and coffee table accoutrements, a Matisse print in the bathroom, wooden stools and fancy cupware. Yulia and Selma had cooked mussels in wine sauce and made a radicchio salad. Meadow had offered to make drinks, as he'd been whiling away free time at the office browsing cocktail recipes.

"So what do you say, Meadow?" Selma asked after putting down the last plate at her dining table. Yulia was seated and distributing utensils.

"Hmm?" In the kitchen, he looked up from peeling the rind of an orange. "Sorry, I wasn't listening." Lately he'd often found himself tuning out like that. No matter if it was during a conversation with a friend or coworker, or while he was walking the streets or taking the subway, a shapeless fog could descend on him for an intractable moment. He'd look up, listen in again, and wonder how he'd gotten where he was.

"A weekend getaway," Yulia laughed. "We're inviting you to come on a mini–road trip next weekend."

Meadow wiped an orange peel on the rim of the tumblers before him, then slipped one into each drink. The liquid in the glasses was ruby red, shimmering cold. "Ah," he said, bringing two tumblers over and setting them next to the salad bowl. "What's the occasion?"

Selma raised her eyebrows and gave him the recap. She was friends with an older couple, a retired professor and curator, who were heading to Italy for the month of August. Normally they did an apartment swap with someone from the European side, but this year that didn't come through. So the couple had offered their beach house on Cape Cod to Selma for the month. How about Meadow join them for a few days, at least?

"Oh," he said, taking a seat at the table. "Sounds nice. Can I let you know?"

"Sure, Meadow," Selma said with a resigned smile on her face, sitting down as well. "You can let me know. Thanks for making us negronis."

"Thanks for this dinner," he returned. "Smells amazing. Cheers."

Selma had a habit of always calling him by his full name, Meadow, and never Med, as Peter and a few others liked to shorten it. Meddy was an appellation that belonged to the realm of college friends, maybe a long-ago lover. Bobby sometimes called him Medame, especially after midnight. Meh–*damn!* he'd screech each time Meadow returned from the bathroom or buying another round.

That night he was lost in thought throughout most of dinner. He overheard snippets of Selma vacillating over whether to invite Simon to Cape Cod. She hadn't ever anticipated forming a relationship with him, but now they'd been seeing each other for almost half a year. Though he'd officially separated from his wife, Selma still felt unsure about her romantic future with him. Meadow listened, nodding occasionally. He drank the first negroni super fast, got up to make another round. He couldn't stomach the idea of dating again. He'd been single for just a few weeks, and already the last relationship—if it could even be called that, lasting only three or so months—seemed distant and unreachable. As though it had happened to someone else, had been mere fiction. He had been a good man, this plainspoken activist ten years Meadow's senior. Meadow remembered shopping for groceries in Chinatown with him. The way he inspected daikon or held mesh bags of garlic, knew exactly which brand of soy sauce to buy. The activist, chopping ginger in his kitchen, always the perfect amount. The kind baritone of his laugh, the quickening pulse beneath his jaw, soft ecstasy of his body. The body that held Meadow, that sundered and made him whole, over and over again. That night, home alone at an unexpectedly late hour, he squeezed his eyes shut and called up these images again, of the two of them together, groping in the darkness, short of breath and drunk with desperation. Their bodies had moved in concert, tumbling in joy. He had been a good man, though they'd had their differences, but would that not always be the case, that you simply had to try and try until—

Until Meadow was alone again.

The next week, Peter had a last-minute business trip to Detroit and flew out on a Wednesday. Meadow couldn't bear the thought of stewing in the apartment by himself for days on end. Though he hadn't really been inclined to go to Cape Cod, it dawned on him that an escape might be just what he needed. He texted Selma to ask what time she was leaving and whether he could still hitch a ride.

Hello darling, she replied immediately. *Can you take Friday afternoon off? I've just secured a vehicle.*

Selma picked him up from his office on Friday. He'd packed a weekender with clothes and toiletries, and brought it to work with him. As he exited the building into the glaring midday sun, he gawped at the sight of a boxy red convertible idling by the curb. Is that— It can't be—

The woman in the driver's seat turned her head toward him and smiled. It was Selma, all right. She wore a black-and-white polka dot scarf around her hair and diamond-shaped black sunglasses. Her lips were a lush scarlet that matched the hue of the Mercedes-Benz, which had to be at least twenty or thirty years old, in spite of its fresh paint and wax. Selma was wearing a white tunic and black palazzo pants, looking as though she'd walked off the set of an old Italian film. In the back seat was Yulia, in a sleeveless sky-blue sundress.

"Meadow," purred Selma. "You made the right choice to come with us. Now get in the front and help me navigate."

They threaded their way north between elegant redbrick buildings and glass monstrosities until arriving in the Bronx, where they hit a surprising snarl of traffic. Selma kept changing the music as they crawled across the pavement, extricating themselves from the grip of the city inch by inch. There was a half-empty pack of Seven Stars on the gearshift, right behind a coffee mug and tall bottle of Perrier in the cupholders. She smoked several cigarettes in succession, asking Meadow to light them for her so she could keep her hands on the wheel. Selma was in an unusually chipper mood, singing along as her playlist cycled from Alanis to Radiohead to Bob Dylan. "It's such a beautiful day, isn't it?" she kept saying. "Even with the traffic."

Meadow found his spirits lightening as they drove. He'd been so preoccupied with work and his general melancholia that he'd scarcely even thought about what it might feel like to get out of town. Now here he was on the road, talking about his favorite music in high school with Yulia and Selma, the three of them lazily wondering what time they might reach the Cape and where they might eat dinner or, at the very least, grab an afternoon snack. A friend owed me a favor, Selma had said of the convertible when Meadow asked. Other motorists gawked enviously as they slid past, some of them whooping with glee as their gazes danced between the body of the car and the sensual insouciance of the chain-smoking driver in her polka-dot headscarf.

"I'm so happy you could make it, Meadow," Yulia trilled. "Now the road trip feels more complete."

"Thanks for having me," he said with a grin, turning to face her in the back seat.

"Originally, Brigitte was supposed to come, too," Selma added, "but unfortunately she has to be at a funeral somewhere out west."

Soon they were speeding up I-95, surrounded by greenery on either side. The scarf managed to stay secure on Selma's head, amazingly, although she yelped occasionally when she thought she felt it slip, bringing one hand up to her hair as the car swerved blithely onto the shoulder of the freeway. They drove for hour-long stretches, stopping regularly to get gas, find bathrooms, or procure snacks. Selma eventually decided to forgo the headscarf, stuffing it into the glove compartment and unpinning her hair, which had been coiled into a tight bun. When they were cutting through Rhode Island, they pulled over at a liquor store in Providence to pick up some supplies. A while later, they passed through the town of Sandwich, Massachusetts, which Yulia thought was the funniest thing ever.

"Homestretch!" chirped Selma. "Let's find a grocery store and stock up for the weekend."

After the shopping errand and a few wrong turns, it was past six by the time they found their way to Yarmouth. The house was located in a sleepy Colonial Revival neighborhood, with generously sized lawns lined with tall trees along the perimeter. The dense cluster of bushes made the driveway difficult to find. Selma had to step on the brake and slide the sunglasses low on her nose, squinting at the wooden mailbox shaped like a duck, an emerald-green head and dull yellow beak protruding at the top. "And here we are," she announced.

They made their way up a winding driveway that led to the back of the house, wobbling gently as the gravel crunched beneath the tires of the Mercedes. Behind a wall of shrubbery, the house was a squat two-floor building with tall windows overlooking a sloping backyard. A row of pine trees stood guard behind the house and delimited the yard, which sparkled under the August sun. Selma parked the convertible where the gravel ended. Right at the edge of the yard, a vegetable garden with tiny green tomatoes and clumps of herbs bursting from the soil swayed happily in the breeze.

"How lovely!" exclaimed Yulia, clapping her hands together. She scrambled out of the car and took a few steps back to gaze up at the house, hands on her hips. Meadow joined her, placing one hand over his forehead to block out the sun. The air smelled of sea salt and a touch of mulch from the garden.

Selma ran a hand through her windswept hair and went to open the trunk. "You'll like the inside even more," she said cheerfully. "Help me unload these groceries, and I'll give you the grand tour."

Within the hour, they were basking in the shade of the back porch, nursing ice-cold beers from a local brewery and picking at a plate of olives, almonds, and cheese that Yulia had selected from the grocery store. Meadow couldn't remember the last time he'd felt so relaxed. A light layer of sweat coated his body, but it was still significantly cooler there than in New York. An earthy calm pervaded the house, which was suffused in the fragrance of citrus.

Selma was explaining how she'd met the owners of the house some years ago, during a residency she did in Hudson. "They came to the open house we had at the end of the summer," she said, lolling her head back dreamily. "I'd spent six weeks weaving masks out of straw and hemp and scraps of clothes from my ex-boyfriend. Victoria was a curator at a local gallery then and sniffing around for new work. I met her and Enrico separately at first, so I had no idea they were married until they came back to my studio at the end of the night. They plied me with prosecco until I agreed to drive up with them the next day."

"To here?" asked Meadow, glancing at the house looming behind him.

"Yes," said Selma. "To be honest, I . . . I wasn't sure what their motives were."

Yulia popped an olive into her mouth. "What do you mean?" she asked.

"Oh, you know. They were both perfectly respectable. Enrico was flirtatious, but in that European sort of way. I knew that he taught art history. Maybe I was in a weird state of mind because of the man I'd just left a few months before. Though we weren't compatible, ultimately, and I was glad to be single again, I found myself thinking about our physical relationship a lot. It practically consumed me during my residency, when I had all that time alone to work feverishly on the masks. It was like a . . . sex hangover, or something."

The three of them laughed at this comment.

"But really," Selma went on, "no man had ever had that effect on me before. By the time I came up here with Enrico and Victoria, I felt completely fried. They're in their late sixties or so now, and both of them keep quite trim and energetic. Anyway, we get here and Enrico immediately sets to work, whipping up some amazing puttanesca and a fish salad. He insists that he can do it alone, so Victoria and I end up sitting out here"—she gestured at the porch—"with a bottle of wine. I wasn't sure if I was projecting or not, but it suddenly occurred to me that maybe . . . That maybe they'd invited me up for some kind of *tryst*."

Selma was staring into the distance, glass of beer in hand. Yulia and Meadow exchanged a glance. "So, *was* it a tryst?" Meadow pressed.

"Well," Selma continued after a pause, "we stayed up late, drinking more bottles of wine and listening to records. We shared some delicious tiramisu that we'd picked up on the way here. Victoria just held it in her lap, on a plate, and the three of us went at it. She had this beautiful silver hair that shone in the soft lighting. At some point, Enrico disappeared down the hall. I was pretty drunk by then and thought to myself, *This is it. This is when the proposition is going to happen.* I felt like Victoria was sitting so close. Or maybe I'd moved closer without realizing it?

"'I get the feeling you've just fallen out of love,' she said to me. I was floored. All night we'd kept things professional, talked about my work, their work. A bit about family and travel. Then out of the blue, this. I told Victoria she was right on the nose, in fact. That I'd spent the whole time at the residency—and then some—trying to untangle the knotty feelings I had about my relationship that had just ended. My heart was pounding. I was half expecting Enrico to appear in a robe and beckon us both to the bedroom . . ."

Selma picked up an almond between her thumb and index finger, examined it for a second, and then bit it in half. "Nothing happened, in the end. We talked about relationships for a while. Victoria told me how she finally agreed to date Enrico after he doggedly pursued her for a year. That had been over thirty years ago. At some point, she looked at the clock and said, 'Oh my, it's nearly three. Maybe we should give it a rest?'"

"So anticlimactic!" laughed Yulia. "That was it, then?"

Meadow poured the rest of his beer into the glass and took a foamy swig. Even though this was only their first drink, he felt strangely tipsy already. The world had grown soft at the edges while they'd been listening to Selma's story. There was a sheen of unpredictability that danced in the air, across her face, in the sunbeam that shone on the white paint of the back porch.

"Well, nothing untoward happened," Selma said. "She showed me to the guest bedroom—where Yulia is staying now—and we said good night. I decided I was too exhausted to shower, so I would do it in the morning. I washed my face, brushed my teeth, and slipped into bed. I fell asleep almost immediately, which you both know is uncommon for me. It usually takes me forever. Must have been the drinks.

"And then I had the most vivid sex dream that night. I never knew my subconscious to be that erotic. It's hard to describe . . . The dream was so lifelike in a way, but I couldn't tell you who I was with or what exactly was being done to me. I remember the texture of the wall, the floorboards, the feeling of warm skin. I woke myself up when I knocked the clock off the nightstand in my excitement. The duvet was a mess, the pillow was on the floor with the wooden clock. It was early morning, crack of dawn. A bit of blue beginning to seep into the edges of the sky. I was still breathing heavily, and could feel that . . . that *pleasure* pulsating in my body, along with loneliness. Or rather, the loneliness and the pleasure were one and the same."

"Wow," said Yulia.

"So this is the house of unconsummated desires," offered Meadow.

Selma laughed. "Anyway, it's just a story about my first time here. Victoria and Enrico have been wonderful friends ever since."

It was evening, but the sunshine showed no signs of abating. Meadow and Selma moved out to the yard to smoke cigarettes, while Yulia cleared the bottles and went to look at what they had in the fridge. Selma held her arms out and spun in the grass, smiling toward the sky. "We should take some photos here," she said. "Don't let me forget."

"You brought your camera?" Meadow asked, taking a puff of the Seven Stars she'd given him.

"Yeah, just a point-and-shoot," Selma said. "Black-and-white film. I haven't shot anything in a while, so I'm excited to take it for a whirl."

She went on to tell Meadow that she would be staying on the Cape until the middle of the month. Simon would be joining them, as well, but the timing of his arrival was unclear—most likely Sunday or so. As for getting back to New York, Yulia would drive Meadow home in the Mercedes whenever he needed. But maybe he could enjoy an extra-long weekend up here if he called in sick for a day or two. A respite from the city could do wonders.

"Don't I know it," Meadow sighed. "I feel better already."

For dinner, Yulia made an Odessa-style eggplant spread that they smeared onto crusty slices of baguette, along with pickled herring. Selma contributed a Japanese potato salad and miso chicken cutlets, while Meadow mixed gin gimlets for all. The dining area was simply a table next to the modestly appointed kitchen, but it was the perfect vantage point to take in the rest of the house. Situated near the door that led to the back porch, the table also constituted the far end of the living room, which had a high ceiling that sloped upward to the second floor.

Selma had put her belongings in the master bedroom on the ground floor. Meadow had volunteered to take the day-bed in the study upstairs so Yulia could have the official guest bedroom next door. The house was rather sparsely decorated, at least compared with what Meadow had imagined for an art history professor and his curator wife. As they ate dinner with relish, Meadow's gaze drifted onto the massive woven tapestry that hung on one wall, a riot of colorful birds and geometric shapes. Tall windows overlooked the greenery of the yard shimmering beneath a mauve-colored sky. Like something out of a storybook, Meadow thought. This scene, this whole setup, was almost too pristine, the tasteful but eclectic home furnishings, a slightly crooked picture frame, everything lived-in to just the right degree. He'd never once heard Selma mention anything about Cape Cod in the years they'd known each other, and now she'd conjured up this perfectly sculpted world as though it were a parlor trick, a mere afterthought.

Meadow made another round of gimlets as dinner wound down. "So what's on our agenda for tonight?" Yulia asked with a cryptic smile.

"Oh, whatever we feel like," Selma lilted. "There's a screen that we can pull down over on that wall. Meadow, I might need your help in setting up the projector."

"Sure, sure," said Yulia. "A movie or whatever. How about our other entertainment, though?"

"I was thinking we'd save it for tomorrow," Selma said. "But no harm in having a little taste tonight."

"Wait a minute," said Meadow. "Are you guys talking about what I think you're talking about?"

Both women looked at him. "I thought we mentioned it when you were over for dinner last week," Selma said. "We did, didn't we?" She raised an eyebrow at Yulia. "Didn't we?"

"Who knows?" Yulia shrugged.

"Let's just dip our toes in the water tonight," Selma said. "Tomorrow we'll drive into town, have a nice breakfast, maybe buy some fruit from the farmers market. Then we can plunge right in with the whole day ahead."

Meadow furrowed his brow and took a hurried gulp of his gimlet. "And by 'dip our toes in the water,' you mean . . ."

"I mean, let's have some after-dinner tea!"

They decided to tidy up, do the dishes, and have a quick rinse before getting down to business. Night tumbled quickly over the Cape. The sunset felt like it had lasted an eternity during dinner, the verdant scenery outside glowing gold and then amber. The next time Meadow looked out, the sky was a dark jewel behind the silhouettes of the trees lining the property. Selma was fumbling through Victoria and Enrico's record collection for some background tunes to put on, murmuring to herself. She chose an Otis Redding album. As "These Arms of Mine" rang out, the wooden frame of the house seemed to shrink, suffused in a warmth not unlike that of a fireplace in winter.

The same record was still on by the time Meadow went to shower in the upstairs bathroom. He could hear the muffled croonings of Otis over the splash of hot water, through the steam rising around him. Even though they'd been there for mere hours, he already felt an immense distance between him and life in the city, and all that it entailed: more absence than substance, his sad singledom, lonely apartment, and shitty job. From disheartenment he'd risen anew, crossing an invisible boundary in the span of an afternoon into someplace softer and more neutral. Aching, but whole. And he had Selma to thank for making space for him here.

Selma. She'd been nothing short of stunning the moment he saw her in the convertible that afternoon. Like a pinup girl, a rollicking woman of the winds. She'd looked like she wouldn't think twice about driving that car off a cliff à la *Thelma & Louise*. Earlier, on the porch, talking about erotic dreams, her sex hangover. He'd barely ever heard of anyone in her life prior to Fawaz. What kind of person could cast a spell on a woman like her Meadow found hard to imagine. He squeezed his eyes shut and rinsed the shampoo from his hair.

"All yours, Yulia," he called as he stepped out of the bathroom. He went to find a clean shirt and put on some shorts in the room where he was staying.

They gathered downstairs again once everyone was dressed. While the water was boiling, Selma picked out an album that simply read *Moondog*. The cover featured a photo of a wizened man with a long white beard in a Viking hat. "Have you listened to this before?" she asked Meadow and Yulia. They both shook their heads. "Well, you're in for a treat."

The music was antiquated, a bit baroque, alternating between a full ensemble of instruments and minimalist dirges. It made for a very different mood than Otis Redding as they sipped from mugs of mushroom tea. Yulia and Selma curled up together on the living room couch, while Meadow sat on a colorful throw rug by their side. He absentmindedly thumbed through a book on Japanese interiors that was on the low table before them. The tea was earthy and pleasant, sweetened with honey and a bit of mint that Selma had procured from the garden. It sat warm in Meadow's belly as he lazed on the rug. Eventually he had the inclination to lie down as he listened to Selma and Yulia reminisce about a trip to Corsica the previous summer. He could picture the two of them wandering from town to town like island spirits, with long hair and flowy robes. "Maybe we can do Sicily next time," Selma was saying. "I think Enrico's family is from Palermo, actually."

Meadow blinked at his surroundings. Suddenly all the colors of the room seemed faintly brighter than they had been a minute ago. The bird tapestry on the wall looked particularly vivid and beautiful, fluttering faintly—or was that just his imagination? The rug beneath him was a bit scratchy, but not unpleasant. A whimsical piano tune punctuated the mood. He wiggled his toes, feeling a hotness in his extremities. "That was fast," he heard himself say.

"You feeling it already, Meadow?" Selma asked.

Meadow sat up and saw her smiling gently at him. "Metabolism," he replied. "I forgot it always hits me so fast."

"I don't feel anything," complained Yulia, looking somewhat like a grumpy teenager in her oversized T-shirt and cotton shorts. Selma wore the same white tunic as earlier but had also changed into shorts.

"It's going to be light," said Selma. "I didn't put too much into the tea."

Meadow declared that he was nibbly and went to the kitchen to fetch some snacks, gourmet crackers and dark chocolate and the like. He brought it all back on a tray that was leaning against the toaster, along with a bottle of seltzer and three glasses. The tray had a floral print that looked a bit out of place in the house, too heavy-handed with its bright greens and garish flowers. Still, he became entranced by the details of the artwork and found himself wondering where Enrico and Victoria had picked it up, whether it was of European provenance, or perhaps from Latin America, Southeast Asia? He poured seltzer into the glasses and handed two to Selma and Yulia.

"Such a gentleman," Yulia said approvingly.

"No sweat," he said, grinning.

In his peripheral vision, the room seemed to contract a bit. He looked outside and saw that it had grown completely dark. The trees were hard to make out against the night sky. Instinctively his breath caught in his throat. He had to remind himself that there was nothing to be afraid of. They were in an unfamiliar place, the sea just half a block away, now cloaked by nightfall. But the house itself was a place of warm protection. Just in case, he got up and walked over to the front door to make sure it was locked. He gulped down the glass of seltzer, the bubbles tickling his throat, and poured another.

That night, after listening to the Moondog record, they decided to put on a movie to ride the gentle wave of the mushroom tea. Selma dug the projector out of a trunk in the corner of the living room. It took all three of them a bit of trial and error to hook up the hardware and position the device properly. There was a screen that descended over one wall with the flip of a discreet switch. Once they finally got everything powered on, it took another few minutes to find the right remote control. Selma finally found what they needed inside the ottoman, on top of a stack of DVDs.

"This is all so confusing," Yulia said, collapsing onto the couch. "You two can pick a movie. I can't think anymore. Please."

"I'm also burnt out," laughed Meadow, flopping back onto the rug. "Selma's pick."

"Silly rabbits," said Selma. "I'll take care of you."

She maneuvered through a series of incomprehensible screens with the remote control until coming to a movie catalog. After what seemed like a blindingly fast scroll through the titles, she went all the way back to the beginning and hit play on *L'Avventura*. "This is more for ambience, really," she said.

"Thank God," said Yulia. "I'm definitely feeling something now and don't know if I can read subtitles."

"Good thing we're starting light," Selma said, reaching for the crackers.

Amid their meandering conversations, all three of them getting up and moving about the room, going to the bathroom, looking into the fridge, the plot of the movie was indeed a lost cause. But it was, as Selma had suggested, a beautiful atmosphere, with the pitter-patter of Italian in the background, the doleful beauty of the actors, the sea and sun, rocky cliffs, old buildings. While gazing fixedly at the black-and-white visuals, Meadow found himself zoning in and out and thinking about other things. There were layers and layers of stories forming an invisible mesh around him. The tale that Selma had recounted on the porch, the friendships that he had with both Selma and Yulia. The end of his journey with the activist, the story of his twenties in New York City. This Italian woman wandering on-screen, at once severe and sad. Could she have imagined that her face could be conjured up at will like this, over half a century later, to haunt the quiet spaces of a cabin she'd never seen? But, in a way, this was like all manner of relationships in this world, Meadow thought. People finding you, whether you were ready for it or not. People changing you, and being changed by you.

They called it a night after the movie was over. In reality, Yulia had already started puttering around the kitchen long before, while Selma was reading something on her phone. Meadow retired upstairs to brush his teeth and wash his face. Once he slipped into the study and closed the door behind him, he let out a long yawn, stretching his arms and flexing his toes. The study was lined with floor-to-ceiling bookshelves against three walls. Near the windows overlooking the front yard was a daybed in a handsome mahogany frame, with a patterned duvet and royal-blue sheets over a pleasantly hard mattress. Next to the bed was a writing desk with a hutch, a few stacks of notebooks and documents immaculately organized.

He noticed now that there was a framed photo on one of the shelves of the hutch. His eyes were still tingling, the colors of the book spines and the linens unusually bright. Picking up the frame, Meadow brought it closer to his face and saw that it was a black-and-white photo of a couple, presumably Victoria and Enrico in their younger years. A casual portrait, most likely taken by a friend or family member. He sat in an armchair by a window while she stood by his side, one hand placed on his shoulder. Judging from the clothing and hair, Meadow thought it might be the late '70s or early '80s. The woman had long flat-ironed hair that hung down to her waist and wore a light denim outfit with a chunky statement necklace. The man had on a paisley shirt, unbuttoned to reveal curly tufts of chest hair. His handsome face was concealed by a thick mustache. Victoria's eyes seemed fixed on a point behind the photographer, while Enrico's gaze was emphatic but warm as he stared right into the camera.

Meadow wondered what they looked like now, or when Selma had met them for the first time in Hudson. He felt a flush of heat remembering the story she'd told earlier and set the photo back down on the shelf. Crickets were cheeping rhythmically outside. He could hear the sound of movements downstairs, then someone ascending the steps to come up to the guest bedroom. A heaviness was forming in the back of his eyes. He stripped down to his underwear and plunked himself onto the bed. The duvet smelled like it had been freshly laundered and hung to dry in the sun. There was a whiff of nature in it, something piney, with the fragrance of soil after a fresh rain.

Meadow climbed under the covers and turned off the lamp on the writing desk. The mattress was sturdy against his back. He could make out the blue-black sky through the windows, the pinpoints of starlight over the trees. He drifted off to the sound of the night breeze, the gentle lap of the tides on the sand, and the creaking footsteps of his two friends downstairs.

HE AWOKE EARLY the next morning to brilliant rays of sun shining directly onto his face. The eastern-facing window revealed a lush expanse of green beneath, a blue sky dotted with powdery puffs of cloud. It wasn't even nine yet. He drew the sheer yellow curtains and tried to go back to sleep. But he discovered that this was not possible after twenty minutes of tossing and turning. His mind was already buzzing with some excitement he couldn't name, perhaps at the mere feeling of being on vacation—when was the last time he'd gotten out of town?—or the promise of the day ahead, some remnants of last night's mushroom tea.

Yulia was grinding coffee beans in the kitchen by the time he made it downstairs. "Morning," said Meadow.

"Hi," she replied. "Did you sleep well?"

"Pretty good, in fact. How about you?"

"Like a log," she laughed. "I still feel it in my bones. That's why I need this coffee." She gestured at the backyard. "She's having a cigarette outside, but wants to head to breakfast at this place. We have to arrive by the time they open or there'll be a wait."

"Wait a minute, I thought we left Brooklyn so we wouldn't have to worry about things like this . . ."

Yulia widened her eyes dramatically. "That's what I said!"

"Must be some really good breakfast." Meadow shrugged.

They left at half past nine so as to give themselves a cushion for getting lost or finding parking. Selma hastened them out of the house and into the convertible. Today she wore a red halter top and a flouncy black skirt, while Yulia was in a linen romper. Meadow had thrown on a pair of faded shorts and an old T-shirt. They sped through the sleepy residential neighborhood until they reached a main thoroughfare lined with mom-and-pop stores, bakeries, pharmacies, hardware shops, gas stations with weatherworn wooden signage. Selma's face lit up as they approached an intersection, blazing through and swerving onto a road that branched off to the right. Some five hundred feet later, they arrived and pulled into a tiny parking lot beside the restaurant.

Sure enough, there was a line gathered out front for the commencement of breakfast service at ten, mostly local types who peered at the three of them with a mixture of curiosity and mild disdain. The crowd's attention was disrupted by a heavyset woman with a mop of curly hair who propped open the front door with a brick. "Good morning, folks! Come on in. Nice to see you all."

The restaurant sat no more than fifteen or so, including the counter spots. Meadow, Yulia, and Selma were shown to the final open table by a smiley teenaged server who couldn't stop staring at the two women. The cacophony of the diner was a world away from the solitude and serenity they'd grown used to. Selma told them how she made it a point to get breakfast there ever since her first visit with Enrico and Victoria years ago. "They're old friends of the owner," she explained. "This place is a great dinner spot, too, actually. I would've suggested dinner for tonight, if we didn't have our other plans—"

The curly-haired woman was just passing by their table when she did a double take. "Holy moly!" she crowed. "Selma, is that you?"

"It sure is, Flora!" Selma stood up and was immediately pulled into a bear hug.

Flora leaned back with her hands on her hips and clucked affectionately. "Little lady, it's good to see your face around here. Are you visiting Rico and Vic again?"

"Ah, sort of," Selma said. She gestured at the table. "Flora, these are my friends Yulia and Meadow." They gave sheepish waves. "They're staying with me at the house. Rico and Vic are off gallivanting down the Amalfi Coast right now."

"That figures, for them," Flora said. Turning to Yulia and Meadow, she added with a wink, "Welcome to my eatery, you two. A friend of Selma's is a friend of mine. Make sure she tells you what's good on the menu here. Just kidding. It's all delicious!" She roared with laughter at her own remark. "Selma, you go on and sit," Flora continued, pressing Selma back down into her chair. "Someone will be right here to take your orders." Her eyes flashed as she looked around with mock seriousness. "If he knows what's good for him. I'll see to it that you all are taken care of."

"Thanks so much, Flora," Selma replied gratefully. "It's really lovely to see you again."

"You too, girl. Come back in the evening sometime so we can catch up proper."

With that Flora vanished from their midst, leaving only the stupefied gawks of the other patrons in her wake. "I've gotten drunk here a few times with her," Selma said coyly. "We have more in common than you'd think."

Their breakfast was a savory assortment of eggs every which way, sourdough toast with locally produced strawberry jam, applewood sausage, superbly crunchy watercress salad, and coffee, freshly squeezed orange juice, and Bloody Marys on the house. It was all divine. "I don't think I've ever tasted a tomato before today," Meadow said as he worked his way through the salad.

"I want this Bloody hooked into my vein," moaned Yulia.

"Told you so," said Selma, looking very pleased with herself. Halfway through breakfast, she disappeared for a long spell. Meadow needed to go to the bathroom and was waiting for her to return. Then he realized she was out front, smoking a cigarette with Flora. The two of them were laughing like old chums and even talking with some other locals who were drifting in and out of the restaurant. Selma should have looked out of place among them, in her outfit that was more suited for walking the cobblestone streets of SoHo than hanging around in a Cape Cod breakfast joint. But, even from afar, Meadow could see something sincere and compassionate about the way she engaged with Flora and her ilk. Selma's gesticulations and earnest repartee simultaneously commanded their attention and ingratiated her with them.

After breakfast and a hearty send-off in the parking lot, they decided to make a pit stop at an antique store on the way home. It was surprisingly large, filled with ceramic tchotchkes and lamps, and they spent a while wandering through the cramped aisles, running their hands along the lacquered wooden furniture, riffling through shoeboxes of old photos and postcards. Yulia bought a pair of drop earrings she'd procured from another room that Meadow hadn't even seen. Exiting the store was like returning to the realm of the living. The world was flooded in sunlight and sound and sensation. As though a nameless weight had been lifted, they clambered back to the car with a skip in their step and got on with the day.

There were some household things to take care of, per Victoria and Enrico, some upkeep of plants and a flower bed on the other side of the yard. Selma dispatched Meadow with a watering can to attend to the flowers while she located the seeds and nuts to refill the bird feeders. Meanwhile, Yulia decided they ought to have a light lunch, or at least prep some food for the eventuality of hunger. By the time they reconvened in the kitchen, she had a spread of small sandwiches and bowls of sliced fruit for the picking. They ate some of this as Selma boiled water for tea. "This time, the tea's just to wash down the good stuff," she said as she tilted a ziplock bag of dried mushrooms onto a decorative plate. She partitioned the mushrooms into three relatively equal portions with a knife, then presented the plate to Yulia and Meadow at the dining table. "Have at it, lovelies."

The mushrooms were grayish brown and not very pleasing to look at. Each pile was roughly the size of a palm. Meadow looked up from the plate and saw that Yulia seemed rather intimidated. "This looks like a lot," she said. "Is it a normal amount?"

"Pretty standard, I'd say," Selma replied. "Meadow?"

"Yeah, it's about right," he said.

"Okay, well, just don't let me get naked or anything." Yulia picked up the largest cap and sniffed it. "Cheers," she said, locking eyes first with Selma, and then with Meadow.

They each held a dried cap, knocking them together for good luck, then started chewing. The kettle began to whistle. "Perfect timing," said Selma.

They ingested the rest of the scattered stems and caps with a lot more ease, thanks to the rooibos tea that Selma prepared. "Ah, my camera," Selma said suddenly, standing up. "I'll be right back. Why don't you two put on some music before we get silly?"

Meadow picked out an old Caetano Veloso album and put it on. "You get the next one once this is done," he said to Yulia.

"Sounds good. Now what?"

"Now we wait," said Selma, returning to the living room with a slim black-and-silver Pentax slung around her shoulder. "Why don't we go relax on the porch again? It's gorgeous out there."

Meadow sat on the sunny side of the porch, feeling the warmth envelop and then permeate him. Sweat began to bead on his arms, the back of his neck. He imagined the heat cleansing his body, dissolving all trace of doubt, scrubbing away sadness. He closed his eyes and listened to Yulia and Selma talk about childhood summer vacations and road trips. Sometime later, when he went inside to drink a glass of water, he realized that he was already on his way. The tiles of the kitchen counter were shimmering in his peripheral vision. A technicolor glow pulsed at the edges of everything from the fruit bowl to the handles of the cabinets. Meadow spread his fingers and examined the back of his hand, his old college trick for confirming his state of mind. Sure enough: he was about to trip balls.

When he went back out to the porch, Selma was taking photos of Yulia in the lounge chair, leaning back with one arm slung over her face. "Guys, I'm starting to feel it, I think," Yulia said, eyes closed. "It's like a fun house behind my eyelids."

The next thing Meadow knew, there was a rising sensation in his stomach, a pocket of heat and air that buoyed him and pushed him from place to place. He found he couldn't sit still on the porch with stuporous giggles alone. He was walking along the edges of the yard, wondering if tree bark had always had this lavender tinge. The leaves overhead swished in synchrony, a faint neon afterglow lingering in the sky. He took in a long, deep breath and expelled a cloud of gray particles that scattered into nothingness.

Meadow decided to lie down at one end of the yard. He could see the house in its entirety from here, picturesque against the tall trees that formed the border of the property. The grass felt prickly and pleasant. He heard a faint rumble and made out the metallic slab of an airplane crossing a distant corner of the sky, drawing farther and farther from him. The sight of it elicited a silvery sigh from his chest as he slumped down onto the ground and breathed in the aroma of the soil. The image of the plane, even as a tiny gleam of light that he could block out with his fingertip, wriggled into his brain, resurfacing memories of departure, separation, absence, loneliness, the mundane experiences that ruptured his childhood, disjointed him as an adult, the cycle repeating on infinite loop in his patterns and predilections now—

Fuck.

He imagined flicking away the tiny plane in the sky and turned his attention to the grass and the soil again. Every breath he drew was dry as brambles. The sea, he thought, the sea. The sea was nearby. That was where he ought to go for some clarity, for solace. Rising unsteadily to his feet, he inhaled another long breath and stretched his arms out to the sides, then up to the sky. He walked around the house and through the front yard, looking at the grass sprout between his toes with every footstep. He could hear the swish of the tide more clearly now, could make out a sliver of gray-white water in the distance. The promise of watery redemption awaiting, he trotted barefoot across the street and down a short slope to the beach. There were a few properties right on the water, houses much grander than the one they were staying in. The sand was warm beneath his feet, but he could feel the cool, salty kiss of the breeze against his face and arms. By the time he reached the shoreline, he was hugging himself as he looked out across the mournful expanse. The water that swept across the sand and stones stung his feet with cold. A moment later, he felt his heels sink into the muck as the tide swashed out again.

It had been a memorable getaway already since leaving the city only one day ago. Riding with Selma and Yulia in the convertible, sun in their hair, smoking Seven Stars all the way from Manhattan to the Cape. He really ought to quit smoking, he thought while gazing at the wavelets roil and churn. He'd been telling himself this for years, but the habit just dragged on and on as he tumbled through life with no sense of direction. He would be thirty soon enough. And then what? Would he be able to curtail these unhealthy tendencies? Would he have someone to love? He felt as though the sea were mirroring his inner tumult, swells and bursts folding back into the same flat plane. The moon, he thought, the moon creates the tides. So wonderfully mystical a notion, nearly absurd, that an orb many millions of miles away be responsible for the disturbances that were manifesting in front of him. "Oh my God," he heard himself say aloud. Too much time alone. He turned around and hastily made his way back up the slope, away from the beach.

He always got lost in himself when alone. Padding back toward the house felt like a salvation, as though returning to shelter after a monthslong voyage. It was an uncannily perfect tableau, the house a boxy structure set against an idyllic swath of green, brimming with hidden magic. Rather than go around to the backyard, where he'd come from, he decided to try the front door, which was a brilliant jewel-tone magenta. Had it been this color yesterday? It must have been. The things you noticed, or didn't. They'd forgotten to lock the front door after returning from the antique shop, and so he stepped into the cool of the house. Yulia must have changed the music to the song playing now, an operatic, melodramatic piece. But where was everyone? An aria, gilded by wind instruments, a violin. The woman sang so beautifully, tempered by some sadness; her voice was a silken peacock feather, deep purples streaked with lime and cobalt. Transfixed, Meadow stood in the doorway.

"Hello?" His voice sounded as though it belonged to a stranger. Blades of grass and bits of sand were still stuck between his wet toes, he noticed. The living room was bright, the florid tapestry on the wall too dazzling to behold. The opera record crackled onward with great romance and melancholy. He started to move toward the sofa, thinking of lying down for a bit, but the music was too loud. He heard laughter down the hallway and headed in that direction instead.

The door to the master bedroom was open. He'd caught only a quick glimpse of it yesterday when Selma was showing them around the house. As he approached, he saw there was a duffel bag at the foot of the bed. The bedspread and matching duvet were a deep indigo that contrasted beautifully with the rosewood of the frame. A smartphone atop the duffel bag lit up with a notification. It was a text message from Brigitte. *Absolutely incredible*, it read. "Meadow?" He looked up and saw Yulia crouched on the opposite side of the bed with a black makeup brush in her hand.

"I'm being subjected to an experiment," came another voice. "She won't let me move." It was Selma who spoke. Meadow saw now that she had her back against the bedframe, facing Yulia.

"I wanted to touch up her eyelashes," Yulia explained. "Come look. It's so fun to have a live model. Isn't she beautiful?"

Meadow floated over to where Yulia was and tilted his head down to examine the fruits of her labor. Selma was sitting cross-legged before her, eyes downcast. She looked up at Meadow with a shy smile. That morning she hadn't been wearing any makeup. On most days, Selma kept a rather austere cosmetic routine or skipped it entirely. There was a natural glow to her, as Yulia and some of her girlfriends liked to point out enviously. Her features were striking, if a bit severe. Oftentimes her temperament itself seemed to be amplified by the tense line of her jaw or the sharp angles of her cheekbones. At other times, when she allowed herself to embrace ease, these edges could become a surprising harmony: inviting and sympathetic, imbued with an understated glamor that verged on pain, like that of an old Hollywood film starlet.

The face that looked up at Meadow now was supple and even coquettish. Her eyelashes and brows had been accentuated under Yulia's brush. The effect was subtle yet powerful. Neurons firing, Meadow felt like he was seeing the Selma of the present overlaid with his memories of her, as well as images of other women from elsewhere, from the depths of his imagination. "Well, how do I look?" Selma asked, pursing her lips.

"You— You look fantastic," he spat out, suddenly aware that he was trembling.

"Glad you approve," Yulia said. "Did you go for a walk?"

"Ah," Meadow heard himself say as he stepped back and started shuffling out of the room. "Yeah, I went to the beach. Sorry, I . . . I need a minute."

"Sure," the women giggled as he exited into the hall. "Oh! I'm hungry again," Yulia said.

Without knowing where he was going or why, he found himself retreating upstairs. The opera record played on and on. He shut himself in the bathroom by the study and locked the door. The mirror was almost too much to look at. He stared at his face, blinked, took a breath, looked away. Flashes of light in his head. An image of Selma snaked down from the heavens and electrified the open plains of his mind. Selma, blooming brightness, alternately playful and serious, open and closed. The day he saw her in the SoHo bookstore arguing with Fawaz. Selma hosting dinner, hair in a messy bun, martinis sloshing over the rim. Selma driving with one hand on the steering wheel, the other lifted, palm to the wind.

His heart thudded. Am I— he thought, face in his hands as he sat on the edge of the bathtub, —in love with Selma? He felt close to short-circuiting, some erotic low tide seeping into the peripheries of his consciousness. But no, that wasn't it. That wasn't it at all. He expelled a breath as his rational brain whirred back to life. Still in the bathroom. His bladder was full. That was why he'd come in originally. He lifted the toilet seat and urinated. You're tripping, getting confused.

He flushed the toilet, washed his hands, and crept from the bathroom to the study. He closed the door and decided he needed to lie down. It had grown overcast outside. He curled up on the daybed, tugging at the edges of the pillow, the bedding, rubbing his face into the pleasing solitude of now. Yes, sometimes it was good to be alone, he thought. He closed his eyes. The music had stopped. He felt himself slipping into a fugue state that was at once monochromatic and glimmering with extraordinary color. Thunder rumbled. It had been so bright and beautiful earlier. Where did the clouds come from? Ah, but it was so peaceful to be alone in this gray space of potentiality.

He lay there for a while, sailing over the choppy seas of his thoughts. More flashes of light brought a white-hot glow to the study. He thought it was his mind sharpening under the influence of psychedelics, a knife scraping the whetstone, until it hit him that what he saw in the room was not imagined but rather— "Lightning," he whispered. And then a tremendous crack of thunder seemed to cleave the sky. Meadow looked out the window and saw that it was raining now. Fat clouds of gray smothered the sky and weighed heavily on the greenery out-side. From a gentle drizzle, the rain picked up intensity until it was pouring down in sheets and pounding on the house. The cabin percolated with energy. Meadow sat up and listened to the melodic drumbeat of the rain on the roof, against the windows. He closed his eyes, letting the sound scrub deep inside his ears. Another thunderclap jolted his eyes open again.

Standing back up, he crossed his arms and began to pace the room. The bookshelves looked flat and unreal. He cautiously went over to one, chose a book at random, and flipped it open to make sure there were words inside. It was some text in Italian that hurt his brain to look at, so he closed it and tried another book. Meadow gradually descended into a vaguely self-aware frenzy, inspecting all facets of the room, pulling out drawers in the writing desk and rifling through loose change, sticky notes, stacks of envelopes. Meanwhile, the rain continued to unleash its fury. At some point he had the brilliant idea to turn on the desk lamp. There were books on the floor, a few strewn on the daybed. The drawers of the desk were open, the chair askew. He had the feeling that he shouldn't touch anything else, that the room should be left just like this. There's a door, he thought to himself. I can go through the door and leave.

So he did.

In the bathroom again, he felt like it had been hours since he'd last been in there. He started to hear sounds from downstairs again, some commotion, more music. The music was familiar, but it was too muffled for him to latch on to. Eventually it clicked in his head with the refrain. Something by Prince. The refrain sounded like something about a raspberry beret. Meadow laughed out loud to himself. "Raspberry beret," he said. A phrase so nonsensical that his mushroom-addled mind couldn't even picture it. He wondered what the real lyrics were. When he left the bathroom and shuffled down the stairs, he found Selma and Yulia twirling in the living room and laughing like two forest nymphs. They'd swapped clothes, or something: Selma had her hair in an elaborate braid now, while Yulia let hers hang loose. They swept their arms out to beckon Meadow to join them, and they were singing, and the song really was called "Raspberry Beret," which was absolutely hilarious, he thought, as he moved into their midst and began to dance and laugh with them.

Right as rain he felt the rest of the day. From pensive solitude to exhilarated companionship. The comedown from mushrooms had always been one of his favorite parts. Everything was as it should be, anxieties and strange thoughts conquered, fears allayed. They chattered happily and openly as the thunderstorm ran its course, laughed so hard that tears burst from their eyes. Soon the golden glimmer of afternoon was visible again, with a sheen of rain that made the whole world appear even glossier and more vibrant than before. Selma was especially radiant, doubling over with laughter when she informed them that Simon was actually en route and would arrive by dinner that night. She'd gotten his text hours ago and kept forgetting to tell them. They dissolved into further fits of giggles.

"Jesus Christ," Meadow said sometime later. "I didn't know how much I needed that."

They were standing in the yard smoking cigarettes, even Yulia, buoyant and satiated in each other's company. The amber light in the sky made the green of the trees around them look even more majestic.

"Yeah, it was pretty good, wasn't it," Selma said softly. "It was pretty good." She let out a small gasp. "Look!"

Meadow and Yulia saw she was pointing at the porch directly in front of them, where a burst of vines hung over the wooden frame near the vegetable garden. There was a single hummingbird that was hovering around the red and orange honeysuckles on the vines, a fantastical creature with gleaming green feathers and a persimmon-colored throat.

"Wow," said Yulia.

"So tiny," Meadow sighed.

Selma said nothing and crept a few steps toward the porch. The hummingbird whizzed between several flowers, then turned to look at the three of them, it seemed. It flew close enough for Meadow to see the yellow white of its underwing shine in the fugitive afternoon light. An instant later, the bird disappeared in a flash. "It's an omen," Selma declared. "A bearer of good tidings."

Once they confirmed that they had the wherewithal to cook again, they moved back inside to start prepping for dinner. At the grocery store the day before, Meadow had assumed they were just picking out haphazard ingredients, but apparently there had been a plan all along. He marveled as Selma gave them specific instructions about which vegetables to wash, how many cloves of garlic to chop, which saucepan to use for what. Midway through cooking, as the pasta was boiling, she opened a bottle of white wine without asking anyone and poured glasses for them all. Simon pulled up in his BMW just as they were mixing the tagliatelle with the garlic tomato sauce in a Dutch oven and drizzling olive oil and grinding black pepper over a huge bowl of caprese salad.

Simon greeted them warmly with his cheesy smile, characteristic tight hugs, a kiss for Selma. He was a quintessential vacation dad in his boxy shorts, small belly visible against his dark tee, curly locks of hair matted against his forehead beneath a red baseball cap, redolent of cologne. There were so many complications, Meadow knew, and Selma was not sure of what possible future, if any, lay ahead for her and Simon. But it seemed like they were all too eager to put it aside and play house for at least this one night. Still buzzing from the afternoon, they sat down to dinner and put on more tunes, poured Simon a glass of wine, regaled him with stories of all they had seen and done in the past day.

It may have been one of the happiest days of his life, Meadow thought back later. Passing the salad bowl back and forth, the dining table drenched in the blazing gold of late afternoon. Simon had brought treats: an enormous chocolate babka, kopi luwak, ice wine, and Japanese craft gin. Later that night they would all curl up again in the living room, Selma nestled against Simon, Yulia and Meadow under thin blankets. Meadow would have the strange feeling, some residual psychotropic fantasy, that they were a family, that Selma and Simon were his parents snuggling comfortably behind him as they watched a horror movie. He would make gin rickeys and mint juleps, passing them around the room, and Selma would thank him with a languid smile like that of a perfectly contented cat lying in a patch of sun.

That night the four of them walked to the beach and stood before the sea, Selma and Simon with their arms around each other's waists, Yulia and Meadow donning the blankets from the couch. The full moon over Yarmouth was pale as the pebbles in the sand, poignant in its circular perfection in the black velvet sky. They'd fallen into quiet contemplation after dinner and wine, and now simply stared out at the moonlight glistening on the water, the immaculate lunar orb still tugging on the surface of the sea.

In the silence, Meadow would look at his companions and see Selma in profile as she faced the water. How beautiful she was, he'd think, her porcelain skin and self-possessed manner, remembering with amusement and shame the terror he'd felt that afternoon at the possibility of being in love with her himself. If nothing else, the weekend had reminded him how grateful he was for her friendship and the life she'd invited him to embrace, the person she saw he could become, or had always been. He would wonder if Selma were not, in fact, the single most important person to him in New York, more so than Peter even, not for anything material in the way their friendship developed but simply for the grace with which she accepted him and led him to believe that there could be beauty and magic in living, and still.

And still.

These memories formed only one part of Selma's complicated topography. Shifts in her temperament were as regular as the tide, and unpredictable for the intensity by which she would be pulled into a different current, rendering her by turns sanguine or frantic, stupefied or anguished. She excelled at maintaining surface appearances, above all. She might be drifting hopelessly into a whirlpool of despair, but one would never know until the moment she disappeared and reached a hand up in panic.

Meadow would remember the sublime ease of that evening in Cape Cod with the same purity of fondness as he did that first time he'd been invited over to Selma's for dinner on a January evening years ago. By the same token, the memory of finding her catatonic at her birthday party would live alongside another episode some months later. It was late October, a sense of fore-boding weighing heavily on the city, and Selma had invited him to take refuge at her apartment with a few others as Hurricane Sandy approached. A state of emergency had been declared that week, train services suspended, grocery stores all but cleared of household provisions.

Meadow and Peter found themselves at Selma's with Brigitte and Wei-Ning. They helped Selma tape crosses to her windows and locate candles in preparation for the possibility of a power outage. Though somewhat tense, they were mostly enjoying the copious bottles of wine that Selma had procured for the occasion and joked about reversing a biblical miracle should the water stop running. The lights occasionally flickered as rain lashed down from the skies, wind thumping against the windowpanes. They played card games while tuned into the news on Selma's laptop, none of them paying much attention to what was going on. With people moving around between the living room, kitchen, and bathroom, none of them noticed at first when she disappeared. The tenuous security they'd felt in being together all but evaporated upon realizing she wasn't in the apartment with them anymore.

They searched high and low for her, calling her name in the stairwell, texting her phone only to discover it was still on her bed. This whole ordeal probably lasted no more than fifteen minutes, but it felt interminable at the time. Again? Meadow thought. Was this something she just did whenever she wanted? To disappear like so, with no consideration for others who might be concerned about her safety and well-being. Flustered, drunk, he opened every closet in the apartment to make sure she wasn't hiding behind a suitcase or a rack of clothes. Peter and Wei-Ning even circled the block, checking for her in McGolrick Park, at the bodega.

In the end, she was much closer to home than any of them had suspected. Meadow heard Brigitte shriek and immediately ran out of the apartment, heart pounding. He thought the sound had come from downstairs, but then he heard the metal grate above his head creaking and banging in the furious winds. The roof. Without waiting for anyone else, he scrambled up the rickety metal ladder that descended from the grate and hoisted himself onto the rooftop. Brigitte was a foot away, staring straight ahead. Meadow suspected the worst for a second, his heart in his throat. But then he saw that Selma was still there. She was sitting on the ledge, legs dangling off the roof, looking out at the treetops of the park before her. One unsteady movement and she could topple three floors down to the concrete. He stood next to Brigitte, who looked at him with tears in her eyes, mouthing incomprehensible words as rain continued to fall and thunder rumbled overhead.

Selma's back was incredibly straight, hands clasped in her lap. It was impossible to tell what she might be thinking, how her face appeared. But, without even needing to look, Meadow could already picture it: the unfocused eyes, the strange smile on her lips. Oblivious to the wind and rain, the lightning in the purple-black skies. These haunted memories would beget more haunted memories over the years, nesting into one another like matryoshka dolls. He had given himself to her in the name of friendship, and she'd reciprocated with so much tenderness and empathy, coaxing him outward into a new bloom. She'd never demanded anything of him, except it became clear that she was in desperate need of someone to both fortify and restrain her, to prove that her wild beliefs were viable. And in spite of the world she'd painstakingly constructed for herself, the characters she easily assimilated into it, what Meadow finally understood on the rooftop that night—for the first time, but certainly not the last—was how deeply lonely she was. How she constantly struggled against the black currents and boundless depths that threatened to swallow her whole.

12

MEADOW WAITED A GOOD HOUR AT THE AQUARIUM THAT
day. Diego wasn't always the most punctual, but he usually gave
notice if he was going to be significantly late. No word this time.
Meadow decided to call him at two thirty. The phone rang for
an eternity, then went to voicemail. *I'm outside the aquarium*,
Meadow texted. No reply.

It wasn't warm enough for the beach. Meadow decided to
go for a walk nonetheless, taking in the slit of brightness at the
horizon where the clouds met the gray water. He stopped checking his phone after a while. Then he decided to send one more
text. *Are you okay?* Surely Diego would call him any minute
now, apologize for keeping him waiting. Or he'd show up on the
boardwalk, waving from a distance, and rush over to give him a
kiss. Eventually, Meadow got tired of waiting. He walked back
to the aquarium, bought a ticket, and went inside.

He had never imagined things could go to ruins so abruptly.
He staggered through the darkened halls in disbelief, past luminescent tanks of silver minnows and snapping turtles, coiled
eels, sharks with skin sleek as marble. Their colors were so beautiful that he practically choked in wonder, in spite of the despair
gnawing at his insides. He stood amid this alien seascape, awash

in blue tones with glimmers of electric yellow and neon pink, wondering if this was really how things would end.

A slight nausea came over him, black dots bubbling at the edges of his vision. He stopped in front of the tank of moon jelly and pressed a hand to his chest to feel his heartbeat. Maybe he had always been a fool in love. But to love at all, to become a fool for the sake of loving—surely these were noble actions? They were a means of self-preservation, he wanted to believe. It was a way to validate himself, to dream big and persist against all that was wretched in the city, in life.

Meadow watched a group of moon jellies as they undulated and pulsed, tendrils sweeping through water. If only he could be like them and find motion in emptiness, exist elegantly alone. The people around him were featureless shadows whose chirring conversation and whispered exclamations were indecipherable. It felt fated, in a way, to end up like this. Perhaps he had always been meant to come here and skulk through this underworld. As he stared at the diaphanous dance of the jellyfish, the darkness of the aquarium enclosed him, sealing him in this nowhere-space between muffled shrieks and watery silence.

Weeks later, when Meadow had mustered up the mettle to relate this whole tale to Peter at the bar in Koreatown, Peter had given him a look and asked, "What if something happened to him?"

Meadow shook his head. "It crossed my mind. But to be honest, I doubt it."

Peter leaned back in the booth, clasping his hands behind his head. "What makes you so sure, Med? From everything you've told me, it sounded like you guys were really hitting it off. I mean, I know dating is brutal these days. But do people just drop each other like that, after you've made plans for the day? Without even the courtesy of a text?"

Meadow wanted to tell him that he had searched online that night for subway accidents. His mind started wandering in all sorts of crazy directions. He had tried calling Diego one last time when he left the aquarium—straight to voicemail. But as half a day passed, then a full day, he had to rein himself in from the impulse to keep reaching out. Self-consciousness swept over him. There was a thin line between reasonable concern and pitiful inability to accept reality. There was only one truth: Diego never once contacted him that day, or in any of the days since.

"People get cold feet," Meadow said with a sigh. "I don't know. Life's weird like that sometimes."

PART IV

The Lunatic

13

"SELMA," HE HEARS HIMSELF GROAN, HIS BODY HEAVY against the front door.

In the smothering darkness of the apartment, Meadow suddenly finds it hard to operate his limbs. He swivels his head away from the peephole and tries to reach for the doorknob, only to miss and lose his balance instead. He crumples to the floor and feels nausea rise in him. Whimpering with frustration, he flops onto his knees and struggles to stand. I have to get up, he tells himself. I have to let Selma in.

The shadowy hallway spins around him, a sour reek in his mouth. Head lolling in all directions, he catches a glimpse of the kitsune and demon masks on the living room wall. He feels like they are watching him, even though their eyeholes are fixed straight ahead. There's a rustle of a night breeze through the window screen. Or is it a voice? Still kneeling by the door, Meadow strains to listen, to ascertain if Selma is speaking to him through the door. If she is, it's in the barest whisper, more like a razor scraping across a wooden floor than a human voice.

Another sound disrupts his concentration, a blaring pulse in the distance. Meadow moans as queasiness roils through his belly again, clenching his eyes shut. The sound is persistent and painful, jabbing him in the brain. A car alarm. Make it stop, he beseeches. Make it stop. The water he gulped earlier sloshes inside him. Fuck. He needs to vomit. Fluttering his eyes open, he flails his arms out to the wall and manages to stand upright. Selma, hold on, he entreats silently as he staggers down the hall, wincing at the car alarm. He flings open the bathroom door. Before he can even turn on the light, he falls to his knees in front of the toilet bowl. Selma. It occurs to him only now, as he opens his mouth and lets loose a stream of sour liquid. Could she really have come back from Shanghai already? His stomach contracts and he throws up again. Why wouldn't she have a key?

He vomits several more times until he's retching bitter bile from his throat to the edges of his mouth. The stench of it is everywhere. He reaches a trembling hand to flush the toilet, his head pounding. The noise of the toilet is intolerable. He knows he should get up and go to the front door again, see if she really is out there. But he feels so weak and dizzy, hot and cold at the same time, limbs heavy as lead. Almost without volition, he lies down on the bathroom floor in the darkness. Just a moment, he thinks to himself. I just need to rest. The cold of the tile is soothing, in a way, cutting through the dull pain of his headache, pressing against his cheek. Cold and hard and simple. That's all he wants. Things to be simple, straight. Sleep for just a moment, now, just sleep. Sleep.

MORNING LIGHT STREAMS into the bathroom from the window. Meadow awakens with the base of the toilet in front of his face, the tile floor unpleasantly hard against his rib cage. The overwhelming nausea has subsided into a mere burble, but now it feels like someone is taking a pickax to his head every few seconds. "Jesus Christ," he rasps. He can feel the heat of a July day already permeating the apartment, brushing its tendrils against him. His rational mind tells him he ought to get up, drink some water, and go lie down in bed, but it takes him close to twenty minutes to budge. When he finally heaves his body upright, pressing against the sink cabinet for support, he's stricken by a momentary guilt as he remembers Selma was standing at the front door.

But it couldn't have been her. Could it? The marginal clarity he has gained by daylight allows him to assess the situation with more logic, or at least without the intoxicated haze of last night. At first Meadow wonders if it was all a dream, but then he realizes his being in the bathroom, and the telltale signs of his fit of regurgitation, is evidence otherwise. His reflection in the mirror is a ghastly sight: bleary eyes, a dense mess of stubble on his chin and above his lips, sunken cheeks. The headache is atrocious yet familiar. He can recall so vividly the image of Selma through the peephole, standing in the hallway with her face in shadow. No way he could have imagined that or conjured her up out of nowhere. Could she still be there?

With a twinge of apprehension, Meadow plods down the hall and to the front door again to press his eye to the peephole. The vestibule is empty. Grasping the doorknob in one hand, he turns the deadbolt above to its unlocked position and opens the door. No one and nothing in sight, the atmosphere exuding an innocent serenity. A mournful groan escapes his throat.

Meadow crosses into the kitchen and discovers a broken glass in the sink, the shards still cluttered at the drain. Cursing his drunken antics, he manages to collect most of the pieces into a plastic bag, which he places on the counter. The oven clock shows that it's not even seven in the morning. It hits him that he has to work in the afternoon at Barley. He ought to get some proper rest in bed before, especially if he wants to run back into the city to investigate the Embarcadero Theater. Nonetheless, he basks in the satisfaction of having slept a few hours at night at long last—even if it was an ignoble, whiskey-induced sleep on the bathroom floor.

The bed is in a slovenly heap. Despite feeling in shambles, he finds the softness of the sheets against his back to be a revelation, and the curtain of sleep descends with merciful speed once more. Perhaps this, too, is because of the physiological rhythm he's grown accustomed to over the past weeks, a Pavlovian conditioning that equates clambering into bed by daylight with releasing his body and mind to the sweet darkness between worlds.

He drifts in that abyss, untroubled by the dreams or malformed dramas of the human soul, for a comfortable eon. When he comes to, the first thing Meadow notices is that he neglected to set an alarm. The second thing is the difference in the quality of light, the hazy brightness an indicator of midafternoon in the New York summer. Scrambling upright, he checks his phone. It's quarter till four; he has fifteen minutes until his shift starts. "Fuck fuck fuck," he cries, springing out of bed. A residual dullness lingers in his stomach, but thankfully it's nowhere near as bad as the morning. He throws on the nearest T-shirt he can find, summons a rideshare vehicle on his phone, sprints into the bathroom to brush his teeth quickly, then scampers down the three flights of steps right on time to catch his driver pulling in next to the curb.

When he makes it to Barley just in the nick of time, he exhales and lets his shoulders slump again. Monique peers at him, hands extended toward the ends of the counter. "How's tricks?"

"Mo," he sighs, "I don't even know how to begin to answer that."

It's by and large an uneventful shift, and for that Meadow is grateful. He spends a breezy afternoon and evening pouring beers and mixing cocktails for regulars and new faces alike, groups of friends who idle by the window booths, lonesters reading in the back, young and old, men and women in all shades of summer. Even Meadow finds it impossible to be in a bad mood on this Saturday afternoon, in spite of the questionable way he started his day. When the wincing hint of his headache finally dissolves, he scrolls through his phone to find something more upbeat and puts on Fela Kuti, the whole bar perking up from a hit of aural caffeine.

At eight, Monique taps out and Damian, a singer-songwriter from Atlanta, takes her place. The weekend revelers start to come in. A birthday party arrives and occupies most of the back tables, a raucous but respectful group congregated by a rosy-faced woman wearing a Burger King paper crown on her head. When the birthday girl's best friend orchestrates a round of tequila shots, everyone erupts into cheers. They suck dutifully on their wedges of lime and bring the empty glasses back to the bar, one by one.

Meadow heads home at midnight, surprisingly invigorated by the shift and grateful for the social interaction at the bar. There are still plenty of people roaming the streets of Crown Heights and Bed-Stuy at this hour, and so he walks back to Selma's untroubled, stopping by a bodega to buy a seltzer. Amid the activity of the day, he almost forgot about the Embarcadero. Now that he has regained some of his headspace, he resolves to go back tomorrow to follow through on his original intention.

When he gets home, the apartment looks innocent and inviting, completely devoid of the leering shadows and strange vibes he's been feeling for days. He decides to make himself some chamomile tea, pop a melatonin, and read *The Masquerade* until he gets tired. With any luck, he'll be able to coerce his body and brain back to a normal sleep schedule. The bottle of Four Roses on the counter, he notices, is half-empty. No fucking wonder. He's taken aback by how much he drank in one sitting, and also unsurprised in some measure. The vision of Selma must have been no more than an alcoholic hallucination—his first, and hopefully also the last.

Meadow succeeds in reading just a few pages before the enticement of sleep starts to drag his concentration away. How simple, and yet what a relief, to feel tired at a normal hour. He brushes his teeth, then slips under the covers, eager to release himself into the unconscious.

THE NEXT AFTERNOON, after preparing a simple lunch at home of miso salmon and grilled vegetables, Meadow gets dressed and heads into the city. In Manhattan, he catches his reflection in a storefront and chuckles. It was not his intention to go incognito, but he barely recognizes himself in his baseball cap and sunglasses. Otherwise, he wears a totally standard outfit, a patterned shirt in hues of green and yellow, flowy trousers, and woven loafers. The stench of the city wafts around him as he maneuvers up Second Avenue past slack-jawed tourists and university students dawdling with their iced coffees. By the time he turns onto Second Street, he has pushed all uncertainty from his mind. Take it one step at a time, one thing after another. He trusts the right course of action will reveal itself to him. After a brisk walk, he comes to a stop in front of the art deco building with an arched doorway, its display case bearing the Embarcadero Theater name. The same poster he saw two nights before still hangs behind the glass, the same set of faces—on the bottom left, Matthew Morales—peering out at him with their suave smiles.

It has to be Diego, no doubt. Meadow takes a deep breath, sweat sliding down his neck. It's not as hot as the previous day, but summer is still in full swing. The gate leading into the theater is ajar. He squeezes past the black iron, walks up to the front door, and pushes it open.

Meadow stands in the lobby as his eyes adjust to the interior dimness. On the far end are steps of smooth stone that look freshly mopped. Weak light filters in and illuminates the staircase area. A darkened hallway next to the stone steps leads to an elevator. There's a pair of double doors on the other side, presumably the entrance to the theater itself. Meadow takes stock of these surroundings, then ventures toward the booth that sits before the double doors.

The booth is encased in glass that could use a good scrub. An ancient woman sits inside, looking somewhat sickly under the waxy, fluorescent lighting. Meadow thinks she's staring into space, but then realizes there must be a computer directly in her line of sight. Her eyes move back and forth, as if reading. She does not acknowledge his presence. Suddenly feeling awkward, he pretends to examine the pamphlets on a folding table nearby. There are business cards, takeout menus, and brochures for local businesses, including florists, barbershops, Chinese restaurants, and wine stores.

He glances back at the booth and notices a letterboard behind the old woman. There's only one line on it:

MOON GARDEN   THU FRI SAT   730PM

Meadow walks over to the booth. The old woman doesn't look up. A thin layer of red lipstick covers most, but not all, of her lips. Her short white hair is brushed back behind her ears, a nearly shocking contrast to her thick, dark eyebrows. She wears a silk shirt that seems incongruously youthful. Meadow gawks at her, dumbfounded. Finally, he clears his throat.

"Excuse me."

The woman's eyes flick up and lock him in her gaze. A strange smile spreads on her face. "Oh, hello," she says warmly. Her voice, too, sounds like someone decades younger. "My apologies, I didn't see you standing there."

"Ah, it's okay. Is this . . . is this where I can get tickets for the Embarcadero Theater?"

"Why, it certainly is, young man."

Meadow shifts his weight. Stupid question to lead with, he thinks to himself. "Great. And I take it *Moon Garden* is what's showing now?"

"Yes. *The Moon Garden*, that is," she adds helpfully.

"I see." Something about the woman's demeanor creeps him out. He realizes it's because she hasn't blinked once. Her eyes have been staring at the same spot without moving since she's turned her attention to him. "In that case, could I get a ticket for the Thursday show?"

"Absolutely, you may. That'll be twenty dollars. Cash only, please."

"Got it." Meadow fumbles in his pocket for his wallet and discovers he has enough cash, thankfully. He slides a twenty under the glass partition. When the woman snatches it with a surprising ferocity, he sees her nails are also painted a bright red. She turns back to face the computer screen. He hears her type something with painstaking effort, one keystroke at a time. Then there's the sound of printing from below.

She deposits a rectangular slip of paper under the partition and pushes it toward him. "There you are." Her leering smile reveals a row of tobacco-stained teeth.

"Thank you," Meadow says. "Um, do you happen to know what the play is about? Or where I can find more information?"

The smile disappears from her face like a candle being snuffed out. "Oh no, dear. I'm afraid that's not my area of expertise at all."

"Okay, no problem. I—"

"They just pay me to mind the box office." She laughs. "Nope, don't know anything at all."

"Got it. Thank you. I guess I'll find out."

"Yes, you will, dear."

"Huh?"

"Thank you for your patronage."

Meadow nods at the old woman as he backs away from the box office. He stumbles out into the midafternoon heat, blinking wearily at his surroundings.

He spends the rest of the day, and most of the next, deep cleaning Selma's apartment. He vacuums all the dusty corners, wipes down the shelves and countertops with a rag, and waters all the plants. The strange bloom of celadon next to the rubber tree has grown even taller, the petals having opened to reveal thin tendrils of vibrant gold within. In between washing and drying his clothes in the basement laundry room, he puts on Whitney Houston, cleans the toilet with bleach, and scrubs away the mildew between the bathroom tiles. It's gratifying to refresh a living space, even a temporary abode, in this way. He feels a weight lifting before he's even finished the job, as though the heartache and maudlin energy of the past months have been banished by the chemical products he's deployed.

After he finishes, he decides to jog to Prospect Park. The temperature has cooled down a touch and, importantly, it's less humid. So even though he knows that it will be punishing to exercise outdoors, he does so anyway. His hands itch from the cleaning supplies, he realizes as he puts on his running shorts and stretches his hamstrings. He hasn't exercised in ages, but he's already looking forward to the shower later, which will undoubtedly feel divine.

By the time he reaches the park, nearly two miles away from Selma's, he's pouring sweat, red in the face, and mildly euphoric. He does a full lap inside the park, all the way down to the lake and back up again, occasionally wiping his forehead but otherwise paying no mind to how he must look. Plenty of joggers and cyclists are doing their own circuits on the paved paths, while hundreds more people lounge on the greensward, throwing

Frisbees, playing loud music, barbecuing gleefully. Meadow feels reassured by the city pulsing with life as he runs steadily onward, squinting in the sun.

As he winds back toward the way he came, he decides to stop at a water fountain and catch his breath for a while. The water is cold and sweet. He cups his palm to catch a small handful and splashes it on his face. Exhilaration. The breeze picks up just then, whipping around his taut legs and against the back of his shirt, which is totally drenched. He walks away from the fountain into the grass, finds a sunny patch, and plops down happily, face toward the sky. The smell of grilled chicken, fresh-faced girls in elaborate dresses celebrating a quinceañera, a neon-colored kite soaring on high, teenagers on skateboards, groups of friends pouring wine and whiskey into red plastic cups. The whole of the park is bursting at the seams.

On the way home, he passes a florist and doubles back on a whim. He buys a bouquet of randomly selected flowers, single stems of freesia and dahlia mixed with some green stalks, and decides to walk the rest of the way home. Happy even just to hold the flowers, he brings the bouquet to his face every so often and inhales their fragrance. When he gets back to the apartment, he throws the bundle into a blue vase sitting in a corner of the credenza, an irregularly shaped glass piece that Selma was using as a pencil holder. He places the pencils in one of the coffee table drawers, then moves the vase to the windowsill, admiring the bloom of brightness it adds to the living room.

For dinner, Meadow whips up a batch of Bolognese and pours the sauce over a generous helping of spaghetti. He grates cheese and tears basil leaves over the pasta and eats it with a salad of herbed tomatoes. Meadow chugs a cold lager with his meal. He puts the bowl and chopsticks in the sink when he's done, deciding to shower first before cleaning up. As he walks into the hallway toward the bedroom, his eyes happen to glance at the console table, where he has been depositing mail over the past weeks. He didn't touch this table during his cleaning and there's quite a pile. He checks the mailbox only every few days and never bothers to look that closely at the incoming missives, but now the top envelope catches his attention for its irregular size and vertical postage stamps that depict miniature natural landscapes of jutting rocks and spindly trees over inky currents of water. Then, in the spillover of light from the kitchen, he sees that the name written on the envelope is not Selma's, but his own.

He snatches the envelope from the table, hands trembling. There is no return address, but the red ink of the postmark indicates that the letter was sent at the end of June—from Changchun, China. Before he even tears open the letter, he knows whom it's from. He reads the two pages of careful penmanship on parchment paper:

Darling,

Thank you so much for taking care of my home. I hope you're finding it to your liking and that my ghost hasn't been bothering you too much. I write to you from northern China. Please excuse my abrupt disappearance. After I last saw you in Shanghai, I was overcome by the impulse to make this journey. No, I shouldn't call it an impulse. It was more like something compelled me, that I had no say in the matter. As though my Brooklyn ghost had followed me to this part of the world and dictated my every action.

Rather than fly or even take the train, my ghost insisted that I move slowly so I could see the landscape change. It took me so long to make my way out of the forest of a city that is Shanghai. Then I wound through Jiangsu province, northward to Shandong and farther east, deeper and deeper into the heart of Manchuria, until I arrived here in Changchun at last. My ghost knew that I would end up here someday. Perhaps that had been my ulterior motive all along, the reason why I applied for this residency in the first place.

There's a book that I've wanted to talk to you about for the longest time, but I never knew where to begin. Forgive me for being so vague. When we saw each other in Shanghai, I thought surely you would have said something about it, had you found it already. Since you didn't mention it, I felt I should keep quiet and let it come to you. Do you know what I'm talking about? It's a book called "The Masquerade." If you have been reading it, you probably have questions about it. I do, too. More questions than answers, I'm afraid.

You see, this novel was written by my maternal grandfather. His name was Yanagida Yoshitaka. His parents migrated to Manchuria from Japan in the early twentieth century, and he was born in Changchun in 1910. He went on to attend university in Shanghai and never even set foot in Japan until after the war, as far as I know. My mother was the youngest child from his second marriage. She barely knew him either—he died when she was still a young girl. I imagine you're well aware of the Manchurian region's fraught history. The city called Changchun, where I am currently staying, and where my grandfather returned after his time in Shanghai, was declared the capital of the puppet state known as Manchukuo and renamed Shinkyo 新京. "New Capital."

Only in recent years did I discover that my grandfather had been a writer, and that he had penned an underground novel when he was a young man. In Shanghai he was *involved in literary circles and even knew some filmmakers, I'm told. He wrote exclusively in Chinese, though he was fluent in both languages, adopting a pen name of sorts using the characters of his surname, Yanagida, by their Chinese reading: 柳田 Liu Tian. The novel was just a piece of family lore, washed away by the tide of history, until a translated copy of it turned up as my relatives were cleaning out the home of a recently deceased great-uncle of mine. I happened to be visiting my father's side of the family in Kamakura—it was earlier this year, if you recall. I knew I had to get my hands on the book when I heard the news. My family members were happy to pass it off, considering the book simply to be an oddity or worthless relic.*

I read through "The Masquerade" quickly just once. I don't think I understood the story, or why my family only had this English version and not the original in Chinese. To be honest, part of me is afraid to ask more questions. I'm not sure what the answers might reveal about my grandfather and, by extension, about me. Of course I always had you in the back of my mind. You would be the perfect person to untangle things with, given your academic background, but I could never figure out how to broach the subject.

Maybe you have no idea what I'm talking about still. No matter. I trust that my ghost will make sure the book comes to you. I feel as though this story holds the key to understanding something about myself and where I come from. And maybe you, too, will be able to find something illuminating or evocative in the book. When we meet again, I'd like to spend some time talking about it with you.

Yours,
SS

Meadow puts the letter on the kitchen counter, steadying himself. The symphony of crickets and traffic rumbling down the street outside sounds artificial all of a sudden, no more than recordings piped into this space. Around him, the apartment seems to contract, all the carefully laid out furniture and decorations a stage set. Even the letter itself, despite its postmark, feels like a prop that someone planted for him to find, that he retrieved exactly according to plan. What on earth? In all the years he's known Selma, she has never once mentioned that her family had such an intimate connection to China. Why would she have kept this from him? Was it truly as she said—that she didn't know enough to talk openly about her grandfather and his legacy? Or is something darker afoot, with all this business about her ghost? A ghost that somehow has been directing and manipulating the both of them. What was once an inside joke they'd shared now feels awfully disconcerting, a crude cover for superstition or, worse yet, episodic bouts of lunacy. She hasn't mentioned the ghost in years, ever since she first moved into this apartment. To see her write so casually about its influence in a half-serious manner absolutely floors him.

Yanagida Yoshitaka. Meadow storms over to the living room, where *The Masquerade* is lying face down on the coffee table. He seizes it and peers at the cover, where the author's name is romanized, clear as day, as his own: Liu Tian. The second character is indeed exactly the same as his given name, but the *Liu* is written differently, per Selma's letter, with the character denoting "willow" instead. He shakes his head, wondering how much of the letter to believe. What does Selma mean that this book was an "underground novel"? How and why would such a work be translated into English, to say nothing of the supposed translator's name echoing that of a library in Vermont? And what the hell do the symbology and synchronicity of the book—the

German man in the beaked mask warning of elemental forces, the pervasive riddles and deceptions—mean to Meadow?

He flips open the cover again. The book was purportedly printed in Manchuria in 1940. Does the pristine quality of its pages betray its ersatz provenance? Meadow feels like he's still missing a glaring anachronism or obvious clue. A wave of uncharacteristic anger rises in him at the absurdity of it all: this explanation, which feels disingenuous at best; the situation he has found himself cornered in; the fact that all of the precipitating factors leading to this moment were things he'd blithely agreed to, if not the consequences of his own actions. He grits his teeth and finds himself flinging open the kitchen drawer and reaching for the switchblade. Without even having a clear intention in mind, he presses the button on the handle and lets physical instinct take over. The blade whips out of its ivory carapace.

Meadow releases a shriek of frustration and plunges the knife into the soil of the rubber tree in the hallway. Narrowing his eyes at the strange bloom, its greenish-white petals fanned open, he pulls the blade out, presses his thumb and index finger against its stalk, and unceremoniously severs the plant at its base. The flower goes limp, deprived of life in an instant. Then something white and slippery falls onto the back of his hand. He yelps and recoils, only to see the maggot that was nesting inside the flower fall from his knuckle into the pot. Within an instant, it wriggles into the soil and disappears from sight.

14

ORCHID IS WAITING FOR HIM IN THE HALLWAY WHEN HE STEPS out of the bathroom. After Spiegel brusquely left the room, Mizuno had to take a few moments to steady himself. What sort of subterfuge could be underway at this party tonight, with all these cryptic messages? First a warning from Dahlia not to trust Spiegel; Luna telling him to watch for a conspiracy by Orchid and Peony. Then the business about mirrors being doorways or instruments of deceit. "Yueh-Lan," Mizuno says hollowly when he sees her standing in front of him, leery that she may be an apparition or doppelgänger. "Is that you?"

"Why, of course," she says softly. "Come with me, my sweet man. You look like you need some air."

He falls in step with Orchid as they descend the red-carpeted staircase and head out the front door. They pause on the veranda, taking in the scenery of the cool spring night, the moon casting a silvery sheen on the cement and surrounding foliage of the Du estate. Along the path that leads to the circular driveway, a marble fountain with cherubim sculptures still spouts water lazily into the air at this late hour. A single Rolls-Royce sits in the driveway, its black varnish gleaming wickedly beneath the moonlight. Mizuno and Orchid walk in silence, moving from the veranda to a cobblestone path. At the end of the path is a walled entrance with a circular opening, leading into one of the famed gardens of the residence.

He can almost smell the dewy grass as they walk along the cobblestones. The light and energy of the masquerade ball seem to be concentrated in the house proper. Mizuno feels relieved to have some distance at last, the night air punctuated only by the sound of crickets and his rasping breaths. When he and Orchid reach the wall with its distinctive circular entryway, he recalls that this structure is known as a moon gate.

The garden is empty. A paved path encircles the perimeter, with a bridge providing a walkway over the pond in the center of the garden. At last Orchid speaks. "I'm glad we could come here for some privacy," she says in a hushed voice. "I understand you may have been told some disturbing things. And because of that I wanted to give you something. For protection." Mizuno lets her lead him around the garden at a relaxed pace. The silver disc of the full moon casts a cold light on the greenery and the pale petals that open into the spring night. Far from the party and its oppressive cheer, Mizuno feels as though he has entered a fantasy realm. He is about to lift the mask from his face, but Orchid stops him. "No," she says. "Not yet."

Orchid gestures at a stone bench on the opposite end of the garden, with a view directly onto the pond. "You want to give me something?" he repeats, his mouth dry. "For what?" He stops in front of the water, noticing how the reflection of the full moon is startlingly clear, as though the glowing orb were floating at the bottom of the murky waters. Taking one step closer to the edge, he rests his hand on a rocky outcrop. On the black surface of the water, a few lily pads drift idly by. "I'm afraid I really don't understand."

The moon's reflection seems to stare back at him, impelling him to draw nearer. Mizuno finds himself stooping beyond his own volition, then lowering himself to his haunches. Enchanted by the lustrous perfection of the circle, he reaches a hand out toward the water, his body leaning forward bit by bit, completely magnetized. Only when a dragonfly skims over the surface of the pond and the reflection dissolves into streaks of silver does Mizuno pull back with a gasp, startled by his behavior. He rights himself and sees Orchid beckoning to him from the bench.

He makes his way over to her and sits down. "Yueh-Lan," he says. "Help me understand."

Orchid doesn't look at him. She stares straight ahead instead and speaks in even, unhurried tones. "Midnight approaches. When the clock strikes twelve, Du Kuo-wen would like to see you in his study. It's on the second floor, at the end of the corridor. I believe you may have been there already." She sighs. "It's imperative that you go to the study as soon as the clock chimes. I can't disclose to you the nature of the meeting, but it directly concerns your livelihood and well-being. But there may be some trouble afoot. That is why I have asked you here. So I can give you this." Orchid presents an oblong case of pearlescent white in her palm. He takes its cold weight into his hands.

"It is a blade," she whispers, leaning closer to him and running her finger along the outer edge. She presses a button on the handle and a sharp flick cuts through the silence of the garden, the metal gleaming beneath the moonlight. "Use it for protection. The study at midnight. Shut the door after you. Please don't draw any further attention to yourself. I must take my leave now."

THE DAY BEFORE the play at the Embarcadero Theater, Meadow goes on a long and aimless walk through Clinton Hill and Fort Greene, then north on Flatbush toward downtown, zigzagging along the busy summer streets. It's a beautiful Wednesday afternoon, the kind of day when all of life's blemishes and impurities, be they physical or spiritual, seem to be effaced by the crisp light. Eventually he realizes that he's drawing close to Boerum Hill, where Diego lives. Part of him fantasizes about walking past to see if anyone's home. Diego wouldn't be off work yet, he supposes. He could find somewhere to pass the time. A coffee shop or, better yet, a bar. Or he could just buy a bottle from a liquor store, stake out a spot across the street. He could wait until Diego gets home, and then—

And then what?

Meadow shakes his head. He's not sure whether this train of thought is more pathetic or psychotic. Either way, even imagining such behavior is laughable. He veers away and back northward again, tracing a hook on the map as he draws closer to Brooklyn Bridge Park. On the way there, he buys chocolate soft serve from a food truck and finishes it before he even reaches the park, the pillowy sweetness melting into his mouth with the same satisfaction as a good kiss.

The rest of the day passes with remarkable swiftness and a peace that he hasn't felt for a long time. He may or may not see Diego, or Matthew, in *The Moon Garden* tomorrow; the mystery of Selma's whereabouts is partially settled for now, if not fully resolved. After reading her letter, Meadow had typed out a quick message to tell Anya that he'd received a communication from Selma, and that she appeared to be in China still. He found himself almost apologizing on her behalf, but he deleted this part. Best to keep it brief. Summer is already half over and it's time to move on, move past, move into the new. That's his new mantra, at least for this next stretch of the season, he decides. Let the universe guide you, let the answers come. Decide for yourself the story you want to live in.

It is this spirit that dominates his thoughts as he gets dressed the following afternoon, in preparation for the show at the

Embarcadero. After trying on a number of outfits, he decides to wear a dark blue shirt with shiny silver buttons and high-waisted black linen pants. He examines himself in the mirror, assessing the serious, thoughtful expression of his gaze. Serious and thoughtful, but not sad, at least. With a spritz of cologne on his neck and a quick swipe of his wrists against the fragrance, he stuffs a light jacket into a tote bag, slips on black moccasins, and bounds out the door.

Early evening in the summer is bright and brisk, as people transition from work to leisure, spilling out from offices and into bars and restaurants or returning home to cook, order in, take it easy. Without time for a proper meal, Meadow grabs a pastry from a local coffee shop on his way to the C train and finishes it before he even reaches the subway station. Dinner can wait. He finds himself thinking back to that morning just weeks ago when he reached into Selma's coffee table and found *The Masquerade*. It's not as though the book had anything to do with his stumbling upon Diego's photo outside this small theater in Manhattan. Nor was it the book's fault that whatever relationship he had with Diego evaporated spontaneously over a month ago on a dreary and unremarkable day at the aquarium. But somehow these things all feel connected. He can't quite parse out the reasoning for it, let alone how Selma figures into the picture, if at all.

When he arrives at the theater, he walks past an older man smoking a cigarette by the railing. Tall and clean-shaven, he has the look of a mercurial orchestra conductor in his crisp white shirt and cuff links. His eyes sweep over Meadow for just a second before he looks away. Meadow wonders if he might also be one of the actors in the play. Inside the lobby, he's surprised to see a line forming at the box office. It's no longer the strange old woman selling tickets, but rather a sleepy-looking teenager with Hello Kitty earrings. Meadow moves past this scene and rummages in his pocket for the ticket. He finds it just in time to present it to a smiling young man at the double doors that lead into the theater.

"Thank you," the guy says, opening a door. "Please watch your step as you enter."

Pushing aside a heavy black curtain, Meadow steps into a surprisingly spacious theater with a square stage illuminated in the front. Three sections of folding chairs are arrayed across the room, the rows descending toward the stage with black curtains drawn. He hesitates, then picks a seat in a middle row on the right, where he has a reasonable view but can remain relatively discreet. The entire theater looks like it seats more than a hundred. It seems to be only at one-third occupancy, but more people trickle in by the minute. An impressive showing for a weekday performance at an obscure theater, Meadow thinks. Then again, it's not like he knows anything about this business.

There are program leaflets on each of the seats. Meadow picks up the folded paper and examines all the text printed on it. A list of individual sponsors and supporting organizations is on the back. Inside is a brief description of the Embarcadero Theater and a statement from its artistic director, a person by the rather improbable name of Dmitri Suzuki-Alvarado. The language is florid and even academic, invoking the notion of the theater as refuge and heterotopia, a compression of temporalities, and ideas in that vein. Meadow can't help but grimace. The cast list of *The Moon Garden* is short, fewer than ten names in total. In the middle of the page, a dotted line connects the name Matthew Morales to two characters called Sojourner #2 and Horticulturalist. Meadow raises an eyebrow. On the one hand, he's mildly relieved to find Matthew's name at all. He had a brief misgiving about whether he'd made the right choice in coming. What if Diego, or Matthew, simply wasn't a part of the play that was showing? Thankfully, this isn't the case. But, by the same token, it means that the inevitability of their encounter draws ever nearer. Meadow's heart speeds up as he imagines how it might play out. Calm, calm, he tells himself. Nothing to get worked up about. Or at least not yet. He has the whole play to watch first, and then he'll have to make a choice about the confrontation. How, where to handle it. What to say, when.

Meadow takes a deep breath. For now, all he has to do is sit back and watch what unfolds.

People filter in for the next few minutes, an eclectic crowd that includes some college-age students, older couples, middle-aged men with dreadlocks, women in severe business suits, choosing their seats carefully across the expanse of the room. Nobody ends up sitting in the same row as Meadow, and for this he is grateful. The last thing he needs is a bout of claustrophobia to agitate his nerves and distract him from the experience.

Suddenly the lights go dark and a hush falls over the audience. Meadow feels like a child, brought to witness some spectacle at the planetarium or amusement park. A single, circular spotlight illuminates the stage. From behind the curtains emerges a man dressed in a black fleece shirt and black jeans, the glasses on his face sporting asymmetrical lenses. He strides into the spotlight and, with a dramatic pause, brings a wireless microphone to his lips. The fringe of his hair is glossy and of uniform length around the circumference of his head.

"Greetings," he says in a surprisingly deep voice. "Welcome to the Embarcadero Theater." He licks his lips, gazing into the audience. "I am Dmitri Suzuki-Alvarado, artistic director of this small but stalwart bastion of the dramatic arts."

Of course this is what he looks like, Meadow thinks to himself. A walking stereotype if there ever was one.

"The show you are about to witness is a very special one," Dmitri continues. "Although we have been rehearsing it for only a recent stretch of time, the writing of the play itself was a long endeavor on the part of a visionary artist . . . who just so happens to be a debut playwright." He goes on to postulate about the exceptional formal and aesthetic qualities of the work while speaking in generalities so as to not spoil the experience. Meadow squints in the darkness at the program leaflet to locate the name of the playwright: Catherine Clearwater. Something tickles the back of his brain, but he can't coax it out while Dmitri Suzuki-Alvarado is still speaking briskly and with great pageantry. When he finally falls quiet, Meadow snaps back to attention. The artistic director stands before the audience with head bowed, in a pregnant pause. "Dear friends and patrons of the arts," he says at last. "Without further ado, I present to you *The Moon Garden.*"

The spotlight turns off the instant he utters his last word. Twenty seconds pass in complete darkness and silence, save for a muffled cough and the sound of people shifting in seats. Then a crack of thunder trembles through the room with such intensity that Meadow feels the vibration humming in the legs of his folding chair. A pale green light illuminates the stage, where the curtains have just opened to reveal props arrayed into two discrete sections. On stage left is an interior space with a freestanding wall and picture window that looks out onto a photorealistic painting of a sloping pasture. An actress playing an elderly woman sits in a rocking chair, her face turned away from the audience and looking out the window. A potted tree, ten feet tall, is on stage right, surrounded by a row of smaller plants. A low stone wall divides the two settings from each other.

The old woman rocks back and forth in the creaky chair, saying nothing. Finally, she turns to face the audience. A caricature of a grandmother, she wears thick glasses and a curly white wig, a shapeless dress draping all the way down to her feet. She reaches for the cane next to her and struggles to her feet, taking tentative steps to the front of the stage. When she opens her mouth to speak, an unlikely samba track begins to play instead. The woman casts away her cane and begins to dance. Her movements are jerky but hypnotic at first. Then these motions become rhythmic, more fluid and expansive, as a deep-throated male voice begins to sing dolefully in Portuguese. Before the refrain, the old woman takes the glasses from her face and flings them off the stage. The color shifts from green to a majestic purple with golden backlight. She dances sensually now, her movements clearly that of a much younger woman, gracefully arching her back and falling to her knees. Legs fluttering rapidly, fists clenching and unclenching as her arms fly to either side in step with the music.

And then another boom of thunder reverberates through the room. The music stops abruptly as the woman falls backward and lies still. The light changes to a grim blue halo. Two figures dressed entirely in black, mesh bodysuits covering even their heads and faces, prance onto the stage on all fours and encircle the woman, limbs rising and falling in ritual. They close in on her body and double back several times as dissonant piano keys sound at irregular intervals. Eventually, the two figures in black huddle over the woman, obscuring her from view as they thrash and writhe, a gnashing sound growing louder and louder in step with their movements. A fog shoots from the bottom of the stage and envelops the theater as the gnashing and piano chords continue in parallel. The whole of the auditorium grows hazy. Meadow looks around in a minor panic, even glancing up at the ceiling. Then all the lights cut out. A warm, unpleasant void swallows the entire theater. He squeezes his eyes shut and can't tell the difference. The darkness is like that of a tunnel in an ancient mountain, black skies above an unknown ocean. For a scary few moments, he feels detached from time and space altogether.

When he opens his eyes again, the lights have returned and the fog has mostly dissipated. Up on stage, the same woman—at least he assumes it's the same one—stands erect before the audience, not as a hunched grandmother, but as a regal goddess-like figure in a shimmering robe. She begins delivering a monologue, her voice unaided and yet powerfully resonant. The show proceeds in this manner for the next hour and a half. Meadow watches, entranced, as surreal images unspool before him like a kind of dream consciousness. He is only able to catch the vaguest thread of a plotline, something about an island colony populated exclusively by people looking to recapture lost love. Most of the scenes represent the interior worlds of the characters, it seems, dreamscapes and fantasies, unfulfilled wishes, alternate realities. Occasionally the stage is set up to convey the eponymous moon garden, a nocturnal landscape with flowers in riotous bloom, sentient vines slithering at their feet while the actors deliver soliloquies or gyrate to strange melodies. The music is a curious mix of baroque piano, folk songs in unrecognizable languages, experimental jazz. In the same vein, the actors cycle through nonsensical bits of dialogue and strained discourses about their childhood or past lovers, lamentations on their lot in life. The actors themselves never sing, but they frequently break into dance not unlike the old woman's in the beginning.

Within the first half hour of the show, Meadow thinks he spots Diego on stage. But it's only a hunch. The actors all wear elaborate costumes, and it's impossible to determine based on context who Sojourner #2 or Horticulturalist is, even by voice—each character in the play speaks in affected accents, alternately bellowing or gurgling their lines, panting and shrieking as they go along. The play culminates in an ensemble dance in which all the actors don costumes and makeup to resemble stylized flora: bodysuits in shades of green with roots of brown fabric splayed on the floor below, colorful petals and fronds fluttering like wings on their arms, clouds of confetti whirling from elaborate headdresses. They pirouette on stage, drawing close to one another and then spinning outward while an acoustic cover of "Moonage Daydream" by David Bowie plays. As the song finishes, the actors each freeze in position, while three of them—including a person Meadow thinks may be Diego—take turns reciting stanzas from a poem.

The entire cast repeats the last line in unison, two more times:

"And binding with briars my joys and desires."

"And binding with briars my joys and desires."

The theater goes dark, to rapturous applause. Meadow is surprised by the swell of emotion that he, too, feels at the conclusion of this bewildering experience. As the stage lights come on again, he stands and continues clapping, like most everyone else, for a long, long time. The actors trot back out on stage from behind the curtain in their final costumes and give a deep bow of gratitude, hands interlinked and faces beaming at the attendees, who are still whistling and hooting with appreciation. The applause grows even louder when a man clad in black—Dmitri Suzuki-Alvarado—appears alongside them. With a broad sweep of the palm, he gestures at the row of actors, inviting the adoration of the audience. Finally, Suzuki-Alvarado twirls his hand in a few circles, then places it flat on his stomach and bows deeply from the waist.

The actors file offstage, followed by Suzuki-Alvarado, and the houselights come on. Meadow rises from his seat and goes to the lobby to find a bathroom. "Gorgeous," he hears people tittering.

"What a beautiful journey that was," another sighs. Only one sullen voice mutters, "I don't think I understood anything I just saw."

Meadow breathes deep and steadies himself as he washes his hands. The play may be over, but now it's truly showtime for him. He returns to the lobby and loiters awkwardly for a few minutes, watching as people come out from the theater. Pretending to study the pamphlets by the box office again, he overhears snippets of other people's conversation about Suzuki-Alvarado, the artistic director. A genius, they declare, but how did they ever manage to get him to come to New York? They say he hates it here.

He came to work with Catherine Clearwater, someone surmises. What a fabulous imagination she must have.

I heard he brought a few of the actors with him from the West Coast, another person pipes up. He refused to start from scratch with this company.

Meadow grows woozy standing in the lobby. He backs up against a wall and glances nervously at the crowd, but doesn't recognize anyone. Then he realizes he hasn't even thought through what it might look like when he accosts Diego in their midst. What is he going to say? Nice play, now tell me the truth about why you dumped me? He shudders and flees the building, fumbling in his tote bag for the red pack of Chunghwa cigarettes.

He stands outside the black iron gate with a cigarette in his mouth, trying to look casual. Part of him wants to go for a walk around the block and come back ten or fifteen minutes later. Surely the actors won't be leaving anytime soon, since they have those costumes to change out of, friends and well-wishers to greet. But he's scared of Diego slipping away somehow. Stepping away from the theater for even a minute would risk such misfortune.

So Meadow resolves to stand there for as long as necessary. The theater doesn't seem to have any other public entrances or egresses. For now, he stands with his back turned, facing the street, idly looking at his phone to pass some time. Occasionally he glances up when he hears the door to the building open, chattering voices carried aloft by the nighttime breeze. It's still the members of the audience leaving, as far as he can tell. It may be a while yet before he has a chance to make his move.

Some minutes later, Meadow is startled by the sudden presence of a person who comes straight up to him. But it turns out to be a bearded white guy, looking somewhat like Jesus with his shoulder-length hair, asking for a cigarette. "Nice pack," the guy comments when Meadow fishes out the cigarettes from his bag. "Chinese?"

Meadow nods.

"I dated a Chinese girl once," the guy offers. "She smoked these red packs exclusively. Either that or the Panda brand."

"They're a national favorite," Meadow says neutrally. "Need a light?"

"Nah, I'm good," the guy says, walking away. "Peace."

Left to his own devices again, Meadow turns so he's facing the entrance to the theater. As he lights up another cigarette, he thinks about the show he's just watched and whether there are any connections to *The Masquerade*. A moon garden, perhaps similar to the scene where Orchid brings Mizuno out for some air on the Du estate. A tale of deviance and deception. Mirrors and dualities, secret identities. The play was very much about interior worlds; if not deceit and performance, then at least the disconnect between desire and reality. How would he describe these works to someone else, in a nutshell? Flickers of academic parlance and armchair criticism light up in his mind. A postmodern play about colonial pasts, about exile and yearning, searching for consolation in an unfamiliar land. Directed by one Dmitri Suzuki-Alvarado, based on a text by Catherine Clearwater. Meanwhile, the other one is a book, written in Chinese by a Japanese man, the grandfather of Selma Shimizu. Translated by Barnaby Salem. A story about freewheeling Shanghai in a time of contained violence. Masks and disguises, illusions and fantasies.

Meadow's halfway through his second cigarette, lost in this swarm of ideas, when a group of people emerges from the building, moving past the iron gate to stand in a circle less than ten feet from where he is. He takes a long, hearty drag and turns his head to face them. His vision is briefly obscured by the white cloud of smoke he exhales. But then he sees in the group, facing in his direction, though talking to someone else, none other than Diego. Or Matthew Morales.

These must be the actors. Though they are back in their street clothes, T-shirts and shorts, one-pieces and miniskirts, there are telltale vestiges of makeup on some of their faces, crimped hair or chunky headpieces. Meadow takes another puff of his cigarette, fixing his gaze on Diego. He thinks about waving, as silly as it feels. But in the end, he doesn't need to. In the midst of the conversation, as he listens to the woman next to him speak, Diego's gaze shifts to the solitary figure standing nearby. The smile on his face vanishes like the sun disappearing behind a cloud. Meadow simply tilts his head and continues to look in Diego's direction. So he does recognize me, he thinks.

He sees Diego excuse himself from the group. "I have to talk to someone," he overhears, just before Diego slips out from the circle and tentatively makes his way to Meadow. A few of his compatriots gaze over at them, but lose interest and return to their conversation. With no glasses, Diego's eyes glimmer in the darkness, a nervous, somewhat pained look on his face.

"Hi," Meadow says, frozen in place. The reality of what's happening hasn't quite hit him yet, this scene that he's imagined dozens of times in any number of contexts.

"Hi," Diego says. Silence accretes in the air between them. Then, he adds, "You must hate me."

"I don't, actually," Meadow hears himself say. "I wasn't sure I'd be able to see you at all, to tell the truth."

"Were you at the show?"

"Yes." He takes a final drag of the cigarette, crushing the nub on the metal fence next to him. "It was a beautiful performance."

The tension on Diego's face eases somewhat. "Thanks." A pause. "I know that it's not something I mentioned to you before, and that—"

Meadow holds up a hand. "Please. Can I have just a little bit of your time? Right now, if you can spare it." He looks at the group of actors. "I don't want to keep you from celebrating with your friends, but I also don't want this thing to hang over us any longer than it has to. Or hang over me."

"Of course," Diego says. He hesitates, looking behind his shoulder. "Let me just tell them I'll catch up later. Be right back."

They walk over to Second Avenue in silence, Meadow scanning the street for a suitable bar or restaurant. He gestures at a gastropub that looks low-key, and Diego nods in agreement. Now that the initial adrenaline of their encounter has worn off, awkwardness with a hint of dread lingers between them—that distinctive apprehension before a breakup, a feeling Meadow remembers well from past lovers. A bubbly blonde hostess greets them as they enter, asking if they'd like a table. "We'll grab seats at the bar," Meadow tells her.

"Sure thing," she chirps. "Take whatever seats you like."

Thankfully, there are empty stools at the far end, away from the dude bros congregating by the door and girlfriends dishing gossip in between. They order vodka sodas, which arrive mercifully fast and plenty strong. Finally, feeling as though he's a teacher who is about to reprimand a disobedient student, Meadow sighs and turns to face Diego.

"So I guess the first thing I want to know is," Meadow says, enunciating and choosing his words carefully, "should I still call you Diego? Is that your real name?"

A worried look comes across Diego's face. "It is," he says quickly. "I mean, it's my middle name."

"Huh." Meadow nods. "I guess I should have assumed that."

"My full name," he continues, blinking rapidly, "is Matthew Diego Morales Selva. I can show you my California driver's license if you'd like, although it doesn't have 'Selva' on it. It's my maternal surname, you know, something that's customary in Span—"

"Okay, fine, got it. But you can imagine my surprise when I saw your photo outside the theater, just walking by one day. I thought I was going crazy, or that I'd found your doppelgänger." He turns to take a sip of his vodka. "Do you go by Matthew usually though?"

"I . . . Yes and no."

Meadow shakes his head. "What does that mean?"

"When I moved to New York, I wanted a fresh start, you know. I thought about it for a long time. Especially as an actor, as someone who's trying to work not just in theater, but in film and TV, I decided that 'Diego Selva' was a much more memorable name than 'Matthew Morales.' Or at least less common."

"You never told me you wanted to be an actor. Or that you were in a play. And even then, if you're telling me this is your stage name, why does the poster list your other name?"

Diego slumps back, biting his lip. "The long and the short of it is, I began working in this production as Matthew. It wasn't as easy to toss aside as I'd thought—the name, that is. But I have been going to all my auditions as Diego since May. As for my being in theater . . . There are lots of things we never talked about, Meadow. I mean, we knew each other for just how many weeks?" Seeing the look on Meadow's face, he softens and adds, "Look, that's not to say I didn't enjoy what we had together. And, for what it's worth, I didn't intend to disappear from your life like that."

"That's comforting. So what did you intend?"

Diego takes a sip of his drink, then rests his chin on his hand. "I think I should tell you about how it all happened. You can believe me or not, but this is really how it went down."

He takes a breath, then begins to recount everything that happened after the last time they saw each other, a month and a half ago. The day he and Meadow were supposed to meet at the aquarium, he had an accident. He was on his way to catch the Q train at Atlantic Avenue-Barclays Center and had just stepped into the crosswalk when a bicyclist zipping through the red light slammed perpendicular into his side. The collision knocked him several feet away. There was so much blood that he ended up going to urgent care, where he was diagnosed with a concussion and received stitches on his forearm.

He shows his right arm to Meadow, a band of shiny skin with a faint row of vertical lines notched along its length. Meadow simply raises his eyebrows in response.

Diego had his phone out at the time of the accident. The impact from the bike sent the phone flying through the air and onto the pavement. He was able to retrieve it, but the screen was shattered and nonfunctioning. He went without a phone for a full week, until his parents sent him money to replace it. "You and I never exchanged emails," Diego says. "You're not on social media. I basically had no way of contacting you."

Except you knew where to find me, Meadow thinks.

As if reading his mind, Diego says, "Yes, I guess, eventually, I could have gone over to the bar and looked for you or left a message, at least, to let you know what happened. But then . . ."

But then things took another complicated turn. The urgent care center had let Diego use their landline to call someone. The only person he thought to reach out to—the only person whose phone number he could recall by memory—was his ex. The way Diego talks about the guy is rambling and circular. It takes Meadow a while to realize that this wasn't an ex in California, but someone he was seeing in New York. And now he comes to understand that Diego had been in a relationship with this guy pretty much right up until the spring. Not long before Meadow met him at that party in Chinatown. He was certain they were broken up for good, Diego says. There was no ambiguity in his mind about it. But when his ex came to tend to him that day, meeting him at the clinic and escorting him back home after the concussion, watching over him for hours on end, something shifted again between them.

"I never knew you were seeing someone in New York," Meadow says finally. "The way you and I talked, I always figured I was the first. At least, the first semiserious thing."

A helpless expression comes across Diego's face. "I'm sorry I kept it from you," he says. "To be fair, we never got to talking about our past relationships that much."

"So you rekindled things with your ex," Meadow states simply. "Through the accident."

"Yeah," Diego says, taking a breath. "That's how it ended up happening. And by the time I was back up to speed, with a new phone and everything . . . Meadow, I knew I owed you an explanation. I didn't want you to think I'd ghosted you. But the more time that passed, the weirder I felt about trying to contact you.

Maybe I was biding my time, trying to feel my way through the ambiguity with Dmitri, but—"

"Dmitri? You mean, the director?"

Diego winces as though he's let a valuable piece of information slip. "That's right," he concedes.

"So that's who you're back together with."

Diego gives a solemn nod. It wasn't just any relationship, Meadow finds out. Diego had been with Dmitri for almost two years, working under him in an independent theater in downtown Los Angeles. He was a big part of the reason Diego moved to New York to begin with, though Diego tried to establish autonomy to the extent possible, with his day job, studio apartment, social life. Dmitri is nearly ten years older than Meadow. He's at a different stage of life, professionally, romantically, and otherwise. But he and Diego are giving it another go, trying to make things work again.

At this point, Meadow's heard enough. Everything Diego has told him is logical, even if the explanation feels a bit airtight for his liking. "Just one question, though," Meadow interrupts. "What's the deal with his name? Like, no offense, but 'Dmitri Suzuki-Alvarado' sounds totally bogus as a name."

"And what about 'Meadow Liu'?" Diego smiles. "Just kidding. Yeah, I know, it's strange. Well, his mother's side of the family is Chilean. His father is half-Japanese, half-Russian, but grew up in Argentina."

"So it all checks out in the end," Meadow says with resignation. All the turmoil he felt while reading *The Masquerade*, the paranoid headspace and weird experiences at Selma's, turned out to have absolutely nothing to do with this. He's tempted to tell Diego about the book, the other strange things that have happened: the encounter with the hatted eccentric, Selma's letter. Tailing his own doppelgänger through the Lower East Side. But another part of him wants to end this interaction as soon as possible. "This really had nothing to do with Selma, then," he says aloud.

Diego furrows his brow. "Your artist friend? What about her?"

"Never mind," Meadow mutters. "It's just been the strangest month of my life house-sitting for her." He flags the bartender to get the check. Diego insists on paying for the drinks, slipping a twenty onto the counter. The two of them walk out past the same blonde hostess, who wishes them a beautiful evening ahead.

Outside the night air is heavier and damper than it was earlier, clouds gathering in the western sky looking sickly and bruised in hues of orange and purple. Meadow lights another cigarette when they step onto the sidewalk. "You meeting up with your friends?" he asks, trying to be nonchalant.

"Yeah, I think they're having drinks around here."

"Well, thanks for letting me literally ambush you," Meadow says. "I know it was a bit of a creep move, but . . . you already know why."

Diego shakes his head. "It's kind of a relief for me, too, to be honest. I'm glad we saw each other again."

Before the moment drags on any further, Meadow begins walking south. "Congrats again on the show," he calls out. "Good luck to you and Dmitri."

"Good night, Meadow," Diego replies, looking somewhat startled. He adds hastily, "Take care."

An airtight explanation, Meadow thinks to himself again as he walks down Second Avenue. He can't tell if he feels any better for knowing what he knows now, but it can't be undone. At least it offers him some semblance of closure. So much in the world rests on the unspeakable and the unknown. A million different decisions and details, within one's control and completely beyond fathom, have conspired to create one's reality. And this reality continues to twist and tremble with every passing moment, like shapes and colors transforming within a kaleidoscope, fractals of light strobing through a thick fog. Profundity and meaninglessness woven into a gossamer web. What he thought to be love was, in the end, just another fantasy.

15

IT'S FIFTEEN MINUTES TO MIDNIGHT BY THE TIME MIZUNO
returns to the house. He fingers the switchblade in his pocket,
his hands clammy and uncertain. Inside, the party guests are still
mostly in the ballroom, where a number of revelers are dancing
the foxtrot to the lilting music of a reassembled band. A woman
on stage belts out a familiar tune by the popular young singer Bai
Hong. Or could that be Bai Hong herself? Mizuno doesn't pause
long to consider this, moving swiftly from ballroom to parlor
to grand foyer. When a waiter comes by with a tray of drinks,
he takes another Phantasm and drains it quickly for courage.
Is Orchid involving him in some kind of conspiracy? Or is it
Spiegel who is truly planning something devious? Mizuno had
originally hoped to gain an audience with Du tonight. Now,
according to Orchid, Du had planned for the same. But what
could he possibly have to discuss?

Mizuno slouches against a wall and watches the masked
partygoers move around him. The Mexican heiress bantering
with a Hong Kong playboy, the American dowager trading
barbs with that suspicious Italian, Luna. How preposterous
a scene, that they could all convene here on this night. The
absurdity of this city, Shanghai. Glorious and unhinged, this
meeting of mankind. Mizuno feels, with more conviction than

ever, that modernity is truly chaos and seduction entwined. At the stroke of midnight, the grandfather clock in the foyer begins to chime. Instinctively, Mizuno glides up the staircase and into the second-floor hallway by the sixth chime. By the ninth chime he has reached the study. By the final chime he has closed the door behind him.

A cool wind blows in through the window. Mizuno hears footsteps plodding down the hallway, drawing closer to the study. The person stops outside the door. Then the knob turns and the door gradually swings open. "Master Du—" Mizuno begins, but he stops the moment he sees who has opened the door. It is not Du Kuo-wen who stands at the threshold. The man who has come to the study is Mizuno himself: clad in a tuxedo jacket and white mask, a red rose pinned to his breast pocket, patent-leather shoes. Worse than anything is the doppelgänger's leering smile. As he steps in and closes the door, Mizuno chokes and reaches for the knife in his pocket, his whole body trembling. He removes it fumblingly and locates the button to snap the blade out. When he looks up again, he sees his doppelgänger pointing at him with an identical knife in his hand. *Mirrors can also be doorways.* The smile on his double's face widens. *Instruments of deceit.*

Mizuno backs up against a bookshelf, glancing around him. There is only one door to this room, and a single window that is too high to safely leap from. His double takes a step closer, crouching his posture with the grace of a trained fighter. "Wh-Who are you?" Mizuno gasps. "What is this?"

The double says nothing, edging toward him with the knife still in hand, his arm taut and ready to strike. Just then comes the sound of footsteps in the hall again. I'm saved, Mizuno thinks. When the door flings open, it turns out to be Du Kuo-wen—or at least, the man in the pig mask. "Mizuno?" says Du, looking at the Japanese editor by the shelf. "I heard you wanted to see me?" He steps into the study, not seeming to notice the other man waiting in the shadows.

"Master Du—"

Before Mizuno can say any more, his doppelgänger leaps toward Du with frightening speed, sinking the blade into his gut with the same ease as slicing through a bolt of fabric. In the commotion, Mizuno loses his wits and lets his own knife clatter to the ground. Du makes a gurgling sound as he crumples to his knees. Below his rib cage, a massive scarlet stain colors the crisp white shirt like a profusion of rose petals. The doppelgänger slides the blade in and out of Du's stomach with horrifying squelches, then turns to face Mizuno again. The smile on the double's face has disappeared, replaced by a sneer. As he approaches, Mizuno falls to the ground in a fright. Only then does he notice one notable difference between their appearances: his double is wearing gloves. The double simply snaps shut the bloody switchblade that he used and places it on the table. Then he picks up the knife that Mizuno dropped and returns to crouch by Du's side. The pig mask has slid partially off his head. Du chokes on his own blood with an awful gurgling until Mizuno's double takes the knife and unceremoniously slits his throat. He then tosses the blade to the ground and steps calmly out of the room, closing the door behind him.

A SCREAM CUTS through the cheerful commotion of the masquerade ball just as the band concludes one song and the singer on stage is offering her thanks to the audience. "Master Du!" wails a distant voice. "Master Du!" The guests who are spectating on the sidelines are the first to leave, followed by pairs of dancers who unclasp their hands and murmur to each other as they scurry across the parquet. The current of partygoers follows the sounds of distress upstairs to the corridor leading to the study. A crowd of people gathers on the stairs, anxiously talking to one another. Eventually the hubbub dwindles into stupefied silence, save for the sound of a woman weeping inconsolably. Du Kuo-wen's lifeless body is slumped on the carpet inside the study. The pig mask lies nearby, its features made more monstrous in its flat and misshapen state.

"What's happened here?" demands a man in a Peking opera mask.

"What do you think happened?" mutters someone else.

"Master Du," sputters Orchid, ripping off her mask as she kneels by Du's corpse. "I-I was told to meet him in the study at midnight. And when I came, there was already a confrontation underway. Master Du was in a heated argument that ended only when he was *murdered*"—a collective gasp goes through the crowd—"by him!" She points an accusing finger at the man in the white mask and tuxedo jacket who cowers against the bookshelf.

The stony silence gives way to a chorus of voices. "Who's the murderer?" cries the American dowager with bejeweled fingers. "Apprehend him at once!"

"It was Masatoshi Mizuno, the newspaper editor. A monster of a man!"

WHAT A FOOL, Mizuno-san. So enchanted he was by a pretty face that he could scarcely fathom the scheme that had long ago been concocted. Du Kuo-wen was always the target, that conscienceless financier all too keen to protect himself by cozying up to the Japanese. What Orchid and her compatriots needed was someone to take the fall for Du's murder—and this diffident editor who claimed to look past politics was the perfect prey. Not only was Mizuno a regular fixture of the Shanghai social scene, he was also naïve enough to play right into their hands without realizing it.

The scheme had been set into motion well over a year earlier. Orchid and Peony, or Yueh-Lan and Hsiao-Dan, had already auditioned their way into the ranks of Wonderwood Studios by then, under the guise of modern girls who prized glamor and amusement above all. With their womanly charms, they flattered and cajoled Boss Du, joining him for lavish dinners on the Bund and banquets with his European and Japanese business partners. They gained his trust, little by little, and bided their time. When Du declared he would host a masquerade ball in the spring, a most insidious plan began to take shape.

Yueh-Lan knew plenty of this man Mizuno, alternately pitying and despising him for what he could so easily overlook. Though she knew him not to be a strident imperialist per se, he was all too happy to pretend that his nation was not carrying out a murderous campaign throughout all of Asia. He behaved as though he could simply glance away, whistle a few bars, and dance a few rounds, and then the whole messy business of war and bloodshed could conclude and a new era of peace would prevail. What a farce. Mizuno deserved his fate for this selfishness alone. Shanghai was being crushed under the military occupation of the Empire of Japan. Men like Mizuno would rather see it as but a minor inconvenience, filling their time with their gin rickeys and horse races, movie premieres and garden parties. Meanwhile, the chokehold of empire tightened by the day in the form of curfews and checkpoints, clampdowns on social life, the exploitation and reallocation of business and industry. In the face of this injustice, Yueh-Lan took cold comfort in the fact that she had, in her student days, found her way to a coalition of leftists and intellectuals fighting against fascism. She refused to believe this state of indignity could be their collective destiny. She was nothing if not patient.

With an unlikely band of international compatriots adopting the identities of Luna, Spiegel, and Dahlia Derby, Yueh-Lan set out to monitor the party as it unfolded and draw Mizuno, her unwitting accomplice, into a state of perplexion. She would invite him to a game of mahjong and ply him with drink. Along with her coconspirators, she would fill his head with all manner of fantasies and intrigue. Then she or Hsiao-Dan would arrange for Mizuno to meet Boss Du in the privacy of his study—just in time for the double to arrive and carry out the assassination. The man that Mizuno took to be his doppelgänger was simply another collaborator from Yueh-Lan's coalition. It had been simple enough for Yueh-Lan to learn the whereabouts of Mizuno's tailor, vain man that he was, and commission an identical outfit under the guise of a romantic gesture.

All that was left then was for Yueh-Lan to convince Mizuno that she was but only a taxi dancer this whole time, spellbound by the worldly Japanese editor and the ostentation of the social world within which he dwelled. This part of the plan was simple enough. He could not have fathomed how much she abhorred him for his arrogance. In an era of subjugation and humiliation, and the Chinese to whom this land belonged at the mercy of foreign occupiers, a man like Mizuno was only too content to peddle entertainment to the masses: the latest starlets and soft films, perfumes, fashions, expensive hotels and luxury steamers. The audacity to present a veneer of peace and prosperity when the world was anything but. At a time when Yueh-Lan's countrymen were suffering insult and injury alike. For that alone, Mizuno deserved his fate. Thus, by these collective machinations, on the night of the full moon, on the serene grounds of a German-style villa, the woman known as Orchid succeeded at felling not just one man—but two.

16

THAT WEEKEND, MEADOW MAKES A TRIP TO FOREST HILLS FOR the barbecue that Peter and Annika are hosting. A waxing moon rises in the sky over Queens, adding a silvery sheen to the soft glow of string lights that illuminate the backyard. It's an exuberant, intimate affair of a dozen or so people, most of whom Meadow met at Peter's birthday party the month prior. He makes lackluster conversation with the lot of them in between Annika's interrogations of his trip to Shanghai and Peter's murmured reactions to Selma's letter, the experimental play, and Diego's alibi. "That sucks, Med," Peter says simply, flipping over the sliced portobello mushrooms on the grill. "Even if everything he says is true. Especially if it's true."

"I don't even know if this qualifies as bad luck," Meadow mutters. "We only dated for a month, but it felt so solid, so . . . *real*. Now it makes me wonder how much of it was in my own head." He takes a sip of his beer and frowns. "Anyway, sorry to be a Debbie Downer. I just figured I owed you an update."

"Don't sweat it, man."

Annika materializes and places her hand on Peter's back. "Babe, all the veggies and fish are here now, but I'm afraid I left the freezer bags of meat in the kitchen. I'd rather not touch them."

"No worries," Peter says. "I'll go get them."

"Ah, let me do it," Meadow pipes up. "Be back in a sec."

Even though it's a midsummer evening, Meadow can't shake the feeling of finality that looms over the party. It's hard to pinpoint the source of this apprehension. Usually he starts to get restless right before a trip, when he imagines blazing through the sky in a silver jet, compressing space and time to traverse this plane of earthly existence in extraordinary fashion. But he has been back from Shanghai for weeks now, with no more travel planned for the year. Maybe he is responding to the stifled smallness that New York has suddenly revealed, now that he has been at Selma's apartment for over a month, and the hurt of Diego's absence is no longer as fresh. It all begins to make sense when he considers that he is rounding the bend on ten full years in the city—the minimum time it takes to claim the mantle of a true New Yorker, so they say.

He doesn't know anymore if he belongs here. There was a period around his late twenties when he felt that this was the perfect and only place for him, comfortable as he was in the Greenpoint apartment with Peter, where they got high and watched Werner Herzog movies, or buoyed by Selma's flighty charms and quixotic passions, the fiery fabulations of Bobby over happy hour and on nighttime prowls around Alphabet City and East Williamsburg. He felt so grounded in their midst, in the reflection he saw of himself in each friendship, by the way they revealed aspects of him he could not otherwise grasp or acknowledge. The naïve notion that this could all continue in perpetuity somehow took hold in the back of his mind, that he might stay in this city forever, riding the L and Q around town, enjoying oysters and cocktails, meeting men who provided some semblance of love. All of these trappings of urban life were enough to allow him to craft a narrative of sufficiency, if not fulfillment.

But now here he is, standing in Peter's backyard eating a skewer of grilled scallions and mushrooms while the poppy rhythms of "Lovefool" stir something in him. The song reminds him of being a prepubescent teen in Shanghai, the portable CD player he brought with him on the bus every day, the great romance and loneliness that filled his head, having traveled thousands of miles away from everything he'd ever known to plant himself in this whole other world—a world that he'd inherited, supposedly, but which he could never comfortably claim as his own. Peter and Annika look so picturesque in their backyard, raising their glasses for a toast, barreling toward the heteronormative bliss sanctioned by society. He feels halfway between a proud family member and a pariah, slinking in his corner, still mired in solitude. He wonders vaguely how Bobby is doing in Portland and decides to shoot him a text to say hi. Then his thoughts drift to Selma; God knows where she is, when she'll be back. He wouldn't be surprised to find out that she went to North Korea or Iceland. Or maybe she's still in Manchuria, wading through a sea of ghosts, looking for clues to her personhood in the new capital of another era.

When he takes the F train later that evening, Meadow gratefully plops into a seat in the mostly empty car. He is wistful and wobbly, head against the window, as the train plunges through black tunnels on its subterranean journey. A stuttering zoetrope of columns gives way to a platform and white-tiled wall in the distance. The doors open, close, and then the train continues on, tearing through the darkness, wheels clattering beneath. His reflection in the window looks ill-defined and uncertain, transposed onto the liminal space of the tunnel. The din of transit and the quiet conversations of other passengers blend into a low buzz around him.

What if there really is a ghost in Selma's apartment, he wonders lazily, and everything that has befallen him over the past weeks has been a kind of message? The letter she wrote was so casually emphatic. That she may have been living with such a ghost for many long years, had even accepted it into her life, might not be the most implausible thing in the world. Perhaps the ghost had lain in wait and seized upon Selma the moment she moved into her apartment. She would have been the perfect target, imaginative and suggestible, prone to flights of fancy and periods of seclusion. The minor mishaps and scattered focus of her first months in the space so many years ago, then, had been a warning. It must be the same phantom as of late teasing Meadow, instigating his vivid dreams, manifesting as Selma herself during his drunken stupor.

Alternatively, Meadow considers, it might be even likelier that the ghost attached itself to Selma long before—a dark power precipitating her unnameable sorrows and catatonic ruptures, giving rise to her whims and methodical madness. Maybe her grandfather's spirit had traveled through time and space to demand reconciliation, if not penance, an acknowledgment of the world in which he'd once dwelled. To warn her—and Meadow, by extension—that humankind lives always on a razor's edge, that unfathomable catastrophe is imminent, or is already beginning to unfold. Meadow's mind becomes swarmed with haphazard images from his own life and the world of *The Masquerade* overlaying one another as he follows this train of thought. He pictures himself in Douglas Koh's home, wearing a tuxedo jacket and one of Selma's masks, a switchblade burning a hole in his jacket pocket. Selma on a stage, hands clasped at her stomach as she bows to the ecstasy of the crowd. Selma spinning around in a dimly lit library to face a man in a beaked mask. He hears Bobby's voice ring out from a conversation they had countless years ago: *She wants something from you.* Diego's dream of being lost in a forest, fish flying through the air. Diego unmasking himself on a balcony as a full moon rises in rapturous iridescence behind him.

On the train, in his softened state, Meadow finds his mind drifting further and further back, recalling the road trip to Cape Cod years ago, and then a conversation from a few months after that. He'd been on a second date at an upscale Greek restaurant in Astoria, pleasantly tipsy from Aegean wine, stomach satiated with grilled lamb and lemony potatoes. While his date was in the bathroom and Meadow was contemplating whether they truly had any relationship potential, a woman strode by his table, did a double take, and stopped in her tracks.

"Meadow?"

He recognized the shock of white hair and red glasses right off the bat. "Brigitte!"

"Wow, it's been a while," she said, giving him a once-over. "You look good."

"Ah, thanks," he chuckled. "You, too." Brigitte was adorned in a shapeless woolen smock that he presumed to be some expensive designer piece. "I'm on a date," he offered sheepishly, by way of explanation.

"Then I won't get in your way," she said with a knowing smile.

She looked like she was about to excuse herself when Meadow blurted out, "I'm so sorry for your loss." He remembered Selma mentioning that there had been a death in Brigitte's family, or something to that effect.

Brigitte's expression hardened. "Loss?" she repeated.

In his state of mild inebriation, Meadow felt his face grow hot as he became aware that he was stumbling into a precarious topic of conversation. "I mean, the road trip you were supposed to come on. Selma told us . . ."

"Selma." Brigitte sniffed, eyes darting back and forth. "She's just full of tall tales, isn't she? So she told you someone died?" A staccato laugh escaped from her lips. She seemed to hesitate for a moment. But when she spoke again, the words came spilling out even as her voice quavered with intensity. "The truth is, I can't be friends with her anymore. I take it you two are still close, so I'll keep this diplomatic. I think it would be in your best interest to be careful around someone like her, who has a very . . . *strange* sense of boundaries.

"A small thing here and there, I could forgive. But so much of what she told me never added up. When we met in Providence way back when, she got into my good graces by telling me she was a cousin of my colleague who'd just retired. Then I found out years later that this was a flat-out lie. Turns out he had no idea who she was. I mean, can you believe it? The audacity to build our whole friendship around that kind of utter fabrication?" She shook her head. "That was the last straw for me." As Meadow opened his mouth to say something, he noticed his date making his way back to the table. "You don't need to answer for her," Brigitte added curtly. "And I'm sorry to heap all that on you. I just thought maybe you should know." She seemed to take her cue from the look of confusion or discomfort on his face. "I'll be out of your hair now. Take care, Meadow. Have a great night." With that, she vanished from sight before he even had a chance to properly say goodbye.

None of what Brigitte had told him was a major surprise. Ultimately, whether he was aware of it or not, he dismissed her warnings about Selma's questionable or disingenuous behavior because, as far as he had experienced, her most egregious offenses had no direct bearing on him. Then there was the plain truth that he cared greatly for her, could scarcely imagine New York without Selma in his life.

In the years since, it has been all too easy to persist in this dance of mutual dependency and containment, to mistake stasis for security. The train is already at Court Square–23rd Street. It takes a second for Meadow to register that he needs to get off. "Shit," he mutters, gathering himself and bounding up. He exits just barely in time as a melodic tone sounds and the doors of the train slide shut.

THE NEXT MORNING Meadow awakens with an idea tickling the inside of his skull. It's as though a wisp of a proposition floated in on a night breeze and wriggled into his ear, burrowing deeper and deeper until lodging itself into his subconscious. He feels like the universe has been beaming a message to him, all summer and then some, through a series of setbacks and cryptic encounters. Now he considers the proposition that has organically emerged in his mind as he gets dressed in Selma's apartment, and for a moment wonders if it's too easy a solution to his existential frustration: to simply up and leave New York City. It seems so delicious and freeing, this idea, even while being riddled with its own problems. For one thing, where can he possibly go? Though a few cities flit through his mind, an instinctive answer that comes to him is Shanghai. When his mother casually suggested he consider living in China just weeks ago, he brushed it aside without much consideration. But now it seems like the only logical choice. To journey back to the city where he experienced his first rupture, was cloven into two. Going back means he could find the fault line in his core and retrace its jagged path; he could devise a means to rehabilitate himself into wholeness. He resolves to think it through over some coffee, somewhere out of the house. The less time he spends at Selma's, the better. He steps out into the swelter of Sunday morning, a tote bag slung over his shoulder out of habit, nary a destination in mind. For a while, he simply trudges aimlessly on the concrete while smoking several cigarettes in succession. He could ship his things back to his parents, close out the storage unit. Or just ditch and donate everything, taking nothing but his suitcases with him. His stomach turns from the giddiness of possibility. Nothing and no one binds him to this city, single man and free agent that he is.

The day is bright and beautiful, not a cloud in the sky. Meadow eventually draws near a popular brunch spot on Fulton Street and dips in, nabbing a counter seat and ordering a black coffee. Across the length of the bar stretches a horizontal mirror in which he observes the hip clientele, casual chic in silk blouses and linen shorts, drop earrings and gel nails, designer tops and ripped jeans. Des'ree on the sound system, ice crackling in cocktail shakers, the teasing laughter of groups of friends, couples sitting cozy in booths. Meadow is in their midst and yet completely detached.

As he's hanging his tote bag on the hook below the bar, he notices the familiar faded green of *The Masquerade* inside. He slips the book out and sets it on the counter. He'd nearly finished it yesterday before the barbecue at Peter's. There was just a single page left, but he decided not to read to the very end. It didn't feel right. Now, as a server brings him a large mug of steaming black coffee, Meadow turns the book over to the back cover. Maybe it doesn't matter whether what Selma says is true or not. Regardless of its provenance, the book came to him and cast its spell on him, lulling him into a state of astonished imagination—that a story could possess such power, or that Selma could have engineered his fate. Now it's time to let it all go. The sun is shining, his mind is clear, the coffee plenty strong. Meadow opens the book to the last page:

Our tale comes to a close here, as night covers the wicked metropolis like a sleek garment and our hapless young man Mizuno is relinquished to the destiny that always awaited him. A magnificent full moon shines above like the lumines-cent pupil of a celestial eye—all-seeing and all-knowing. Since the dawn of man she has incited his folly and yearning, been cast as accomplice to his fear and fantasy. She teases and taunts from the black firmament, watching silently as the agonies of our existence flare up and extinguish, then flare up once more.

You may wonder, dear reader, what moral lies in a story such as this. What arrogance, you may scoff, for a man such as myself to dictate the fate of another, even in a fiction. But I will consider it an accomplishment if even the most trifling feeling has fluttered through your heart, be it curiosity or revulsion, compassion or contempt.

For you, dear reader, are the true author of this tale. I have constructed only a bare frame, while you have filled it with glorious color, sound, and texture. I have sketched shadows into which you have breathed life, that you have endowed with motion. I have provided the masks, and you the voices. Clear as water is the surface that divides us, and smooth as a mirror that reveals we are but one and the same.

Stories, like people, have different fates. Perhaps this one will ultimately be consigned to oblivion, or the nebulous space between creation and annihilation: as real as flowers glimpsed in a looking glass, as untouchable as the moon's reflection on the sea. To know my intention, dear reader, you need simply look into the mirror. If any trace of doubt remains—then write this story anew. Write a story that feels just and true.

But first, look into the mirror.

Meadow turns the page and finds that it is indeed the last leaf. There is no more printed text, no further information about the author or translator. He closes the book, shaking his head and drinking more of the coffee.

A buzz comes from his pocket. Retrieving his phone, he sees that it's Bobby responding to the text message he'd drunkenly sent last night.

Miss u too, bitch, it says. *You owe me a visit. Call me sometime?*

Meadow smiles. It's true that he has yet to follow through on his promise to see Bobby and Rebecca in Portland, though they've been talking about it for years now. He starts to tap out a reply, but decides to wait a minute and get his head in order. After all, there's nothing stopping him from flying out there sometime soon if he really wanted to. Maybe he could even take an extended vacation in the Pacific Northwest on the way to Shanghai, if he truly ends up moving.

His stomach gurgles as he finishes the rest of the coffee. *But first, look into the mirror.* What a weird last sentence, he thinks. A little too on the nose. He stares blankly at the brunch crowd reflected in the mirror, faces enlivened by tasty food and good company, egos and energies competing for dominance at each table. Then, as his eyes sweep from one end of the room to the other, his gaze alights on a man sitting at the counter, chin resting on his clasped hands, a studious, solemn expression on his face, a book with a faded green cover and an empty mug before him.

Write a story that feels just and true.

Meadow pays for his coffee, slides off the stool, and exits the restaurant. He begins walking up Fulton without thinking about where he's going. Surely there's some kind of story to be told about this summer, but even now he doesn't fancy himself a writer, or imagine that it's in his future. Maybe the perspicacity will come to him with age and experience. Maybe it will never come, and the experiences of this summer will fade and warp like a photograph left under the sun. He'll begin to question whether it all really happened, the book and the play, ghosts and doubles and mirrors. Perhaps the dreams and stories that trouble him now will continue to bleed into one another until they become one seamless delusion, these years of ache dwindling into a distant memory against the fullness of some far-flung, and as of yet unimaginable, future.

Another buzz in his pocket alerts him to one more message from Bobby: a link to a web page. *Found u online lol.*

Meadow stops in the middle of the sidewalk, lighting a cigarette and squinting into his phone. Bobby's link takes him to a gallery of thumbnail photos. Then the featured photo loads: it's a picture of him and Selma, standing on the balcony of somebody's apartment in the evening. Why does this look so familiar? He can't quite place it.

But then Meadow begins to click through the other photos, which mostly show the interior. It comes flooding back to him in an instant. The party in Chinatown, a spring evening almost three months ago now. Selma had insisted on taking him there. And sure enough, it was at that party that he ended up sitting on a couch with Diego, striking up a conversation while flipping through Nobuyoshi Araki photos.

This was a memory Meadow recalled fondly for some time, when Diego was still in his life. Now the party simply reminds him of loss, of the beginning of yet another fizzled romance. He hiccups, cigarette in mouth, leaning against a tree. Despite the slight sadness he feels, he can't help but keep scrolling through the photos, hoping to catch a glimpse of himself or Diego. He finds himself in the background of one or two more snaps, then a couple more of Selma talking to different people. She looked dramatic that night in a woven red sweater and matching lipstick.

Wait a minute. He scrolls too quickly past a photo and has to flip back a few. It's a photo of the living room, where quite a few people are lounging, neither Meadow nor Diego anywhere to be seen. But Selma is in this photo, standing against a massive poster of Jodorowsky's *The Holy Mountain*. What catches his eye, though, is the person Selma is talking to. The man has glossy black hair in a kind of bowl cut that would look ridiculous on most anyone else, but seems appropriate given the whole of his sartorial sensibility, an embroidered shirt and tight black pants.

Where have I seen this man before? Meadow wracks his brain. He squints, wondering if he's come across his image in a show or movie somewhere. But then the answer comes in a flood of recognition, pulling him into a current of confusion and disbelief. The cigarette drops from his lips as Meadow opens his mouth and speaks the name aloud:

"Dmitri Suzuki-Alvarado."

The artistic director, Diego's erstwhile, and once-more, lover. He was at the party where Meadow and Diego met. Not only that, but he and Selma know each other? The image on his phone screen begins to blur. It takes Meadow a moment to realize that it's because his hand is shaking violently. All sorts of misgivings and half-truths and wild conjectures fill his mind again. His breath quickens. He tastes tobacco and coffee on his breath, smells the grit and exhaust of the city around him. Meadow takes several steps with a brutal clarity flashing in his mind, only to double over as though struck. At the edge of the sidewalk, between two parked cars, he leans forward, panting, until he finally musters the wherewithal to make a phone call.

"Howdy," crackles the voice on the other end.

"Bobby!" he shrieks into the phone, oblivious to the gaze of passersby. "I went to see this play recently, and that guy in one of the photos— Standing next to Selma, you see. I didn't meet him at the party, and I guess I still haven't really met him, but . . ." He tries to form a cogent narrative but it all comes out a jumbled mess. Where to begin? How can he even start to tell this story? Meadow talks fast and feverish into the phone, so engrossed in his own excitement that he barely hears Bobby try to cut in several times. "Fuck," he says, trying to slow down. "Fuck, I'm sorry, Bobby. It's just been a weird few months. Yes, I'm still staying at Selma's, but she's . . . off doing something, somewhere. God, I'm such a shithead. I'm sorry. We haven't talked in months. I haven't even told you about my whole mess with Diego, and here I am wailing about something that probably makes no sense to you." Meadow catches his breath and starts walking again.

"Girl, yes, you have."

"I have? What do you mean?"

He finds himself on Atlantic Avenue beneath the glaring afternoon sun. Bobby is saying something to him that he doesn't quite comprehend. "We talked for a long time that night. Don't you remember? You were going to Shanghai the next morning, had just stuffed your face with pizza. You told me about Diego then, getting ghosted and all."

"Oh, shit."

"I guess you really don't remember, huh. So the sketchy vibes were for real then?"

"Who was sketchy?"

"The house-sitting. Selma. You had a weird feeling about it—"

On the crosswalk, Meadow nearly collides with an old woman coming the opposite direction. He mutters an apology and trots ahead. A weird feeling about Selma? "But that was before I even found the book—"

"Book? What are you talking about?"

"Listen," he hears himself say, "I-I can't talk right now. I'm . . . I need to get something to eat." The words tumble out of him a moment before he realizes that he is indeed famished, his knees buckling. Black dots appear in his peripheral vision. He careens down the sidewalk and staggers into the nearest bodega that he sees. He has dealt with the occasional bout of low blood sugar, but the hunger that engulfs him now is an entirely different entity. A colorless void has opened in the core of his being, a vacuum of meaning that threatens to expand and swallow up his entire existence if he doesn't fill it in time. He can hardly keep his eyes focused as he stumbles down the narrow aisles, his breaths heavy and hands shaking as he grabs at whatever objects his body seems to crave. As he brings a pile of things to the register, he feels the bewildered gazes of the cashier and the other people around him, faceless and formless but for their eyes. None of it fazes him. Before he even exits the store, he finds himself tearing into his purchases, feverishly unwrapping a chocolate croissant from its plastic packaging and stuffing it into his mouth. Buttery sweetness melting on his tongue, he devours the whole of it in less than a minute.

Names are important symbols, are they not?

The words of the hatted eccentric suddenly echo in his head, clear as the tolling of a bell. Meadow quivers as he stands in the street, fragments of past conversations whispering in his ear. Names. Long ago, when he was still a child, his mother liked to ask him if he knew why he was named Tian. It would happen on his birthday or another special occasion, or when she was in a sentimental mood—doting on him as he recovered from the flu, a heart-to-heart before bed. *Tian* as in *field*, she would go on, always as though explaining it to him for the first time. Remember that your heart is expansive as a field, stretching as far as the eye can see. Like a field grows crops, you provide nourishment to others. But you must also learn to nourish yourself. The earth may not last an eternity, my darling Tian, but it persists through unimaginable change. You are sturdy and solid as the ground beneath your feet.

Meadow huffs and squints against the heat and bright colors of the world outside. He opens a bottle of kombucha and quenches his thirst with a long, fizzy glug. Nourish yourself first, he tells himself as he tears into a slab of beef jerky. Leave this city to find that vitality again and transform your life. For this long, messy slog of a summer, he has been transfixed by the mystery that has been unfolding insidiously around him, unable to escape the machinations of Selma or some deranged god, futilely attempting to scrabble together any sense out of it all. Only now, as he hobbles down Atlantic Avenue in a delirium, has it become glaringly obvious that this can't go on—that he needs to wrest control of his story again. And he can do that so easily. The answer has been there all along, and it asserts itself to him once more, like a shaft of light slicing through the heavy hours before dawn. It's time to get the fuck out of New York.

The hot sun beats down on him as he reaches into the plastic bag and produces a nectarine. Without even wiping it on his shirt, he bites into the tender skin of the fruit and tastes its juices gushing onto his tongue, trickling out the edges of his mouth. He doesn't pay any attention to which direction he's walking. It matters not, since he has nowhere to go. He simply plods through the city and fills his hunger, one bite at a time. Expansive and resilient as the earth, he reminds himself. Steady and free. A whole new decade is just around the corner, a different self lies ahead. It's high time to take control of his own narrative again, rather than let the whimsies of others decide his fate. This story belongs to him alone, Meadow reminds himself. Every day, a new beginning. Time to invent a different story—a story that feels just and true.

REFERENCES

THE HISTORICAL PERIOD OF 1920s AND 1930s SHANGHAI HAS been examined, dramatized, and romanticized in many sinophone films of the past decades, such as Chen Kaige's *Temptress Moon* (Feng yue), 1996; Hur Jin-ho's *Dangerous Liaisons* (Weixian guanxi), 2012; Ang Lee's *Lust, Caution* (Se, jie), 2007; Lou Ye's *Purple Butterfly* (Zi hudie), 2003; and Zhang Yimou's *Shanghai Triad* (Yao a yao, yao dao waipo qiao), 1995. While Wong Kar-wai is not among the filmmakers who has directly taken up this subject matter, his aesthetic influence in the domain of global visual culture cannot be overstated.

The poem Meadow quotes while discussing his name with Diego is "Marriage Morning" by Alfred, Lord Tennyson.

The lines of poetry offered by Du Kuo-wen for the parlor game are my rendition of the final couplet of a Song dynasty poem by Ye Shaoweng, about visiting a garden.

Contemporary artist Zhang Huan's *1/2 (Meat and Text)* is the print that hangs in Douglas Koh's home.

Tang Seng is the name of the protagonist monk of *Journey to the West*, considered one of the four great classic novels of Chinese literature. One of his travel companions on his pilgrimage to India is an anthropomorphized pig named Zhu Bajie, sometimes translated as "Pigsy" in English.

Footlight Parade (1933), directed by Lloyd Bacon, is a quintessential example of Busby Berkeley's choreography.

The closing line of *The Moon Garden* is from "The Garden of Love" by William Blake.

ACKNOWLEDGMENTS

THIS BOOK WOULD NOT BE IN YOUR HANDS WITHOUT THE unwavering faith of Heather Carr, my agent, who connected with me across thousands of miles and a dozen or so time zones several sweltering summers ago. I am immensely grateful for her intuitive understanding of this novel, the rigorous feedback she offered as it expanded and contracted dramatically over successive drafts, and her indefatigably cheerful disposition as we navigated the submission cycle. Any writer would be lucky to have a literary partner of such savvy and grace.

Similarly, it's been a pleasure to collaborate with Elizabeth DeMeo, whose astute editorial sensibilities and judicious interrogations from sentence to structure alike helped me perceive aspects of my characters and story anew. The shape and texture of the novel have tremendously improved as a direct result of her nuanced interventions and incisive inquiries, as well as the congenial dynamic that undergirded our mutual enterprise.

I consider myself incredibly lucky to join the Tin House family for my debut, and have been buoyed by the enthusiasm of Becky Kraemer, along with Masie Cochran, Nanci McCloskey, Jae Nichelle, and Jacqui Reiko Teruya. Beth Steidle's brilliant cover design perfectly captures the mood and mystique of the world I strove to create, and I simply can't sing her praises highly enough. Meg Storey and Lisa Dusenbery's sharp eyes during the copyediting and proofreading stages helped polish and elevate *Masquerade*, for which I hold them in the greatest esteem. I offer further thanks to Hannah Brattesani and Lucy Carson of the Friedrich Agency and Jiah Shin of Creative Artists Agency for their ongoing efforts to introduce *Masquerade* into other cultural spaces around the world.

Republican China and the popular culture of Shanghai in the 1920s and '30s have transfixed my imagination ever since my undergrad days in California as a lackadaisical film student. More recently, my writing about this era has been informed by academic texts including *Shanghai Modern: The Flowering of a New Urban Culture in China, 1930–1945* by Leo Ou-fan Lee and *An Amorous History of the Silver Screen* by Zhen Zhang; nonfiction narratives like *Shanghai Grand: Forbidden Love, Intrigue, and Decadence in Old China* by Taras Grescoe; and works of fiction such as *Mu Shiying: China's Lost Modernist*, collected and translated by Andrew David Field, and *Shanghai* by Riichi Yokomitsu, translated by Dennis Washburn. Any factual errors or historical inaccuracies are entirely of my own making.

My dear friends Orion Jenkins and Xuan Juliana Wang read and commented on a partial draft of a novel I toiled over for a year, back when we all lived in New York. Though I abandoned that sapling of a story long ago, many of its seeds drifted onward, found fertile soil again, and bloomed into this present work. I thank Orion, Juliana, and Juli Min, another longtime companion and creative colleague, for graciously reading both snippets and full drafts of *Masquerade* and offering their feedback.

It's an honor to have such beautiful praise from Jinwoo Chong, Juli Min, and Xuan Juliana Wang attached to this book. I am thrilled to be in community with them, as well as with other queer and Asian diasporic writers around the world today.

I am indebted to Maaza Mengiste, my MFA advisor, and think fondly of the long conversations we shared more than a decade ago, which cemented the foundation of my narrative sensibilities. Nicole Cooley, Kimiko Hahn, and Roger Sedarat were also an indelible part of my MFA experience, along with my beautifully diverse cohort of peers in all genres.

My family's transnational movements have fundamentally shaped my worldview and cultural sensibilities. I also like to believe that a primal predilection for storytelling has existed within the bloodline for countless generations. I thank my parents and sister for their steadfast support, and for giving me the space to grow fully into the person I am today.

To Christopher Yosuke, I'm so heartened to make a life with you and our kitties. Your patience and kindness, not to mention confidence in my potential as an artist and human being, have fortified me immeasurably over the years. New York will always be our beginning, but I'm ever eager for the adventures ahead. Thank you for being with me on every step and every day of this journey.

Mike Fu is a writer, translator, and editor based in Japan. He has studied in Los Angeles, New York, Paris, Suzhou, and Tokyo. His Chinese-English translation of *Stories of the Sahara* by the late Taiwanese cultural icon Sanmao was named a Favorite Book of the Year by *The Paris Review* and shortlisted for the National Translation Award in Prose. He is a cofounder and former translation editor of *The Shanghai Literary Review*, and recently completed his PhD in cultural studies at Waseda University.